Olga's Egg

Sophie Law

London | New York

Published by Clink Street Publishing 2018

Copyright © 2018

First edition.

ISBN:
978-1-911525-09-7 - paperback
978-1-911525-10-3 - ebook

for Henrietta

When you touch or hold a Fabergé object, you are in contact with something, coming down to you, not only from the era of the Tsars, but of an ancestry far more ancient; for it is typical of all the Imperial courts there have ever been.

Sacheverell Sitwell

A note on Russian Names

Russian names consist of a first name, patronymic and surname; for example, from *War and Peace*, Nataliya Ilyinichna (daughter of Ilya) Rostova, sister of Nikolai Ilyich (son of Ilya) Rostov. The majority of Russian names have a diminutive, mostly formed with a range of contractions and suffixes, which can be varied according to familiarity, hence 'Tanya' for 'Tatiana' with 'Tanyusha' being one of the more familiar variations. Other examples are 'Olya' for 'Olga,' 'Vika' for 'Viktoria,' 'Alyosha' for 'Alexei' and 'Kostya' for 'Konstantin.'

Prologue

Oxford, 1929

Set them, Lord, in bright places of light, in places of green pasture, in places of rest whence all pain, sorrow and sighing have fled away, and where the light of Thy countenance shineth and gladeneth forever all Thy saints.

Grant unto them Thy Kingdom and participation in Thine ineffable and eternal blessings, and to delight in Thine unending and blessed life.

For Thou art the Life, the Resurrection and the Repose of Thy servants who have fallen asleep, O Christ our God, and we render glory to Thee, with Thine Eternal Father, and with Thine All-holy, Gracious and Life-giving Spirit, now and forever and unto ages of ages.

Amen

Father Alexei's voice was not deep but it was strong and sure. Finishing the prayer, he raised his head to behold the icon of the Vladimir Mother of God before describing the Sign of the Cross, sinking to his knees and prostrating himself so that his knuckles shone white as he clenched his fists on the cold floor. He stayed there for longer than necessary before getting up and moving towards her image. The flames of the candles flickered as he approached and her face was dappled with the light, her eyes alive with tears. He closed his eyes and kissed her.

I

A black cab ran through the blue neon shimmer of the Curzon sign which floated in a shallow puddle on the road. A London sound if ever there was one, thought Assia. There was something very soothing about a city that had just been rained on; heavy umbrellas shaken down, tyres spraying through puddles, sodden coats peeled off in warm, steamy halls. That feeling you get when you have finished crying.

As she shuffled into the cinema lobby next to Ben's damp woollen shoulder, Assia watched as rich Russian after rich Russian rocked up and rolled out of Porsches, Bentleys and any other Mayfair car you could think of. This was an event to which they brought their wives, not their girlfriends. Assia had begun to respect the men who had retained their first wives but kept mistresses openly; it showed a kind of reverence for the women who had borne their children all those years ago. Russians married when they were very young and often oligarchs-in-the-making had had children in wedlock by the time they were twenty. Then they did a front-wheel skid into money, and everything changed.

'This place is quite extraordinary, *n'est-ce pas?*' Assia cast her eyes around the lobby of the Curzon Mayfair before taking a sip from a squat glass of icy sludge layered with exotic leaves, the sort of thing that was offered by expensive caterers desperate to do something different. 'Different' was essential because the people who made it their job to cater to the very rich had realised that when you serve expensive champagne to

Russians at drinks parties they slate it because being rude about what you drink shows off your sophisticated palate. Assia had become very used to drinking the finest champagne while the Russian guests complained: *This champagne is disgusting, I can't drink this filth! How can you drink such dish water?*

Ben nodded in agreement. 'Hmm, yeah. Very 70s, very retro. Quite a time capsule.' He paused and crunched a mouthful of ice while surveying the guests as they arrived. 'Normally you can rely on the Russians to look pretty vintage fashion-wise but this lot seems to have come on. In fact, you could say they're giving you London girls a run for your money.'

'You really don't get out much, do you?' said Assia. 'Rich Russian girls, mostly second generation oligarchy, have been elbowing their way to the front of the fashion pack for a while now.' Assia lowered her voice. 'It's the girls who are new to money who slip up: the Oligarch Girlfriends or Second Wives who take the Versace route, thinking that you can't look like a hooker if your dress is expensive.' With her eyes she steered Ben's gaze to a tall woman with a high ponytail of long peroxided blonde hair. Wearing a thigh-length white snakeskin coat with gold studs around the collar, entire stretches of long leg emerged where the coat ended prompting doubt as to whether she was wearing anything underneath. She was standing next to a dark bull of a man who looked as surly as she did.

'That coat is probably fresh from the Versace Autumn/ Winter 2016 collection and I bet it cost thousands, but she still looks like a tart from Volgograd. You can take the girl out of... and all that.'

'You might want to be careful what you say, young lady,' said Ben smirking and rubbing the sleeve of her coat between his fingers. 'From looking at your coat... hmm... There's got to be a drop of Russian blood there. In fact, you've got to be half-Russian, am I right? Am I right? This coat is just that little bit too sexy on you.'

'Shh, for goodness's sake!' Assia swatted Ben's hand away and avoided his gaze. 'I would say something foul to you in

Russian, but I don't want to offend my fellow countrymen.' She laughed and stirred the melting pile of ice in her glass with the stubby straw. She hadn't admitted it to herself, but she didn't like it when Ben tried to seduce her, even jokingly. He turned into a man she didn't recognise and she felt tricked in some way, as though all he had ever wanted was to get her into bed. Her eyes wandered over his shoulder and she looked suddenly preoccupied. Ben followed her gaze.

'What is it?'

'Tanya's here with some man.' Assia sighed. 'Great. Just what I feel like on a Friday night. Get ready for the *Tanya Show*.'

A beautiful woman with dark shoulder-length hair and fierce eyes came towards them followed by a red-headed man in a pinstripe suit. The man smiled at Assia when he saw her.

'My sister!' Tanya pointed at Assia while beaming at her companion expectantly. Her smile split the deep red of her full lips and her eyes wrinkled beguilingly.

'How do you do, I'm John.' The man with red hair stepped forward and grasped Assia's hand warmly. 'It's quite incredible meeting Tanya's doppelganger. I mean, I understand the science of it but it never fails to be utterly surprising to see identical twins. Am I allowed to say it? You are just like her!'

'*Real* twins' said Tanya looking serious, her dark brow furrowed. 'Not those fertility-clinic multiple-birth type twins.'

'Well, quite' said Assia, nodding with mock concern. 'It's lovely to meet you. And this is Ben.' Assia ushered Ben forward and watched as the men shook hands and muttered the platitudes of greeting. She had no idea where her sister had found him, but she liked John immediately. It was hard to put her finger on it but something about him seemed warm and authentic.

'Little sister, how are you?' Tanya opened her arms extravagantly, sweeping her fur-trimmed pashmina around her twin. Assia allowed herself to be embraced. It felt strange hugging like this in public; a display of affection for everyone except her. Assia knew that Tanya was just playing to the crowd, to John specifically, showing him how much she loved her darling, sweet identical sister – *aren't we a scream?* – and yet a part of her longed to please Tanya again and so she went along with the display of sisterly love.

'Yes, good, good, thanks.' Assia wriggled out of the pashmina and folded it back onto Tanya's shoulder. 'What are you doing here? We don't normally see you in the halls of art. Has its siren call seduced you at last?'

'Hang on, *little* sister? You just called Assia your *little* sister. How can that be? Are you really twins?' John caught Assia's eye as he asked the question and she grinned at the faux inquisition intended to wind up Tanya.

'Yes, *John*,' said Tanya, knowing she was being played, 'Assia was born six minutes after me and therefore she is my younger sister.' She addressed John as a headmistress would a naughty child and he pretended to look chastened.

Tanya continued archly, 'And to answer your question, Assia, we are here because one of John's friends is a producer of the film we're all going to see and obviously I am interested in Fabergé because of Mama. Apparently they are showing a clip of her.'

Assia felt a flare of acid blaze in her stomach. Her cheeks flushed. She was sure that Tanya was studying her, looking for a reaction and her cheeks throbbed even more in defiance. Turning to John she said casually 'Our mother is in the film?'

John appeared to dip his head in a reverent little bow. 'Yes, my friend Sam is very much in awe of your mother and he wanted to feature her in the film. He just loved learning about Fabergé and said he devoured her books while he was researching. In fact, he was quite stunned when I said I was stepping out with one of Olga Wynfield's daughters!'

At this Tanya threw her head back and laughed loudly while John continued. 'I understand that you work with Fabergé, like your mother did?' Again, he seemed to bow to Assia and she wondered whether he knew what had happened and was trying to be sympathetic towards the vulnerable twin who had ruined everything.

'Yes, I do,' she said and smiled back into his eyes. 'I consult for a few clients on the acquisition of Fabergé pieces and I curate their collections. I spend half my life on a plane.'

Ben stepped in. 'Assia is also editing Olga's *Encyclopaedia of Fabergé Eggs* for re-publication, aren't you?' He touched her arm lightly and moved next to her protectively.

'*Are* you? I didn't know that! Why didn't you tell me?' Tanya snapped shut her Bottega Veneta woven leather clutch. The move was strangely aggressive.

'Thames & Hudson want to update it,' said Assia matter-of-factly. 'Obviously there are some recent discoveries to add and new information which has been uncovered since Mama wrote it in 1991. It's been twenty-five years after all!'

As they followed the drift of people towards the screen doors, Tanya said to Assia under her breath 'You should have told me that you were editing Mama's book. I have a right to know!' Assia looked at Tanya sharply and was about to speak before she was shunted away from her sister by the stop-start movement of the crowd. She knew Tanya wanted to cause a scene but couldn't and she drew some small satisfaction from this as her sister pursed her beautiful lips and glared at her when she thought John wasn't looking.

II

The door clanged shut and silenced the whine of the freezing wind. It was as cold inside the building as it was outside, but Konstantin Stepanyan didn't notice. He knew what a Russian winter was, the fight it demanded, and he had no time for it anymore; no time for the fatty food which his sister nagged him to eat to ward off the cold and no time for the snow which had arrived for its long stay in the city. Standing on the steamy trolleybus on the way there he had thought about all the struggles today's generation had ahead of them and he pitied them. Russia felt like a new beast now. The status quo had shifted since Communism fell and all the old paths in the snow had gone. Konstantin would never have called himself a die-hard Communist - he was anything but - and yet he couldn't help but feel that the better devil was the one you knew.

He made his way towards the lift which stank of urine and pressed the stiff button with a well-insulated finger. A tinny noise approached and hovered behind him, accompanied by the sound of chewing. Konstantin turned and saw a youth with shiny black headphones playing with his phone. The boy didn't look up at him but carried on swiping at the screen of his device. Konstantin hoped that he was good to his grandparents and listened to them. They would tell him that young people spent too much time on their phones and that when they were young they had read or discussed art and ideas with their friends as a way of passing the time. *Our world was materially poor but rich in thought,* they would say. *You young people disappear down a black hole when you're playing with your phones. You find it impossible to concentrate on anything for more than a minute. How will you ever learn anything?*

The lift arrived with a muffled thud and only one of the stiff, metal doors drew back as the other was jammed shut. Konstantin and the youth stepped in and jabbed the button pad on the left to request their floors. Konstantin noted that the boy was going two floors above him and that he would have to hear the incessant bass beat which leaked from his headphones for the whole of his journey up to the eighth floor. When the lift stopped abruptly at his floor, Konstantin got out and turned left down the concrete corridor, wondering at the source of the acrid smell. He was just a few doors away from the door to his daughter's hallway when he realised that he could hear the sound of the youth's music behind him. He turned around, baffled because he thought the boy was travelling two floors further up, and saw him ring the bell of an apartment a few doors away and wait for an answer. Pausing a second, Konstantin concluded the boy must have pressed the wrong lift button and carried on to his daughter's door. She had opened the door to her hallway and was crouching down arranging a series of little shoes and boots on the brown carpet.

'Vika.' He bent a little to touch her shoulder and she stood up immediately and hugged him.

'*Pap. Oy, spasibo, Papochka.*' She spoke with her face pressed into his broad chest and then drew back, sniffing loudly. She wiped the tears from her cheek, shut the hallway door and led him into the apartment by his hand. She helped her father take his large shearling coat off and hung it by the door.

'Alyosh, Papa's here,' she said calmly, poking her face around the door frame of the living room. A thin man sprang up off the sofa and embraced Konstantin.

'How can I thank you, Kostya?'

'You don't need to say anything, Alyosh.' Konstantin patted his son-in-law on the back and smiled softly at him before moving to the corner of the room where a little boy was sitting, propped up by a cushion. Konstantin lowered his large frame slowly so that he was resting on his knees and looked into the face of the blond child who was inspecting a teddy bear.

'Grandpa's here, Mishenka. And I've brought something for you.' He plunged his large hand into his pocket and pulled out a small gold sphere. The gold was matt and smooth and Konstantin opened his grandson's palm and placed the sphere in it. The boy curled his fingers over it and looked up at his grandfather's grey face. He looked down at his hand again and his lips rounded with concentration, a stream of dribble flowing out of the corner of his mouth.

'Look inside it, Mishenka.' Konstantin delicately unfurled his grandson's fingers from around the yellow orb and, cradling his small hands, helped him to pull its two halves apart. As he did so, a little golden hen with pink eyes rolled out and fell onto the floor on its side. Misha made a gleeful noise when he saw the hen and stretched his arm out to retrieve it. He strained unsuccessfully and his little face reddened with the effort.

'Careful, Mishenka,' said his mother. She had appeared next to Konstantin and handed him a glass of amber-coloured tea before picking up the gold hen. 'Pap, what is this? It's beautiful.'

'Don't worry, he won't break it. It's a present for the boy. I wanted him to have something that will last, something that will make him think of me when he is older.'

'You've already given him enough. Did I tell you that we have a date now? – I can't believe it. I had a Skype conversation with Dr Macfarlane and we will take Misha to see him in Boston next month for the pre-surgery assessment. Then, all being well, they will do the operation three days later.' Vika stroked her son's left foot and gave it a squeeze.

'That is marvellous, darling. I am so pleased.' Konstantin got to his feet and leant down to pick up Misha. He lifted the small boy up with ease and Misha, still clutching his little gold hen, giggled as his grandfather whisked him about the room in his arms as though dancing a waltz.

'Thanks to you, Kostya, he may walk one day.' Alexei didn't look at anyone as he said this. He was standing by the window of the living room, gazing out at the stretch of brown-streaked snow outside their block of flats. A little child in a psychedelic green ski-jacket was running around holding snowballs, flitting to and from its mother as they walked the frosty paths across the vast complex of hive-like buildings.

'Don't say that, Alyosh. You'll tempt fate.' Vika stood up and went to the small table in front of the bookshelf where a number of small icons were laid out on a square of pierced white cotton. She blew dust off the wooden icons and straightened their already neat arrangement.

'Fate has nothing to do with it' said Alexei, turning from the window and addressing Vika sharply. 'If Dr Macfarlane can help our son walk, it will have nothing to do with whether we uttered this wish or not. Why is it always this doom-laden outlook?' He crossed his slim arms and went to sit on the sofa.

Vika glared at Alexei and went over to her father and took Misha from him. She stroked the baby's soft white cheeks and kissed his nose while Misha played with her hair. Konstantin felt suddenly that he had to leave, that he couldn't stay a moment longer with this little family that he loved so much. He had done what he came to do and lingering would do no good.

'You are exhausted, my sweet, I can see that,' said Konstantin. 'Worrying wears you down but have faith. Have faith in this marvellous American doctor and let him deal with your worries.' He touched Vika's cheek with two fingers and kissed her before kissing the top of Misha's head. 'I must go, I am afraid.'

'So quickly? You have only just arrived! Let me give you something to eat, Papa, you are looking thin.'

'There's no chance of me starving when I live with your aunt, believe me! No, I must go, darling, I have to meet someone. I just wanted to see you and Misha and give him his present. Please look after yourselves. Alyosh, goodbye.' The urge to absent himself was so strong that Konstantin grabbed his coat and started putting it on hurriedly while making his way to the door of the apartment. Vika followed him and stood in the little hallway with Misha on her hip, watching her father anxiously as he laced up his boots.

'Pap, are you OK? You seem bothered by something.'

Konstantin's large but deft fingers tied a small knot in his thick laces. He avoided Vika's worried gaze and fumbled in his pocket for his phone. Eventually he met her eyes which searched his face hurriedly for clues.

'Is it your health? You don't have to hide anything from me just because of Misha. I can cope with bad news. I'm used to it.' She smiled wryly and shifted Misha up her hip.

The worried expression on his daughter's face made Konstantin temper his swift exit. Vika's pale skin and the heavy bags under her eyes wounded him and he longed to carry her load for her. He knew that no amount of money would ever stop her worrying about Misha but he wanted to give her hope. Hope was everything. He wanted a new horizon to appear for her and the boy, to give her a reason to get out of bed and go and lift her little disabled son from his cot and tell him that everything was going to be alright.

'My darling, I didn't mean to alarm you. I am absolutely fine and nothing's wrong. I just need to be somewhere and I'm late.' He held her forearm firmly and pulled her towards him gently, pressing her head onto his chest with his other arm. He stroked her hair and repeated his prayer, knowing that she would be listening to his voice reverberating through his chest as she had done when she was a little girl.

'Lord Jesus Christ, Son of God, have mercy on me, a sinner.'

He said it three times and then Vika said it with him. Misha looked at them both enquiringly and his bottom lip began to protrude before his face crumpled and large tears fell quickly down his cheeks. Konstantin and Vika laughed at the sorry sight and stopped the recitation.

'Poor baby, he doesn't like prayers yet, do you, munchkin?' Vika hugged him tightly and swayed from side to side to soothe him. 'I love you, Pap. Please don't rush in this weather. The ice is not kind.'

'I know, my love, I know. I am careful, I promise. Take care of yourself too, and the babe. Goodbye.' He kissed the air and nodded the kisses towards them while pulling the door closed. He stopped in the corridor outside and breathed deeply, hunching his shoulders to prepare for the cold. He walked towards the lift, in his mind's eye picturing Vika talking to the surgeon and hugging him with gratitude. She would be watching Misha in his little hospital bed and crying joyfully as he wiggled his toes. American nurses would be crowding round the little boy and giving him lots of toys and wholesome food.

He had climbed into the thought so completely that he didn't look back when the tinny beat from the shiny black headphones positioned itself behind him.

III

The veil of blue light over the walls seemed to pulse and then dimmed. Gradually, people stopped talking and only the sound of icy slosh being tipped up and drained from the bottom of glasses could be heard. The orangey-red curtains which hid the screen were drawn back with a click and an electric hum to reveal the title of the film, 'Fabergé: Revolution and Romance,' on a black background above the spiky white signatures of the people from the Board of Film Classification. The title page seemed to swim on the screen for a long time and people started turning round in their seats and staring up at the white light of the projector box as though something had gone wrong.

Suddenly a cymbal clashed. The screen was filled with pinkish grey grains which began to get smaller and smaller and rush away before it emerged that the camera was zooming out from what at first looked like a mountain but turned out to be the Thunder Stone, the colossal granite base of Falconet's monumental bronze statue of Peter the Great in St Petersburg. Snow lay in the grooves of the rock and the tsar, against a bright blue sky and atop a rearing horse, surveyed the world from the edge of a vast and treacherous mountain top. As the camera continued to stream backwards, the primrose yellow walls and white Corinthian columns of the Admiralty rose up behind Peter who, for a split second, appeared to mount the building as perspective threw it under the hooves of his horse. The questing, wintery notes of Tchaikovsky's Symphony No. 1 trickled in to accompany aerial views of St Petersburg in all its snow-draped glory. Gradually getting louder and louder, a rich male voice reciting in Russian slid under the music as the camera studied views of the Neva and the palaces that sat on her banks. Assia recognised the insistent iambic pulse of the Introduction to Pushkin's *Bronze Horseman*, and noiselessly she chimed in, whispering the lines with the narrator.

In the dim light Ben turned to study her face when he saw her mouth moving out of the corner of his eye and he smiled as he realised that she was joining in. She was entirely at home in this lost world of pre-Revolutionary romance and fantasy, he concluded. Watching her face illuminated by the bright light of the million snowy pixels on the screen, he saw her as a creature distinctly separate from him. All he had ever done was study her and take his cues accordingly. She had never moved in time with him, but then, he had never asked her to. Their whole relationship had been sculpted around the fact that she was going to fall and he was going to catch her.

> *City of nights, your crystal dusk*
> *Moonless nights, still, clear and bright ...*

An English voice was translating Pushkin's verse and extolling the virtues of Peter's great city while the audience was shown views of the Neva and her many bridges beneath a sky heavy with milky light. Assia knew St Petersburg well and had told Ben about the White Nights in June when the sun never dips far below the horizon and the coalescing dusk is as dark as it gets. Ben had thought it sounded like an insomniac's nightmare but he had come to realise there was so much about Russia, and Assia, which he didn't understand.

'Only a city like St Petersburg could have given birth to a jeweller like Carl Fabergé,' began the narrator who had a richly timbred voice and was probably a famous actor. 'A city of the impossible: a northern Venice built on a Finnish swamp. A city which looked to the West but was founded by Russian ingenuity and determination and built on the backs of Russian peasants: a city of contradictions.'

Suddenly Fabergé egg after Fabergé egg appeared on the screen, the image of each one appearing quickly on top of the other so that only glimpses of gold, diamonds and enamel could be seen. It was like looking through a kaleidoscope: at that moment when the brain begins to decipher the snowflake patterns, the picture changes again and moves just outside comprehension. The knowing voice continued, 'The Easter eggs of Carl Fabergé represent the opulence, beauty and inevitable tragedy of Tsardom in miniature form. Epitomising the art and tradition of Russia in many-faceted ways, the eggs symbolise a time and an age at its peak, on the verge of combustion. No other century could have produced the eggs, and none shall be able to produce them again. Considered to be some of the most valuable works of art on earth, their story began with a disgruntled Tsarina and a small golden hen.'

The film took its audience on a gentle walk through the fairy-tale ascent of Carl Fabergé's star: the rapture of the Tsarina Maria Feodorovna each year on receiving yet another captivating Easter egg, the many presentation boxes and charming presents which Fabergé's workshops created for the Imperial family to give as diplomatic gifts, the exceptional skill of the workmasters who oversaw the vast and various output of their craftsmen and the astonishingly modern management style of the man himself. Footage of an interview with Marius von Tiesenmeyer, the slim, aristocratic Fabergé guru of the 70s, made Assia smile as she recalled his tapering Beerbohm-like limbs which he would fold elegantly when sitting. He was speaking about the inspiration for the design of some of the eggs and the painstaking, sometimes year-long, process of making them. He used his left-hand to gesticulate as he talked, turning it elegantly from the wrist as if he were practising a regal wave.

'The tradition of giving lavish Easter eggs was not begun by the last Tsars, you know. In the 18th century, the goldsmith Jean-Jacques Duc produced an exquisite egg-shaped incense-burner of gold and pale lilac enamel with a painting *en grisaille* celebrating Catherine the Great. It's in the Hermitage, should you care to go and inspect it.' On his knee, he placed one long hand on top of the other. 'Fabergé, however, made the revival of the practice entirely his own. Over the course of thirty years he made fifty eggs for the Tsars to present to the Empress and the Dowager Empress and even before he had delivered the eggs for one year, he was working on the next year's creations. Anything could inspire him: the seasons, religion, history, engineering. He made an egg commemorating the Trans-Siberian Railway with a working miniature golden train inside it which winds up with a tiny key, I mean – could you imagine? There was nothing he couldn't turn his hand to.'

Marius had adored Assia's mother and they had co-authored a number of books on various Fabergé specialisms with an especially popular edition published to accompany an important exhibition of the Fabergé hardstone animals in the Royal Collection. He lived and breathed Fabergé and had always said that Olga would have to act as the 'keeper of the flame' when he was gone; he couldn't trust anyone else to do it properly. As far as Marius was concerned, Soviet scholarship on the master and his work was dubious at best, while the Americans were far too keen to use Fabergé to promote themselves. 'They plaster their names all over their collections and bequests. It's so immodest and so *revealing* about their origins, or lack of them, I should say.' He would shake his head very slightly when something irked him, almost as if he were shivering with distaste.

The reach of the film so far appeared to be quite broad, focusing on all of Fabergé's output, from the delicate cufflinks and charming bell-pushes for St Petersburg's upper classes to the more popular and affordable silver cutlery made with Moscow's merchant classes in mind. As the camera lingered on a rainbow display of guilloché enamelled cigarette cases, the narrator elaborated on the point that Fabergé, while designing a vast array of *objets*, had also pushed the boundaries of craftsmanship. Fabergé chose materials which could be found in Russia's rich Jurassic quarries, such as moss agate, nephrite and Alexandrite, and he used them inventively. The curator of the Royal Collection was shown at this point talking about Fabergé's genius for selecting hardstones. Before the camera, in the palm of his hand he held a hardstone toad which he stroked while waxing lyrical about Orskaia jasper, selected by Fabergé for rendering the glistening skin of a brown toad and making it pleasing to touch. Then very carefully, as if cradling a butterfly, he picked up and presented to the camera a sprig of something in a small clear vase. 'Just look at this spray of wild strawberries made from enamel, hardstones and gold. If you look at the gold stalk in the water, which is rock-crystal, you can see that Fabergé has mimicked the way water distorts the appearance of the stalk, so that it appears to split. Everything is artful and considered; for example, the nephrite leaves allow a certain translucency and the natural inclusions simulate the texture of real leaves. The piece has been made to delight and deceive.'

In the row behind her Assia could hear a Russian with a very deep voice saying loudly that he had a better one in his collection and that in fact his Fabergé pieces were better than the Queen of England's. His girlfriend laughed and said that he was richer than the Queen of England too. Assia turned around and tried to identify the treasonous couple but it was too dark. Ben put his hand on her knee and mouthed 'Are you OK?' Shifting in her seat, Assia nodded and shot him a quick smile before turning back to the film.

'… it is thought that only fifty Easter eggs were produced by Fabergé for the Imperial family,' continued the narrator, 'but this number has been challenged by a number of Fabergé scholars and many believe that Fabergé made two eggs for the Dowager Empress and the Empress in 1917 which were never delivered. The question of whether Imperial eggs were made only for the Empresses has also been asked…'

Her stomach tightened and her heart thumped a steady pace, heaving blood up to her neck and her cheeks. *They're going to show her now*, she thought, as she breathed out and acknowledged the chill inevitability. She willed the film to freeze on the Mosaic Egg which was being rotated gently on a spinning socle, its pixel gems mesmerising the auditorium.

Then she saw her mother on the screen. Her name appeared in white letters in the lower left corner before disappearing again: 'Olga Morozova Wynfield, Fabergé expert, interviewed in *The Hunt for Fabergé's Eggs,* BBC One, 2001.'

Olga was sitting on a salmon-pink armchair in front of a bookshelf crammed with large tomes. Her thick blonde hair was twisted into an elegant chignon and she wore a pair of gold and amethyst drop earrings. A raw silk navy blue Nehru-collar jacket framed her neck and emphasised its slender lines.

Olga was nodding as she spoke and her earrings quivered. She sounded defiant.

'Yes, I believe that there is an Imperial Easter egg made by Fabergé which no one knows about.' She was looking sharply at the interviewer who was off screen. He must have been expecting her to say more because there was a long silence and then he asked a question hurriedly.

'And why do you believe this to be the case?'

She smiled now as though indulging a child. Her high cheekbones shone and her eyes narrowed benignly.

'Alma Pihl. Fabergé's best designer. She was a genius. A young genius. Do you understand? She designed an egg for the Grand Duchess Olga and it has been a great secret for a long time. I believe that it was the most beautiful of all Fabergé's eggs.' She continued in a conspiratorial tone, a Russian accent only faintly discernible.

'Little Alma Pihl fled Russia for Finland after the Revolution. She made a new life for herself there teaching art in a provincial school and no one knew that she had worked for Fabergé designing Imperial Easter eggs. Can you imagine? She taught calligraphy and drawing for twenty-four years and no one other than her family knew of her former life. But…' Olga punctuated the air with her index finger. 'But, one of her students contacted me. She had seen me speaking about Fabergé on television, so she wrote me a letter and told me that she had been a favourite student of Alma's. In order to encourage this student, Alma had told her about her career as a designer for Fabergé. She confessed that, *as well* as designing the Mosaic Egg for the Tsarina in 1914, she had designed an egg for the Grand Duchess Olga and that Fabergé himself had said it was the best egg he had ever produced for the Imperial Family.' Olga stopped speaking as though weighing the significance of the revelation she had just uttered. She moved her hand to rest at the top of her neck, just by her jaw, and a gold bracelet slid down from her wrist and disappeared beneath the sleeve of her jacket.

She continued slowly, confessionally. 'And so I went to the Holmström albums and began to look at Pihl's designs again in the light of what this student had told me. These sketch books are the most amazing resource – full of beautiful watercolour designs of jewellery produced by Albert Holmström's workshops between 1909 and 1915. There was one small sketch for a brooch which leapt out at me: white daisies, rendered almost geometrically, not in the lifelike fashion. You could see that Pihl was experimenting with an idea, playing with the materials and the design. She was working with the motif in the round.' At this point Olga leant forward slightly in the armchair as though she were uncomfortable.

'The white daisy, the *Beliiy Svetok*, was a symbol of "White Flower Day", an important charitable event in Yalta which was started in 1911 by the Tsarina Alexandra. On that day, the nobility who were holidaying in the Crimea and the townsfolk – everyone – would buy a bouquet of white daisies from the Tsarina, the Grand Duchesses and the Tsarevich who would mingle with the crowds, their baskets full of the flowers and carrying staffs wreathed with them. It was a very happy occasion and the Grand Duchesses loved helping their mother, Olga in particular. Now, call it a hunch, or whatever,' she waved her hand dismissively, 'but I believe that the brooch design with the white daisies grew into Pihl's design for the egg which was made for the Grand Duchess Olga.'

'Is there any evidence that this egg existed?'

'There is no evidence, otherwise we would know for certain this egg existed. There are only clues, breadcrumbs. But you know what's surprising?' Olga clasped her hands together earnestly. 'The Imperial eggs are so famous now, it's hard for us to imagine that they were made, delivered and then simply enjoyed in private by the Imperial Family. There was no fanfare and no public announcement about any of the eggs. There was an exhibition of some of them in 1902 and in 1915, but otherwise they only came to fame after their original owners were slaughtered. Many of the eggs that we know were made were never photographed so we don't even know what they looked like, not least because very few of the records from Fabergé's studios survived the Revolution. For me, the biggest clue leading to Olga's egg lies in the Court Ledgers for 1914. Accounts for that year show that Fabergé was paid over 68,000 roubles, a sum substantially higher than that paid by the Imperial Purse in previous years and the payment is described as having been made for "eggs". The eggs in question are not itemised and I believe that it was this year that *three* eggs were made: one for the Dowager Empress – the Catherine the Great Egg; one for the Empress Alexandra – the Mosaic Egg; and one for the Grand Duchess Olga. At the time when they were presented, Easter 1914, Olga would have been eighteen years old, a woman who could receive an egg in her own right, like her mother and grandmother.'

'And where is Olga's egg now?'

'Where are any of the missing eggs? Don't we all want to know?' She shrugged as she spoke and wore an apologetic look on her face. 'It may not have survived the Revolution. It may be in a tin box somewhere waiting to be discovered or it may be part of someone's collection and they don't want to share it with the world. It will be difficult to trace something we hadn't known existed. This is why I am talking to you: if the egg can exist in our consciousness then it is more likely to be found.'

The clip finished and the narrator began to talk about recent Fabergé discoveries. Ben, who had been holding Assia's hand throughout the interview with Olga, kissed her wet cheek and offered her his handkerchief. She took it without looking at him and buried her face in it. Tanya, who was sitting next to Ben, leaned over him and said loudly to Assia 'Are you OK? It must be hard seeing Mama. It's hard for me too.' Assia knew that Tanya was pretending to be sympathetic for John's benefit, to make herself look like the caring and concerned sister. They were so unlike the average expectation of twins that Assia found herself disappointing people when she said that she rarely saw her twin sister. She knew that they wanted to believe in the unbreakable bond between twins, how Tanya would know instinctively that Assia was in trouble through some telepathic channel, but she had given up trying to please people on that front and just said, truthfully, that she and her sister led very different lives. She omitted to tell people that she and Tanya had been closer than she ever thought it was possible to be to another human being until the accident had happened and their mother had been killed.

'Do you want to go?' Ben squeezed her hand. He knew Tanya was upsetting her and he didn't want Assia to make a scene that she would regret later.

'No, no, I'm fine, thanks,' she whispered back. She didn't want to go into it with Ben, not here. She smiled meekly, trying to sniff as quietly as possible into the spotted handkerchief. Someone from Wartski was on screen talking about the discovery of the 1887 Egg in Midwest America. She knew the story inside out but it never failed to thrill her. What if the dealer who had bought the small gold egg from an antiques stall for just a few thousand pounds had managed to sell it for its scrap value to be melted down, as he had planned to? What if he *hadn't* decided to research his egg on the internet and *hadn't* seen an article identifying his item as a missing Fabergé Imperial egg? The intricate ribbed gold egg with a watch inside would have been lost for ever and the ordinary man from America would have destroyed his £20 million golden ticket.

The film had finished and the credits began rolling. The hum of people chatting rose immediately and guests began to get up from their seats. Suddenly a spotlight was trained on a handsome young man in a dark blue suit at the front of the cinema, just in front of the screen. He began to address the audience.

'*Damy i gospoda!* Ladies and Gentleman! Grant me your attention, please! I have something important to tell you.' The man translated what he had just said into Russian and the whole cinema fell quiet apart from a group of Russians who were chatting and laughing until they were hushed. Assia realised she knew who was addressing them and, without meaning to, she felt excited.

'Ladies and gentleman, thank you for taking the time to listen to me. I am speaking on behalf of the St Petersburg Museum, a museum which, of course, needs no introduction. The Trustees of the Museum have asked me to make an announcement to you before a press release is issued to the world first thing tomorrow. They wanted this esteemed audience, this august group of Fabergé collectors and experts to know what I am about to tell you before the general public knows it.' He repeated his speech in Russian while those who had understood what he had said in English began to chatter in anticipation.

'I am delighted to announce that the egg which Olga Morozova Wynfield was talking about in the film was not a figment of her imagination. Quite the opposite, in fact. The Grand Duchess Olga's Fabergé egg has been discovered.' The words hung in the air before being greeted by gasps from the audience. No one had expected this. It was as though a golden ball had been tossed into the air and everyone had watched its beautiful progress as it fell and smashed on the floor. The man appeared to smile and waited before translating the announcement into Russian, drawing out the suspense as much as possible.

'And to whet your appetite, here is the egg.' The eyes of the audience followed the man's outstretched arm as it gestured at the screen behind him. Before she knew it, Assia was looking at the most beautiful thing she had ever seen. Spinning on a socle, the egg which appeared on the large screen was a pink, green and white confection of what appeared to be ribbons. Plaits of coloured enamel were gathered at the base of the egg and unravelled across a body of chequered enamel with painted flowers before gathering into formation again to crown the egg with a bow. Where the ribbons had unravelled in the middle of the egg they framed four golden cyphers of the Cyrillic letters 'ON' which stood for 'Olga Nikolaevna,' surmounted by a little golden crown. The egg rested on a small gold stand constructed of miniature Doric columns divided by arches. People gasped as they watched the footage and one woman standing a few feet behind Assia began to sob. 'Such beauty!' she cried out, 'Such beauty!'

Assia felt as though her head were in a vice as she looked at the screen and her breath quickened. She didn't know how to interpret the beautiful egg that was spinning into a blur in front of her. The only thought that kept running through her mind was that this was not the egg that her mother had imagined. This egg did not feature the white daisies which her mother had believed were part of Alma Pihl's design for Olga's egg. *My mother was wrong.*

The egg stopped turning and the camera moved closer to it. As if by magic, the gold cyphers which were situated on the bulbous part of the egg at intervals, moved clockwise on a hidden axis at their base so that they parted to reveal four miniature paintings of moonlit scenes.

Tanya, open-mouthed, was holding up her phone to record what she was seeing on the screen. The hubbub in the room swelled and then died down when it looked as though the man was going to say more.

'The egg has been acquired by the Russian Federation and generously gifted to the St Petersburg Museum where it will be unveiled in one week's time. We look forward to seeing you there. Thank you for your kind attention.' As he finished speaking, the man put his hands together as if in prayer and nodded slightly, paying homage to some kind of Asiatic gesture of thanks. He looked towards the door of the cinema, wondering if he could make an escape before being grilled by eager Fabergé scholars, and as he did so caught Assia's eye while she edged out of a row of seats towards the back. He held her gaze and smiled nervously, expectantly, before mouthing to her to stay where she was.

Amid the people jostling around her to get out of the cinema, Assia felt as vulnerable and frail as an old woman. She thought she might be crushed to powder as a large Russian pushed past her in the row and for a second, as Tanya kept repeating 'Mama was right! Mama was right!,' her line of vision folded into a blackness which bore down on her. She gripped the seat in front and felt the red plush of the upholstery feed through the gaps between her fingers. She knew she had to pull herself together and leave the cinema before Edward – the young man who had just been speaking – reached her. She hadn't seen him since she had left Oxford and she just couldn't face him and his announcement and his egg.

'Assia, what's wrong with you? They've found Mama's egg! Aren't you happy? Rather cheeky of him to have said that it was no longer just a figment of Mama's imagination, though. She didn't just dream it up – she did all that research and was positive it existed.' Tanya put her arm around Assia's shoulder and pulled her sister towards her as an over-keen toddler might hug an unsuspecting baby.

'It's an amazing discovery.' Assia pulled back and turned to face her sister directly. 'But you know it's not Alma Pihl's design. It's not what Mama predicted and I can't understand why. The language of the design is totally unexpected. It's not what I had wanted it to be.' She paused. 'Could you send me that video you just took of the egg? I want to study it properly.' It wasn't easy to look her sister in the eye but Assia made herself engage with her twin as a way of repelling her, the way similar ends of magnetic bars bounce off each other.

'Well, it's fabulous news. And I would have thought you would be pleased on many counts: for Mama especially but also because there is a new egg out there. Fabergé is your thing, isn't it?' Tanya took her arm off Assia's neck and brushed a strand of dark hair behind her ear as though licking a wound. They had managed to move out of the screening room and into the passage leading to the lobby. Edward hadn't caught up with Assia yet and she hoped that she might be able to leave the cinema without bumping into him.

John, who had gone ahead of everyone to make a phone call, was pacing about in the lobby. He was still on the phone when Assia emerged and he rolled his eyes and smiled at her to indicate that he was stuck on an interminable call. Assia wondered what he must think of her and Tanya, the identical twins who never saw each other. Had Tanya told him about their mother? She couldn't tell whether he was behaving sympathetically towards her or just being a gentleman.

The lobby was still brimming with people: Russian girls looking at each other's furs, their men muttering into phones; grey-haired European collectors who didn't want to linger with the Russians but didn't want to venture into the rain either, and a few American pensioners who sat on the only available chairs.

'Is Assia OK?' John asked Tanya as he helped her on with her coat. 'She looks a little upset.'

'Oh, God knows!' Tanya sighed loudly, glancing at her sister with an admonitory brow. 'She's having a tantrum about the newly discovered Fabergé egg. It's not what she expected apparently, even though Mama has just been vindicated in her prediction of its existence. As if life should be all about what *Assia* expects!'

Assia felt a cold stone drop inside her. She couldn't believe that Tanya was speaking about her in this way, as though she were just a spoilt child who didn't like her birthday present, as though the accident hadn't changed her life for ever. She stared at her sister, trying not to let the quivering ball of upset reach her bottom lip.

'I think you misunderstood what I was saying, Tanya.' Her voice was shaking, but she spoke loudly. Loudly enough that the man with a shaven head standing a few feet away and pretending to talk on his mobile could film her conversation surreptitiously with his other phone.

'I was just saying, because you asked me back there, that the egg strikes me as a little unusual.' The quiver had smoothed out of her voice and she could sense other people in the lobby had quietened to listen to her. 'It's like being shown a painting by Manet while being told that it's an unknown van Gogh. I feel as though I've seen bits of it before and it all jars somehow. It's as though the egg has been put together in a dream, one of my dreams, and I don't know whether to feel enthralled or repulsed.'

Ben came up to Assia and held her coat up, guiding her arms into it. He put his arm around her waist proprietorially.

'Bye, sis' said Tanya breezily when they were outside, leaning out from under the umbrella which John was holding over her. She was behaving as though they hadn't nearly locked horns or scratched each other's eyes out inside the cinema. Her face had softened since the beginning of the evening: her eyes were less narrowed and she had relaxed the pout which she normally assumed as a sort of armour. 'Will you let me know more about Mama's book – the one you're working on? Involve me in your life, please. She would have wanted it, you know.'

'Yes, I do know, Tanya. I do know what Mama would have wanted.' Assia couldn't bring herself to smile back at her sister. Tanya had dressed the sentiment as sisterly concern but the admonition was there all the same. *I am the keeper of our mother's memory, not you.* The girls did the mwah-mwah kiss on each cheek and agreed that they would have to get together soon to talk about Olga's egg. As they all stood outside and contemplated how to get home in the pouring rain, Ben held open the door for two smartly dressed women, one wearing an Hermès scarf around her neck.

'Thank you' said the one with the scarf, nodding to Ben before continuing her conversation loudly '... yes, it's true. And did you know that Olga Wynfield was killed in a car crash not long after she gave that interview we saw? Yes, awful, I know. *And* it was one of her twin daughters at the wheel, poor thing. I believe she now works in the Fabergé world too. Making up for her mother's loss, I dare say...'

IV

Alexander Palace, St Petersburg, 8th March, 1917

The Grand Duchess Olga Nikolaevna opened the door and closed it softly behind her. She glanced at the man in the dark suit who was reading aloud, but he did not look up. She sat on an upright chair next to her brother's bed and listened. Mr Fairfax, her English tutor, had a strange way of reading stories, she thought. He projected his clipped voice without looking at his audience which had the rather odd effect of making her want to close her eyes to shelter from the bluster. He also emphasised the last word in every sentence, for some reason, which deprived the listener of any attempt to linger in the words and the story.

'... seeing this, the king took it into his head to take a dip himself. He jumped into the cauldron and was boiled alive! And after he was buried, the archer was chosen to rule the realm in his stead. He married Princess Vassilissa and they lived together for many long years and were as happy as happy can be. The end.' Mr Fairfax looked up. 'Good afternoon, Your Imperial Highness. I hope you are sufficiently recovered to be walking about. He does not appear to be troubled by any pain at present but he refused his lunch.' He turned to the Tsarevich, propped up in bed by a bolster underneath a thin pillow, 'That was a short one, I suggest we have one more. Fenist the Falcon, perhaps?'

'I don't want any more stories.' The Tsarevich's bottom lip protruded ever so slightly.

'Alexei, don't be rude,' Olga said quickly. Mr Fairfax had folded his hands on top of the book of Fairy Tales and was looking down at them.

'But I don't! I don't want to hear about magic feathers or happy endings. Why should I? I can't go back to Mogilev with Papa, I don't have my regiments anymore and we cannot see the *Shtandart* again. What is the point? – there *are* no happy endings!'

Olga narrowed her blue eyes and snapped at her little brother in Russian. 'Papa will be furious when I tell him what you just said. We have to behave better than the soldiers outside the palace, do you understand?'

Alexei's eyes filled with tears and he looked at Olga pleadingly. She got up from her chair and leaned over his bed to embrace him, pressing her cheek against his and stroking his soft hair. Over and again she said 'God grant us strength, God grant us strength.' She saw that Mr Fairfax had lifted his head and closed his eyes. Finally, he spoke:

'Think not thou canst sigh a sigh,
And thy Maker is not by:
Think not thou canst weep a tear,
And thy Maker is not near.

O He gives to us His joy,
That our grief He may destroy:
Till our grief is fled and gone
He doth sit by us and moan.'

V

Ivan Borisovich Denisov fiddled with his Fabergé paper knife as he watched the news on a vast television in his study. He held the silver blade in his right hand and used its tip, without looking, to scratch repeatedly at the blotting pad on the huge partners' desk in front of him. Narrow little pulpy trenches had already been dug in the pad so that it looked as though a tiny mole had been excavating a white field. To the front of the mahogany leather-bound desk stood a scale model of Falconet's Bronze Horseman, a gift from the President. It was one of only a few smaller versions which had been made at the same time the famous bronze of Peter the Great had been constructed and which had been made from pieces of the very Thunder Stone itself.

His youngest daughter, a dark, slender girl of ten, was sitting on the chair on the other side of her father's desk as though she were about to have a meeting with him except that she was engrossed in a game of Candy Crush Saga on her far-too-large phone. The relentless stream of glittery electronic sounds which issued from the game seemed not to bother Ivan and yet when his phone rang he clicked his fingers insistently and pointed to the door. Without looking up from her computer game, she slid off the gilt chair upholstered with white leather and walked slowly out of her father's study. The way her shoulders sloped tugged at his heart. She misses her mother, he thought – she needs a woman to love her. His wife, Maria, had been predictably furious when he had announced that his illegitimate daughter was coming to live with them because her mother had been blown up in a terrorist attack. Maria had always known about his mistress Svetlana and her child with Ivan – she had tolerated it – but caring for the child was a step too far. To her credit, on the face of things, Maria had tried to care for Alina as best she could, but Ivan knew that the arrangement wasn't going to last. Some nights he could hear Alina moaning in her sleep and wondered if she was having the same nightmare that so often came to him, that hellish scene where Svetlana reaches out to him and mouths his name before being engulfed in a column of flames.

He continued to watch the plasma screen mounted on the wall, holding the large Samsung phone away from his ear because General Arkady Nikolaevich Kolesnikov, the Director of the FSB, had a tendency to raise his voice when speaking on the phone.

'Good morning to you, Arkady Nikolaevich. I take it you're watching the news.' Ivan drummed his fingers on the desk.

'The footage was sent to me last night. Filthy little Muslim satrap,' spat the General, 'he's humiliating us again.'

The General was not so loud this morning and Ivan moved the phone closer to his ear. 'Most men are not aware of their fatal flaw,' he said. 'The philosophers call it *hubris*.'

The General coughed; a small volley of strangely effeminate noises. Ivan wondered if he was, in fact, laughing, and pulled the phone away from his ear again.

On the plasma screen a news report was relaying footage of a concert which had taken place the night before in Chechnya. A flashy laser show played on the back of a large stage while a famous American songstress twerked in a leotard. She put her hand out to a red-bearded man in a navy blue shirt and a karakul waistcoat, pulling the Chechen leader onto the stage and grinding her shimmering haunches against him. The man laughed and exhorted the star to continue at the same time as gesturing lewdly to the audience.

'The man is a beast of the orient, Arkady Nikolaevich. I've said it to you before: he plays us with two hands. He can be an ogre when it suits him and a clown the next time. On this occasion, he is the jolly tyrant, and he has invited Hollywood to play with him.'

The camera hovered on famous faces in the audience: an action movie veteran beamed and clapped his hands while a black rapper in a ripped T-shirt had his hands on his knees and appeared to be uncomfortable. An actress from one of the Transformers films kept crossing and uncrossing her legs, looking round the stadium anxiously.

'Damn Hollywood' said the General. 'We are waiting; Russia is waiting.'

'It has begun, Arkady Nikolaevich. Everything has been set in motion.'

Ivan finished the call and picked up the Fabergé paperknife, threading it through his fingers so that the fleshy pads of his fingers cooled on the polished silver. He still couldn't be sure whether the General had known about Svetlana and her death or not. He was probably kidding himself that he had managed to keep it all under wraps – the man could find out anything he wanted after all. But keeping her a secret was the only way Ivan could continue to possess her, to protect her. The General had referred to the recent Domodedovo Airport bombing frequently in their conversations at his dacha in Barvikha, perhaps too many times.

'Ivan Borisovich, we – you, me, Russia – are paying the price for that Chechen fool Dudayev's failure to suppress Islamic militants in his own back yard. Not only do we pay him untold millions to prop up his regime, but we pay with Russian blood when he cocks up. Eighty-three dead at Domodedovo. Eighty-three precious lives. *Eighty-three loved ones!*'

The General took a swig from his bottle of beer, keeping his eyes on Ivan as he threw his head back and the liquid slopped down his throat.

'I am more concerned about the Dudayevtsi. No other governor in this country has a private army of 30,000 bloodthirsty men armed to the hilt,' said Ivan. 'They swear allegiance to Russia and the President but Dudayev parades them as a provocation and uses them to assassinate his enemies in Moscow. If we do nothing, one day we'll wake up and the Dudayevtsi will control Russia.'

No, he hadn't given a thing away; the General was not going to have her: to hold her over him and use her existence and death for political purposes. Svetlana was his, and his alone. Aslan Dudayev had allowed her death to happen and he was going to pay for it soon.

What was to come would be her memorial. This was for Sveta, his love.

VI

Assia had read the same line in her heavy biography of Pushkin at least five times and closed the book with a dramatic flourish, garnering a few looks from her fellow passengers at the airport gate. She couldn't concentrate. Her mind felt insubstantial, like powder; as soon as a thought took shape, it collapsed again in her hands.

The new egg had unsettled her. She knew she was meant to be thrilled about its discovery but something felt wrong. Instinct, the restive cave-dweller in the pit of her stomach was telling her to reject the egg. She was the mother bird who looks at the cuckoo's egg in her nest and knows that the markings aren't right.

She had thought about calling her friend Angie, a former colleague at the V&A, to talk through the egg with her. Very often she found that a conversation with the right person could pull observations and ideas out of her – a protracted process in which she caught a thought and wound it out of her innards like an unfurling tapeworm. She and Angie had used Socratic debate when deciding if something was really a piece of Fabergé or Fauxbergé. Assia would begin by saying 'All pieces by Fabergé are exquisite' and then they would examine the small box or hardstone figure before them and hunt for details which either proved or refuted the statement. 'Assia, don't be silly, this chasing is sloppy – the border between this leaf and that is too blurred. Not exquisite to my eye,' Angie might say, shaking her head. Or Assia might exclaim 'Come on, Angie, the translucency here is exquisite! There are at least seven layers of enamel here. Only Fabergé could do that.' Although each had disputed what the other said on occasion, they had always ended up agreeing unanimously in the end.

Unlocking her phone, Assia tapped at the screen and brought Angie's number up, ready to dial. Her index finger hovered. Did she really want to speak to Angie? Did she really want her to walk roughshod over these delicate and rather uncomfortable misgivings she had? A colleague at the V&A had told her that Angie often moaned about what she called Assia's 'Fabergé dynasty,' the fact that her mother had become a kind of saint-figure in the Fabergé world. Angie would definitely labour the point that Olga had been wrong about the design of the egg and Assia didn't feel up to a large dose of 'smug' right now.

She didn't know what prompted it, but a picture appeared in her mind's eye as clearly and unceremoniously as though someone had inserted a slide into her mental projector. There it was: gloriously technicolour and absurd, the 'Trinket Seller'. Assia saw it in detail that she had not previously been able to recall: the weave of his golden basket, the delicate layer of green enamel on his jacket, the gold bows on his shiny black shoes. She laughed to herself at the surprise her mind had sent her, the silly little Baroque pearl model of a trinket seller with a Dalmatian next to him, standing on the lid of a gold and jewel-studded casket. The Galanteriewarenhändler was an early 18th century piece by an unknown maker from the Green Vaults in Dresden which Assia and her mother had always admired when they looked through the large book of *Treasures from the Dresden Green Vaults*. Olga had even had a postcard of the Trinket Seller on the pin-board in her office. The Dalmatian, whose little spotted face and body were made from bulbous baroque pearls, had amused Assia when she was little and she had enjoyed looking at the miniature trinkets for sale in the seller's basket. Now it rose before her like Banquo's ghost, its presence a protest.

Of course. Yes, it makes sense. The decorative pattern on the body of this new egg – that chessboard enamel – is lifted directly from the pattern of light and dark chequered enamel on the casket, the one on which the Trinket Seller stands. The pattern of painted flowers is virtually identical. I knew I'd seen it somewhere before and the sense of déjà vu was bothering me.

Assia leant forward and placed her head on her knees, breathing deeply, as though recovering from the effort of having scratched her mental itch. She realised that she was frowning. She could feel her pulse swelling and falling away with steady pressure at the top of her head and she blinked away the sting of tears. She felt an unbearable sadness when she thought of how pleased her mother would have been to know that this newly discovered egg had elements of the Trinket Seller. Olga loved the Dresden Treasures and had explained to Assia that much of the young Carl Fabergé's education had been conducted in Europe and he had studied many of the masterpieces in the Green Vaults.

'And so when he designed the Renaissance Egg, no one who knew Fabergé's background would have been surprised that it was almost an exact replica of Le Roy's crystal casket in the Grünes Gewölbe, the Green Vaults in Dresden.'

'You mean he copied it?' Assia's nose wrinkled as though something displeased her and she looked back and forth at the photograph of the Renaissance Egg and the photograph of Le Roy's casket. She was sitting on her parents' bed, the large book of Fabergé eggs balancing on her bare outstretched legs. Watching her mother putting on her makeup before she went out was one of her favourite things and this evening she got to be with her alone while Tanya was at a swimming competition. Olga was tying her blonde hair into a ponytail and securing it with a black gauze ribbon. She looked at Assia in her dressing-table mirror and smiled at the young girl perched on her bed.

'It certainly wasn't regarded as copying then, my darling. Being able to reproduce something from a bygone era was considered a mark of great skill. In fact, it was how the Emperor Alexander first came across Fabergé's work. He so admired Fabergé's reproductions of Scythian goldwork at a fair that he decided there and then to buy some cufflinks designed by him and later came the commission for the first ever Fabergé Easter egg.'

'I like that idea,' said Assia looking earnestly at her mother's reflection. 'At school copying is considered to be lazy. The teachers want us to have our own ideas.'

'And so do I,' said Olga, holding her daughter's gaze in the mirror while applying lipstick. 'It's very important to think originally and to have ideas that other people don't have, but it's just as important to recognise what Fabergé was doing. He wasn't copying Le Roy, he was paying homage to him and acknowledging what he had inherited culturally from Europe.' She plucked a handkerchief from the box next to the mirror and slid it between her lips. She then held it up and admired the pink pout which had stained the tissue. 'In fact,' she continued, applying another coat of lipstick, 'he was showing that he – and Russia – appreciated what Le Roy did and could enhance it. If you compare the Renaissance Egg with Le Roy's casket, you'll see that Fabergé's egg is more delicately curved and its flared foot is more pronounced. He also represents the date "1894" at the top of the egg in rose-cut diamonds. It is quite breath-taking to see the egg in the flesh.'

Over the Tannoy it was announced that her flight to St Petersburg was delayed by forty minutes. Assia felt the onslaught of a migraine. Hunting for some ibuprofen in her bag, she popped two pills out of the blister and felt the chalk at the back of her mouth as she swallowed a few mouthfuls of water from a plastic bottle. She threw her head back to try and swallow the pills and had to take another mouthful of water to get them down. It had always annoyed Olga that she threw her head back so dramatically. *You're just making it difficult for yourself, darling. You don't need to move your head to swallow them. You don't throw your head back when you're drinking lemonade, do you? No, you're doing it again!* Assia would protest that she couldn't help it and in a funny kind of way she had come to own this exaggerated movement, even though it irritated her mother and made her sister laugh.

She tried Konstantin's number again. He hadn't answered his phone for the last two days, but she was desperate to speak to him about the new egg and she wanted to meet him when she landed, before tonight's unveiling. He must have seen the photographs of the egg and she wondered if he had also made the connection with the design of the egg and the Dresden Trinket Seller – not many people knew the collection in the Green Vaults well. She had pulled up a photograph of the model on her iPad and felt a thrill of excitement at pin-pointing the similarity between the pieces. *This must be how Mama felt when she got her teeth into a lead.* Her exhilaration was blunted when she heard the officious female voice announcing that Konstantin's number was unavailable. She began to think that perhaps she should have been concerned when she hadn't been able to get hold of him a few days ago. But he was probably just very busy. Everyone would have wanted his thoughts on the egg and he wasn't wedded to his phone – so many of his generation weren't.

The airport gate was full now and some people had already begun to queue to board, even though there was nobody at the desk. Assia hated queues. She had laughed out loud on reading Dmitri Bykov, one of Russia's most famous modern poets and artists, saying 'Seeing any line, our people will go and stand in it.' Queueing was both a Russian and an English pastime. The Russians did it to get whatever was at the end of the line and the English did it to avoid arguments. Either way, thought Assia, I'm not getting up until the last moment.

In front of her seat, a gap in the queue yawned where a group of people chatting hadn't noticed that boarding had begun. To the right of someone's leg, Assia saw a man on the opposite bank of seats looking down at his phone. There was a slight shadow on his scalp and she guessed that he shaved his head. She was sure that she had seen him at the screening of the Fabergé film last week and when he looked up, she smiled faintly, politely. He caught her glance and looked down again quickly.

VII

In its stone bed, the Neva looked as though it was frothing; little white eddies and peaks billowed along weightlessly. Staring at it for more than a few seconds though, Assia saw that the river was, in fact, static and cracked: the fizzy froth of waves just clumps of snow and ice blocks. The coursing of the great river had been stilled by winter and the frozen expanse was surprisingly soothing to look at. The milky St Petersburg sky was as white as the ice-bound river but the cold did nothing to dampen the headache which had got worse on the flight over.

Drawing her silk scarf up so that it covered her lips, Assia sighed and felt her breath warm her face. It was bitterly cold and part of her longed to go inside and warm herself inside the Hermitage, in the all-consuming unfaltering warmth that every Russian building generated in the winter, while another part of her wanted to linger here outside the Hermitage and settle into the historical grooves which had been worn into the ground by so many feet. Here was where Father Gapon and his peaceful petitioners had been heading in 1905 on Bloody Sunday, holding icons before them and hoping for sight of their Little Father, the Tsar. He would listen to their grievances and right the wrongs they suffered as toiling workers. *If the Little Father only knew of the injustices we bear, he would relieve us of our burdens!* And yet the Tsar was not in the palace and the Cossacks charged on those marching, threshing the crowd with their sabres while the Preobrazhensky Guard peppered them with bullets. Assia thought of the bodies strewn in the snow and the icons lying scattered like shields discarded on a battlefield.

Icons that couldn't protect you from slaughter were somewhat redundant, she thought. Shouldn't light shine from them, emanating as bright white spears which run through those doing wrong, piercing them? She recalled an icon in the chapel at which her mother used to worship in Oxford. It was a copy of a famous 16th century icon in Yaroslavl which depicted the Transfiguration. Jesus shimmers in a white robe, his Godhead radiating from a star-studded aureola with geometrical perfection, like the golden spokes of a wheel. The mountain rocks over which Jesus, Elijah and Moses float are sharp and spiky, as jagged as the limbs of the stunned Apostles which are frozen into arthritic angles as they cower before the Son of God. It was a beautiful icon and she had spent many hours staring at it during innumerable services. Olga had taken the twins to the Chapel of St Alexis the Wonderworker in Park Town every week for as long as they could remember, and the iconography and music had formed a significant part of the tapestry of Assia's consciousness. She hadn't been back there since Olga's funeral because she was furious with God. God had allowed her to be her mother's executioner; he hadn't stopped the van from pulling out on that slip road and for that she just couldn't believe that he loved her.

In the distance, a man emerged from a side door at the Western end of the palace building and Assia's eye fell on the figure as he walked across the forecourt. His gait was lumbering, as though he could barely bring himself to pick up each foot as he leaned into the wind. He was tall with dark hair and Assia ran towards him as he stopped to put on a leather cap.

'Kostya, Kostya!' she yelled, trying to pick up her pace without slipping on the icy must of the ground. 'Kostya, wait!' Her cheeks flaring pink, she approached the man who was now standing still, cap on, straining his eyes to see who was shouting at him. The look of confusion remained on his face and it was only when she was a few feet away that Assia realised she had the wrong man.

'Oh, gosh, I'm so sorry,' Assia said politely in Russian, 'I thought you were someone else.'

The tall man looked her up and down and walked away slowly, shaking his head. Assia felt stung by his disapproval and she was shaking a little as she pulled her phone out of her bag and removed her glove to dial Konstantin's number.

'Kost, where are you?' her words spilled out as steam in the cold air as she muttered into the phone. The line clicked into the same brisk declaration of unavailability which she had been getting every time she had dialled Konstantin since she had arrived in St Petersburg. She wondered if perhaps he was trying to avoid her, even though she couldn't think why he would do so now. They had managed to repair their relationship after Olga's death even though Konstantin couldn't bring himself to speak to Assia at the funeral. When, eventually, they spoke again, eighteen months later, he explained that he had gone through all the stereotypical things that grieving people go through: shock, boiling rage towards Assia for taking Olga away from them and then a deep, dark depression which made him feel so needy that he continued a relationship with a girlfriend who was totally inappropriate. He had only relented when he listened to a tearful voicemail Assia had left him in which she begged him to forgive her and explained that she was pulling her life together and wanted to begin a career in Fabergé. She had said that he was the only person who still refused to talk to her after the accident and that his silence was making her ill.

She decided to go to the flat Konstantin shared with his sister on Ulitsa Zhukovskovo. She couldn't bear any more second-guessing and unanswered questions. Her brain felt as though it might short-circuit if she didn't find out where he was. For some reason, Konstantin had become a kind of touchstone and if she didn't see him while she was in St Petersburg, she felt as though she couldn't address anything else. She wondered if it was because he had grown up with her mother and that she needed to pay a sort of atavistic homage to her family roots in the city by seeing him. *No, it's not that.* She tried to put her finger on what was bothering her as she headed towards Nevsky Prospekt, leaving behind her the white and Eau-de-nil palace of the Hermitage and its golden-topped Corinthian columns. The Russian flag flying on top made a snapping sound as the wind parried with it and Assia looked back quickly when she heard the noise.

She picked up pace along Nevsky Prospekt where the heavy footfall from shoppers had melted little paths through the snow. Wires crisscrossed overhead, dangling from one neoclassical palace to the other across the broad plain of the street and giving it a slightly destitute look. The neverending straightness of the street and the expanse of white sky above made Assia conscious of the size of Russia's vast lands. Nothing seemed to begin or end but just went on and on and on under the same yawning, pitiless sky. As she passed the Kazansky Cathedral on her right with its large dome floating on a crescent of soaring columns, Assia felt her nose tingle and tears rush to her eyes. Her face crumpled into that involuntary expression of crushing anguish which so often accompanies tears and she had to stop and mop her face with the fur rim of her gloves. She felt in her pockets for a handkerchief and pulled out a scrunched-up blue and green paisley silk square which she had unwittingly acquired from her father's huge collection of handkerchiefs. Dabbing her face, she saw a few passers-by glance at her without turning their heads, their eyes so swiftly averted that you could not say for sure that they had seen her. For the first time ever in Russia, she felt insignificant and unsure of herself. Ever since Olga had taken her and Tanya to St Petersburg as teenagers, Russia had become a real place for her, not just some land behind a chainmail curtain where people queued to look at empty shelves. The twins spoke Russian like natives and knew the local rubrics: how to kiss in greeting, when to use someone's patronymic and how to cross themselves in an Orthodox church. There was no custom or tradition which would have caught the girls out and yet Assia, in this moment, felt isolated and vulnerable. Seeing her mother in that film clip had taken her by surprise and she supposed that this had rattled her more than she had realised. Olga's legacy had been appropriated by the news of the egg's discovery and while she knew her mother would be pleased to be remembered, Assia couldn't help but feel that she had been supplanted as the keeper of her mother's flame.

It took her a little while to reach the Anichkov Bridge and its famous bronze Horse Tamers which represented the harnessing of nature by man. Two couples were embracing by the pedestals of these colossal sculptures, one couple on each side of the bridge, and posing for a friend who was photographing them. The friend called out adjustments in Italian and got the girls to stand on tiptoes and flick up a leg at the back. To Assia, shrouded in anxiety, this seemed almost perverse: the horses were on the verge of smashing their hooves down on their mooning tourist faces. The tamers were athletic and cast in attitudes showing them reaching up to hold the horses and contain their strength. Assia wanted to approach the lovers and twist their jaws upwards so that the bellies of the horses bore down on them, hooves poised to crush.

She hurried across the bridge and tried to dismiss her urge to scream. Tourists and people going about their everyday business angered her periodically: they didn't seem to appreciate that tragedy was just a whisper away. The psychologist at the Warneford had told her that people who had undergone a trauma often felt this way. Russians, of course, were different – they understood. The older generations which had been born and brought up in the Soviet Union knew all about loss and grief. Although Assia had never met her grandparents, she knew that her grandfather had been a young man during the Siege of Leningrad and her mother had told her of the deprivations he and his parents and sisters had endured and the awful, awful things they had witnessed. Olga had related his experiences not just as matters-of-fact but as though she herself had suffered through them as well and Assia was convinced that this preservation of experience had become a kind of ancestry for Russians under Soviet rule: these events had to be revered and remembered as one would recall a family tree. Added to this, the close quarters in which everyone lived provided the kind of clinical conditions in which memories could thrive: communal living meant that if you had lost grandparents or parents, other people's relations would tell you their memories. Assia used to think that although the circumstances were awful, at least in those crammed apartments there would always be somebody to notice your tears. A person had once said to her that the nice thing about having a twin was that you were never alone: you would have someone who knew what it was like to be you and who would wake in the night if you were in trouble. At the time, Assia had just smiled and agreed, thinking to herself that they couldn't be more wrong.

On Liteyniy Avenue, Assia crossed at the lights so that she would be on the right side to see the southern wing of the Sheremetev Palace, known as the Fountain House because of the multitude of fountains which used to adorn its gardens. The legendary poet Anna Akhmatova had lived here with her third husband and this part of the palace had been turned into a museum dedicated to her life and works. Assia had only been here in the summer when a canopy of green leaves shaded the columns of the house. Now the winter-stripped trees stood bleakly beyond the green railings and the Fountain House looked beautiful but forbidding. Akhmatova was one of Assia's favourite poets and she treasured her particularly because her life and art seemed to straddle both Imperial and Soviet life. She had been only a few years older than the Grand Duchesses and grew up near them at Tsarskoe Selo, and yet she had lived beyond the Revolution only later to see her son being dragged off to the gulag because his father was an aristocrat. Their blue blood could not be expunged, reflected Assia, peering through the railings surrounding the palace. For Lenin and Stalin, an accident of birth was a crime of birth and their cold god would only be appeased by a bloodletting so vast that the soil swelled like a full sponge.

A cloud of Assia's warm breath melted past the cold green metal railings and evaporated on the other side as if encountering a vacuum. The melancholy poet still lives there in those rooms, thought Assia. She is sitting on a divan, her long neck and profile set into relief by the pale light from the window behind her. She is magnificent in her dignified silence. Set apart from the bustle in the crowded apartment, she is a strange and fearsome prophetess. High-pitched laughter from a young woman passing by and chatting on her phone brought Assia back from the tableau of sadness just beyond the windows. She bowed her head for a second or so in obeisance to the Russian goddess of poetry and then carried on to the corner where Liteyniy Avenue turned into Ulitsa Zhukovskovo.

Konstantin's sister's apartment was not very far up the street on the right-hand side. The building was about four storeys high, honey-coloured with a large door and big windows. If viewed with one eye closed to the surrounding buildings, one could almost imagine that it was a Georgian building in a market town in England. Assia had been here once before, a few years ago, and she had remarked upon the impressive location of the apartment to Konstantin. He had explained that his sister had been married to a *chinovnik*, a senior government bureaucrat, and that although now a widow, his sister had the right to live in the flat for her lifetime. Konstantin had moved in with her fifteen years ago, at her insistence, when she had found him living in his tiny studio after his wife had chucked him out.

Assia looked up at the building and tried to remember which floor the apartment was on. It was either the third or the fourth but she couldn't be sure exactly and she couldn't recall Konstantin's sister's married name. She tried the buzzer next to the name 'Petrovichev' and leaned next to the speaker to hear a response. She waited for thirty seconds or so and was about to press the next buzzer when she heard a muffled noise and an anxious-sounding '*Allyo?*' came through the little metal grille next to the buttons.

'*Allyo?* Who is it? Who's there?' It was not a man's voice but it was surprisingly deep and clear. Assia assumed it was Konstantin's sister speaking into the intercom and she explained herself.

'Hello, my apologies for disturbing you. My name is Assia Wynfield' – she pronounced it as *Vinfeld* in Russian – 'and I am a friend of Konstantin Alexandrovich. I have been trying to get hold of him for a few days now but he is not answering his phone. I know he lives here and I was hoping he might be in?'

A buzzing sound and the muffled crackling noise of the intercom phone being replaced. Assia realised almost too late that she had been granted admittance and she pushed urgently at one of the heavy brown doors with flaking paint. The door slammed behind her and the noise reverberated around the cold hallway she was now standing in. Assia could hear the rattle of a door being unlocked at the very top of the stone stairs ahead of her and she walked towards them and peered upwards, hoping to see Konstantin looking back down at her. She couldn't see anything beyond the grey stone above her and she stepped back and pulled open the small metal door of the tiny lift which had been grafted into the body of the stairwell so that the stairs snaked around it. The lift juddered up to the top floor and arrived at its destination with an unceremonious jerk. Assia pulled the door back quickly before it could transport her back down again and she stepped out onto the top floor of the building.

The door to Konstantin and Yelena's apartment was ajar and Assia made to peer round it tentatively but she gasped and stepped back when she saw a woman's face loom suddenly before her.

'Oh, I'm so sorry!' Assia smiled apologetically and put her hand on her chest to indicate shock. 'Forgive me. I was wondering if Konstantin Alexandrovich was here? I haven't been able to reach him on the phone. Am I right in thinking that you are Yelena Alexandrovna?'

The tall woman nodded and ushered Assia into the apartment, looking around the small landing outside anxiously before closing and bolting the door quickly. Assia went through the second door into a narrow, rectangular hallway with a high ceiling. Paintings crowded the walls making the ceiling seem even higher than it already was. From her previous visit to the apartment with Konstantin when Yelena was not there, Assia recalled that the sense of space imparted by height of the rooms was the reason why the place was given as a trophy flat to successful bureaucrats.

'I don't know where he is,' said Yelena Alexandrovna, shaking her head and pulling Assia's coat gently off her shoulders. 'I haven't heard from him for four days. You don't know, do you? No. Otherwise you wouldn't be here, would you?' She paused before Assia, absent-mindedly holding her guest's coat in her arms and looking into her face with a worried expression as though she were about to learn something awful.

Assia mirrored Yelena's concerned look and felt an overwhelming need to comfort her. She hadn't met Konstantin's sister before but she could see a strong family resemblance which made her feel that she knew the woman already. Yelena was tall and her dark hair, worn up in a bun, was streaked with grey. She had Konstantin's heavy brow and deep-set eyes, her high cheekbones still attractive even though her skin was worn and lined.

'You are Olga's daughter, of course,' said Yelena smiling weakly and putting her hand on Assia's arm.

'Yes. How did you know?' Assia was surprised that Yelena knew who she was but then felt foolish immediately. She had forgotten that Yelena would have known her mother way back when.

'You look like her; you have her beauty. Please come and sit in here and I will bring us some tea.' Yelena led Assia into the sitting room before going into the kitchen. A pale gauze curtain hanging over the large window hid the street from view but allowed the lemon-coloured light to stream in. The walls of the room were hung densely with paintings of various sizes and Assia could see that they were all painted in the same immediately recognisable style. The bright colours and thick brushstrokes were characteristic of Socialist Realism, which typically depicted young girls in patterned cotton dresses or thoughtful-looking sailors and miners. Assia wondered if Yelena's husband had collected the paintings; high-ranking bureaucrats were encouraged to display portraits of everyday heroes and happy children living the good Soviet life.

Hanging just below the ceiling on the far wall was a painting which stood out from all the rest. A snow-capped mountain loomed on the horizon and flat, rich, green fields with poplars and blossom spread out before it. A train of yoked oxen pulling a plough ran into the foreground of the painting and processed off into the lower left corner, their humped backs and lowered necks ever so slightly menacing. The blue of the mountain and the hot oranges and greens of the landscape had an intensity that was lacking in the all the other paintings in the room and Assia couldn't stop gazing at it.

'Mount Ararat,' Yelena said as she walked in with a tray and placed it on a small table in front of the sofa. She came over to Assia and handed her a glass of tea.

'It's utterly beautiful' said Assia, still looking up at the painting. 'Who painted it?'

'Martiros Saryan, Armenia's most famous painter. My father bought it from him and it hung in my parents' bedroom until my father was taken away; then my mother couldn't bear to have it anymore. My husband hated it because it reminded him of my father, the troublesome dissident. I like it for that very reason.' Yelena sat down on the low sofa, her hands placed primly on her knees. Assia didn't know whether to ask more about the father who was taken away in the night. She knew what had happened because Olga had told her; it was every family's worst nightmare and many children had avoided Yelena and Konstantin at school as though the disease of a missing parent could be caught.

'Have you been to Armenia?' asked Assia, sitting down gingerly next to Yelena and trying not to spill her tea as she lowered herself into the deep basin of the sofa.

'Never. My father fell out with my grandfather, who was a very religious man, and so we never saw our family there. But I always wanted to go. Kostya and I had a plan to go one day but I think I'm too old now. I always remember being told a story about a poor Greek couple who dreamed of going to Paris all their lives. Finally, when their son said he would pay for them to go, they turned him down. He couldn't understand why but they explained that going to Paris would mean that their wish, which had become as familiar to them as a member of the family, would evaporate.' Yelena was looking up at the painting while she related this. Suddenly, she turned to Assia with panic in her eyes.

'I am so worried about him. Four days is a long time. It's just not like him to disappear in this way. He knows that I would worry. He would get in touch if he was going away somewhere.'

Assia leant forward, placed her cup on the table and turned to face Yelena. She felt that the woman was longing to be reassured and that not to do so would be cruel. 'Really, I wouldn't worry. I'm sure that he's absolutely fine and that all will become clear when he walks back in. What was he doing when you last saw him?'

Yelena spoke calmly now, as though reasoning with herself. She must have rehearsed this over and over in her mind, thought Assia. 'He was excited because he had managed to get Vika a loan for Misha's treatment and they were going to take Misha to the States for an operation. He was so happy about that because he felt that it made Vika soften towards him. Things had been so bad between them ever since the divorce.' Yelena looked up towards the window and paused, deep in thought. Assia watched her, biting her lip as she did so. She felt a rising sense of panic about the situation and Yelena's mixture of distracted calm and wild anxiety was alarming.

'Have you spoken to Vika?'

'Yes.' Yelena nodded.

'And what did she say? Had she seen him?'

'Yes.' Yelena put her cup back on the tray and threaded her fingers together tightly as if in prayer. She looked up at Assia with tears in her eyes. 'She saw him on Tuesday, which was when I last saw him. Vika said she thought he was acting strangely when she saw him.' Her bottom lip quivered. 'She said he had seemed a little withdrawn and that he didn't want to stay long. She was worried too.'

'Ah, I see. Well, still, you mustn't worry. I'm sure there's a perfectly good explanation.' Assia slid a hand under her thigh – a prop, of sorts. 'My theory is that perhaps he was called away on a Fabergé restoration emergency. I work in the Fabergé world as well and I know that when an important collector has a problem, they always expect it to be sorted immediately.' She rolled her dark brown eyes exaggeratedly and smiled. 'You know that kind of person: the kind who thinks that their Fabergé frame is more important than your night's sleep.'

'I don't actually,' said Yelena soberly. 'Kostya's world is completely alien to me. But there is one thing I know. My brother is also the child of a man who was taken away: he would never disappear without telling me where he was going because he knows what my first thought would be. We suffered so much from not knowing where Papa was and Kostya just wouldn't do that to me willingly.' She shook her head vehemently as though she could not brook the prospect of such cruelty.

'Yes, but mobile phones die and modern life leads to all sorts of inconveniences that prevent us from being able to get in touch when we want to. I am sure everything will be fine.' Assia was about to touch Yelena's arm gently but thought better of it. She couldn't be sure that the older woman wouldn't flinch if she reached out to her and she could tell from Yelena's expression that nothing she had said had assuaged her worries.

'Actually, I forgot something.' Yelena stood up, a triumphant look on her face. She smiled at the revelation and began to pace around the room, drawing the recollection out. 'I had forgotten that Kostya did disappear once, for a while. It was when your mother died and I didn't hear from him for two days. He had gone to his studio and drunk himself stupid and then he reappeared again, looking like hell. Why didn't I think of that?' She shook her head as she racked her brain for an explanation. 'Yes.' She answered herself slowly, nodding. 'Yes, I think it was because I was very busy at work then and I didn't even notice that he had gone. That must be what has happened; he is sad about something and has gone into hiding.' Yelena looked expectantly at Assia, waiting to be congratulated on her sleuthing work.

'I think you are probably right.' Assia nodded softly and smiled indulgently at Yelena. She was stung by the casual mention of her mother's death but decided not to make anything of it. From what she could see, Yelena had lighted upon this episode as a way of stemming her anxiety and she wasn't about to upset her hostess further by picking apart her theory.

'*Gospodi!* I am sorry. I did not mean to bring up your mother's death. You look sad. I have just remembered what happened and that...' She drew a long breath and stopped pacing the room. 'Please forgive me. I think meeting you reminded me of how sad Kostya was at the time. I had forgotten it all.'

'It's quite all right,' said Assia, mollified by the apologetic look on Yelena's face. 'It was a long time ago and occasionally, on a good morning, I forget for a little while too.' She paused. 'May I pop to the loo?'

Washing her hands, Assia felt frustrated with herself. Why did she always try and relieve other people's discomfort? Why couldn't she just be one of those people who allowed others to stew in their own awkwardness when they stuffed their great big feet in their mouths? Just now she had tried to make Yelena feel better by saying that sometimes she too forgot that her mother was dead. The remark had no bearing on the truth at all – so little, in fact that she was rather embarrassed at having told such an untruth. And all to please others! Her matricide didn't exist just because she remembered it: it existed because she had become that person, because it was a fact that she couldn't escape. She was the person who killed her mother in both her dream-life and her waking-life. No matter that she hadn't *intended* to kill her and, oh, it wasn't your *fault*, Assia. It had still happened and she had been the one moving and propelling her mother's cells and particles towards destruction.

She, *Assia* had wanted to go to Waddesdon and see the murals painted by Leon Bakst. *She*, *Assia* had said that she would drive because she had just got her licence and she needed the practice and she liked having someone experienced next to her. Everyone had told her to keep driving when she passed her test and not to lose momentum as so many road-fresh drivers did. She hated driving on the fast roads and stuck to city driving where possible but that day, *that day*, she had made a conscious decision to listen to all the sages who had urged her into her motor and thought that she would dare to tackle the wretched slipstream of mirrors and signs and metal and exhaust. Bursts of ineffectual adrenalin had sprayed and sprayed into her system like a worthless chemical oracle as she saw the white van speeding along the slip road which ran into the A34.

She had known that something would happen. The ever inaudible Cassandra shriek had left echoes of echoes in her ears. She had tried to move into the fast lane when she saw the van but she wasn't decisive enough and missed her chance as a Range Rover paced her. She was about to ask Olga, her passenger, what she should do but she faltered, unable to decide if her mother wasn't saying anything because she thought she was driving well, or maybe her mind was elsewhere, spinning the colour wheel of the 144 different shades of enamel which Fabergé's workshops produced.

She couldn't recall any longer; she had worn the memory threadbare. But her brain, her God-awful augur-wise brain, had tripped her up. It was like thinking about running down a flight of steps while you're doing it. *Try it! At first you feel invincible, supra-human and then… foot meets step, foot meets step, foot meets… foot meets edge, foot edge meets, step edge foot, foot, foot…* Your instincts tumble before you like as many dominoes and you're a piece of jelly.

She had pressed over-ride and put her foot on the pedal.

Looking at her reflection in the tiny mirror in Yelena's bathroom, Assia wondered how many masks she wore to cope with the real world. The pretty woman with brown almond-shaped eyes and a perfect little nose was still - after all that therapy - someone whom she didn't really know. It was only at moments like these, when she tried to peek behind the exterior, that she spied glimpses of her true motivation: sparks flying from the hard drive. She had always thought that the reason she told white lies, like the one she had told Yelena, was because she was someone who couldn't bear another's discomfort and would rather bend the truth than hurt someone. But at this moment, in the narrow, high-ceilinged loo, Assia wondered if, in fact, she was just incredibly selfish and the white lies were entirely for her benefit.

Sometimes I forget that she is dead too.

There it was: a not-so-little white lie which she could crawl into like a cool, smooth cave. What she really needed was one of those witness-protection programmes where she could become a lie entirely and the escapism would be complete.

On her way back to the sitting room, Assia peered into what she determined was Konstantin's bedroom. Stacks of books on Fabergé and Russian silver covered every flat surface except the bed, which was made neatly and without a crease – Yelena's handiwork, Assia suspected. A beautiful icon of the Kazanskaya Mother of God hung over the bed and she tiptoed into the room to inspect it. The large, stylised head of the Virgin leaned protectively over the small Christ, whose hand was raised in blessing. Their delicate faces were painted in ochre colours which contrasted with the rich pastel colours of the enamel work on the silver *oklad*. Assia absolutely adored cloisonné enamel work and she took the icon off the wall to inspect the shading of the glossy cloisons. The Virgin's halo was intricately embellished with blue and pink enamel which sat within tiny little cells of twisted wire. The craftsmanship was staggering. Assia had seen many examples where the enamel was gloopy and heavy and had bled from one wire cell into another, but this one was exquisite. She wondered if it was an inherited piece but decided not to ask Yelena who would have thought she was snooping.

As she put the icon back on its hook, she noticed a small round wooden frame with a photograph of two young people. The frame was on a pile of dusty books on the bedside table but it wasn't itself covered in dust. She thought the girl looked like her mother and on closer inspection she realised that she was looking at Olga and Konstantin as teenagers. The picture was black and white and the two young students were sitting on a wall next to each other, her mother wearing a dark polo-neck and Konstantin in a snug-fitting short-sleeved shirt with a pocket on the chest. The pair were not smiling and their expressions were serious but not severe. They seemed to be posing in the way that people did back then when a snap was more of a portrait than something supposed to illustrate your mood. There was none of the grinning and gooning and fish-bowl closeness of a modern selfie. Olga had her head turned slightly towards Konstantin but she wasn't looking at him. Her pose was apparently self-conscious but she seemed perfectly at ease, almost languid. Blonde hair parted in the middle framed her pale, delicate face and her mouth was closed although, looking closely, Assia detected a slight tension around her lips which could have been a smile or a grimace suppressed – she couldn't decide. Next to her, Konstantin had the easy grace of a handsome man. From under his dark brow and mop of wavy hair, his gaze was angled beyond them, as though scanning the horizon protectively. He was remarkably attractive, with the cheekbones and jaw of a young Paolo Pasolini. His arms were strong and tanned and there was the suggestion of dark chest hair among the top buttons of his shirt. Armenian men had always held an attraction for Assia, partly because of Konstantin, she supposed. It felt like a dirty secret to admit it, as though she were a blonde maiden in a tower who longed to be ravaged by a marauding invader from The Orient, but there was something about the dark colouring and expressive eyes: forbidding masculinity and emotional intensity warring with each other.

Assia had never seen a photograph of her mother as a young woman in Russia, from the time before she had met her father and moved to England. When she was much younger, about twelve years old, Assia had asked Olga if she could see some photographs of her as a young girl and Olga had told her that her mother – Assia's grandmother – had had all the photos in a box somewhere in their flat in St Petersburg and that she didn't know what had happened to the box when her parents died. Her young self had been so surprised back then that her mother didn't seem to care what had happened to those photos. As far as she was concerned, such photos were sacred and she had always loved looking through the many huge cloth-bound albums Olga had made with photos of the twins. The photos had been carefully secured on each page with paper mounts and almost every photo had a neat little inscription next to it stating who was in the photo, the date and where they were. These books were the foundation stones of Assia's internal architecture and she would study the photographs with fascination and reverence. Were there any differences between herself and Tanya when they were born; did her mother look happy; who was baptised first at their Christening; what was their nanny like? These were questions to which the photographs couldn't provide all the answers but Assia would sit down, legs crossed, with a pile of the albums and feed her curiosity with the grainy lens of 1980s photographs.

Tanya hadn't been interested in these meticulous records but for Assia it was a way of setting her parents and her early life at one remove. The parents she gazed at on stiff page after stiff page were as unfamiliar to her as the people in the old *Picture Post* magazines she loved. Her parents – those young ones in the photos – had a glamour then that the chaos of daily life forfeited from them in their present lives. Her mother looked so fresh and pristine and English in her floaty floral dresses with big Laura Ashley collars; she had thrown herself fully into the Sloaney Princess Di look and even had the hair to match. A string of pearls and high-necked frilly shirts appeared to be her staple wardrobe and she perfected the fashion in a way that must have made all the other mothers jealous.

While Olga looked perfectly at ease as a doting young mother with a babe on each hip, Richard, her father, looked stiff and uncomfortable in the posed photographs. In one particular photo taken in the kitchen of their house in Oxford, Olga is sitting on a wicker chair in a long sugar-pink cotton dress with puff sleeves and a Peter Pan collar. Her slim brown feet are in a pair of white leather pumps with gold links on the front. She looks pretty and poised with one toddler on her lap and another standing, resting dimpled little elbows on the arm of the chair. Richard, in a checked flannel shirt of 80s distinction, stands behind the maternal tableau, one hand on Olga's shoulder. He looks stern but proud, as though lining up in the First VIII's College photograph. Everything was the long game with him, Assia had thought. Photos were just records of milestones for your biographer – you posed and then you un-posed again. In his head Assia knew that her father would have captioned this particular milestone as *Richard, 28, Senior Lecturer in Mathematics at St John's, with his beautiful Russian wife, Olga, and their twin daughters, at home in Oxford.*

Up until she had seen Olga in the photo on Konstantin's bedside table just now, Assia hadn't even considered that her mother might have had a Soviet look, a Soviet self which she had shed and stepped out of when she moved to England. She had, of course, wondered about her mother's life in Russia but Olga had never wanted to talk about it and the young Assia had fenced off this part of her imagination's cartography and that was that. The Olga in the photograph was an incarnation of her mother which undoubtedly belonged to Konstantin, and Assia felt as though she was committing an illicit act in studying it. Sitting on that wall then and there, Olga would have known nothing of the life she would eventually lead in England. Richard and the twins did not exist for her and she had other dreams and fancies: moons that orbited entirely different planets.

In addition to her family photographs, Assia had always been fascinated by the family albums of Nicholas, Alexandra, the four Grand Duchesses, Olga, Tatiana, Maria, Anastasia ('OTMA,' as they referred to themselves) and the Tsarevich. The young girls had been given Box Brownie cameras and had taken vast numbers of photographs of each other, their brother and their parents at rest and at play. As a young girl, Assia would sit on the sofa and flick through a book of these photographs for hours and hours: the younger pair of sisters cuddling a dog, Olga next to a favourite officer on the *Shtandart*, Maria smiling broadly on the sea shore. She inspected every image of these young princesses knowing how their story would end and it was this knowledge that gave their beauty and innocence a fatal quality which pricked her, even at a young age. The weight of inevitability gave their lives an other-worldliness; like looking through binoculars the wrong way, their existence had a remoteness. Assia wanted to shout through the small lens of the Box Brownie and warn them of what was going to happen, but they couldn't hear her. They just carried on playing with the officers on the deck of the *Shtandart* and posing sweetly in the gardens of the Alexander Palace. Olga had described to the twins one evening what had happened to the Imperial Family at Ekaterinburg and she and Tanya had cried when they learned how the family were executed. The young Grand Duchesses, the Tsar and Tsarina had been awakened in the early hours of 17th July, 1918, and been ordered to dress and go down into the basement of the Ipatiev House on the understanding that they were being sheltered from a possible artillery attack. The women had donned their stays which had bracelets, necklaces and all sorts of heavily-carated diamonds woven into the seams and, weighted down like deep-sea divers, they processed across the small courtyard of the house and down into the basement rooms where they were told to wait for a truck which would take them to safety. After more waiting eventually some guards walked into the room and announced summarily that the Tsar had been sentenced to death. Without further ado the family was gunned down with volley after volley of gunfire. The jewelled corsets of the women only served to prolong their torture as the bullets ricocheted off the stones and the guards resorted to stabbing them with their bayonets as though they were no more than dolls stuffed with wool. Even Tatiana's Pekinese, Jimmy, was not spared and his tiny little body, as offensive to the Bolshevik cause as his Imperial mistress, was tossed onto the truck that bore the last of the Romanovs.

'She couldn't bring herself to stay in Russia.'

Assia started and turned to see Yelena standing in the doorway.

'I'm sorry, I wasn't snooping. I just saw this icon as I passed and I wanted to take a closer look and then I couldn't help but notice the photograph.' Assia gestured loosely at the photo and then put her hand up to her cheek which had flared pink.

Yelena walked over to the table where she picked up the frame and appeared to study it. 'I always knew that she would leave – it was just a matter of when – but it was the way she held herself, as if she was too good to be among us.' She addressed herself to the photograph. 'It didn't bother Kostya, of course; he loved being around her and he would have done anything to get her to stay but I was pleased when she went. She was holding him back.' She looked up at Assia defiantly now, the bitterness which had lain dormant for so long smouldering like a touch paper. Her mouth hardened into a line.

Assia had clasped her hands together and put them down in front of her like a naughty schoolgirl surprised at the tuck box in the middle of the night. As Yelena spoke, she dug the nails of her right hand into the fleshy pads of her left palm and maintained the pressure so that her knuckles whitened.

'I can only apologise on behalf of my mother, Yelena Alexandrovna. Perhaps it would be best if I left now.'

VIII

It's him again. What is he doing here?

Assia wanted to believe that the man with the shaven head on the Troitsky Bridge was just admiring the view. He was standing by one of the low seats carved out of granite which flanked the corners of the bridge and – she thought – looking out over the river. Like her, he was a Fabergé enthusiast who had come over for the unveiling of the egg and was killing time before the grand event tonight. *Yes, that had to be right, didn't it?*

She decided that she wouldn't try to call Kostantin again. She was still smarting from the way Yelena had turned on her just now, baring her teeth so unexpectedly. To begin with it had seemed as though their mutual concern for Konstantin was enough to smooth over any scars from the past. What an idiot she was. She of all people should have known that old wounds never stopped weeping.

A matt black Bentley purred along the snowy embankment like a panther in stealth. She couldn't see anything through the tinted windows of the car but guessed that the passenger in the back of the car was probably an oligarch who was going to the unveiling of the new egg tonight. She loathed that kind of car; the type which oozed money like sticky sap. The smell of newness inside made her feel sick and the squeak and squish of the leather seats was enough to bring her out in a rash. She leant over the balustrade taking deep breaths and feeling her shoulders rise and fall. She felt concerned about something but couldn't quite put her finger on it; something somewhere was off-centre and this sense of imbalance was disarming. She squinted at the river in a half-hearted attempt to gain a new perspective but had to sit down on a bench when she felt that she might lose her balance.

She thought she felt the buzz of her phone in her bag and she patted it to feel the vibrations and confirm her suspicion. Sometimes she imagined her phone was buzzing and scrabbled to reach it only to find a blank screen. She wasn't sure if these phantom vibrations were indicative of a deep desire to be contacted or a fear of the same. She rummaged through the deep pockets and pulled out her phone. She almost didn't answer when she saw who it was and she felt her stomach drop.

'Edward, hi!' She took a deep breath. 'Gosh, it's been so long since I spoke to you! How are you?'

'Assia, hello! I got your number from Madéleine Roseman. You're in Piter now, I hope? I'm fine. Tired – it's manic at the Museum. Last-minute everything. Where are you? We must have a proper reunion tonight.'

She loved his unapologetically upper-class voice. It suited him better now that he was older. 'Just strolling along Dvortsovaya Naberezhnaya and inspecting the river. I'm going to pop into the Hermitage at some point and catch up with their new keeper of Western Art.'

'Well don't spend all your time with Leonid Evgrafovich; we want to have the chance to get to know you and to charm you this evening. You're down to come to the dinner after the unveiling tonight – you are still coming, I hope? Oleg Dmitrievich, our curator, is very keen to speak to you and tell you more about the egg.'

Assia tried to dampen the excitement she felt, to make sure he didn't hear it in her voice. 'Yes, of course,' she said coolly. 'What time does it all kick off again?'

'I'll send a car for you at seven. You're in the Kempinski, aren't you?'

'Yes.' She wondered how he knew this and then felt silly for wondering: they were in Russia, after all. 'Sounds good. See you this evening.'

'It's wonderful that you're coming. Bye.'

She thought he sounded moved just then, his assured timbre softening ever so slightly as he signed off. Perhaps not; perhaps he was smiling at a waitress or waving to a girlfriend as he spoke, but it was the possibility, the guessing of the odds which thrilled her. She hadn't expected to be taking part in a kind of fan and dance-card waltz when she flew out to St Petersburg and yet here she was, wondering if her dress for tonight was right and musing about Edward's reaction to her outfit. It was so long since she had felt stomach-plunging excitement that she had forgotten how wonderful it was, how it added a piquancy to everything.

IX

Assia had changed since her student days. It was not just that she and Edward had taken separate paths until now, it was the fact that the accident had had a mutating effect. Living at home in Oxford with a mortified father who made clumsy attempts not to blame her for his wife's death had provided anything but a platform for recovery and Assia had abandoned all attempts to go back to Worcester and finish her degree. She didn't feel she had the right to grieve; grief was her father and Tanya's alone and while her father hid his mourning from her, her twin could not bear to be in her presence. Gradually, Assia had begun to doubt if she were human any more.

For a long time after the crash, even when she had recovered physically, Assia was absolutely sure that she had cancer. In the shower she would feel cancerous lumps in her armpits and breasts where the doctor assured her there were none and she became particularly obsessed with the idea that her lymphatic system was clogging up. Mysterious pains would trouble her and she was convinced that she could feel her cells multiplying and hardening into tumours. It seemed as though everyone – including Tanya – had finished their degrees and were pursuing sensible careers in London. They were all living in shared flats in Clapham while Assia was analysing lumps in a stale room in Oxford. In her sister she saw a much healthier version of herself and there was a particularly dark period when she thought that it would be altogether easier if Tanya could just live her life for her.

It was a psychologist at the Warneford Hospital who had encouraged Assia to pursue the love of Fabergé which she and her mother had shared.

'Think about something which you both enjoyed, something that was just between the two of you.'

He had said this in a beige room with a spider plant and a box of tissues. She had ignored the suggestion at first and dismissed it as something only morons needed to do, but sitting in her mother's study on the top floor of their house in Jericho and plucking books on Fabergé off the shelves, she thought of the keen interest she had once had in her mother's world and their long conversations about Fabergé and his workmasters. Her mother had been ecstatic when she had got a place at Worcester to read History of Art and she had arranged for Assia to spend a couple of weeks in Moscow after her first term at Oxford working with a friend who curated the Kremlin Armoury's Fabergé.

'I'll come out to Moscow with you and introduce you to Larissa,' said Olga skewering an olive onto a cocktail stick as they waited for their drinks at a smart brasserie in Oxford. 'She's very old but widely considered to be the best expert on Fabergé in Russia and you ought to meet her and pick her brains while she's alive.'

'But you hate Moscow!' exclaimed Assia, smiling.

'Moscow is a necessary evil, darling,' said Olga choosing to ignore Assia's amusement 'and I don't *hate* it, I just prefer Piter. I'm monstrously biased, of course: as a native of Piter I was never going to love Moscow more.'

'You *do* hate it. You never stay there for more than a day and you're always drawn back to Piter like a moth to a flame. Anyway, Mama, your friend at the Armoury won't want me hanging around bothering her all day.'

'Such reticence from an Oxford student!' Olga pretended to look horrified but took Assia's hand and squeezed it. 'Larissa Mikhailovna will adore you, not least because you're my flesh and blood. She'll take you under her wing and be a mother to you as she was to me when I worked for her. She knows so much and is quite messianic about passing on her knowledge. It will be such a treat for you: the Armoury has ten Imperial Easter eggs!'

Assia recalled the way in which the aged Larissa Mikhailovna had heaved her large frame out of the uncomfortable wooden chair in her magnificent office at the Armoury when she saw Olga and embraced her with tears in her eyes. When Olga introduced Assia to her, the old woman took her face in her hands and kissed her forehead.

'*Takaya krasotka, Olyusha!*' she had said and kissed Assia again. 'Only you could produce such a beautiful Russian girl with an English man!'

'My other twin, Tanya, is just as beautiful but has no love of the arts,' said Olga. 'She is a boring old mathematician like her father and my father, if you can believe it!' Larissa Mikhailovna was tickled pink by this comment. She laughed so much she had to sit down again, her eyes and nose wrinkling as though she were a maniacal putto.

Watching her mother and Larissa Mikhailovna discussing the restoration of a magnificent emerald-green enamel presentation snuff box which had been badly damaged during cleaning of one of the display stands, Assia marvelled at the two women's knowledge. In spite of the derogatory remark pitching science versus art, both Larissa Mikhailovna and Olga demonstrated a knowledge and appreciation of the restorer's skill in repairing the engine-turned ground which created the guilloché effect. The talented restorer had also managed to match the new enamelling to the original colour and had applied the modern enamel so it exactly replicated the translucency of the enamel which remained with barely a hairline crack visible.

'This is really excellent work, Larissa Mikhailovna. This restorer understands the chemistry of old enamel,' said Olga, examining the box with her loupe. 'Who did you use?'

Larissa sighed heavily as though troubled by the question. Her huge bosom heaved and the spectacles hanging from a ribbon around her neck slipped to the right, 'For this piece we could only use the very best because of its value. His name is Pyotr Shemetilo and he was recommended by your friend Konstantin Stepanyan. He was Konstantin Alexandrovich's apprentice.'

'Kostya's apprentice? I didn't realise he had any protégés. Well, the best could only be trained by the best and there is no question that it was always Kostya. I will be seeing him in Piter in a few days and I'll congratulate him on his student.'

'Yes, please do. And tell him to train more young restorers. There are too many charlatans out there who ruin good pieces because they don't understand Fabergé's designs and techniques.' Larissa Mikhailovna had looked distressed by the unpalatable thought of masterpieces being butchered by talentless cowboys.

When Assia had told the psychologist that she had been thinking about things she enjoyed with her mother and that their shared love of Fabergé had inspired her to consider a career in that world, he had nodded and scrawled something on his clipboard.

'I was sitting on the floor in Mama's study, looking at all the books on Fabergé which she had written and, for the first time since the accident, I felt excited by something.'

'Could you say what it was that excited you?'

'Fabergé was a genius at turning ordinary things – a photo frame, a letter-opener – into beautiful things. It just… I don't know. I suppose I felt that there are small openings for little bits of beauty in my life: delicate things, miniature things that one can cope with every day. That thought excited me.'

'And you couldn't look at these things before now? What would you say has changed?'

Assia turned to look out of the window at the view of a red-brick paved path enclosed by high glass walls. Whenever she spoke in these sessions, she tended to address the furniture or the window, finding it easier to speak to something inanimate and then glance at her psychologist to see what reaction her words had engendered. 'Beauty makes me feel guilty. It reminds me of what I took from her.' She turned and looked again at the man opposite her. He shifted in his chair and crossed his legs. 'I regret that I killed my mother when she had so much more to offer the world. I took away all the possibilities she had to research Fabergé, to discover more things and share them with everyone. You know, if I had killed a murderer or a paedophile, I don't think I would regret that.' She smiled wryly and checked to see her interlocutor's reaction. 'No, I would regret it, but you know what I'm saying, don't you? I wouldn't have deprived the world of something.' She paused. 'What do I think? I think I mean that it would be a lot easier to bear, what I did, if Mama had been just another ordinary housewife. That sounds awful, doesn't it?' She bit her lip and fiddled with the cotton handkerchief in her lap.

'What you are saying is not awful. You are telling me that you feel aggrieved on a number of accounts: you feel pain because of the loss of your mother and you feel guilt for being involved in the death of a talented woman. It is important that you separate these things in your mind.' The psychologist took off his steel-rimmed glasses and rubbed them with a cloth. He put them back on and looked at Assia kindly.

He continued. 'I think a part of you is struggling with the idea that you miss your mother in her professional capacity just as much as you miss her as a mother.'

Assia sighed and bit her lip again. 'Gosh, I don't know. I hadn't thought of it like that. I'm not sure I can separate the two in my mind. Mama wasn't particularly maternal, really. I mean, her way of mothering myself and Tanya was to be ambitious for us, to ensure that we were well-educated and that we pushed ourselves and realised our potential. Perhaps it was because she was brought up in Soviet Russia.'

'So she wasn't a cosy mother? Not someone who would comfort you if you did badly in an exam?'

'Well, no, she wouldn't. She always expected us to do well, and we did. I don't think I would have told her if I did badly at something because I would have punished myself enough first. Tanya and I competed with each other at school – total over-achievers. Maybe Mama encouraged that, I'm not sure.'

'Did you resent your mother for pressuring you all the time?'

'I'm not sure. But it wasn't really like that. Yes, she was a demanding mother, undoubtedly, but Tanya and I put the pressure on ourselves. We were at a very academic school with lots of dons' daughters who were also very clever. It was a bit of a pressure cooker and everyone wanted to go to Oxbridge. Mama liked our successes; she liked the fact that we were top-of-the-class and that we were thin and pretty. We were known as the Russian Princesses at school and I think Mama liked that. More than anything, I liked pleasing her.'

'And did you feel that she favoured one of you more than the other?'

Assia smiled at the question while gazing at the print of a sunflower on the wall. 'Hmm. I don't think she had a favourite, really. Both Tanya and I got into Oxford which is what she wanted for us. Tanya got a place at Merton to read Maths and I got into Worcester to read History of Art. I think Mama thought I had her sensibilities because I was studying the Humanities whereas she always said Tanya was like her father, our grandfather, who was a Maths professor at St Petersburg State University. Our father also teaches Maths at Oxford but Mama was convinced that Tanya's maths skills were from her own Russian genes. I don't know, maybe Mama did prefer Tanya because she is more like her than I am. More hard-nosed. Are you more likely to hate someone who reminds you of yourself or love them? I don't know, but I'm sure Mama saw more of herself in Tanya than in me.'

'And was it exhausting trying to please your mother?'

'Well, as I said, Tanya and I put pressure on ourselves. Mama encouraged us to have high standards but we wanted to meet them, so they became our own bars and not hers. I could never have been happy without something to aim for in my old life and I think, perhaps, that I am feeling like that again, like that person I was.' Assia raised her head tentatively to see the reaction of her psychologist; she felt as though she were confessing something shameful. 'I want to take on Mama's mantle and continue her research into Fabergé. It will give me a reason to get up in the mornings.'

The psychologist took a few moments to write on his clipboard before putting it down on the table next to him. He folded his hands and placed them on his knee. 'I want you to be careful how you approach this, Anastasia. Yes, it is good, undoubtedly, that you have found something which you are passionate about, but there are things we need to take into consideration. I want you to be aware that people in your position very often feel that they need to live two lives: their own, and that of the person who has died. This can often bleed into perfectionism, to which I think you are susceptible anyway. My main point here is that you mustn't confuse a healthy interest in Fabergé with the impulse to make up for the loss of your mother's life.'

Assia nodded earnestly as she listened. Her thick, dark hair was tied in a low ponytail which sat elegantly on one shoulder, its tip curling up. She played with the tip, weaving its perfect, glossy curl through her fingers. She frowned before beginning to speak.

'The thing is, I don't really see how I can separate the two things; it's not that simple. My passion for Fabergé is so intimately bound up with my mother that they might as well be welded together. I'm not the kind of person who has "hobbies", which is what I imagine you would call a "healthy interest". I don't do healthy interests – you will know as well as anyone that high-achieving girls are total failures at doing anything moderately.'

X

'All v. busy here but having an interesting time. Hope you aren't working too hard. Will send some pics of the egg when I see it. A Xx'

Assia pressed 'Send' and her phone made the noise of a stone plopping into water as her message sped through cyber clouds to Ben's phone. She had only sent a few cursory replies to his many enquiries about her 'Fabergé adventure' and she knew that her intention to keep him quiet with paltry scraps of information was not a good sign. To her dismay, Ben replied straight away and the thought of him waiting patiently online for a missive from her was surprisingly irritating.

'Longing to know what my gorgeous expert thinks of the egg in the flesh. Bxxx'

Assia sighed and closed the app on her phone so that Ben could see that she had gone offline. She didn't feel like telling him about anything that was happening at the moment; it was like being asked to show your hand to someone who was learning about the game when all Assia really wanted to do was to press her cards to her chest and guard them closely. Ben didn't understand the Fabergé world or Russia but she knew that he longed for her to include him in these parts of her life. Sometimes he would flick through her books on Fabergé and ask her to tell him about various pieces and occasionally, she would indulge him and talk him through the finer points of Rappoport's creations in silver for Fabergé. Ben would sit there listening with a smile on his face and then tell her how clever and amazing and beautiful she

73

was and on those days, the days when she didn't just bob on the water but felt the alarming and persistent tug downwards into the depths, on those days Ben's admiration and encouragement would reassure her that she was safe and loved. Yet there were times when Assia felt that she was coping with things – doing well, even – and it was then that she just wanted Ben and all his love and understanding to jump off a cliff. She knew he thought she was this perfect girl who had been felled by the great tragedy in her life but he didn't know – and sometimes she felt that he refused to know – that she wasn't spotless. She was aware that she used him far too much to bolster her confidence when it suited her and then bitched about his dependability behind his back. Guiltily she thought back to the time that she had been so anxious before giving an important lecture at the V&A to curators from the Fabergé Symposium. Ben had arrived early full of supportive pep-talk and helped her set-up her laptop and connect it to the projector. After the lecture, when she had been richly applauded and presented with a bouquet by the museum, she had pretty much ignored Ben at the reception and then told him that she had to go on to a dinner and asked him to take her flowers back for her. She knew she had to end things with him but she couldn't quite think how to do it.

'What is the occasion tonight, Miss?

Assia looked up from her phone and saw the young driver looking at her in the rear-view mirror. His eyes were wide with gentle curiosity.

'It's the unveiling of Olga's egg, the Fabergé egg which was made for the Grand Duchess Olga Nikolaevna.' Assia smiled into the mirror. 'It's a very exciting discovery.'

'Oh, I heard about that. I don't know anything about the Grand Princess, but I do know that Fabergé is worth a lot of money. What would this egg be worth then?'

He kept his eyes on Assia as they drove along Naberezhnaya Kutuzova and approached the ornamental green ironwork of the Liteyniy Bridge. He was chewing gum and she could see the top of his jawbone flex through his close-cropped blond hair as he ground the gum about his mouth. He wore a diamanté stud in his ear and a thin leather jacket which he had zipped all the way up to his throat. Assia was amused by his youthful acquisitiveness and decided to oblige him with talk of numbers.

'Well, it's rather hard to say because there is nothing comparable to this egg out there. It's about as rare and precious a discovery as you could hope to make, but if you were talking about retail value, I would say it would cost you about sixty million dollars to buy this today.'

'Seriously? That's insane!' The man's eyes creased with humour in the mirror and he turned briefly to look back at Assia. He was smiling broadly and his teeth looked bright against his honey-coloured skin.

'But I don't think the St Petersburg Museum is in a rush to sell, even if you did have sixty million dollars kicking around.'

'Who's to say I don't, eh?'

Assia laughed and looked out of the window. Across the Neva, the domes of the Kresty Prison chapel loomed, ghostly white in the dark.

'You know,' the driver continued, 'when I was told to collect a Miss Wynfield' – he pronounced it slowly as *Wine-fill* – 'from the Kempinski, I assumed I would be collecting an English woman. No one told me I would be driving a beautiful Russian girl. Are you married to an English guy?'

'No, my father is English and my mother was Russian. I'm only half-Russian, I'm afraid.'

'Your good looks are from the Russian side then. English guys always come over here and take our girls – they flash a credit card and the girls are in love. Russian girls all want to drink tea with the Queen so they marry these guys and go and live in England. In my opinion, they don't deserve to live in Russia if they want to leave it. Our President is making Russia great again; they'll be sorry they left, one day.'

Assia realised that the young chap wasn't bright enough to realise that he had just insulted her parents – the pillaging Englishman and the materialistic Russian girl – and she decided not to hold it against him. In some ways he was right; Olga probably had noticed her father's rarefied English pedigree. The younger son of the 13th Lord Carmichael, the Hon Richard Digory Selton Wynfield was a scholar at Harrow and Trinity College, Cambridge, where he took a distinction in Part III of the Mathematical Tripos. The Wynfields had run through their ancient fortune and sold the family seat in the 50s but great things were expected of Richard and his large brain. When he met Olga in 1979, Richard was lecturing at Leningrad State University in the Faculty of Mathematics as part of a programme established by the British Government to facilitate the thawing of relations with the Soviets. Before he took up the position he had studied Russian and arrived speaking the language flawlessly – so much so that the Deputy Administrator in the Admissions Department refused to believe that he was English when he registered. Inevitably, rumours abounded at the University that Richard was an English spy and in spite of his bookish awkwardness, he would have cut a rather mysterious figure.

Assia wondered what her father was doing now and pictured him walking along St Giles in Oxford, his long legs encased in dark green corduroy and his upper half in tweed. He would be carrying his battered toffee-coloured leather briefcase and would duck his head just before he reached the narrow opening of the dark wooden doors which led into St John's. Once in his College rooms, he would sit at his desk and work with brief interruptions for tutorials and PhD students. On leaving his rooms once, Assia had passed three very anxious-looking students who had gathered outside her father's door. She heard one of the students knock and then an impatient-sounding 'Come in!' She imagined her father to be an exacting tutor: hard to please and quick to criticise. He had always been thorough with the twin's school reports and would sit them down and ask them to explain every apparent failure: 'Why is this "A" not an "A+"?' Aged sixteen, when Assia told him she had dropped her extra French classes because she had already taken her French GCSE and was not going to continue with the subject, he refused to allow her to do so, 'Assia, you don't study a subject just to get good marks in it. Good marks show that you have mastered something, but they are not a reason to relinquish it and move onto something else.' When Assia protested that all her friends had dropped the class, her father countered with 'Just be exceptional, Assia.' He had said it with a sigh, as though exercised by her ordinariness and the casual delivery of the exhortation had cut Assia to the quick. Tears stung her eyes and fell down her cheeks, the weight of her frustration and the desire to please breaking behind her eyes like a wave crashing onto the shore. Her chest strained for breath and she issued a strange panting noise as she sobbed.

'Oh, Assia. Come on, there's no need to cry.' He touched her arm gently and frowned. 'Let me get your mother.'

Ruefully Assia recalled the time her father had asked some students over for supper to celebrate the end of their Prelims, their first year exams.

'He can't stand women crying,' a teenage Assia had told one of the female students over their pre-dinner drinks. 'Just burst into tears if something goes wrong and I guarantee he'll give you a very wide berth.'

Her phone purred in her hand and the screen lit up in the dark of the car. Assia glanced at the message, expecting it to be from Ben. Her heart did a somersault when she saw it was from Edward: 'Held up at the press conference, but I'm coming. Don't go anywhere! E x'

She smiled at the frozen river through the car window. Light shone onto it in soft pools of yellow. Before the great river freezes over, reflections of the sky and horizon in its waters gleam and sparkle with a brightness which is almost fierce. Now, the snow which lay on the iced water blurred the reflected light like blotting paper, its softness at once absorbing the light and emitting it. For the first time in a long, long while, Assia allowed herself to feel moved by the beauty of her surroundings. She felt a certain tautness releasing: muscles, cells, clenched jaw, fossilised thoughts. Tonight, she wanted to live.

XI

The taxi had arrived at the St Petersburg Museum. Assia smoothed out the invisible creases in her red and gold dress. The material was scratchy to touch but the dress was magnificent with red silk and gold thread roses which looked slightly smeared, as though they had been crushed into the weave. It was by Frank Usher and had belonged to her paternal grandmother. Assia had seen her wearing it in photographs and had always admired her grandmother's small waist and delicate arms. She hadn't realised that the dress still existed until her father told her that her grandmother had left it to her when she died, and she had only tried it on for the first time yesterday. She thought that her grandmother would be smiling down at her from on high, knowing that she was giving the dress an outing in St Petersburg at a very lavish party where the Russian President was going to make an appearance.

Ben had told her she looked beautiful when she had tried the dress on at home and she had to agree it was a bit of a knockout number. The low scoop neck gave her a décolletage worthy of Jayne Mansfield, while the fullness of the skirt emphasised her tiny waist. Even with her long and unstyled hair, Assia resembled a dark-haired beauty from the red carpet of Grauman's Chinese Theatre. The other Russian women at the party tonight had gone for modern designer numbers which were all about sparkle and scant material and Assia stood out with her pale skin and richly-dressed curves.

Someone in the queue at the entrance was wearing Paloma Picasso scent and Assia was immediately plunged into atmospheres of the past which weren't quite memories and weren't quite dreams. Her mother had worn the scent and every time Assia smelled it, which wasn't very often as it was not a fashionable scent, she had to stand still and savour everything. She inhaled the faint memory of her mother in a crepe silk black dress with a large gold choker and she could almost taste the nights when she and Tanya were tucked up in bed and kissed by their mother as she went out to some glamorous event somewhere in the dark night. Assia had often considered buying a bottle of Paloma Picasso and using it to summon her ghosts on lonely evenings but she knew that, like all precious things, memories and feelings fade after too much exposure.

Ever since the announcement of the discovery of the Grand Duchess Olga's Egg, Assia had been trying not to think of her mother in spite of the fact that all the articles about the momentous find in newspapers and magazines cited her mother's research and her prophetic insistence that the egg existed. Her mind was frantically sealing up any nasty thoughts that would seep through her porous consciousness and prick her with the realisation that she had cut short her mother's starry life. Assia didn't want to imagine her mother's joy if she had still been alive to witness the discovery of the egg; she knew Olga would have been over the moon to have been part of the biggest find of the 21st century. It was just too painful to acknowledge that her own mistake behind the wheel had ruined four lives instantaneously. In fact, Assia had often thought that her life had been many-times ruined when she killed her mother. Not only was she a victim of the great tragedy of losing a parent when young, but she was also the perpetrator of the crime and had no one but herself on which to blame her horrific loss. Naturally, Tanya only ever saw Assia in the perpetrator guise and refused to believe that she had the right to claim she had suffered anything after what she had done to their family. *Tonight, I shall imagine that Mama is here*

with me and seeing everything through my eyes. I am living for her.
As Olga's earthly representative, Assia felt suitably charged to go
and face the evening.

A tall, lean girl with a severe black bob and bright red lips looked
at Assia with forensic eyes for a few seconds before lowering her
chin to check the guest list.

'Vinfeld, *da?*' She almost sneered as she inspected her
clipboard. Assia pressed her tongue to the roof of her mouth
as she waited for the gatekeeping bitch (a Russian speciality) to
grant her entry. Someone had told her once that the pressure
of the tongue on the palate could stop your eyes watering and
since that point Assia had used the rudimentary technique to
suppress any kind of emotion that she felt would write itself on
her face. Perhaps it was the illusion of control but she had come
to believe that the method worked and she felt it gave her an
inscrutable expression at very useful times.

'That way.' The Gorgon with red lips pointed down the
marble gallery without looking up from her clipboard. Assia
was about to ask her if Kostantin Stepanyan had arrived but
thought better of it and said only a gracious 'Spasibo' before
starting along the vast passage, her heels clicking pleasingly.
She passed portraits of the great and the good of Peter's Russia;
men in various affectations with open books and instruments
of wisdom – globes, telescopes, compasses – each and every
painting a paean to Western enlightenment. As a door at the end
of the gallery was opened and closed, the noise of conversation
roared and faded. Assia felt her stomach fizz. She hadn't been
able to eat much all day and really she wasn't all that hungry
right now; food was a distraction, a heavy, cumbersome anchor
she didn't want at the moment even though she probably ought
to eat something.

The door opened again and the noise of laughter seeped
out. Assia identified a wheezy laugh, like the noise that issues
from something which has been punctured and, for just a
second, she wondered whether she wanted to go into the room.

Wouldn't it be better if she simply turned around and walked away from everything, from all the uncertainties which would confront her when that door was opened? Did she really need to know if Konstantin was in there? There was bound to be a perfectly logical explanation as to his whereabouts, and as for Edward – she had Ben at home: devoted, understanding and loving Ben – why stir any embers from past flirtations which felt like a lifetime ago? The past was the past and 'if only's were dangerous. *Go home, Assia. Go back to Ben, back to your fabulous job and publish your precious little* Encylopaedia of Eggs. *When was it ever a good idea for Pandora to play with boxes?*

A lavishly dressed couple overtook her in the gallery, the woman all molten silver in a sheath of steely sequins. She balanced on metal spikes which looked thin enough and hard enough to pit the marble floor while her other half walked reverently beside her, occasionally proffering an elbow when needed. As they passed, the man turned back to look at Assia. His slicked-back hair formed a little duck's tail at the nape of his neck which curled over the dark blue collar of his Brioni suit. He smiled knowingly at Assia and nodded his head towards the room as though to chivvy her along. Assia smiled back softly and hurried her pace. On reaching the large, smooth wooden door, he pulled the brass handle and opened the door slowly, head in the air, inhaling the atmosphere of the room he was about to grace with his presence. His metallic goddess went in, her hips sashaying so that her dress flashed like the scales of a snake in motion. The man waited for Assia, holding the door and bowing as deeply as a Versailles courtier as she passed.

The Great Hall was heaving with guests in all their finery. Even the museum appeared to have put its best foot forward for the evening and the marble floor and Corinthian columns shone glossily. At every angle there was one of the President's heavies standing against a wall and muttering into their black suits and although they looked somewhat absurd, their presence escalated the already hysterical excitement.

Assia tilted her head up to admire the elaborate ceiling. The Greek key pattern which was picked out in gold was mesmerising and she felt slightly dizzy as she followed its geometrical train around the perimeter of the ceiling. The rotunda in the centre was clearly inspired by the one in the Gardens of the Villa Borghese and painted with gilt hexagons and decorative roundels within, which decreased in size as the eye travelled up to the centre of the dome. The *trompe l'oeil* was an homage to Fibonaccian beauty and the room really was the most appropriate place to display an egg which was also testament to the twin beauties of symmetry and design. In the middle, right above her head, a golden Imperial Eagle was set into a circular recess which was surrounded by a thick wreath of gilt acanthus leaves tied at intervals with trailing ribbon. The eagle's tongues protruded, snake-like, from each of its throats and reminded East and West of the awful majesty of Imperial Russia. It occurred to Assia that this evening's guests made up much of the court of Capitalist Russia, from the President (who was yet to arrive) and his Ministers, to the many oligarchs, all of whom had carved up Russia between them in the way that it had been held by the princely families of old. As she removed her gaze from the ceiling, Assia caught an admiring glance from a man in a shiny suit and looked away quickly.

Taking a glass of champagne from an expressionless waiter, she moved to the left of the hall, maintaining her pace so as to give the impression of someone with purpose. Guests hovered and leaned against the chairs which surrounded a vast table covered with a beautiful tablecloth with embroidered flowers. The table appeared to have about 200 place settings and was crowded with glasses and porcelain and vases with teetering displays of flowers. A little further behind the table security guards surrounded the corners of a tall glass cabinet in which sat the new egg. People gazed into the glass box and thronged around the egg, jostling for a view with such neck-craning insistence that Assia feared the cabinet might be crushed. She longed to see it but thought she would wait until the hordes receded and she could snatch a moment with it alone. She turned her attention to the paintings which hung at eye level on the walls of the hall which were lined with eau-de-Nil moiré silk. Small plain black wooden frames surrounded chalky landscapes constructed of smooth shapes in cool, deep colours: promontories, shallow hills and low, mirage-like horizons floated before her. Inspecting the labels next to the paintings, Assia determined that she was looking at a series of views of islands on Lake Ladoga in north western Russia by Nicholas Roerich, one of Russia's most celebrated painters. Gazing at the water in the luminous gouaches was like bathing one's eyes in a stream; the works had a soothing, glacial quality in which Assia felt she could easily lose herself.

To find yourself, you have to lose yourself.

Assia muttered this refrain before realising that she couldn't remember if someone had said it to her or if she had just made it up there and then. It sounded like the sort of spiritual guff spouted by LSD enthusiasts but for a moment, meditating on the deep stills of the lake waters, she thought it made perfect sense.

'My number one favourite, Roerich. We have one of his Himalayan views at home; I had it put opposite our bed so that it's the first thing I see when I wake.'

Assia turned from the paintings and looked to her right to meet the voice. A blonde with a pale pink gauze scarf tied high up around her neck with a little bow was standing a few paces behind her. She was wearing a turquoise dress with a bright paisley pattern, the twisted droplet shapes picked out in tiny brightly coloured beads – so many of them it would have taken a whole couture workshop to sew them on. The dress was 60s-inspired: long sleeves which flared at the wrists and a short A-line shape which showed off her shapely legs. A Russian Catherine Deneuve, thought Assia admiringly. The woman had folded her arms and held her empty champagne glass by the stem, twisting it occasionally.

'We bought it before the Russian art market boomed, so it was a good investment as well as something I adore. I love their *otherness*.'

'How wonderful to own a painting by him. These are just mesmerising; I can't take my eyes off them. I'm sorry, I'm Assia Wynfield.' Assia laid her hand on her chest as she said this in what was both a childish and modest gesture.

'Maria Denisova, Ivan Denisov's wife.' A shallow nod of the head and a faint smile as introduction. Her eyes crossed the room, presumably to ascertain her husband's whereabouts and as she turned her head to the left, Assia noticed a stretch of mottled skin on one side which ran from the only bit of her neck which her scarf hadn't covered, up into her jawline. The skin on her left cheek was pitted and uneven and the corner of her mouth looked as though it had been smeared into her face, pulled down so that the natural definition between lip and cheek was blurred. The Janus-like effect of beauty-slash-disfigurement was disarming.

'Will you excuse me?' Maria looked distracted. 'I can see that my husband wants me. A pleasure to meet you.'

'And you too, Maria.' Assia wondered what had happened to her beautiful face. It looked as though an invisible hand was reaching up from her chest and tugging at a mask, trying to drag it off in one corner. Presumably a burn of some sort would have caused such damage but had it happened recently or when she was a child? It must be hard to wield beauty for years and years and then have it snatched away from you. Assia watched Maria weave her way past people, twisting her body neatly wherever necessary in order to reach her husband who must have been at the furthest end of the room. Assia noticed some people trying to hide their reaction on seeing her ruined face; their gaze lingering for longer than was considered polite.

Ivan Borisovich Denisov, Maria's husband. Of course, she had known the name was familiar. People muttered his name softly at parties, trying to dampen its power. Denisov was the 'grey cardinal', the President's ideologue and puppet-master.

An Aide in the Presidential Executive Office, he was a strange combination of horse-whisperer and strategist. He was seen in public very rarely but featured in all sorts of editorials in the Russian press. Journalists liked to speculate about the kind of power he wielded over the President, dubbing him the 'modern Rasputin'. Inches and inches of column space had been devoted to the story of Denisov's and the President's childhood which had been granted a sort of fairy-tale status in the media. They had grown up together in St Petersburg: their fathers working together in the KGB and their mothers the best of friends. They were judo devotees and school buddies and later both studied law at university. When the President cemented his political career by becoming Mayor of St Petersburg, he often consulted Denisov who was at that stage chairman of a major Russian television channel, and when the move to the Kremlin occurred, Denisov and his wife were summoned to Moscow as well. Highly religious, Denisov's practice of Orthodox Christianity was rumoured to border on the fanatic. He always accompanied the President to Mount Athos and was a member of an ultra-conservative religious group called The Icon Bearers who were nationalist, xenophobic and very, very traditional. The Patriarch was one of his closest friends and it was believed he donated many millions of dollars from his mysteriously deep pockets to the Russian Church. Occasionally he was spotted in Moscow putting his very deep voice to use singing the Rachmaninov Vespers in the choir of the Cathedral of Christ the Saviour, a vast gold-domed church which was rebuilt in 1990 after the Soviets had demolished it and used the foundation pit as the world's largest open-air swimming pool.

A hush spread throughout the packed hall and it was apparent that the President had arrived. Assia couldn't see him but a parting in the crowd to her left suggested that he was somewhere in the vicinity. She saw a young security guard watching her as she looked around and she decided to make her way towards the front of the hall where a podium had been placed in front of a large screen.

'I was wondering where you had got to.' A tall blonde in sequins came to stand beside her, refusing to whisper like everyone else just because the President had arrived. Assia turned to see one of her clients, Madeleine Roseman, and embraced her fondly. Madeleine had a Fabergé Museum in Washington DC which housed an egg her father had bought and she commissioned Assia to buy Fabergé for her regularly at auction.

'Did you know about this one?' The question was faintly accusatory.

'This new egg? Olga's egg?' Assia met Madeleine's penetrating gaze and held her ground. 'No. I didn't know a thing about it. No one did. But it's been acquired by the Russian nation for the Russian nation and will be housed here at this Museum when it's not on tour. It's not up for sale.'

'OK,' said Madeleine, pursing her lips and nodding thoughtfully. 'That makes sense. Keep the Fabergé in Russia, its birthplace. I understand that.'

The speeches began. Mounting the podium without fanfare, the Director of the St Petersburg Museum, Sergei Vinogradov, thanked everyone for gathering to mark this 'good news story' for the Museum and for Russia. He then made a small bow to the President and said how grateful the Museum was that he should attend the event. A young male interpreter stood beside him and translated his speech into English without any making any attempt at preserving cadence or intonation. The Director introduced the Museum's Fabergé curator, Oleg Sablin, a small man with a diamond-shaped face which was emphasised by a neat, dark goatee beard. Although Assia had not met Oleg, she had dealt with him when she was working at the V&A and had found him to be deliberately obstructive when she was trying to arrange the loan of some of his museum's Fabergé. Sablin waited for the excited chatter to die down, glaring at the audience with the authority of a headmaster. He nodded respectfully to the President, pressed his hands together and took a deep breath, as though troubled by the enormity of what he was about to say.

'Here, at this museum, on this night, you are going to witness a story of good news – the unveiling of Fabergé's most significant creation. In years to come people will talk about this evening with the envy of those who long to be a part of cultural history. I can describe to you the exquisite beauty of this object but you will not believe me until you see it yourself. When I saw it for the first time,' here Sablin paused and closed his eyes dramatically, 'I was so moved by what I was seeing that I had to sit down.' The young interpreter failed entirely to capture the theatricality of Sablin's speech and Assia had to suppress a smile as she listened to his rhythm-less monotone.

The curator went on. 'For many years Fabergé had made Easter eggs for the Dowager Empress Maria Feodorovna and the Tsarina Alexandra and he employed all his ingenuity and that of his craftsmen in these creations. When he received the commission from the Tsar to make an egg for the Grand Duchess Olga, he knew that he had licence to design something out-of-the-ordinary, something that would please a young woman. What you are viewing tonight is an egg which celebrates the vitality of Olga Nikolaevna and the joy and hopes of youth. The egg is displayed in this cabinet here but right now, I am going to show you video footage of the egg in the round. Mr President, ladies and gentleman, feast your eyes on Russian genius.'

The eyes of the audience followed Sablin's outstretched arm as it gestured at a screen behind him. Suddenly the lights in the hall were extinguished and the egg appeared on the screen which glowed in the sepulchral darkness.

Sablin's face was now illuminated by the small lamp on the podium and the upward cone of light lent him a Mephistopheleian appearance. He spoke into the microphone while looking up at the screen.

'The body of the egg is a silver-gilt ovum which bears eight ropes of triple plaited guilloché enamel, using never-before seen shades of enamel-work. It is small, about 7½ centimetres, the same size as the 1895 Rosebud Egg. We believe Albert

Holmström to be the workmaster and it is marked 'Fabergé' under the lid. Each of the small watercolours under the articulated cypher is a different view of the Livadia Palace at night. The Livadia Palace in the Crimea was a favourite holiday destination of the Imperial family and it was the setting for Olga Nikolaevna's "Coming Out" party to celebrate her sixteenth birthday. The stand of the egg echoes the columns and arches in the Italian courtyard at the palace.

'You will see now that the egg fans out, like segments of an orange, to reveal its surprise.'

Assia stared as the egg was filmed opening up like a flower receiving the sunlight with its petals. She found herself going into autopilot and cataloguing the surprise inside the egg as though she were preparing an exhibition description:

The surprise of the egg is a miniature fan with two-colour gold-mounted mother-of-pearl guards with the diamond-set cypher of Olga Nikolaevna applied to a diamond-bordered translucent rose-pink enamelled medallion on sunburst guilloché ground, below a rose-cut diamond-set ribbon bow and suspending bow-tied chased green gold foliage set with amethysts. The parchment fan leaf hand-painted in watercolour heightened with white depicting sprays of brightly-coloured flowers tied with vari-coloured ribbons.

There were more gasps from the audience as they saw the fan surprise and some subdued chatter. Sablin paused until the crowd quieted and then took in a shudderingly slow meditative breath which gave the impression that he could barely tolerate the disorderly crowd. He opened his eyes and resumed. 'The flowers on the fan leaf are flowers unique to the Crimea: the Shrenk tulip, Kuznetsov cyclamens, pasqueflowers, wild irises and asphodels. Combine this with the painted views on the egg and its architectural stand and we are presented with an egg which sings of the Crimea. Naturally, we are reminded that the Crimea was as important to the Imperial Family as it is to all Russians now. It has always been and always will be a part of our cultural and historical heritage. The egg encapsulates everything that was beautiful about the Crimea – this magical place that had once been part of the Russian Empire before it was given away in an exchange which made no sense to anyone. The handover of the Crimea to Ukraine in 1954 was like giving a beggar a diamond when all he really wants is a loaf of bread. The…'

A tentative clap from someone at the back of the hall was bolstered by more and more applause until the entire place was clapping vigorously and people looked around to see who was cheering and who was not. A man shouted '*Krym Nash!*, Crimea is ours!' and a few bold souls stepped out from the edge of the assembled crowd to peer at the President's reaction to the outburst, however the man himself was set back among a semi-circular retinue of cronies and guards and his expression could not be seen. Sablin smiled from the podium, his eyes dark smudges in the yellow light.

'Your reaction proves it to be true: Fabergé was the consummate master of making statements with beauty. You only have to glance at the Romanov Tercentenary Egg to see a classic example of exquisite craftsmanship and design declaring the Romanovs masters of history and masters of the future. The egg we have here tonight was designed for the Grand Duchess Olga to remind her of her coming of age and that moonlit night at the Livadia palace when her sixteenth birthday was celebrated with dinner, dancing and flowers. The fan represents the grand balls she would attend now that she was no longer a girl and the Crimean flowers painted on it allude to the Midsummer tradition of putting flowers under a girl's pillow so that she may dream of her future husband.

'Research into this egg is ongoing but is proving rewarding. We did not even know that it existed until the Russian Fabergé expert Olga Morozova Wynfield said that she believed Fabergé made an egg for the Grand Duchess and even she could not find evidence at the time. We have found Fabergé's original invoice for the egg and some of the designs – a process made much easier now that we know what the egg looks like.'

Assia jumped as though she had been stung when she heard her mother's name and she looked around anxiously. She wished that Konstantin was with her right now – he would help her talk through the strange feeling she had about this new egg. Somehow the vice-like pain that had been crushing her head earlier that morning had migrated to her feet and she longed to remove her heels and sink into a chair.

'It was almost impossible to believe,' Sablin continued, his voice a little louder as he moved closer to the microphone, 'that this egg had been sitting, cocooned in its case, in a cardboard box in the cupboard of an old lady in an apartment in St Petersburg. It had been hidden from sight ever since this old woman's father, a museum-curator with White Russian sympathies, had taken it for safekeeping from the Baryatinsky Mansion, the palace of the Grand Duchess Olga Alexandrovna, Olga Nikolaevna's aunt. It is presumed that the young Olga had given the egg to her beloved aunt on one of her last visits to see her when unrest in the city was palpable. It was discovered when the nephew of this old woman cleared out her apartment after her death and realised that what was in the dog-eared box was not just any old trinket. After the egg was appraised, a private sale was negotiated with the Russian Treasury and it was agreed that it should be donated to the St Petersburg Museum on behalf of the Russian nation. We are incredibly lucky to count this egg, which is henceforth to be known as "The Livadia Egg", as part of our collection. I have taken too much of your time, so I shall finish now and allow you to admire the most important artistic discovery of the twenty-first century.'

The lights went on again and applause for Oleg Sablin resounded through the Great Hall but of the Russians gathered, none were foolish enough to be seen to applaud a man who was not the President too excessively.

XII

The Forbes Galleries, Forbes Building, Fifth Avenue, New York, 1989

'Mama, it's such a shame that it's behind glass. I want to feel it in my hands.'

'I know, darling, but there's a very good reason it's locked away. This egg, all these eggs, are very valuable.' Olga knelt down behind Assia, who was peering into a cabinet on tiptoes, and kissed the back of her head. 'But you're quite right, sweetheart, the eggs were designed to be handled. Once upon a time, the last Empresses of Russia would have felt the weight of the eggs in their hands and then held them up to the light to examine the exquisite craftsmanship of Monsieur Fabergé.'

'This is the one that *I* would have, Mama!' said Tanya excitedly, reaching up and pointing at an egg, tapping on the cabinet glass loudly.

'Careful, please, my darling.' Olga got up and rushed over to Tanya. 'Mr. Forbes won't let us see his collection in private again if you ruin the display.'

'I think this one is the best because it's the cleverest. See, it's not even an egg, it's a small tree! If were a princess, Mama, this would be my egg.' Tanya held out the corners of her dress as if she were wearing a ballgown and curtsied.

'You are right, sweetheart, it is an ingenious creation. This egg is known as the Bay Tree Egg and, as you say, it's not technically an egg. Fabergé was showing off his creative flair by taking the theme of an Easter egg and applying it to the natural world, so the foliage of a neatly trimmed bay tree becomes an egg. Can you see how the green leaves made from stone even have veins carved into them? Everything that ever came from Fabergé's studios always looked as though someone had breathed life into it. Nothing is ever stiff – even ribbons chased from gold look as though they would flutter if you blew on them. That's one of the ways I can tell if something is fake: it looks flat and lifeless.

'And,' Olga wrapped her hand around Tanya's delicate fingers and clenched them animatedly, 'as if a beautiful egg wasn't enough, there is a surprise hiding in this egg. All the eggs were made with surprises. If you ask Mr Forbes nicely when he comes, I'm sure he'll turn the key and you'll see a little bird come out of the top of the tree to sing.'

'Mama?' Assia put her arms around her mother's slender waist. 'Can I show you *my* favourite egg?' She pointed to an elaborate panelled egg, very different in style to the Bay Tree Egg and comparatively smaller. 'There is so much to look at on this egg I could stay here all day staring at it. Everything is amazing: even the green bits separating the small paintings are beautiful.'

Olga smiled at her daughter, so slight and girlish in her cherry-red coat with its black velvet collar. She was playing with the end of her plait as she stared at the egg, her eyes barely blinking in case she missed the smallest detail.

'Ah, my little expert, this is a very grown-up egg. What sophisticated taste you have! This is the 15th Anniversary Egg and it celebrates the fifteenth year of Nicholas II's reign. The miniatures show significant scenes from his life, for example, this one here shows the Pont Alexandre III in Paris for which Nicholas and Alexandra laid the foundation stone in 1896, and here we can see him being crowned Tsar of all the Russias.'

'I like looking at the portraits of the children. The girls are so beautiful.'

'They are, aren't they? Here is Anastasia, whom you were named after and here is Tatiana whom Tanya is named after. Fabergé was very conscious of the different characters of the

Dowager Empress and the Tsarina; he knew that anything relating to her family would please Alexandra and so he incorporated these portraits of her children into the egg. In fact, my funny little darlings, the eggs you have chosen as your favourites were both presented in 1911, the Bay Tree one to the Dowager Empress and this one to the Tsarina. So these eggs are very different in design but born in the same year – a bit like my twin girls!'

'I want to see all the eggs that Fabergé ever made!' said Assia boldly.

'Then you'll need to find the ones that are missing, sweetheart. Mr Forbes has twelve eggs here – he has amassed more than any other person since the Tsarinas themselves – and I think he'll be delighted if you could find him another egg to buy. The other eggs are out there: they just need to be found by someone who knows what they're looking for, someone who can read their language just as you can.'

XIII

There were only two other people gazing into the egg's cabinet so Assia decided to try and have a good look at it – too many people had been crowding around it up until now. She placed her champagne glass on the tray of a passing waiter and walked towards the uniformed security guards surrounding the egg, their feet slightly apart, hands by their sides ready to grab anyone who tried any funny business. The eyes of one of the guards tracked her from his position. He didn't move his handsome head but his eyes walked all over her, up and down her dress, lingering on her neat little waist, then her breasts before returning to her pretty face. Assia ignored him and put on her metaphorical blinkers; she wanted to see the egg and only the egg. Unlike most people here, she wasn't here to flirt or for social purposes – to be seen posing next to the egg and associated with the exclusivity of Fabergé. She wanted to read the language of the beautiful orb in the cabinet, to dive into the slipstream of the past so that she was transported back to Fabergé's workshops, to the work benches where the most famous pieces of decorative arts the world has ever seen were born.

To find yourself, you have to lose yourself.

The cabinet radiated heat, warmed by the heat of the spotlights within. Assia was a moth, drawn inexorably from afar to the hot, dust-speckled, glass. Pressing her forehead up against the vitrine, she gazed at the egg on its velvet stand. She wanted to inspect the painted chequers of enamel on the body of the egg inspired by the Trinket Seller and she walked as far around the cabinet as she could, her eyes never leaving the egg.

'Isn't this the most exquisite thing you have ever seen?'

She hadn't noticed Heinrich Weber on the other side of the display case and she almost walked into him as she followed the planetary ring of the egg.

'Heinrich, hello! How are you? I'm so sorry, I didn't see you there!' Assia looked surprised and then smiled warmly at the young man with pink cheeks. They embraced politely. 'Have you only just got here?' Assia asked. 'I didn't see you at the speeches.'

'I was one of the first here.' He took his black-rimmed circular frames off his head and pulled a blue handkerchief from his jacket pocket to rub them. Assia hadn't realised how big his eyes were without the glasses, not to mention his remarkably long lashes. He continued: 'I was – how do you say – champing at the bit to see this egg!'

'Oh, absolutely!' Assia beamed, nodding vigorously to express her delight at his use of so English an idiom. 'I still can't get my head round it, really.' They stood next to each other, each with their eyes on the egg, Assia biting her lip unselfconsciously.

'On paper, this is the most exciting discovery to occur in the Fabergé world in our time.' Heinrich turned to Assia. 'Of course, you mother had sensed it, like the clairvoyant that she was. Last night I was trying to think of an equivalent in other fields – You might say it's like your Howard Carter finding another Pharaoh's tomb.'

'But what about the curse?' Assia raised her eyebrows enquiringly, her mouth betraying her amusement. She had always liked Heinrich; earnest to a fault, many thought that he lacked a sense of humour – the stereotypical German who was all about precision and detail – but Assia knew that beneath his rigour and particularities was a comic sensibility. She had heard tell from a Russian friend of a party he had thrown a few years ago to celebrate his appointment as Director of the Kunstgewerbemuseum in Berlin where the cake was decorated with a design from the tondo of an ancient Greek drinking cup depicting an older bearded man fondling a younger one. Heinrich, apparently, almost collapsed with hysterical laughter on seeing the cake and although he claimed not to have known about it, his boyfriend insisted that Heinrich had requested the decoration himself. Assia didn't know if this was just the kind of homophobic rumour which Russians liked to spread but she wanted to think that it was true.

'Will you add it to the *Encyclopaedia*?' Heinrich sipped from his glass and ran his tongue over his lips.

'Yes, I will. But I'm just trying to get to grips with it, for now. I want to handle it. I don't know if I'll be allowed to, but I like to hold pieces and to let them sit with me for a while; I'm sure you're the same. I particularly want to research the Dresden reference in the enamel – to me, that's a really interesting note, a harking back to the Renaissance Egg.'

'I'm not sure I follow.' Heinrich's German accent always sounded stronger when he was anxious.

'The pattern of chequered enamel on the body of the egg is a direct reference to the Dresden Galanteriewarenhändler, wouldn't you say?'

'Yes, you are right! I had not made the connection, but it's there, isn't it? Very Grünes Gewölbe. A really very nice touch!'

'It's a rather retrograde motif for a commission for a young woman though, isn't it? I think that's my only gripe with the egg at the moment. My mother was so convinced that Alma Pihl would be the designer and really she would have been perfect. She was a young woman herself and she would have been able to mine the excitements and hopes of youth and express them imaginatively.' Assia frowned as she scrutinised the egg, touching the glass with the tips of her fingers until a security guard asked her to remove her hand.

'I'm not sure I agree with you actually, Assia.' Heinrich sucked in and then blew out his cheeks while lowering his chin as he considered what he was going to say. The inflation of his pink cheeks made his eyes bulge slightly so that the overall effect was so much like watching a puffer fish in a tank that Assia smiled to herself as she imagined Heinrich's words streaming out of his mouth in shiny little salt water bubbles.

'To my mind, the egg is majestic,' the fish was pouting as he spoke, 'and I think the boldness of design was Fabergé's way of expressing hope in the future of the Romanovs. He was acknowledging the family's historical roots, hence the reference to the past with the Dresden Trinket Seller, while employing innovative touches, like the ciselé work underneath the enamel, as a nod to the new, younger generation of the Imperial Family.'

'Hmm, yes.' Assia was nodding as she listened to Heinrich, her eyes flitting furtively between him and the egg as he spoke, as though anxious that it might disappear. 'So the design is working doubly hard: paying homage to the past while heralding the future. That's a clever way of interpreting it – but then I would expect nothing less from you, Heinrich.' Blushing slightly, Heinrich removed his glasses and wiped them again with his handkerchief.

'The miniatures are exquisite, aren't they?' Heinrich swiped a canapé from a passing tray and popped it into his mouth. Assia could hear him crunching something and then sucking whatever residue the canapé had left on his finger.

'The brushwork is remarkably delicate and precise. It says they are by Zuiev in the monograph on the egg, but I'm not so sure.' Assia straightened her back and pressed her fingers into it, trying to massage the ache in the small of her back away. 'I wish they had displayed the egg slightly higher. The older I get, the less I can stoop.'

'Old, my arrrse,' said Heinrich, lingering on the 'r', probably because he thought it sounded more English to do so. 'You're not allowed to say that word when you're in your twenties – it's not fair.'

'Early thirties, actually. Is that allowed? I feel old anyhow.'

'You need to stop working so hard. Take a sabbatical so you can finish your book. And just have some weekends doing nothing. Marco won't allow me to work on the weekends. He hides my laptop.' Heinrich couldn't suppress a smile at the thought of Marco and his mock bullying – the way he would snatch Heinrich's phone off him when he saw him checking his emails and wag his finger disapprovingly.

'Ha! Madeleine would rather sell her daughter than let me take a sabbatical now. I'll be able to take some time off when the sales slow down in August, but until then, she won't let me sleep while there's Fabergé to be bought. But listen, no deviation from the subject!' Assia raised her eyebrows with an authoritarian air and looked down her nose at Heinrich. 'Who do you think painted these miniatures? Zuiev's style was softer, more romantic, to my mind. These seem to be pointedly architectural, like plans for the palace, almost – even though the scene is bathed in moonlight, they still feel different to his work.'

'I haven't really had a chance to look.' Heinrich flared his fish-like lips again and breathed through them slowly so they billowed. 'These are Zuiev, surely? I can see what you mean about the architectural detail, but I have no problem with saying they are him. How has the museum catalogued them?'

'As by Zuiev. Gladkova wrote a note on them in the catalogue.'

'Oh, well that settles it! Surely Gladkova should have the last word on Zuiev, don't you think? The left corner of Heinrich's top lip curled upwards disdainfully, mirroring the arch of the eyebrow above it. It was clear that he thought Assia was potty ever to have thought that Meister Zuiev might not have painted these delicate little scenes of the Livadia Palace.

'Yes, I know, but I'm just saying that they look a little unusual to me. It's all part of my process – I like to tyre-kick when I'm appraising something. Everything is guilty until proven innocent, as far as I'm concerned.' A fat man in a black suit which was fitted in all the wrong places banged into Assia's side with considerable heft as he waddled up to the cabinet to inspect the egg. He didn't apologise when Assia looked at him reproachfully but continued to stare at the egg, his mouth slightly parted like an awestruck young child.

Heinrich rolled his eyes at this deplorable behaviour but refused to be interrupted. 'And so, tell me, your "tyre-kicking" as you call it, it's nothing to do with the fact that your mother imagined the egg would be completely different is it?'

'No, Heinrich, nothing to do with it.' Assia shot him an irritated look before her expression softened with sadness. 'I won't deny that I was disappointed. As soon as I heard that they had discovered Olga's egg, I thought that it could be a sort of posthumous extension of Mama's legacy in the Fabergé world – you know, she had always said that Olga's egg existed and people were sceptical. I don't know why, but it hadn't occurred to me that it wouldn't be the design that she had predicted, so it was a bit of a shock when they unveiled the egg. I'm not criticising it – well, perhaps I am – but really I am just taking time to digest the whole thing.'

'Things rarely turn out as expected, my dear' said Heinrich, deftly stepping out of the way of the fat man in the black suit as he circled the cabinet with all the grace of a drunken rhinoceros. 'My parents wanted me to be a policeman like my father. That didn't exactly happen, did it?' His smile was rueful but when he wrinkled his nose he looked ever so slightly impish, as though he took pleasure in defying expectations.

'Well, you're a policeman of sorts; you police cultural objects. No faux Cycladic pots in your museum!'

'Absolutely not!' Heinrich pretended to look outraged. 'And no Victorian majolica either. It's not allowed – I can't stand the stuff. I'm a policeman of taste, ultimately.' He looked deadly serious and Assia was about to say that actually she was rather fond of Victorian majolica when she saw the back of Konstantin's head, his distinctive thick dark thatch streaked with grey.

'Thank God, there he is.' She said this quietly, feeding the words through her teeth like the latter part of an incantation designed to conjure his appearance. Of course he was here, it made perfect sense that he would have heard the siren call of the most important piece of Fabergé ever created. He looked smarter than she had thought he might, wearing a dark suit with a black satin stripe running down the outside seam of the leg. Watching his head nodding in conversation with a pretty, tanned blond in a white crêpe trouser suit with a diamond brooch on the lapel, she felt angry all of a sudden. He looked casual and so at ease – hadn't he realised how worried she and Yelena had been? What a bastard.

'Will you excuse me a moment?' Assia said to Heinrich who looked a little put out by the loss of her attention. Her lips pursed, she walked up to Konstantin and touched the back of his elbow, waiting for him to turn around.

The dark thatch turned to look at the distraction by his left elbow, angling his face slowly as he reluctantly withdrew his gaze from his pretty interlocutor. He looked expectantly at Assia.

It took Assia a moment. 'Goodness, I am so sorry.' She put her hand up before her face; a defensive and apologetic gesture at once. 'I thought you were someone else. Forgive me.'

'No problem at all.' The man who was not Kostya looked at her appreciatively, his head tilted back slightly, his eyes narrowed. Dimples at the corner of his mouth betrayed amusement. He was tanned and handsome, with a nose and chin which would have looked fine in profile on a coin – like Alexander the Great, thought Assia. You see them every now and again in Russia and Eastern Europe: faces which remind you of the men in hunting scenes sculpted on Hellenistic tombs. Noble and beautiful – a race of men which looked like gods, long before the Slavs appeared with their high cheekbones and flat faces.

He did not turn away immediately but held an embarrassed Assia captive with his humoured silence.

'I really am so sorry, I thought I might see a friend here and you look very much like him from behind.' Assia began to withdraw humbly, backing away like a courtier anxious not to offend a sovereign body.

'And who is it I resemble so closely?' The look of amusement was now a smile: a cool Apolline semi-circle of indulgence.

'Konstantin Stepanyan. Do you know him?' Assia felt uneasy about saying Kostya's name. For some reason it felt like a betrayal.

'Never heard of him.' The man was dismissive. He was still facing Assia and the pretty woman in the white crêpe suit had disappeared. Assia wanted to retreat to the cabinet with the egg, to Heinrich and the familiar shuttle of their conversation. Right now, she felt an uncomfortable tug deep within her, words being pulled out involuntarily.

'He restores Fabergé and often acts as a consultant specialist to museums. He knows Fabergé inside out. You wouldn't be able to drag him away from the egg if he were here now.' Assia looked over to the egg in its cabinet like a child looking to a parent for reassurance.

'And what do you think of the egg?' The way the man said this, with the tip of his tongue touching the roof of his mouth, suggested that he was more curious about Assia's response than he cared to let on. He crossed his arms and waited carefully for her to answer his question.

Assia could feel the challenge in the delivery of the question – it was implicit in the man's folded arms and a supercilious air, but she sensed it also in the semi-unconscious way that a climber appraises a surface, reaching his arm up and reading the rock with his fingers. Her mind flexed, flicking its tail with vigour as she prepared to answer the demigod.

'Well, where to begin? I am still in shock that such a discovery has been made.' She paused. 'But, forgive me – I don't think we've been introduced, have we? I'm Assia Wynfield. My mother was…'

She felt fingers on the bare skin of her shoulder and she spun her head around suddenly. Edward removed his hand and rested it on the small of her back for a second, a delicate apology for the interruption. He greeted the man Assia had been talking to in Russian, '*Dobry vecher, Ivan Borisovich*' before switching to English and announcing his guest. Stepping back, he gestured towards the tall woman standing next to him:

'Madeleine, may I introduce you to Ivan Borisovich Denisov, a senior trustee of the St Petersburg Museum and an Aide in the Presidential Executive Office.' Edward caught Ivan's eye and nodded imperceptibly as he ushered Madeleine forward into the court of the conversation.

'Mrs Roseman,' said Ivan, lingering on each syllable with his deep voice as though unable to believe that the woman before him was real. 'I have heard much about you and your museum, but we have never had the pleasure of meeting. I hope you are enjoying yourself this evening.'

Assia could see Madeleine was thrilled by Ivan. His height meant that she had to tip her head back slightly to talk to him and already she was giggling like a flirtatious teenager, basking in the sun of Ivan's attention. Assia had stepped away from the couple and was scanning the room, the winged edges of her eyebrows lifting with the effort of scrutiny.

'Hey! I've found you at last. Hello!' Edward wrapped an arm around her waist and walked her up to the wall of the room, right next to a marble plinth which bore a large bronze of mounted Cossacks riding up a craggy outcrop, spears slung across their easy backs, the horses nimble as mountain goats.

'Is everything all right? You look bothered by something

'It's fine, I was just looking for someone.' Assia avoided Edward's gaze and studied the bronze. She was annoyed at the way he had carved up her conversation with Ivan Denisov. She had been on the verge of finding out who he was herself and the compositional balance of their chat had been delicate. The way Edward had barged in and dumped *her client* Madeleine Roseman was grating. He was behaving as if he had proprietorial rights to her and it repulsed her slightly. 'I'm getting a drink,' she said shortly.

She walked over to a waiter in a white jacket and grabbed a flute of champagne from his tray. The glass, matt with condensation, felt cold in her hand and she closed her fingers around it. Edward hurried over to her.

'I'm sorry, can we start again? I've been all over the place with work and I'm probably not doing this in the way I had wanted to. It's so great to see you. It's been a long time.' He moved towards her as if to kiss her on the cheek but clearly thought better of it and drew back. Assia noticed the aborted move and looked down at her drink bashfully. She looked up again and smiled at him and he took the cue to move closer to her.

'It's so strange seeing you in Russia,' said Assia. She felt less on edge, less angry, now that she knew he was anxious about making a good impression on her.

'I'm working on the tour of the Livadia Egg, a kind of PR management role. My brief is to get as many eggs from international private collections and institutions on loan for the Moscow leg of the tour in three months. I've been talking to your Madeleine Roseman, actually – you consult for her don't you? We don't have much time, but we hope that with the addition of the Kremlin Armoury's ten eggs, we should manage a decent showing. It's been getting a little crazy since the discovery of the egg, as you can imagine.' He nodded his head towards one of the bodyguards as though to suggest that his thick-necked presence was a sign of things having boiled over. He paused for a second and his brow furrowed very slightly. 'I tried to speak to you after the film screening in London but you got away from me.'

'Oh, did you?' Assia tried to sound nonchalant and wondered if he had noticed her avoiding him as they left the cinema that evening. She had been very surprised when he had suddenly addressed the cinema audience and was somewhat taken aback to see him in her world, *her* sphere. They hadn't seen each other since Oxford, fourteen years ago, when he had been a finalist and she was in her second year. He was as good-looking now as he was all those years ago, although perhaps a little more thickset. The fashionable Prada glasses he was wearing lent him a cosmopolitan air which he had not yet cultivated as an undergraduate at Oxford. Back then he was part of a small group of Old Etonians at Worcester who spent a lot of time pretending to work in the college library where they spoke loudly and made everyone who was foolish enough to work in the same room as them laugh. Late afternoons were spent nursing pints in the King's Arms followed by drunken dinners at formal hall where they were on the verge of being banned by the Senior Common Room. They were funny and charming and all the fresher girls were a little bit in love with them.

'It's truly an amazing discovery,' said Assia, thinking how tanned Edward was and looking into his face a little longer than she had intended to.

He returned her gaze before breaking the spell with a smile of amusement. 'Sod the egg. How are you? I haven't seen you since you left Worcester, although I did see Tanya at a party a few years ago and was sorry when I realised she wasn't you. How has life been?'

Assia took a sip from her drink and stepped sideways to avoid the woman with the scratchy black dress who kept pressing into her shoulder blade. The crush of people moved Edward towards her so that they ended up standing almost side-to-side amid the excited blend of sequins and suits. Assia looked up at Edward. 'Life is better. It can only get better when you hit the massive low of killing your mother in a car crash and then abandoning your degree. The only way is up, really.' She smiled sardonically and raised her glass. 'Sorry, that wasn't what you meant, I know. But life *is* better. I got back on my feet, eventually, after Mama's death and I worked at the V&A, curating their Fabergé and Russian jewellery and now I work for a few clients, building up their Fabergé collections. Fabergé has become my passion, my obsession.'

'I can see how you could become obsessed with it,' said Edward. 'Before I was taken on board for the Egg Tour, I was working at the British Embassy in Moscow and I met oligarchs who would rather show me their Fabergé collection than talk about trade relations with the UK. One guy I met interrupted a meeting to go and bid on the phone for some Fabergé. He returned with this huge grin on his face saying "I bought byootiful Fabergé frame from Christie for many many thousand pounds." He was a lot easier to deal with after that, I can tell you.'

'For me, I think it was something to throw myself into after the accident and because it was Mama's passion, it allowed me to keep a part of her alive. After she died, I felt this huge and unbearable guilt for depriving her of her future. I felt that I had to live for her and I suppose my obsession with Fabergé grew from that.'

'It wasn't your fault, Assia, you know that, don't you?' Edward touched her shoulder.

'Hmm,' Assia paused. 'You know it becomes a philosophical matter after a while, really. I'm not going to go into it now, but there are many, many reasons why, even though it wasn't technically my fault, I still couldn't get out of bed in the morning.' She looked at Edward and smiled ruefully. In her mind's eye she saw the soft shapes of people in pastel colours standing on a lawn in the sun. The memory played as gently and soundlessly as an old reel projected onto a screen and she felt a painful yearning for those days before tragedy ran over her life with its blunt tram lines. That Trinity term of her second year had begun so gloriously and there had been balls and garden parties every week. Japanese tourists would go berserk when they saw groups of undergraduates heading into various colleges in their white tie and ball dresses and Assia had experienced that delicious feeling of being envied and admired. She was living the life that people read about in tourist guides and it had felt as good as it was meant to.

She walked over to the dinner table and peered at some of the placement cards. The names of guests had been written calligraphically in Latin script on thick cream card with the cypher of Olga Nikolaevna on each side and on closer inspection Assia noticed that the glossy plates laid out on the table were also engraved with Olga's gilt cypher. With the vast arrangement of pastel-coloured flowers and glasses which had been polished to crystal perfection, Assia wanted to conclude that it all looked a little *de trop* but she couldn't help thinking that it also looked rather beautiful.

'What do you think of all this, then?' Edward had reappeared and stood in front of Assia, so closely that he seemed to be mocking her reluctance to talk to him. 'I had absolutely nothing to do with the table stuff – that was Katya in the office. She really got her knickers in a twist about the flowers.' He made a dismissive gesture with his hand and shook his head.

'You should tell her I think she's done a fabulous job. I can see she's used some of the flowers that are in the egg's surprise. That's a really nice touch.'

Edward smiled to himself. Assia was trying to irritate him by taking Katya's side. She was trying to gain superiority as she had done in the old days. He took it as a sign that she was softening towards him and he felt happy. He wanted the old Assia back – it was just a matter of getting past all the scar tissue that had grown over the years.

'Ivan's not a bad-looking chap, is he? I could see you were enjoying talking to him. You know he's revoltingly powerful and rich too. Some people have all the luck, huh?'

Playground games. Assia knew Edward was trying to draw her into a playful duel, that he wanted a reaction from her, any reaction. There she was, the prim little girl with her mouth set in a straight line, a bow in her hair and patent red shoes. And there was Edward, smart in his expensive school blazer, prodding her breastbone with his finger.

'What happened to his wife with the…?' Assia ran her hand from her jaw down her neck and grimaced slightly.

'Acid attack,' Edward said solemnly, looking to see where Maria was in the room. He turned back to Assia and lowered his voice. 'She was a soloist with the Bolshoi. Had acid thrown at her when she left the Bolshoi one night after a performance of *Sleeping Beauty*. She was the Queen, not Aurora, but I don't think the irony was lost on anyone, including her attacker.'

'My God, when did it happen? Poor woman.'

'About three years ago. It was all over the press here at the time. "Jealousy at the Bolshoi" and all of that sort of thing. People were very worried and Government Ministers got involved. They wanted it cleared up because the Bolshoi is a national treasure and can't be played with.'

'I'm sure I must have read about it – I remember there were scandals to do with fighting ballerinas and warring factions. How absolutely awful.'

'She's still a very beautiful woman.'

Assia fiddled with her necklace, rubbing the garnets between her fingers. She was aware that she didn't like Edward acknowledging another woman's beauty, even a woman with only half a face. She continued, refusing to let him know that his hook had already caught her flesh.

'I can't imagine what an attack like that must be like. The shock as something lands on your skin and then the realisation that it is eating away at you.' She shuddered.

'Acid seems like a very feminine means of attack. It smacks of bitchiness to me. Men use guns and brute force to settle things.'

'Oh, I don't know. From what I've read, most acid attackers are men – spurned lovers and jealous boyfriends. It's just that they've worked out that taking away a woman's beauty is the worst thing you can do to her.'

'Would you agree?' Edward looked down at his feet and then up at Assia. He appeared embarrassed at having to resort to this kind of question to engage her.

'What, that depriving a woman of her beauty is a good means of punishment? Do I agree?' Assia frowned and looked at Edward accusingly. 'Yes, of course. I don't think you could ever get over it. Beauty is everything to a woman – not terribly feminist of me, I know, but I think you'd find it's true. Even if a beautiful woman is well-rounded emotionally, I don't think its loss is easy to bear. Somehow she would find a way to despise herself for looking worse than she used to; she would see it as a reflection of her inner turmoil. She'd begin to believe that it was her fault she was attacked. Women are just wired that way.'

The way she sighed and smiled ruefully, resigned to her sex's awkward blueprint, made Edward want to grab her face and pull it to his lips. He wanted to smudge her into himself, to own her and be owned by her. He wanted to take her away, out into Peter's city of stone and ice, away from the absurdity of a small egg and its grotesque admirers. He touched her wrist consolingly with his fingers and held his breath as she allowed them to rest on that most delicate part of her arm. He couldn't think of anything appropriate to say to her and then the moment was packed up and swept out of the way as dinner was announced.

XIV

'... and we would like to invite you to join us for the exhibition of the Livadia Egg in Moscow in April. The egg will be displayed at the Manege and will be joined by the ten Imperial eggs from the Kremlin Armoury as well as, we hope, other eggs from collections abroad. Ladies and Gentleman, thank you, and let us now enjoy this incredible feast.'

The dinner guests clapped politely, applauding Edward for a few seconds before turning to their neighbours and chatting among themselves as a troupe of waiters brought out the first course.

The screech of a chair silenced everybody.

Assia stood up abruptly and the man next to her leaned over awkwardly to catch her chair as it teetered on its back legs. She cupped her hand over her mouth and pressed it to her face so that her knuckles whitened and her face flushed with the pressure of her fingers. With the thumb of her other hand she jabbed at the screen of her phone but she was shaking so much that she dropped it. Edward rushed from his seat to Assia and put his arm around her. He picked up her phone and ushered her towards the door, propelling her gently with his hand on her back.

Snatches of the concerned questions Edward was whispering into her neck, the 'What?' and the 'Why?' and the platitudinous 'Are you OK?' could be heard, but it was clear that Assia was in shock because she couldn't talk and she wouldn't remove her hand from her mouth.

'Maybe she's pregnant?' a Russian woman in an Hervé Léger bodycon dress said loudly to her neighbour. 'I felt so terribly sick with my Kyrill – I was always jumping up and running for the bathroom.'

'It looked like bad news to me,' said a slim man with a shiny pate as he drew his phone out of the red-silk lined inner pocket of his jacket and held it up to his eyes, squinting. 'She saw something on her phone. That's the trouble with these smart phones: you can never switch off unless the damn things are turned off, and I never turn mine off!' He began to laugh and looked around the table for a taker for his joke but everyone had turned to watch Assia and Edward leave the room.

The sound of Assia's heels clicking on the parquet floor echoed above the chatter from the table. The click sounded slightly hollow, as though Assia's feet were suddenly too small to wear the shoes and she was dragging them like a little girl in mummy's high heels.

XV

Didn't you know? I was telling you all along, ever since you arrived. I am quite used to it now – I have seen so much death over the years, borne so many bodies. What's one more? Better to die here than somewhere else. Spill your blood on the stone and let me wash it away with my chill waters. This is my city.

Outside the museum, under the frozen crust, the waters of the river continued their momentous but invisible progress to the sea. The river is a brutal goddess, she thinks. Never ceasing, ever-changing, always adapting, forever present. I can't adapt. I can't change my course to flow around these holes – they just become me. I am being hollowed out.

She feels his hand on her shoulder and she turns her head slightly with a weak smile. She doesn't look at him.

'I'm sorry. It must be such a shock. What a horrible way to find out.'

He hangs his jacket gently on her shoulders.

'You'll freeze out here if you give me your jacket,' she says. 'Go back to the dinner. I'm OK on my own.'

'I'm fine. Stuff the dinner. You shouldn't be alone right now.'

The lights on the embankment appear to flicker. They are just holes of brightness that the darkness hasn't yet filled. It will reach them in the end, she thinks.

'I should have known. I couldn't get through to him on the phone and his sister hadn't seen him for a while. I was walking around following a broken scent – I wanted him to be here, I wanted the city to have him in it.'

'Where did they find him? How did he do it?' His eyes are sad but inquisitive, gently probing hers for clues.

'Shot himself outside his daughter's apartment block. Hell. I just can't bear the thought that I was walking round, head in the clouds, oblivious to the fact that he had gone. He must have needed someone so much.'

'When someone doesn't want to be found, it's impossible to reach them.' She looks up at him now. The corner of her mouth softens apologetically; she knows he is referring to the time when she didn't want to be found, when she didn't feel that she ought to be found. Her teeth begin to chatter as the cold seeps in. Her bones ache. She wants to give in. She wants to be warm again.

'Let's go to the Living Room at W,' he says. 'We can warm you up by the fireplace with a brandy.'

She pulls his jacket closer around her shoulders. The scent of a Trumper cologne opens a door onto a memory: a small Wonderland-sized door, hidden behind many others. Through it she sees a drinks party on the Provost's lawn at Worcester. The light of the sun that day was fierce and bleaching. Ice sweated in the drinks lined up on a starched tablecloth. People stood around in linen suits and society ties. She was excited because he was there.

And here now, they bow their heads to the bitter wind. She reaches for his hand.

XVI

Oxford, 1997

'Hello! We're back!' Assia could hear bags being put down in the hall and keys jangling as they were thrown into the pot on the hall table. Her mother was offering tea and guiding her guest down to the kitchen. Tanya groaned and shut her book with irritation.

'Oh, snore. They're here. I suppose we're going to have to go and say hello, aren't we?'

'Yup.' Assia unfurled her legs and got up off the sofa. She slipped on her shoes and smiled at her sister's graceless sulking. 'You didn't think we would get out of meeting Mama's best friend, did you? No way! This is the famous Kostya, after all!'

'I don't see why *we* have to meet him. Can't they just go off and do their own thing? I have a ton of work to do and I don't have time to be bored by stories about growing up in St Petersburg.' Tanya checked her reflection in the drawing room mirror and pulled her 'mirror face' as Assia called it, pouting and looking as stern as though she were storming down a catwalk.

'Well, he'll probably run away if you look at him fiercely enough.' Assia glanced in the mirror and patted her hair. 'Ugh, my hair is so wavy, but not in a good way, you know?'

'Bullshit. You look like a Pre-Raphaelite beauty. Just use my straighteners if you don't like it.'

Hovering by the door of the kitchen, the girls looked embarrassed when their mother spied them and ushered them in.

'Come in, girls! Come and meet Konstantin Alexandrovich! He's been longing to meet you.'

A tall man with dark hair got up from the kitchen table and smiled warmly at the twins as they walked towards him. With his broad shoulders he seemed to tower over them but he embraced them tenderly and kissed each of them three times on the cheek.

'Such young beauties, Olyushka!' He made a grand sweeping gesture with his large, tanned hand to emphasise the splendour of Olga's offspring. 'Not a surprise, of course,' he laughed and addressed the girls. 'Your mother is a legendary beauty. She had a line of suitors as long as Nevsky Prospect! Now, which one of you is Anastasia and which is Tatiana?'

'Assia is the charming one and Tanya is hard as diamonds. Between them, they'll conquer the world, my girls.' Olga said this while sitting at the kitchen table, resting her chin on her hand nonchalantly.

'Mama! What a thing to say!' Tanya glared at Olga furiously.

Konstantin shrugged and knelt down next to the table to riffle through a black bag on the floor. 'She was never without ambition, your mother! But ambition is hope, remember that, and hope is what we didn't have, growing up in the Soviet Union. Be thankful that you have a mother who wants things for you, good things.' He looked up at the twins who were watching him. His large eyes conveyed a look of anguish, intensified by heavy, thick eyebrows. Assia thought he was rather beautiful, with the air of a mournful Fayum portrait. His long, elegant nose gave him a look of the ancient peoples who had once settled in the land of his fathers, Armenia.

'Right,' he said, standing up, clutching something in each hand. 'I thought very hard about what would be the best present to give to two sixteen-year-old girls and I came up with these.' He opened his hands to reveal two little pale wooden boxes, one resting in each large palm. 'Go on,' he said, seeing that the girls were hesitating to step forward. 'Take them – one for each of you.'

Assia, feeling conscious of her red cheeks and flushed neck, reached out for the box in Konstantin's left hand and avoided his gaze. She held it between her fingers and unhooked the little metal hook which held it closed. Inside the box was a small egg with smooth white enamel resting on a cushion of cream-coloured velvet. She smiled when she saw it and looked up at Konstantin who was watching her. She was about to thank him when Tanya exclaimed loudly.

'Oh, my goodness! Konstantin Alexandrovich, thank you, it's beautiful!' Tanya went over to kiss him, holding the tiny egg up to his face as though it were a piece of mistletoe. 'Look, Mama!' Tanya dangled the egg before the light so that her mother could admire it. Against the light from the window, the delicate lilac egg became luminous and the scales of the tiny gold snake wrapped around it shimmered.

'It's perfectly wonderful, Kostya. You are naughty to spoil my girls like this!' Olga looked sternly at Konstantin and shook her finger at him in mock punishment. There was something about this playfulness which seemed unbecoming to Assia and she felt an irresistible urge to pin her mother's arms to her sides. Konstantin pretended to look chastened by Olga before a large childish smile broke across his face and he was unable to hide his pleasure. His presence was unexpectedly comforting to Assia, almost as though he provided a tonic to her mother's astringency and she felt grateful towards him for being there.

Olga came round to look at Assia's present and draped an arm around her daughter. Assia saw Konstantin studying her mother's reaction, his lips drawing together in taut anticipation of which he was clearly unconscious.

'Oh, isn't this divine!' She plucked the egg out of the case and inspected the marks on it. Assia was aware of nasty thoughts about her mother piling on top of each other in her mind; she found Olga's *oohs* and *aahs* somewhat distasteful and she felt the ripples of a tide of alarm. She remembered feeling the same way when she was ten, when Olga had decided to tell her and Tanya about 'what a man and a woman do to make a baby.' Although everyone at school talked about it in vague and euphemistic terms, having the facts of life explained to her by Olga made her want to scream, and while Tanya laughed as Olga continued her blunt anatomical description, Assia screamed in anger at her mother to stop and put her hands over her ears.

'Now, Assia, look! This egg has a musical score on it, can you see? These tiny little notes and the words underneath are from Alexandre Dubuque's song "Do not scold me, my darling". Oh, it is a lovely song, isn't it?' She addressed Konstantin. 'I can only remember the first verse, but it always reminds me of Natasha in *War and Peace* longing for Anatole. She knows she shouldn't love him but she can't help herself.' Suddenly Olga took a deep breath and startled everyone by launching into the song, holding her arms out dramatically in supplication to her small audience. Her lips curved around the words of the Russian song and Assia thought she was radiant, as though the music and the sad words suffused her with a sort of pinkness. It only lasted for a few moments, but Assia would never forget the way her mother looked at each of them as she sang, her eyes wide and sorrowful.

> *Do not scold me, my darling,*
> *Because I love him so…*

She attempted the second verse but the words wouldn't come and so she smiled and bowed deeply like a conductor, ending her performance. The twins and Konstantin applauded vigorously and Olga laughed, waving her hand to bat away the praise.

'Encore! Encore!' cried Konstantin.

'Mama, I had no idea you could sing so beautifully!' said Assia. She was rather taken aback by her mother's talented performance and she felt just a little bit less annoyed by her flirtatious exuberance because of it.

'Well, I had the privilege of being classically trained until I was your age.'

'And why did you stop? You are so good!' Assia looked questioningly at her mother, wondering why she would hide something as beautiful as her voice.

'Grandpapa stopped my lessons when he found out that your grandmother was having an affair with my singing teacher. They split up because of it. It wasn't a very nice time, actually.'

Olga leaned on the edge of the large, worn wooden table and studied her hands and nails, her lips pursed. She looked wounded, as though someone had been nasty to her in some way. Assia didn't know what to say. She hadn't known that her grandparents had split up because of an affair, in fact she hadn't known that they had split up at all. She had always thought of them as a pair of people she never knew in a land and an age that was far away; that was how Olga had always referred to them.

'Watching your mother sing,' Konstantin said gently, pulling out a dining chair and lowering his large frame onto it, 'reminds me of when we were younger.' He patted the chair next to him to encourage the girls to sit around the table. 'She was so talented at school, always answering everything correctly in classes and passing all her exams with flying colours.' He glanced at Olga to see if she was softening. 'Lots of girls were just waiting for your mother to slip up because they didn't believe that someone could be so clever and so pretty and get away with it. But of course, your mama had her eyes on greater things and didn't even notice the envious chatter.'

'I did notice it,' said Olga, lifting her head suddenly. 'It only really began when I was a teenager, but how could I not notice it, Kostya?' She sounded exasperated. 'Do you remember that time when our oven broke and Mama had to take me to the café near school for breakfast and supper every day for three weeks? Everyone at school teased me for having a lazy mother who wouldn't even cook for me. It doesn't sound like much but it was very hurtful to someone of my age.'

'I know,' said Konstantin, 'I know it was. I spent a lot of time shouting down people who were mean about your mother as well as wiping away your tears, if you remember. All I meant was that you never planned on kicking around with those girls from school once you were at university. You were either going to do something important in Russia or leave it altogether. And you left.'

He looked at her with raised eyebrows which seemed to require a response.

'I did leave, but that was because I met Richard and we fell in love. And of course, the rest is history. Look at my two girls. Never was a mother more proud.' Olga beamed at the twins and stood up, moving away from the edge of the table towards the kitchen counter where she inspected the calendar on the pin board. She leaned up towards it on tiptoes, one foot slightly off the floor as she unpinned it and placed it on the counter. In her figure-hugging stonewashed jeans, black boat-neck top and white bandeau around her blonde hair she looked like a prim and efficient version of Françoise Hardy.

'So, Kostya. I have a few things planned for your visit.' She read off the calendar. 'We're due at high-table at St John's tonight – Richard has arranged that and…'

'You left so quickly. You had only known Richard for three months and you had a wonderful job at the Hermitage. You could have ended up running the place.'

Konstantin had twisted round in his chair to face Olga. He spoke softly, but he knew that his words would have an impact.

'I'm sorry?' Olga lifted her elbows off the counter and placed a hand on her hip as she leaned on the other arm. 'Do we really have to do this?'

Konstantin looked chastened but he didn't say anything. He didn't lift his gaze from Olga as though he were steadily drawing the snake out of her.

'Firstly, I did not leave quickly. Richard and I started seeing each other while he was in Piter and when he left, we continued to speak and write for six months before we got engaged and discussed my moving to England. So it wasn't just a three-month fandango, as you're suggesting. And anyway, forgive me for wanting to leave the gaping black hole of a country that we grew up in. I wasn't going to let it swallow me whole, unlike you, and the opportunities that I had there I have had tenfold in the West and…' She slammed her palm on the counter and took a strained breath, staring at the back of the hand stretched out before her. 'Hell, Kostya, why are you making me go through this? I am *not* going to be drawn into any more of this in front of the girls.' She leaned down and dragged the door of the dishwasher up so that the tray slammed into the back of the machine with the sound of plates and glasses crashing into each other. Then she took the kettle from on top of one of the AGA covers and filled it at the sink before returning it to the boiling plate and standing with her back to the room, her hands gripping the silver bar of the AGA on which the tea-towels hung.

Assia held her breath as she watched her mother lose her temper with Konstantin. She chewed her lip, pressing the soft skin between her teeth until it hurt. Looking at Konstantin she felt anxious and sorry for him; he didn't seem to know where to look or what to do with himself now that he had set the spinning top of her mother going. She caught his eye and he smiled at her awkwardly and looked away as though he wanted to disappear. Assia felt a swell of compassion for him as she watched his large expressive eyes study the table. It was a strange thing to feel so strongly for someone one had only just met but the need to protect him from her mother was overwhelming. Perhaps she was conscious of a violation of that age-old concept of hospitality where your guest was treated like a visiting king and she had to stop her mother from casting out the esteemed visitor.

Her mother had behaved in a way which made their guest embarrassed and Assia was angry because of it. She stared at Olga's back, willing her to turn around and dispel the unpleasant atmosphere. Everyone waited in silence until the kettle whistled and pumped steam into the air. Olga grabbed the kettle off the plate and slammed the lid down gracelessly.

Right, that's it. If she can't behave like an adult, then I will.

Assia stood up. 'Konstantin Alexandrovich, would you like to come with me to the drawing room? We have a new book on Austrian music boxes which I am sure you would like to see.'

Konstantin nodded and stood up slowly. Tanya mouthed 'What are you doing?' with a glare but Assia ignored her. As he sidled out of the kitchen, Konstantin looked back at Olga like a guilty dog but she didn't see his glance because she was busy scrubbing cups in the sink.

XVII

Edward checked his phone and tossed it back onto the lacquered walnut table in front of him. He leant back in the large brown leather chair, the edges of which were dotted with large yellow brass studs whose bosses shone brightly, reflecting the image of the hotel lobby like circus mirrors. The hotel designer's brief had clearly been 'English Gentleman's Club' and this had been interpreted with wood, brass and leather in vast quantities. Everything in the hotel had been panelled with heavy slabs of mahogany and Edward wondered if any of the other guests felt as though they were lying in a coffin when they lay on their beds at night. Huge brass lamps modelled as Corinthian columns were on every table in the lobby – fantastic murder weapons, Edward thought. Perhaps the designer had been told to make everything dual purpose; even the heavy gilt frames on the brand new copies of Dutch Old Masters looked as though they could cause some damage.

Edward didn't like hotels which had no character; this one was about as close to conjuring the atmosphere of a club on Pall Mall as its paintings were to being authentic Bosschaerts. The ambience was too sterile and homogenous for his liking – apart from the Russian staff, nothing in this hotel would suggest he was in Russia – but at least he wasn't paying for it. Ivan Denisov and the Livadia Egg Tour management wanted him to stay here because this was where they had put up the American and English VIPs who had come to see the egg and they needed him to look after them. He had spent the morning taking breakfast with Madeleine Roseman, ostensibly to talk to her about her loaning her Fabergé egg to the Moscow leg of the tour, however he had spent most of his time trying to find a hairdresser for her who could take instructions in English.

'It's the water here, you see,' she had said in her loud and abrasive voice. 'I swear it does something to the colour of my hair. It was like this last time I came here, in the 90s. We had to use sterilising tablets to purify the water then and because the water had God knows what sort of impurities in it, my hair went what you could call a lighter shade of green. I can't have that happening this time.' She snapped her purse shut and cradled some of her bleached blonde hair in her palm.

'I am very happy to translate for you, if we can't find a good hairdresser who speaks English,' said Edward, masking his disdain for Mrs Roseman's pampered priorities. Who would waste their time in a foreign city fussing about their hair – and who did she think he was? Some kind of English elite concierge?

'Uh-uh. No way.' Mrs Roseman shook her head and her helmet of hair shook ever so slightly. 'I am not having *any* surprises. I have had foreigners do my hair and when they don't speak English, they don't understand what you mean and it just *does not work.*' She rapped her long red-lacquered nails on the table as she spoke these last words.

'Right ho, leave it with me, Mrs Roseman, if you will, and I will make sure you are relieved of this concern. We can't have anything marring your enjoyment of St Petersburg.' Edward leaned back in his chair and adjusted his tie. He decided to try a different tack with this one; she was a tough nut.

'You know, when I was at Eton, Mrs Roseman, we were all obsessed with James Bond – not the Pierce Brosnan nonsense, of course – but Roger Moore and his gentle ironies...'

'You were at Eton? Oh, my. I *am* impressed. Did you know Prince William?'

'He's younger than me so we weren't there at the same time. My father is a close friend of Prince Andrew though, so I know the princesses well.'

Hooked, thought Edward. She just needed a flash of pedigree and now she'll give me the time of day.

'But what I wanted to say, Mrs Roseman, was that during my Bond obsession, I encountered Fabergé.' He looked into her eyes and she blinked a few times, suddenly unnerved by his gaze. 'Before *Octopussy*, I had no idea that these amazing objects – the eggs – existed. I mean, we all understand the primordial allure of diamonds and sapphires and rubies, but a Fabergé egg is something else. It's a tiny bit sacred, isn't it? What is it like to own one? Do you feel that it even belongs to you? How can you bring yourself to share it? It's very noble of you, really.'

Madeleine Roseman felt a flutter in her chest. This handsome young Englishman was persistent. Most Englishmen, she found, were very polite but she could see them withdrawing when they met her. They coped with her all-over American-ness by employing more and more of their polished diplomacy. She noticed the gentle smirk behind their aplomb even though they thought she was too stupid and brash to be able to analyse their behaviour. In fact, she thought they were the stupid ones for assuming, with typical arrogance, that she had only one-dimension. Didn't they realise that she wielded her boldness in the same way that they wore their diffidence? This chappie was different though; unlike most people he wanted to know how she felt about owning something so precious. Everyone else wanted to herd her and tell her what to do with her money – this one wanted to know about her feelings. She liked him.

'Edward honey, I approve of your questions. No one has ever asked me in all of my fifty-something years on God's earth what it is like to own important things. They all want to know *what* I own, of course, but they are not at all interested in my thoughts on ownership. I think you would understand if I told you that possessing valuable things has its negatives. I don't want to sound like a poor little rich girl – believe you me, I know my problems are gold-plated – but wealth has its burdens.' She put the embroidered linen napkin on the table and smoothed her plaid apricot Chanel skirt with the flat of her hand.

'I can only imagine, Mrs Roseman.' Edward nodded and a look of concern spread over his face.

'Please, call me Madeleine. You see, my father loved owning things. He dragged himself up from his poor kid beginnings and I think it was no coincidence that he started an elevator business. Moving on up was the only way for him and with the elevation came property and possessions and things, things, things. When he bought the Alexander III Medallion Egg, he referred to it in public as the John D. O'Connor Egg – you English would think that frightfully vulgar but it was my father's way of proving to himself and to the city of Washington that he had arrived. He had the egg on view in his offices and when he became a senator, he moved the egg to a cabinet in his office and insisted that everyone who came to see him admired the egg as well. He left the egg to me when he passed on the proviso that I never sell it.'

'How interesting!' said Edward, folding his arms and narrowing his eyes with apparent concentration.

'I wanted to do ownership differently, however. For me, owning a Fabergé egg was *not* about putting my family's name on it: I believed fervently that the egg had to be shared. I didn't want to make it an exclusive and private treasure as my father had before me and so I built a Fabergé Museum around the egg and restored its original name. People still refer to it as the John D. O'Connor Egg, which is fine, but they should know for whom the egg was made originally and its historical significance. When you are second-generation wealth, you feel differently about making your mark on the world. It was important to my father to scratch his name in the cave wall but I feel that compulsion in a different way; I want to share knowledge and beauty.'

Madeleine folded her hands delicately and pressed her lips together. She had said her piece about why she built the Fabergé Museum many times before but it was rare that she told an audience of one. The last man she had talked to about her project and her interest in Fabergé scholarship had not been even the slightest bit interested. Elliott had closed his eyes and turned over: 'I heard you telling the Trustees about it, honey. You don't need to repeat the speech.' She had been left staring at his rounded shoulder covered in expensive Liberty paisley-patterned silk and had felt sick.

'Madeleine, you know, that is absolutely fascinating.' Edward propped his elbow on the breakfast table and rested his chin on his hand. Madeleine admired his vintage Omega watch and his elegant gold cufflinks. He continued: 'It sounds to me as though you feel that the egg belongs to you in a different way to that in which it belonged to your father. For him it was his to do with as he wanted – and who could argue with him? It was his status symbol, after all – but you have taken a fabulously generous approach to Fabergé; by that, I mean you want to share the workmanship so that everyone can love Fabergé's craft as you do. I think that is truly a commendable vision.' He smiled and nodded at Madeleine as though bowing respectfully.

Madeleine experienced a thrill which she had long thought was denied women of her age; she thought she might even be blushing. All those years spent fighting Elliott in the divorce courts had worn her down and even the papers had got bored of reporting the finer points of the case. It had made the headlines though when Elliott claimed he needed an allowance of $100,000 a month from Madeleine to cover the costs of his sex addiction. Teams of hookers had seen this as the time to share their 'experiences' with Elliott with the papers and Madeleine had had to read about his fetishes for leather, threesomes and whips, not knowing how much of it – if not all of it – was true, and wondering if the man whose proclivities were being laid bare to the world was really the same man to whom she had been married. How could the short young man with a nose like a button mushroom and dark sideburns, who had shed a happy tear when they married beneath an arch of sweet william and gypsophila on her father's Florida estate, have wanted to do all these unmentionable things?

Their daughter Athena was mortified by the claims in the papers and would call her mother in a rage, ranting at Madeleine as if it was her fault that she had allowed Elliott to become so starved sexually that he had been driven to these awful measures. 'How could you have let it happen, Mom? Surely you must have known what he was up to? You must have known he was into this shit, right?' Maybe it *was* her fault, Madeleine had thought, maybe everyone else she knew got their whips out of an evening and satisfied their husbands in ways she had never even imagined, let alone thought necessary. The humiliation of being a well-known cuckquean when all this had been in the press over a decade ago had made Madeleine very sensitive to the fact that she was not only inadequate in the bedroom but totally behind the times. She had decided to educate herself in that arena and acquired a porn video before deciding, half an hour in, that it was all completely animal-like, boring and for perverts only. As far as she had been concerned from that point on, all men were sexual deviants and the women who subscribed to that stuff were welcome to them.

And yet, here was this young English man who was interested in what she had to say – everyone else was just interested in her Forbes listing. Madeleine's stomach wouldn't stop flipping and she felt something sink deep inside her. This was silly: Edward was far more suitable for Athena, wasn't he? But some men liked older women – she knew about cougars from that wretched porn video.

'I would just love for you to come and see my museum, Edward. It's small, but perfectly formed – in my eyes anyway.' Madeleine lifted her chin and looked down at Edward in an imperious way. She thought that perhaps he might like being dominated.

'I would be thrilled to see it, Madeleine, how kind of you to ask.' He took his Prada glasses off and leaned back in his chair, trying to deflect her bizarre gaze. He could see that she didn't really know how to relate to men – her brashness and frosty imperiousness bobbed forlornly on a sea of sadness. Her eyes looked wet. 'In fact, your invitation ties in rather nicely with what we were touching on last night and what I would like to propose to you now. You saw the magnificent Livadia Egg being unveiled yesterday evening: that was something none of us will ever forget. The St Petersburg Museum and the Russian nation – like you – believes that Fabergé's craftsmanship has something more to offer the world than just its phenomenal price tag.' He shifted in his seat as he uncrossed his legs. 'We want to share the joy of Fabergé with the Russian people, to celebrate his achievements as the greatest jeweller the world has ever known. We want to gather the many eggs which were scattered to the four winds after the Revolution and bring them back to their birthplace, Russia. Lend us your Alexander III Medallion Egg. Help us encourage young Russians to be proud of their heritage.'

Edward could feel his phone buzzing in his pocket. He ignored it, not wanting to interrupt this pivotal moment with Madeleine Roseman. A waiter in a white jacket was fussing about the table next to them, sweeping the crumbs from the table into a little silver pan and smoothing the starched white linen with the flat of his hand; he moved away quickly when he caught Edward's eye.

'Listen, Edward, I'm afraid that my Fabergé consultant, Anastasia Wynfield – oh, I forgot, you know her, don't you? You were comforting her at the dinner last night when she got that bad news about her friend? Poor child, what a horrible shock. Anyway, I had wanted her to be here at this meeting because she was telling me that she thinks there is something wrong with the Livadia Egg, but she rang me from the airport this morning and said she had to go home because she was too upset about her friend.' She sounded stern now. 'I'm sorry to be indelicate, but I'm not going to commit to anything until Anastasia is happy that the Livadia Egg is authentic.' Lifting her tan leather Birkin onto her knees, she laid her hands on top of it, defensively. She wanted to please this young man, but she *had* to make sure things were done properly.

Edward felt his heart plummet. Assia had gone. Flown away. She couldn't even stand to be in the same country as him. He had hoped that she might stay on in Piter for a few days and that they could talk over this wretched business of her dislike of the egg but clearly she had just wanted to get away from him.

He paused as a clip of that evening ran in his head. He had already replayed it in his mind so many times that he thought the film strip would be fraying by now:

Assia has turned away from him in the bed. He knows she's awake as he can just see the movement of her eyelashes as she blinks. The eco bulbs in the bedside lamps hum softly. He strokes the top of her pale shoulder and is sure that she shudders slightly. He moves closer to her so that he is pressing, naked, against her back, and he sweeps her dark hair from her neck so that it falls luxuriantly between his chest and her shoulder blade. She doesn't move. He puts an arm around her and asks her which part of the grand tour of the egg will be the most successful. Moscow? Nizhny-Novgorod? Samara? He can feel her writhe as she pushes his arm off and flicks her legs over the side of the bed so that she's sitting up, her back to him.

'I don't want to talk about that wretched egg anymore, OK? It offends me.'

She turns her face to the side so that she is addressing him but not looking at him.

'What do you mean? What's wrong with it?' He sits up against the bedhead.

'It's not right. Something about it jars. I think it's been tinkered with.'

'By whom? Who would do that?'

He looks confused. He can't prevent his eyes from lingering on her dimples of Venus.

'I don't know! Someone. I don't think the miniatures are period and the style of the egg overall just doesn't sit properly. Fabergé was better than that.'

She gets up from the bed and picks her bra and knickers up from the floor.

'Don't you think that perhaps your grief for Kostya is clouding your judgement here?'

He crosses his arms and watches her from the bed.

She sighs and purses her lips.

'Oh, my God, Edward. I can't believe how arrogant you are! You think you know what I'm thinking better than I do! And if you don't believe what I'm saying about the egg, you can listen as I call my friend at the V&A and tell her what I think of it. It might just cause problems for you with the tour.'

She has put on her dress and bends down now to pick up her stilettos. She hooks their straps over her index finger and looks for her clutch bag.

'Assia, please don't go. Can't we talk about this? I'm sorry I upset you, I really didn't mean to. Sod the damned egg, I don't care about it. You're what matters to me.'

He watches as she shakes her head and says sorry but she can't do this. She opens the door and leaves, the stilettos still dangling on her finger.

'Ah, right, OK.' He nods. It feels as though Madeleine is saying that Assia hates *him*, not the egg. He wants to put his head in his hands, for Madeleine to go away and leave him with this ache. He needs to work through it, to size it up and quantify it. He needs to be sure that he can pin it down and stop it turning into something more.

He took a breath. 'Why don't you let me arrange for the egg's curator, Oleg Sablin, to show it to you in private? He'll answer any concerns you may have. And then I think you need to come to and have supper with me at the Literaturnoe Kafe. Pushkin ate his final meal there before heading off to the duel in which he would meet his end. You can't be here in Piter and not go there.'

He grinned in a way that he knew showed off the dimple in his left cheek. Women always lapped it up. The slight smile distorting Madeleine's lips convinced him that he'd got her. The rest was just a matter of finesse.

She wasn't going to smile. 'Yes, please set that up. It would be helpful.' Madeleine swallowed, trying to hide her disappointment at realising that Edward did want something from her after all.

XVIII

The Governor's House, Tobolsk,

17/30 August, 1917

Dear Aunt Margaret,

You must have thought it dreadfully remiss of me for not having written after you sent news of poor Father's death, but the letter took a very long time to reach me in St Petersburg, having been almost two months on the way. On receiving your letter, immediately I began a response but was unable to finish it. I had planned to come home to Cold Ashby to see the house before all is broken up and sold but you will doubtless by now know the position in which we are placed here from the turn of political events.

My duty calls for my presence and I have accompanied the Imperial Family into exile here in Tobolsk, which is in Siberia. Our journey by train was not without event and there was alarm when rail workers at Zvanko held our train, not wanting to let it pass through when they learned the identities of its passengers. The family bear all their troubles with equanimity and apparently without question. They departed from the Alexander Palace with dignity and complete calm. Even the soldiers of the Revolution could not find fault with this dear, martyred family.

The Grand Duchess Olga Nikolaevna concerns me, however. She is dangerously thin and gaunt following a serious bout of measles before exile and, of the children, she appears to be the most affected by events. Of an evening, she prefers to sit and read in isolation from the rest of the family and, being too old to have lessons with me, appears to suffer from pronounced ennui. *She has agreed to read* David Copperfield *with me next week and this shall no doubt improve her English and provide ample diversion.*

I would like to ask whether you could let me have a few things from the Vicarage for remembrance's sake… a few pictures, or a piece of furniture, perhaps? It is more than possible that I shall leave Russia with the family and return to England to spend our exile. I cannot say when that may occur, for at the present time we are all confined to Tobolsk and the Governor's House here.

Ever yours affectionately,
John

XIX

'I'm rather amazed that you decided to tell me at all, actually – I normally don't feature in your Russian life. But hell, that's really awful. Poor old Kostya. Have you told Papa?'

Tanya stirred her cocktail with a neon yellow plastic stick and tapped it on the side of her drink to shake off any remaining drops. She placed it on the small square napkin on the bar and pouted as she fiddled with her straw. This habit of pouting had always irritated Assia ever since Tanya had perfected the art of setting her plump lips into a perfect little 'O' cushion. It had become her default expression from the age of about nine and she would use it for all manner of occasions from sulking to trying to win their father's indulgence. Assia knew that she had a whole range of pouts which she could customise depending on what or whom she wanted. On this occasion, Assia saw that Tanya was wearing her 'wounded rabbit' pout.

'It's no more my "Russian life" than yours. We all knew Kostya. You might not have cared for him but Mama and I did.' Assia could feel the heat prickling up her neck. 'And no, I haven't told Papa. I don't think he'd even react. He won't want any mention of Kostya in his life again. Also, I know you think I don't tell you about anything, but when have I actually ever kept you in the dark?' Assia wasn't going to take this. Tanya loved to cast everyone else as the doer of ill while she was just poor little St Tatiana, a martyr whose beauty was never dimmed by her monstrous sufferings.

'Since you ask: Mama's book – the one you're editing for re-publication. For some reason you neglected to tell me about that, but *Ben* knew everything.' She sucked in her cheeks to emphasise the offence taken.

'Oh, come on, Tanya. Give me a break.' Assia looked pained. 'I had only just been asked to do it by my agent. I hadn't even signed a contract. In fact, Ben probably shouldn't have said anything.' Assia checked her phone and saw that she had a message from Edward. She turned the phone over quickly and placed it on the polished metal of the bar ledge.

'All I meant about Kostya was that you're the one who stayed in touch with him and saw him in Russia. You have the world of Fabergé in common – that's all I meant.' She tilted her head to one side – a gesture which was part sympathetic, part conciliatory. 'And it's always been so complicated with him. He could never accept that Mama had her own life and chose to leave Russia of her own accord. I don't know. I just always felt that he was waiting and waiting for Mama to leave her English life and go back to Piter with him, and it was never going to happen!' She wrung her hands theatrically in remonstration. 'Anyway, how did he top himself? Was he clutching a copy of *Onegin*?'

'Just drop it, Tanya.' Assia turned her head and looked away. She wasn't going to stay if Tanya was going to make snide jokes. She pulled her bag up from the floor and slid off the bar stool.

Tanya grabbed her arm. 'I'm sorry, I'm sorry, Assenka. I don't deal with these things very well. Please stay. Tell me what happened.'

Tanya's grip on her upper arm was strong and Assia knew she had to stay. Tanya was aware that she had gone too far; she wasn't even pouting. Perhaps, thought Assia, she had realised that her desire to provoke had backfired. Their father had always indulged Tanya's theatricality; given in to her over-the-top entreaties for his attention, her 'don't ignore me, dearest, darling Papa' routine. It was hard to inflame him which was probably why Tanya so frequently overdid the provocation. Assia stopped holding her breath and exhaled with relief knowing that if she'd walked out then, the slender thread holding them together would have snapped. She lowered her bag onto the floor and pulled herself back onto the stool.

'He shot himself.' She could see Kostya holding the gun to his temple, his hand shaking, his eyes closed. She kept running the scene in her mind as though trying to glue the cinematic cliché to Kostya.

'Oh, God, that's just grizzly. Why? Why would he do that? It can't just be because of Mama, can it? She's been gone for a long time now.'

'I hope not. I really hope not, because I just can't cope with the implications of all of that.' She scratched at something in the fibres of her pencil skirt. 'You know about the grandson with cerebral palsy though? I think that was very upsetting for all of them and Vika only started talking to him recently after years of silence, punishing him for divorcing her mother. So there are many possible causes. I hope there are, at least.'

'Of course there are, Assenka. This isn't your fault. It really isn't.'

It must have been Tanya's look of earnest reassurance which made something cave within Assia. Her twin's wide-eyed certainty threw her a lifeline which she needed desperately. When her mother was killed, no one in the family – especially her father and sister – could bring themselves to tell Assia conclusively that the accident was not her fault. She was cast out into a comfortless land. But now, with Kostya's death, Tanya was saying that she might not have to go into the maze and face the monstrous logic of cause and effect after all – her sister had given her a thread and was guiding her out of it. She could feel her core liquefying and it was a wonderful, liberating feeling. She shuddered as shew drew in breaths and tears spilled out of her eyes.

'Ha! Honestly, I'm a wreck!' She laughed and wiped her eyes and nose on the sleeve of her jacket. 'Sorry, I'm not sure what happened there. I'm just a little wobbly, that's all. Since I heard of Kostya's death, I've been blaming myself and it all felt horribly familiar.'

'You didn't kill him, Assia.'

'No, but I killed Mama and that broke him. It brought him to the point where he wanted to shoot himself, for God's sake!'

Tanya frowned. 'But you and I are coping, aren't we? I get out of bed every day and so do you and although Mama's loss still hurts like hell, we're buggering on whether we really want to or not. Kostya chose not to.' She picked up the neon drink stirrer and flicked it against her fingers. 'At some point the line of collapsing dominoes takes on a life of its own that has nothing to with the person who pushed the first one.'

'I hope you're right.' Assia put the back of her hand on her cheek to try and cool it down. 'I was never strong enough to research the Butterfly Effect. I thought I had enough Chaos Theory in my life as it was.' They both laughed and Assia, with cheeks stained a blotchy pink from tears, beamed.

'Excuse me. You're twins, right?' A man in a grey suit holding a pint approached them from the end of the bar followed by his friend. Assia had seen them looking at her and Tanya but hoped that they wouldn't come over. She couldn't stand being bothered in bars by men who thought that the sole purpose of their visit was to titillate them with their remarkable similarity to each other.

'Would you both like a drink?' asked the friend. He had loosened his tie and unbuttoned his white shirt at the top. He was sporting the kind of huge metal watch which looked as though it could operate a monster truck remotely. Assia smiled to herself as she saw him looking Tanya up and down: the snakeskin Louboutins definitely attracted the wrong kind of attention.

'No, thank you,' said Tanya curtly. 'We're having an important conversation and we don't appreciate the interruption.'

'No need to get your knickers in a twist, love,' said the man in the grey suit widening his eyes and glaring at Tanya. 'Let's leave these snotty bitches alone, Mark.'

'You probably didn't know,' shouted Tanya at their retreating backs 'that it's incredibly bad luck to ask people if they're twins!'

'Is that true?' Assia raised a quizzical eyebrow.

'Nope,' said Tanya. She stood up on the rung of the barstool, smoothed her skirt and sat down. 'I made it up. But I thought it might protect other sets of pretty twins from being pestered by them.' She smiled and her face brightened with amusement. Assia thought how much she missed her twin and how long it was since they had laughed together. The messy circumstances of their mother's death had lit a series of paper-thin tinders which had smouldered, curled and eventually blackened. There had been no conflagration, no great showdown, but Assia had felt that her relationship with Tanya had burned out and that it would be hard for them to revive a sisterly relationship. She knew that their twindom had died as the ambulance sped to the John Radcliffe with their mother in the back.

'I'm sorry I couldn't bring you with me to see the egg. I know you wanted to be there.' Assia pressed her luxuriant mouth into a conciliatory smile. She was about to take Tanya's hand and squeeze it affectionately but something prevented her from reaching out and touching her sister's perfectly manicured fingers. 'If I could have brought you with me, I would have done, but they wanted to keep the event very exclusive. And anyway, I've rather gone off the egg. I just don't think it's particularly beautiful.'

'Oh, really? I thought it looked rather magnificent in the photos. But what do I know? I'm just a boring old number-cruncher.' She took a sip from her drink, pretending that she hadn't just dropped a little ironic bomb. 'Do you think Mama would have liked it?'

The bar was filling up. Assia looked around before continuing. The men they had snubbed had moved to a table in the corner where they had joined some other women who were drinking shots.

'Hmm, I don't know.' She wrinkled her nose thoughtfully. 'I've been mulling it over a lot and it's tricky. The miniatures on the egg strike me as a little anachronistic – they just don't sit well and I think Mama, like me, would find the whole composition quite heavy. It's full of references to masterpieces from the Dresden Green Vaults which would have pleased her, but really, it's not what I – or she – would have expected. I just have a bad feeling about it – an instinctive one. You know how Mama sometimes talked about her Fabergé compass, the internal guide she had which she trusted innately? Well, the needle on my Fabergé compass oscillates wildly around this new egg. I just don't know what to make of it. I *so* wanted it to be Mama's egg, the one she predicted.'

'Yes, I was going to ask you about that. Why wasn't the egg designed by Alma Pihl? Mama wasn't wrong, was she?' Tanya shook her head delicately as though unable to brook the thought.

'No, she wasn't wrong. She was very right, in fact, because Olga's egg does exist, and she had always said that it did. But it's just disappointing that her prediction about who designed it wasn't accurate. But maybe Pihl did design something and it didn't reach production. I want to look into it further.'

'OK, at least Mama comes out of it well. I would hate for people to muddy her name.'

'It was quite the opposite in Piter, I tell you. People were singing her praises and saying that it was fabulous that it was a Russian who knew all along that Olga's egg existed. I saw lots of her old crew and they all recognised her role in getting the egg found.'

'And are you going to put this new egg into Mama's *Encyclopaedia* when you edit it?'

'I'll have to. It's too important a discovery to omit, and my editor will expect me to include it. But I want to settle a few queries I have first. When I look at it, something doesn't seem right. It's a bit like wearing glasses with a small scratch on the lens. It bothers you so much that you spend your whole time rubbing the glasses with a cloth – that's the stage I'm at.'

A blonde woman in a trouser suit with a large tote bag barged into Assia as she walked past carrying a glass of wine in each hand. The wine splashed dramatically onto the floor, some of it spraying Assia's ankle. The woman stepped back, swore and continued her progress. 'Hey!' yelled Tanya after her, frowning. 'What the hell is this place?'

Assia put her hand to her heart and closed her eyes in relief when she saw it was just a woman who had bumped into her. 'Lord! That gave me a fright. I hadn't realised how jumpy I was.' She took a napkin from the bar and wiped her ankle. 'This will sound mad, but I keep thinking I'm being followed. There was this guy at the film screening – shaven head with fleshy lips – and I saw him on my way to Piter and then again when I was there. It was probably just a coincidence, but something about him alarmed me.' She shook her head. 'I'm behaving like a primitive being at the moment – operating entirely on instinct. First the egg unseats me and then this strange man. I need to move out of the dark ages and back into the world of reason and logic!'

'Well, just be careful.' Tanya scanned the bar with a barely veiled look of disgust. 'Generally, I think the female instinct with regards to men is pretty spot on. If you see him again, you should call the police. Stalkers can be incredibly dangerous.'

'Hmm, yup. I'm not sure he's a stalker. I don't know what he is, but, yes, you're right.' The thought trailed off and she paused for a second before brightening. 'Anyway, you should come with me one day to Piter so I can show you how it's changed since you were last there.'

'I bet the bars aren't like this one. At least most Russians aren't louts.'

'That's debatable, Tanyusha. You've just spent a lot of time around Westernised, educated Russians, like Mama and Dasha. The new young are OK – they've been raised on Western media but the oligarch class is a pretty lamentable breed: not far off loutish, actually. The Soviet chip sits firmly on their shoulders. All their conspicuous consumption is rather depressing, not least because you sense that it doesn't make them happy. The smile would never leave my face if I had all the money in the world.' She beamed and brushed a lock of her dark hair behind her ear. 'But then, I'm not like them because I wouldn't spend it on cars and planes and Picassos. Shall I tell you what I'd do? I'd spend all my money recreating the quarters of Nicholas and Alexandra at the Alexander Palace.'

'Seriously, Assenka, you are mad! I know you're obsessed with the Romanovs, but why would you do that? That's insane!'

Assia laughed and sighed contentedly. She loved talking about the last Romanovs – it brought them closer to her. She could pretend they were alive and that physical distance was all that separated them from her. 'I know it seems odd and slightly morbid, but they were such a close-knit family: entirely insular. Of course their insularity is widely considered to be one of their failings, but compare them to any other European royal family of the age and they were certainly the closest to each other, the most loving and intimate. In her letters to Nicholas, Olga addresses him as "Papa, my priceless jewel!" and "My golden Papa!" Isn't that just wonderful? They were so full of love for each other. Alexandra even breastfed Olga which was scandalous at the time. Queen Victoria was horrified! And Alexandra knew everything about the girls – tiny details which were normally confined to the nursery because an Empress shouldn't have bothered herself with such things.'

'Don't tell me you're hankering after that kind of family life! You hated Mama being so nosy and bossy. She was our own Empress of All the Russias, issuing edicts about what we should eat and wear and study!'

'Ha, I know. She was incredibly bossy, wasn't she? So controlling! No wonder Papa was always in college. He probably didn't want her uninvited input on Fermat's Last Theorem!' They both laughed wholeheartedly, happy to be joking about domestic silliness. The moment fell. Assia asked delicately 'So, how is he?'

'He's fine. Ticking over. College keeps him busy. He's been appointed Wine Steward and so he has all sorts of excuses now for dining in college – "sampling the cellar" and avoiding real life. No girlfriend, of course.'

'Where would you say he is now on the "Anastasia terrifies me with her hysterical female emotions" spectrum? Closer to understanding? Further away?' Assia couldn't quite refrain from sarcasm when she asked about their father.

'I would say…' Tanya paused to consider her line of thought, 'I would say that he's realised that you and I are all he's got, aside from Aunt Belinda, and that he's been thinking about how he treated you when it happened. He's been asking me how you are quite a bit recently and I think – if he felt that you were willing – he would like for us all to get together. Perhaps a lunch in Oxford, or something like that?'

'I'm not against it in principle. But I'd like the invitation to come from him, not you. I don't want to come to some awful lunch at the Old Parsonage where the waiters are the only people talking at our table.' She spread her fingers out on the highly polished artfully distressed metal surface of the bar top. Someone behind the scenes had decided to enhance the atmosphere with some music and a relentless bass beat shook the floor.

'Fair enough. But you have to try and be more understanding, Assenka.' Tanya raised her voice to counter the bass. 'It's been hard for Papa too. And that lunch at the Old Parsonage was probably a mistake. It was all too soon and none of us was ready to address what had happened.'

'Don't tell me to try and be more understanding, Tan'! You make it sound as if I'm the only one who's behaving badly, and Papa hasn't put a foot wrong. He could barely bring himself to look at me at that lunch! How do you think that felt?' Her pulse accelerated; she didn't know if she was imagining it, but it seemed to surge in time with the bass beat rising and falling around them.

'I can't imagine how you felt. I know it must have been awful but my experience is more aligned to Papa's. He lost a wife that day and I lost a mother.' Tanya's lips hardened into a firm pout.

'I lost everything that day, Tanya. Everything. I lost the ability to feel happiness – the kind of happiness you might feel when you see a beautiful sunset or someone makes you laugh. I don't feel I deserve pleasure anymore, or peace from my torment. And the thing which I find most galling is that you and Papa don't think I deserve to be happy either.'

'That's not true, Assenka. It's just not. You're being unfair. Of course Papa and I want you to be happy. And we think Ben is good for you.'

'Oh, I am *so* glad I have your permission to be happy! And what else do "you and Papa" think from on high? Ben is good for me is he? Damn Ben! He drives me mad! He has some kind of fetish for girls with delicate mental conditions and he makes me want to scream.' Assia got off the stool and reached for her bag and coat tucked underneath the bar.

'But really, Tanya,' she continued, 'you needn't stoop to grant me permission for anything, because I am a flint-hearted matricide who really ought to have been cast out long ago, isn't that right? In fact, I should do the decent thing and follow Kostya's example of just making myself disappear altogether.'

Assia wound her way through a maze of city folk who were beginning to cluster in concentric circles around tables crowded with pints and shot glasses. She wore a hassled expression on her face, grimacing as person after person got in her way. Suddenly he loomed in front of her, so close that she could smell his beer-infused sweat and see the weave of his expensive designer shirt. 'Hey, cutie, have you changed your mind?' The grey-suited man laughed and blocked Assia's exit, jumping from side-to-side as she tried to dodge him. 'There's no need to cry, gorgeous, I'll show you a good time! Double fun if you bring your twin!'

XX

Warneford Hospital, Oxford, 2003

'And how did you feel about Kostya – am I saying it correctly? – yes? Right. How did you feel about Kostya loving your mother?'

The psychologist pulled his shoulders back into the spongey chair which was covered in a material which had the colour and texture of oatmeal. He seemed to withdraw into his chair as a way of giving Assia the chance to speak.

'I suppose it always seemed right to me,' said Assia. 'I never really saw it as an affair – more a loving friendship. They were so close to each other – like siblings. They fought like cats and dogs sometimes but they always made up in the end. To me, he seemed to be her connection to Russia. Her relationship with him was her relationship with her native country – it was entirely natural, if you see what I mean.'

The psychologist leant forward purposefully, his hands woven together. 'But it must have bothered you, in some way, because you mentioned it to me when I first saw you. You said that your mother was unfaithful and that it hurt you and your family.'

Assia grimaced as she tried to articulate herself. 'Yes, that's true as well. It's hard to express properly but it wasn't that Mama was cheating really, it was just that she seemed to have passions which weren't myself or my sister – she was ambitious for us, of course, but she loved Kostya and she loved Fabergé more than us.'

'And your father? Where did he come into it?'

'Ooof, well…' Assia sighed heavily. 'Maybe he just chose to ignore how close Mama and Kostya were. This is what I'm trying to say – it was all rather odd, but I never thought it was at the time, when I was younger. I mean, Kostya stayed with us in Oxford – a lot. It was a kind of ménage à trois with the adults, but there didn't seem to be anything wrong with it. Does that make sense?' She looked at the psychologist quizzically.

'Yes. If it makes sense to you.'

'But I think Papa was fine with it. He just wanted Mama to be happy and if that meant having Kostya around then so be it. He was never at home, really – his life was in college and with his research. Having a family was just a box he felt he had to tick – Mama was his trophy, something he could retreat behind.'

'Hmm. I see. So what you're saying is that both your mother *and* your father were self-absorbed and that you and your sister came second to their primary passions in life.' He adjusted his glasses and retreated into the chair and the oatmeal sponge.

The psychologist had placed his watch on the table next to him and Assia realised, in the silence, that it was the first time that she had heard it ticking. She looked at the watch and its tired black leather strap and she looked at the man. A faint smile crossed her face.

'You know, I think you're absolutely spot on. Tanya and I came second in our parents' hearts. Always.'

XXI

Assia picked up a towel which was warming on the radiator beneath the window and wrapped it around herself. She could smell the scent of her shampoo on it and she didn't know why, but she thought of Edward as she pulled the towel tighter around her shoulders. She could imagine him picking up a towel, smelling it and being enveloped in traces of her and somehow that felt like love.

His mouth had turned down at the corners when she had left his hotel room in St Petersburg and her heart lurched to think of it now. His need for her had been cloying, suffocating, and when he held her in bed she had felt so terribly alone that she couldn't hide her isolation and had to get up and leave. He reminded her of her old self, her prelapsarian self, and although she would have given anything to go back to that state, she knew that it was a country barred to her. Her suffering since then had changed her atomic number: chemically, biologically, she was no longer the same person. The girl he had desired back then continued to strut through the quads in her smart little trench coats with a silk scarf and knee-high boots. The Assia he had run to ground in St Petersburg wanted to be outside in the deep chill and fading light of Peter's city – at least she would be together with other lonely people, the ones who lingered on the bridges in a sort of awkward companionship. Strangely, she felt colder now in London than she had in St Petersburg – at least she had been alive when she was there: feeling things, hating things, sensing things. Blood flowed through her in Russia –

it had pace and form – whereas in London it was pooling in stagnant, sticky clots: inconsistent and disturbed.

Edward had tried to call her only once since she had got back. She had been holding her phone when he rang, writing an email, and she dropped it on the table as if it were a hot coal, his name flashing hopefully on the screen, her answerphone briefed to inform him that Miss Assia was indisposed. But she decided now to open an email he had sent which had been sitting in her inbox for a day.

Subject: Re: The Livadia Egg – New development

Dear Assia,

I hope your journey back from Piter was painless. Knowing that there are certain areas of the Livadia Egg about which you would like clarification, I thought that you would be interested to know that the researchers at GARF have found a letter written in 1914 from the Dowager Empress Maria Feodorovna to Carl Fabergé congratulating him on the success of the Livadia Egg which had so thrilled her granddaughter and thanking him for the egg that she herself had received. The document was filed incorrectly at some point in time and has only just now been discovered by an archivist who was looking for papers relating to the Imperial trains.

In the letter, the Dowager Empress describes various parts of the egg which delighted her, in particular the enamel flowers which reminded her so vividly of the wonderful summers she had spent with her family in the Crimea. You would love the letter and if you'll allow me, I'll send you a scan of it.

I wanted to let you know about it before we release the letter to the Press.

With all best wishes,
Edward

P.S. I am sure you know that Madeleine was fascinated by this newly discovered letter and we are thrilled that she will be loaning the Alexander III Medallion Egg to the Moscow exhibition. We were also pleased to secure the loan of the Ferber Foundation eggs and I am awaiting confirmation of the loan of the 1887 Egg.

She re-read the email a few times and then got up to make some coffee. She felt numb, slowed down. It was as though someone had put cotton wool in her ears so that she was insulated from the goings-on in the world. She wondered if she could hear a ringing noise in her head; the noise one expects to hear after the Apocalypse. Events were moving on apace whether she liked it or not – Edward wasn't sitting in his hotel room weeping for her and Madeleine had sought other opinions on the egg, opinions which satisfied her.

In the kitchen she poured the just-boiled water onto the coffee grounds and then leant on the plunger of the cafetière. She pressed harder when it seemed to be resisting pressure and then suddenly it plummeted down to the bottom of the glass coffee pot and burning hot coffee grounds mixed with water exploded onto her and the kitchen floor.

'Ugh, bloody hell!' she yelled and kicked one of the cupboards repeatedly. Plates clattered inside and she kicked harder until she could hear that one of them had slid off the top of the pile.

She wasn't numb any more. She was angry. Furious. Teeth-grindingly enraged at Edward. So, he had been courting her just to get to Madeleine and her egg, had he? And when that hadn't worked, he had just gone straight to Madeleine anyway.

With kitchen roll plastered onto her warm wet clothes, she stalked back to her computer and pressed 'reply' to Edward's email. She just couldn't help herself:

Subject: Re: Re: The Livadia Egg – New development

Dear Edward,
I am so pleased that things have worked out as you wanted and that Madeleine is loaning the egg to the Moscow exhibition.

You know, you needn't have bothered with the tiresome process of wooing and sleeping with me, her consultant. The woman has a mind of her own – but then I don't need to tell you that. You worked it out for yourself anyway.

On another note, I would like to know which expert has confirmed that the letter to Carl Fabergé from the Dowager Empress Maria Feodorovna is authentic? How amazing that such a ringing endorsement of the Livadia Egg happened to pop up just now! I never fail to be stunned by the amazing coincidences that arise in the Fabergé world.

> *Best wishes,*
> *Assia*

The book was slim but of folio size and Assia slid it off the shelf and brought it over to her desk where she blew off the fluff which had settled along the tops of the pages. The disturbed motes of dust seemed to linger gratefully in the strong sunlight which came through the window of her study and Assia watched as they danced, unhurriedly, in some kind of strange suspension. A black and white photograph reproduced on the back of the dust cover of the book caught her eye and she reached over to switch off the radio while she studied the image. Nicholas II was looking out of a window of the Imperial train, his piercing gaze directed at the photographer. The window was a narrow rectangular opening and the Tsar had pulled the top of the sliding window down, the carriage curtains edged in white lace casting a shadow over his face and shoulders. He was always a prisoner, thought Assia. Even before he was taken away by a special train from Petrograd, he felt imprisoned by his duty to his country. His gaze is as knowing and sorrowful as that of Christ in an Icon of the Pantocrator.

Assia flicked through the photographs in the book, pausing on a different page every now and then to look at the snaps of the Grand Duchesses and the Tsarevich. She had picked out *The Private World of the Last Tsar In the Photographs and Notes of General Count Alexander Grabbe* from her library because she knew that Grabbe, as commander of the Cossack unit which guarded the Tsar, had been at the Livadia Palace and she wanted to research something which was gnawing away at her.

She flicked through the cream pages that smelled of age and memories for a few minutes before landing on something which leaped out at her. 'Bullseye! Livadia!' she said, jabbing her index finger at a photograph and catching the splaying pages to hold her place. She balanced her phone on one side of the book so that it was weighted and fell open at the spine. Displayed was a photograph of a white stone church with long arched windows and little graduated tiled rooves which rose up towards a rounded dome and then a larger domed tower with a crucifix. The building was neo-Byzantine and its curves and points contrasted with the straighter lines of the Livadia Palace which loomed alongside it in the photograph.

'Hang on a second,' Assia muttered as she scrabbled through the pages of the hardback catalogue for the Livadia Egg. 'Yep, here we are.' She held the page from the egg catalogue next to the photograph taken by Grabbe of the Livadia Palace chapel and looked and one and then at the other. She lodged her tongue between her teeth as she scrutinised the miniature on the egg and the photograph in the book. She could feel her heart racing and her skin prickling. *Be careful what you wish for*, she thought.

'Madeleine Roseman...' The voice spoke quickly with a hint of impatience, her statement designed to be followed by a hurried explanation.

'Madeleine? It's Anastasia.'

'I didn't recognise your number.' Her voice softened. 'How are you, my dear? I have been meaning to call you and check that you're not still grieving for your friend.'

'I'm OK, thank you for asking. Um, I wanted to speak to you about the Moscow exhibition. I've learned that you're sending the Medallion Egg?'

Assia could hear Madeleine's intake of breath. The woman wasn't shocked. She was girding herself to make an explanation.

'Yes. That's right. I am sending the egg to Moscow, Anastasia.' She said it slowly, slowly enough for a child to understand.

'It's wrong, Madeleine. The Livadia Egg is wrong.' Assia felt acid churn in her stomach as she said the words aloud. She continued. 'I've been poring over books, trying to draw out the splinter which has been bothering me so much.'

'Uh huh. And did you find anything?' Madeleine was a beat too slow. She sounded distracted. Assia heard a mouse clicking.

'Yes. I did.'

'Tell me.' She was listening now.

Assia spoke quickly: this was her one chance to be heard. 'You know that I told you that I didn't like the miniatures of the Livadia Palace on the egg? They're painted in a style which struck me as a little too stiff. It was only when I was looking at photographs of Livadia taken by Alexander Grabbe – commander of the Cossacks who guarded Nicholas – that I noticed that the church which adjoins the Livadia Palace has white-painted roof tiles in Grabbe's photo but dark roof tiles in the miniature painting on the egg. Grabbe's photo was taken in 1912 and I've found a watercolour of the church from 1913, when the egg would have been commissioned and the miniatures would have been painted– the roof tiles are white in the watercolour as well, so why would they be black in the miniature on the egg?'

Madeleine didn't reply immediately. Assia knew that she was thinking very carefully. She always had done: she was nobody's fool and always impressively well-informed. It was one of the reasons Madeleine had a consultant: the fools were the ones who didn't take advice when it came to Fabergé.

Finally, she spoke. 'It could just be artistic licence, couldn't it? In a small-scale painting I would imagine that contrasts work better, otherwise it might have appeared too blindingly white. Wouldn't you say?'

'I can't rule that out, of course. But what I think is more pertinent is the fact that the roof tiles today – in present day Livadia – are black.'

'I'm not following.'

'I think that the miniatures on the Livadia Egg are modern and that they were painted from recent photographs which would show the roof tiles as being black.'

'OK, Anastasia.' She pronounced the name in the American way: Anna-staish-a. 'What about this: what if Grabbe's photo was just poorly exposed or developed. I don't know enough about photography back then, but isn't there a chance that the plate – or whatever they used – was overexposed and shows a blinding white where there would have been a darker colour?'

'I know – that's what I thought might explain it at first. But I'll send you an image of the photograph. You can see that all the different tones of black and white are there. It doesn't look damaged or overexposed to me. Anyway, even if there is something wrong with the photo, why would this watercolour of the church by Captain Westerholz, which I found, also show it with a white roof?'

'Well, maybe the miniature was recently restored and the restorer ill-advisedly changed the colour of the roof tiles? But also, haven't the miniatures been authenticated by Gladorova?'

'Gladkova.' Assia corrected her.

'Gladkova. You should bring this up with her, of course, but I just can't see this being enough to say that the egg is wrong, I'm sorry.'

Assia thought Madeleine sounded patronising, as though she were a petulant little girl who needed to be appeased.

'But that's not what I'm saying.' Assia sighed down the phone. 'I'm saying that this is just the tip of the iceberg. I know more things will come up which will prove it's wrong. I just have a feeling about it – call it instinct, or whatever. I don't *want* the egg to be wrong, Madeleine, but I'm afraid I think it is.'

'That's not good enough for me, Anastasia. You are telling me that I should not take part in the most high-profile exhibition of Fabergé ever held because you *think* the Livadia Egg is wrong. Unless you have cast-iron, knock-me-over-the-head proof, then I can't miss out on this. It's good for my museum and it's good for me.' She sighed heavily. 'Anyway, dear, I'm worried about you. Are you *sure* you don't want the egg to be wrong? Because of your mother? It would be perfectly understandable to feel that way, Anastasia. Grief affects us all.'

'No, no, it's nothing to do with that!' Assia was exasperated. She had lost all sway over Madeleine. The woman used to listen to her. What had happened? Edward had poisoned Madeleine against her.

'Look, Madeleine. If you send your egg, there's every chance you might not get it back. The Russians could change the law any time to suit themselves. They could say that the egg was stolen from the Imperial Family and that it should remain in Russia. They could seize it from you!' Assia was desperate.

'Edward has assured me that won't happen. It's all academic now anyway, Anastasia. The egg was collected by my shippers yesterday.' A pause: an admission of guilt, perhaps. 'I hope you'll come and see it again in Moscow. Edward and I would love for you to be there.'

XXII

An Englishman in Russia is never going to want for female attention. Somehow, the girls can sense there is an *Anglichanin* around. Word spreads – perhaps the *babushki* hear it on the grapevine ('Galya's sister-in-law has got a new job cleaning for an *Anglichanin* on Pavletskaya) and tell their granddaughters, hoping the tip is enough to get pretty Zhenia married off to a good English boy, or maybe the girls are just good at scanning the crowd for a Brit. Either way, Edward found that whether he was sitting in a café or standing on the trolleybus, Russian girls would always arrange themselves in the immediate vicinity. He smiled as he recalled the time a beautiful girl with cheekbones as round and rosy as apples asked if she could borrow his copy of *The Telegraph*. She almost jumped when he replied in perfect Russian that there was a very interesting article on Kate Middleton's favourite dressmaker on page ten.

This morning, sitting in the room outside Ivan Denisov's office in the Mariinskiy Palace, Edward couldn't help but notice the effect his presence had on the team of secretaries and assistants at the bank of desks in the room. A brunette tapping away at a keyboard corrected her posture as he passed a cluster of desks arranged in front of one of the large neoclassical windows, while a pale-faced girl with cropped blonde hair who was riffling through a tall filing cabinet stopped what she was doing and stared at him curiously.

The girl sitting closest to the door of Ivan's office span around in her office chair to face Edward.

'Can I fetch you anything to drink, Mr Baillie Aston?'

She brushed her brown fringe out of her eyes with a red-painted finger nail and uncrossed her tanned legs, ready to retrieve whatever he wanted. The navy linen shirt dress she wore was unbuttoned so that just the edge of a lacy bra showed.

'Oh, no. Thank you very much, I'm quite alright.'

With her foot on the floor, she spun the chair slightly but didn't turn back to her desk.

'What about some chocolate-coated coffee beans? I keep them on hand for when I need a bit of a pick-me-up.' She opened the bottom drawer of her desk, necessitating the squeezing together of her chest. 'I am Marina Surikova, by the way.'

'Hello, Marina. Not for me, thanks so much.' He smiled politely and lifted his hand to decline a chocolate coffee bean when she got up to offer him one. He was amused by her open and informal air; plenty of the Russian young were more laidback in social settings nowadays, but so often the first exchange with a Russian was brusque and business-like. The apparent rudeness was a kind of social vacuum, a way of not being present until it was safe to come out.

'Your job sounds fascinating.' She had tilted her head ever so slightly to one side and her eyes shone with amusement.

Edward noticed one of the other girls in the office rolling her eyes as Marina continued to chat to him. Another was staring at them, listening.

'It is. Truly fascinating. It's an honour for me to be able to promote Fabergé and to garner as much attention as possible for the tour of the Livadia Egg. So much of it is about making the world sit up and acknowledge Russia's skill and glittering heritage.' If this was getting back to Ivan, then Edward wanted to tick all the boxes.

'And what do you think of Russia?' She raised her fine dark eyebrows and crossed her legs.

Edward thought how beautiful she was. Her high and rounded cheekbones seemed to sweep her eyes up at the edges so that they slanted slightly in the Tatar way. He wondered if Ivan was sleeping with her. It was rumoured that he had a thing for his secretaries and that the girls who worked for him had to meet very high aesthetic as well as academic criteria. Edward had heard that one of this secretarial harem had borne him a child and then been killed in the terrorist bombing by Chechen separatists at Domodedovo a few years ago. Ivan had, apparently, been unable to hide his grief at her funeral.

'Russia is magnificent. The language, the history, the art. I've lived here for ten years but there is always a new part of the city to discover, a new tradition to observe, a new phrase to learn. I am never complacent.'

'So Mother Russia has enchanted you?'

Edward saw Marina narrowing her eyes, scrutinising him playfully.

'Of course! But not everything about Russia is romantic. I've lived here long enough to know that.' Edward laughed softly. 'No one told me about the real cold of a Russian winter, even my Russian friends. I had to find out the hard way.'

'That's because we're not interested in the truth.' She swept her fringe to the side of her face. 'The truth is only part of the whole for us.' The phone on her desk rang. 'Oh, excuse me a second.'

Marina span around quickly and was facing her desk, clicking her computer mouse while talking on the phone. Edward was a little taken aback by the strange aphorism she had uttered so matter-of-factly. He tried to recall exactly what she had said and found that he couldn't.

Getting up from his chair, he walked to the window which was furthest away from the desks. Beyond the snow-covered rooves of the city, the polychrome ice cream scoop domes of the Church of the Saviour of the Spilt Blood floated on the horizon, as strange and surreal as a shiny Jeff Koons installation in the middle of a museum full of 19th century paintings. His blood throbbed in the vein beneath his ear and he felt unexpectedly and bizarrely serene as he contemplated this fairground view. When you come to know Russia as I have, he thought, the contrasts and contradictions lose their shock value. You balk at first, when you arrive here: you can't ignore the old women who beg, prostrate on the snow in thin coats; you catch the eyes of people staring from the steamed-up tram into your smart car and your skin stings with a rash from the birch leaves in the *banya*. Everything is as vivid and tart as bright red blood on snow. But then, you grow to need these juxtapositions, your palate alters imperceptibly like a camera lens adjusting itself to focus. This country has altered me, thought Edward, and I couldn't give a damn.

One of the girls had sprung up from her chair and Edward turned to see that Ivan had come into the office carrying a black briefcase, a long beige Burberry coat with tartan lining draped over his arm. Marina took his coat and went over to Edward to tell him that Ivan Borisovich was ready to see him.

'Apologies for my tardiness.' Ivan was sitting at his desk and spoke while looking at his phone. 'I have been in a long meeting.' His voice trailed off as he continued to look at his phone. 'Right, there we are, enough of emails.' He put the phone down.

'So, Eduard,' Ivan pronounced his name in the Russian way, stressing the 'a' in his name so that it was the dominant sound. 'Update me. How many eggs have we got coming back to their rightful home for the Moscow exhibition?'

Edward was sitting in the chair opposite Ivan's desk, his back as straight as a rod.

'I have to confess that it has been a difficult task, Ivan Borisovich. Some eggs have been booked out on other tours – I am waiting to hear back if the schedules of some can be altered and, regrettably, many of the major institutions with eggs are reluctant to send them because of Russia's position geopolitically. But…' Edward tried to stifle any response his boss might have by placing emphasis on the 'but'. '*But*, we've got the Ferber Foundation eggs – they're sending the Mauve Egg and the Royal Danish Egg, and Madeleine Roseman, the owner of the John D. O'Connor Fabergé Museum in Washington DC, is sending the Alexander III Medallion Egg.'

Ivan leaned back in his chair and folded his arms. 'Tell me more about this Madeleine Roseman. I did my best to charm her at the unveiling.'

Edward obliged. 'I know she enjoyed meeting you. She's very high-profile in the States. Her father made a not-so-small fortune and was a Republican senator for thirty years. Her Fabergé Museum is considered to be one of the best in the States and her consultant, Anastasia Wynfield, advises her on how to expand the collection. Anastasia is the daughter of Olga Morozova Wynfield.' He longed to talk about Assia. Just saying her name made his mercury soar.

'Yes, I know. I knew Olga – we were at school together.'

'Oh, really?'

'She was talented but wanted a lot for herself – too much. She left Russia at the first opportunity. Her death all those years later was not an accident.'

'It wasn't?' Edward looked troubled and scratched the back of his neck. He was suddenly conscious of his heart beating, clenching and releasing.

'You can't leave the motherland and get away with it. It was divine retribution.' Ivan crossed his arms and looked at Edward. The right side of his mouth lifted slightly. A faint smile.

'I see.' Edward returned Ivan's gaze. He understood. He was being tried, provoked. Ivan was prodding him to see if he was outraged. But at the same time, a line was being drawn in the sand. Edward was in no doubt that if he crossed Ivan Denisov, he would pay for it.

XXIII

On the other side of the road an old woman shuffles along the pavement pushing a shopping basket on wheels. She stops and smiles benignly as a blonde child on a scooter whizzes past her, its mother three or four paces behind with a mobile glued to her ear. The old woman looks back at the mother and speeding child and then continues to push her tartan trolley, disappearing into the Battenburg cake of the Grosvenor Estate. Assia never tired of looking at Lutyens's wonderful modernist buildings, the vertical white and brick checkerboards built at the end of the 1920s to house workers in Westminster. They should have been ugly, these great *zeilenbau* blocks, nods to the New Objectivity which was emerging in Germany at the time they were built, but Assia thought they were majestic. She liked their boldness, the way the design almost overcame beauty but failed in spite of itself.

Her heart stopped. *Was it him again?* The shaven-headed man was walking quickly towards her on the street as she was climbing the steps to her front door. She rushed up the last steps and fumbled with her keys, putting the wrong one into the door and cursing as it jammed in the lock. She tried another key and whimpered as she struggled to put it in the lock. She opened the door and hurried into the hallway, slamming the door behind her. Her hands were shaking and her breathing was jagged. She leant back against the door and wondered if he was outside, leaning against the door, his body mirroring hers.

Upstairs in her flat, Assia grabbed a cushion from the sofa and held it over her face, screaming into the goose feathers and wondering what it would feel like if someone was actually pressing down on her, smearing her nostrils closed and filling her mouth with material. She tried pressing harder, flirting with the idea until she was distracted by her phone ringing. The screen flashed with a St Petersburg number.

'*Allyo?*' answered Assia.

'*Assia, eto Yelena.* I'm not disturbing you, am I?' The voice at the end of the phone whispered anxiously.

'No, of course not.' Assia sat up quickly and frowned as she strained to hear what was being said.

'Assia, listen, you are coming to Piter for Kostya's funeral aren't you?' Yelena continued to speak in hushed tones. 'Assia, please come. No one wants to come because… because he was a suicide.' She paused and breathed heavily down the phone as though she were out of breath. Assia could picture her thin wet lips pressed against the phone receiver.

'Yes, of course, Yelena. I am definitely coming. Are you bearing up OK?' Assia could feel her heart tighten as she thought of Kostya's lonely, mournful sister.

'I'll tell you when you come. *Vsyo, poka.*' Yelena's husky, quieted voice faded away amid rustling and scratching on the line.

Assia had tried not to think about Kostya and his sad demise. She kept seeing him alone and desperate, snow settling on his shoulders as he held the gun to his head, willing himself to pull the trigger. She wondered if he was thinking of her mother as he closed his eyes and ended his days.

Yelena's call had brought the chill of grief into her sitting room in Pimlico. She supposed that Yelena was unable to cope with the loss of her brother and that was why she had sounded almost scared. Fear of grief was, in many ways, worse than grief itself; trying to step around the yawning, gaping hole of bereavement was far more exhausting and perilous than steeling oneself to look into the dark pit. Really one ought to be like Queen Victoria, thought Assia: wreathe yourself in black, decree that everyone else should do the same, and wallow, wallow, wallow while hymning the incomparable qualities of the recently departed to a world which has moved on. *Easier said than done, of course. If you've killed someone, as I have, your grief can't be something that the world has done to you. Victoria blamed her son Bertie for Albert's death and punished everyone for it, but I didn't have that luxury when my mother was killed – I was the active party, the reaper's agent, so how could I grieve in a normal way? Even when the driver who crashed into us was prosecuted for causing death by careless driving, I still couldn't stop casting back to that moment when I accelerated. I have never stopped wanting to yell at the person that I was then, the Assia who was driving, and tell her to slow down.*

Slow down, Assia! It's OK to reduce your speed. You don't have to keep building speed on a fast road. Slow to a halt if you need to. Let the van go ahead of you!

And just like that, in my mind, the white van pulls out onto the road, ahead of us. I put my foot on the brake and feel the force pushing me into the steering wheel and Mama onto the glove box. I can see Mama is a little alarmed and she comments on the bad driving and dangerous impatience of the 'English white van man.' She lives and I live and fourteen years later Kostya doesn't kill himself.

XXIV

Fat snowflakes spiralled from the sky and settled gently on Kostya's coffin. Assia lifted her face and felt the delicious coldness of the snow on her cheeks. She held a gloved finger out to catch a flake and marvelled at the frozen geometry on her fingertip, staring at the intricate pattern in a bid to hold back the tears in her eyes. It was little wonder that Alma Pihl had used snowflakes in her designs for Fabergé pieces – they were tiny little reminders of nature's genius, the everyday beauty that we miss if we don't look closely enough. The snowflake quickly turned into a quivering drop on the black grain of Assia's leather glove.

The priest looked down at the coffin in its earthy pit and dangled the golden thurible over it while chanting some prayers. The phelonion he wore over his black robes looked synthetic and the golden crosses on his epitrahilion were patches of garish gold-coloured material rather than embroidered gold thread. Yelena had told Assia that she had struggled to find a priest who would bury a suicide. Since the collapse of the Soviet Union and the cementing of the President's rule, the Orthodox Church had formed a natural alliance with the ultra-conservative policies of the state, and a 'selfish' and 'individualistic' act such as suicide was heavily frowned upon. Only a few people had come to the burial at the Yuzhnoye Cemetery all the way out here on Volkhonskoye Shosse and the paltry gathering made the occasion all the more pitiful.

There are only six people here: this is the painful reality of a small life. You mess up your marriage, have a small family, a few relations and friends and you never make a lot of money. People shed a few tears, down a vodka, and that's it.

Assia sniffed and Yelena looked up at her abruptly. She looked offended, Assia thought, reproachful: as though she were taking umbrage at the shabbiness and smallness of this funeral.

Holy God,
Holy and Mighty,
Holy and Immortal,
have mercy on us.

The priest's deep and resonant voice spread beyond the small plot over which he was intoning. Sky and earth merged into one as the snow settled; only the tall trees beyond the clearing fought against this unity of elements, marking the horizon and massing behind into a forest that lined the road for miles and miles.

Yelena and Vika each threw a handful of dirt onto the coffin which was already covered in a light dusting of snow. Yelena, her head veiled in a black chiffon scarf, put an arm on Vika's shoulder as the younger woman began to keen. Her moan rose in tone and turned into a shaky cry of 'Papa, Papa!' Assia lowered her head. She shouldn't really bear witness to this half of Kostya's life – she knew Vika didn't want her there and she understood why. Olga was a dirty word to Kostya's daughter. She was the woman who caused the collapse of her father's marriage and even after her death, she had still continued to influence her father. Vika tossed a photo onto the coffin and Yelena comforted her as they turned and began their walk back to the car park. Assia looked at them as they tottered away and then peered down at the photo which had landed on a corner of the varnished pine coffin. Snow was about to obscure the image but she could just make out a little boy with pale hair sitting on a hospital bed surrounded by teddy bears. He was hugging a bear tightly, a full round cheek pressed into its ear, that look of teeth-gritting possessiveness in which toddlers specialise. His lower legs were encased in plaster up to his plump little knees which bulged over the top of the casts. Assia put her hand over her mouth to stifle a sob which swelled up involuntarily. She turned away from the grave and walked back towards the cars behind the priest who was looking at his mobile phone.

The landscape began to harden and urbanise as they sped back along the Volkhonskoye Shosse. The road widened and the forest fell away without warning so that suddenly Assia was looking out at vast corrugated iron hangars and large hoardings advertising supermarkets and swollen SUVs. The light of the day had faded as quickly as the city had appeared and the little squares of orange lamplight in the apartment blocks on the outskirts of the city looked almost appealing through the snow drizzle. Assia thought of the families squashed into them, living their close and colourful lives in such bland and charmless containers. She pictured herself wearing an apron, her sleeves rolled up, placing a plate of steaming *pelmeni* on the kitchen table in front of a toddler with a pudding-bowl haircut and Edward in a smart shirt. They dig their spoons greedily into the sour cream and she sits down at the table, elbows on the oilcloth, smiling at her feasting boys. Could she smile like that? It was a Madonna-like smile of selflessness and sacrifice. I am trying, she thought. *Just envisioning this scene is a good thing; it might make me want it for myself, I might even come to believe that I could be that woman – that domestic goddess who makes the best of what she has and does everything for her family. I am trying. Reason and good sense will rule my life from now on. I'm going to include the Livadia Egg into the updated version of Mama's Encyclopaedia. I realise that I was trying to find fault with it in the same way that I was trying to find fault with Edward. I want to embrace them both. This is the way I am going to live now.*

'You will come to my apartment and raise a glass to Kostya, won't you?' said Yelena. 'I want to have a little *pominki* and there aren't many of us.'

The car was idling at some lights and the driver was beating some unknown rhythm on the steering wheel. The heating was on and Assia unwound her scarf from her neck. She looked up into the rear-view mirror and saw the driver's dark eyes trained on her.

'I'd love to come, Yelena. Thank you. Are you sure?'

Yelena turned back in her seat at the front of the car to look directly at Assia. 'Of course I'm sure.' She reached round to fix her gaze on Vika who was sitting in the back behind her chair.

'Stop it, Auntie.' Vika glared mutinously. 'I don't despise her, you know. I want her to come. She loved my father too and it's the right thing to do.' Still frowning, she turned to Assia. 'Thank you for coming. You didn't have to and it matters a lot to me and Auntie that you're here.'

'Thank you, Vika.' Assia put her hand on top of Vika's and squeezed it.

There was so much food on the table that Assia wondered if Yelena wasn't really expecting an army of hungry young men to turn up. Bowls of *salat Olivier* and red caviar, piles of *blinchiki* and mounds of pickled herring and dill crowded the surface of the table which Yelena had set up in her sitting room. There was a photo of Kostya in a black frame on the table next to a vodka glass with a slice of black bread on it. Tradition dies hard in Russia, thought Assia. There was no way Kostya was being sent off without Yelena arming him with vodka and bread for the road.

Assia filled a plate and sat down on the sofa. A forkful of *salat Olivier* reminded her so strongly of her mother that for a second she felt quite overwhelmed.

'This is the most comforting nursery food,' she said to Vika with her mouth full. She covered her mouth with her napkin. 'I'm sorry, forgive my greed. I'm just being transported back to my childhood.' She swallowed. 'How is your little boy?'

'He's well,' said Vika. Her countenance softened as she started to speak about him. 'Thank you for asking. He's with my husband in Boston. He's having treatment there which is easing the symptoms of his cerebral palsy. He's going to be able to walk for the first time in his life soon, thanks to Papa.'

'Thanks to your father?'

'Papa paid for Misha to have this treatment. It's very expensive because it's the only place in the world that specialises in rehabilitation for children with the condition. They are taking such good care of us there and Misha is so happy.' She smiled. 'He's not in pain anymore.'

'But… that's wonderful, you must be so relieved. I didn't realise Kostya had done so well. Your aunt had told me it was just a loan. He must have done a fantastic deal to have come into real money.' Assia put her fork down and looked at Vika quizzically.

'I know – it's amazing. He had asked me a while ago how much treatment for Misha would cost and I told him. I never even thought for a second that *he* might have the money. But a few months ago he rang me and told me that the funds for Misha's treatment were in my account.' She shook her head. 'I didn't even want to breathe until I had checked, but it was true. I booked the operation as soon as I could – I was so scared that they might put the price up!' She laughed exaggeratedly.

'And he never told you how he managed to pay for it?'

What seemed like a prolonged silence checked Assia and she added hurriedly 'Sorry, ignore me. I'm being far too nosy.'

'No, really, it's OK. I wondered too.' Vika looked almost apologetic. 'I really did try to find out, but he wouldn't tell me. And I'm afraid I didn't want to press too much – I thought it might make the money disappear if I did. I just told myself that wherever he got it from, at least I was using the money for good.'

'I completely understand – when something like that happens you don't want to scare it away. It must have made him very happy to be able to help you and Misha.'

'I hope so. I did thank him over and over again, but he seemed perturbed by something. That's what made me think that the money might not have been from a legitimate source. And I…' She was whispering now. 'I haven't wanted to consider it, but it bothers me… I am worried that he might have killed himself because of the money, because of what he did for me and Misha.'

Yelena walked in carrying another plate of food which she put on the low coffee table in front of them.

'No, he would not have wanted you to blame yourself, Vikusha,' said Yelena forcefully, 'and I'll tell you why: your father did not kill himself.'

'No? What do you mean?' Vika looked up at her aunt and frowned. Yelena towered above Vika who was sitting on the low sofa.

'Do you honestly think that your father wouldn't have wanted to see the results of Misha's surgery? He was devoted to your little boy and I don't believe for a second that he didn't want to be around to watch him grow up.' Yelena sounded angry. Vika sat lumpenly, chastened by what her aunt was saying.

'So what do you think happened?' asked Assia. 'Could it have been an accident?' She felt suddenly as though she had been awoken from a stupor. She flexed her wrists and sat up on the sofa, her back as straight as a rod.

'Absolutely not!' Yelena said this defiantly. 'He was shot, I am certain of it. Kostya was an aesthete, for heaven's sake. He didn't have a clue about guns, let alone how to load one and shoot himself with it.'

'But why would the police classify the case as a suicide then?'

'Assia' said Yelena looking down at her, hands on her hips, glasses on the end of her nose, 'you were lucky enough to grow up in a country where an expectation of justice is as integral to your sense of self as your consciousness. You feel outraged when you encounter miscarriages of justice and more often than not, you can do something about it. If you saw people clearing out an old woman's flat and taking the keys from her, you'd make some enquiries, wouldn't you? You'd sound furious on behalf of the old dear, wouldn't you? For those of us who live here, curiosity and outrage are luxuries we can't afford – even today, post-Communism. Outrage draws attention to you – it gets you onto people's radars and you don't want that. Here, it's a case of *tak nado*. That's the way it has to be.' She pulled up a chair and sat down opposite the young women on the sofa. 'I did think about trying to contact Ivan Denisov – the one who is close friends with the President. Kostya knew him from school and I thought perhaps he could start a proper murder investigation. The issue is this: I knew Kostya better than anyone – better even than your mother did.' She nodded reproachfully at Assia. 'Yes, he was depressed a lot of the time, but he wasn't decisive enough to take his own life. And he would never have done it by shooting himself – it was far too ugly a way to dispose of oneself, in his book.'

Assia was still frowning. 'I didn't realise he knew Ivan Denisov. So my mother must have known him too, if they were all at school together – and the President. She told me once that she had known the Mayor of St Petersburg from her childhood days – she never lived to see him become President.' Yelena didn't say anything and Assia quickly realised that she should move away from the topic of her mother. 'So, did the police know about the money he used to pay for Misha's operation? Did you tell them it could have been a reason for his death?'

'No!' said Yelena sharply. 'I told Vika not to mention it, and you mustn't tell anyone either. Misha needed that money and it's gone now. We don't want the police sniffing around it. They were happy to choose the way of least resistance and make Kostya the culprit in his own death. Job done, case closed. It's not correct, of course, but I want to keep little Misha out of it, and Kostya would have agreed. I stopped trusting the authorities to help us after they took our father away all those years ago.'

Assia shook her head. 'I was absolutely convinced that he killed himself because he decided that this life was too much and he wanted to join my mother in heaven. And I blamed myself, of course, because of the accident and Mama's death. We're all busy blaming ourselves.' She reached for the little glass of vodka on the coffee table and picked it up, watching the tide of chilled viscous liquid move slowly up and down inside it as she turned her wrist. She tipped her head back and swallowed the cold shot.

Vika was still silent. A lone tear rolled down her nose and settled in the little groove above her lip. She made an utterly affecting vision of despair, her gaze fixed on the photograph of

Kostya on the table in the corner of the room and her mouth open slightly as though she were about to say something. Between her thumb and forefinger she rubbed the pendant of her necklace as though it were a rosary bead.

Assia leaned back a little and pulled her necklace out from under her pale pink silk shirt.

'I didn't realise, Vika,' she said gently, 'that you had one of these too. It's my favourite piece of jewellery. Your father gave it to me when I was sixteen.' She held the little white egg up to the light and spun it on its suspension loop so that the tiny gold notes flashed as they whirled round. 'Does yours have a line from Dubuque too?'

'No,' Vika said so quietly it was barely audible. 'Mine says "The gentle stars shone for us". It's a Tchaikovsky song. Papa loved it.'

'I wonder where he got them from – it was such a generous present. He must have bankrupted himself to buy them. Even back when I was a teenager, Fabergé pendant eggs were still pretty pricey. I don't know how he was able to afford them.'

'He couldn't,' said Vika still staring vacantly ahead. She sighed heavily and manoeuvred herself onto her side, leaning on her elbow to face Assia. 'Papa made them himself.'

'Himself?' Assia froze.

'Yes. I would have thought you knew? Papa made lots of pieces. He was so good at enamelling.' Vika took off her necklace so that she could admire the pendant.

Assia shook her head. She was dumbfounded. 'No, I had no idea at all.'

'It's true' said Yelena as she came back into the room with a plate filled with slices of *cherny khleb*. 'He didn't like people to know – he was worried they would think he was a forger. But it was just his private passion, really.' She put the plate on the already crammed table. 'Look, let me show you how talented he was.' She knelt down, groaning slightly, in front of the huge shelving unit which spread over one of the walls of the room. It was veneered with a pale linoleum with faux wooden grain on it which was beginning to lift and peel off at the corners. She struggled to slide the cupboard door back but with a bit of effort eventually prised it open to reveal piles of boxes and folders overflowing with bits of paper. After a bit of rummaging, she pulled out a small turquoise cardboard box and pulled the lid off gently. Inside, underneath a few layers of crispy tissue paper which had a brownish tinge was a small cigarette case. Yelena cradled it in her hand, out of Assia's line of sight before thrusting it forward on her outstretched palm. 'There!' she said, triumphantly.

Vision slipped away for a second to be replaced by a black pain behind her eyes. Assia blinked repeatedly to steady herself and swayed slightly before Yelena reached grabbed her shoulder.

'Are you all right, my dear?'

The pain drained away through her sinus, taking the grainy blackness with it. As her vision swam back again Assia picked up the case from Yelena's hand and held it up to her eyes.

'I'm fine, thank you. I'm just stunned – I think a fuse blew in my brain.' Her breathing was shallow and she put a hand up to the back of her neck and pressed down on her spine, feeling the outline of her upper vertebrae. 'The colours of the enamel are just like those of Perkhin, one of Fabergé's workmasters. The translucency and its rendering are unmistakable.' Assia didn't know if Yelena was listening to her; she was speaking aloud more for her own purposes than anything else.

'Yelena, are you sure Kostya made this? It's exquisite. The quality of the enamel is quite extraordinary. And it's got marks for Fabergé.' Assia stood up, still holding the case, and looked around her distractedly. 'I need to get my loupe.'

'Yes, I'm absolutely sure Kostya made it. There's a little inscription inside. Take a look.'

Assia pressed the smooth cabochon sapphire thumb piece on the side of the case and it clicked open crisply and keenly, as though it had been waiting to be opened. The interior surface was matt gold with a granulated texture that made you want to run your finger over it. Assia opened and closed the case, weighed it in her hand and pressed it against her cheek – all elements of her tradecraft, the means by which she communed with a piece of Fabergé. With her loupe up to her eye, she inspected the marks on the inside rim of the case: the pleasing little circular lozenge inside which was the profile of a woman's head facing left. Known as the *kokoshnik*, this was a mark which indicated the metal standard, the period during which the item had been assayed and the identity of the assay master. Next to the *kokoshnik* was the small cartouche which held the Cyrillic initials 'MP' for Mikhail Perkhin and then a larger lozenge which was struck with Cyrillic letters which read 'FABERGE'. Mikhail Perkhin was one of Fabergé's workmasters and was renowned for his great skill and flair with gold and enamel. Assia looked for the inscription which Yelena had mentioned and found it inside the rim, just beneath the hinges.

For Yelena Alexandrovna, my 'Lenochka', in memory of our childhood, with love from your baby Kostik, 1987

Assia smiled as she read the text. It was delicately engraved in a beautiful scrolling Cyrillic hand and would be missed by anyone who just opened and closed the case to get a cigarette. Not that anyone used these cases for cigarettes any longer; modern cigarettes were too long to fit. The message was meant to be a secret exchange between Yelena and her little brother.

'You know the inscription could have been added by Kostya to a completely authentic Fabergé case. It doesn't mean he made it – plenty of people added later inscriptions to pieces to personalise them.'

'But he told me he made it and I never thought to doubt him. Why would he say that if he didn't make it?' Assia could hear the rising concern in Yelena's voice. She knew that Yelena was girding herself for an unpleasant revelation of which she would be the bearer.

'It's not a bad thing, Yelena. Don't worry. In fact, it's a bonus – if Kostya didn't make the case, and I don't think he did – then you have a beautiful Fabergé cigarette case, which could be worth several thousand dollars. May I take it away and check it for you? I will take great care of it, I promise you.'

'Yes, of course,' said Yelena, shrugging and waving her hand in a dismissive way. 'Do what you need to do. I'm curious, but I don't want any problems, OK? Don't go digging up things that would best be left alone.'

Putting the case in the turquoise box, Assia pressed the tissue paper on top of it and made sure that it was cushioned and secured before she put the lid back on. She slipped the box into her bag and stood up quickly. She was excited: nestled in her bag she had a thrillingly beautiful cigarette case which was most likely one of Perkhin's finest examples. It would be a pleasure to research it. As she was looking for her mobile in her bag, she heard a sob and turned around quickly.

'Vika, what's the matter?' Assia rushed to the sofa and sat down next to Vika who was wiping her eyes on the cuff of her shirt.

'I'm just so confused. Nothing I thought I knew about Papa was true. Clearly I didn't know him at all.' She sniffed noisily and shot Assia a wounded look. 'He lied to me about his affair with your mother, he wouldn't tell me where he got the money for Misha's operation and then suddenly he didn't kill himself and he didn't make the pieces he gave me and Misha.'

'What did he give Misha?'

'Oh, dear sorry, I'm a mess.' She blew her nose loudly on a grubby white handkerchief. 'Um, he gave him a little golden egg with a gold hen in it. It's really beautiful – tiny little rubies for eyes and it's holding a little sapphire egg in its beak. He told me that he wanted Misha to appreciate beautiful things and that the hen would be an example to treasure. He visited us and gave it to Misha just before he shot himself – or was shot. I don't know! What am I meant to think happened to him? He seemed troubled that day and so I wasn't surprised by it all. I was shocked – horribly, horribly shocked, but not surprised.'

'You've had so much on your plate, I know. This must all just seem like a horrible dream but listen, if your father gave you some pieces which are actually by Fabergé and not made by him, then they'll be worth something, maybe even a lot.' Assia put her hand on Vika's softly rounded knee. 'Let me look into Yelena's cigarette case and then I can investigate Misha's hen, all right? Go back to America and be with your son. Your father is at peace now and has escaped this strange, unhappy world we live in.'

XXV

Assia didn't know why she had been surprised that the coach had arrived so quickly. It was the middle of the day in the middle of a surprisingly hot week in April and there hadn't been any traffic on the roads. There weren't many people on the coach either – it was just herself and a few tourists freezing under the blast of icy cold air conditioning. She didn't normally take the coach to Oxford as it could be so slow but today she took comfort in the presence of the driver and being able to see who got onto the coach at each stop.

Someone had been in her flat.

At first, she hadn't noticed. Arriving back home in London, weary after a much-delayed flight back from St Petersburg, she had parked her wheelie bag by the door and it had immediately fallen over on its front. She had turned all the lamps on and made herself a cup of tea. Flicking through her post which was in a small pile on the kitchen table, it was only on opening an official-looking letter that Assia had stopped suddenly and put the letter down. Her blood drained to her feet. *Who had put her post on the table?*

She looked around the sitting room and open-plan kitchen with a forensic sweep. Nothing looked different. Did it? Her skin crawling, she walked into the bedroom and bathroom and took a look around. Everything looked the same. The dry-cleaning was still hanging on the wardrobe door and the stack of folders on her desk was undisturbed. Perhaps there had been a problem with her flat while she had been away and the caretaker had tried to reach her and when he couldn't, went into her flat and picked up her post as he did so.

Assia grabbed the pile of letters from the kitchen table and balanced them in one hand, weighing them, as though that gentle motion might elicit the truth. Something on the table caught her eye. It was a piece of paper with what looked like some newsprint on it. She picked it up to inspect it further and dropped it immediately when she recognised what it was.

On the table, under the pile of post had been a copy of her mother's obituary from the *Daily Telegraph* in May 2002. Under her mother's name someone had written 'CEASE AND DESIST' in black felt tip.

She hadn't been able to explain that away.

The coach lumbered along the London Road and from her seat at the back, swaddled in a pashmina to stay warm, Assia gazed idly at the busy-ness of the people outside. Mothers with prams and Waitrose bags in Headington, a little toddler scooting along beside them as they walked to the playground, the park full of sunbathers and picnics, young men on their mobiles lingering outside fast food joints; everyone was engaged in being and doing while she, Assia, was watching and observing, stuck on the cold side of the window.

Suddenly the coach crested Magdalen Bridge and began to roll up the High Street like the Greeks' horse being wheeled into Troy. Towers and spires rose up next to her and the sight of the sandy-coloured stone of the colleges was like a soothing balm, quelling some of the hysteria which she had felt pressing at the top of her throat ever since she had run out of her flat and made her way to Oxford.

XXVI

A scratching noise as the little flap of the peephole cover was lifted and then dropped again. She hated this miserly habit of his; the way he decided whom he would and wouldn't be present for.

'You're early.'

He had opened the door a fraction and already begun walking back down the hall again as she came in.

'Oh, sorry, Papa. Are you busy?'

'Yes. I just need to finish something,' he said without turning round. 'I'll be with you presently.' He disappeared into his study and closed the door. Assia was left standing in the cold hallway, wondering if she should just slip out of the house again. When she had called her father to ask if she could visit him at home in Oxford, he had agreed but had been as clipped as ever on the phone. She had prepared herself for his awful phone manner and tried not to read anything into it even though the refrain *He still loathes me* persisted in her mind, like a bluebottle stuck in the corner of a window frame. And here, in the chilly hall of her childhood home, she felt the refrain lodge like a splinter too deep to extract. *Yes, he loathes me; he can't even bear to be around me.*

Nothing in the house had changed. Not only were there no new additions to the walls, no new photographs in frames, but the positioning of everything had not been touched. The entire house had been preserved in aspic; it was just as it was all those years ago when Assia was living in college and she and her mother had got into the car on that fateful day. *He's just like Miss Havisham*, Assia thought, and she almost forgot how dismayed she was as she marvelled at the time capsule she had walked into. With tentative steps, she explored the ground floor of the house, opening doors as quietly as possible so as not to disturb her father. Downstairs in the kitchen, the only new thing was the fridge. The old fridge had been covered with magnets and postcards of Botticellis, Titians and Fabergé pieces – none of these things had been transferred to the new fridge and it occurred to Assia then and there that the reason nothing had changed was because her father couldn't be bothered to change it. He might just as well have moved into college – he doesn't need a house, she thought. It's just the place where he sleeps, not the place where he lives.

Her mother's tins of tea were still arranged on top of the oak dresser above the shelves of her brightly coloured tea glasses. The kitchen had been a cosy place to be when she was growing up; she would curl up in the large patterned armchair by the AGA and do her homework. Occasionally, Olga would ask her what she was studying and they would discuss everything from Tudor history to the atomic number of gold. Tanya, who liked to work in Olga's study, would come in every now and then to forage in the fridge and they would sit and chat together.

'You are so lucky, my girls, to study at your school. The quality of education you're getting there cannot be bettered. I am very envious of you.'

'We know, Mama, you say this so often we couldn't possibly forget.' Tanya was leaning against the AGA, stroking the Labrador with her foot.

'I say it because you mustn't forget and you must be grateful. I don't want you to take it for granted because that will diminish its gold standard. Objectively, you are getting the best education money can buy but you are also being educated in a country where freedom of thought is valued and you don't have to parrot things ad nauseam just because some ideologue says you must.'

'You are a true Anglophile, Mama!' Assia clapped, laughing, but stopped when she saw the seriousness of her mother's expression.

'Things are changing in Russia now, and Yeltsin has a lot to be getting on with, but he only narrowly defeated the Communists in the recent elections. Go to any school in Russia right now and you'll find that very little is changing. The students will still be parroting the dates and names of Soviet heroes long into the life of this new Federation. Go and live in Russia and then tell me why I'm an Anglophile, darling.'

Climbing the stairs gingerly, Assia stopped to look out of the large window on the landing. In summer, tendrils of wisteria would frame the view and she had loved looking out over North Parade with its bunting and shops. She half expected to see their neighbour, an old don with a scrappy Jack Russell, hobbling over to the Rose & Crown as he had always done at three in the afternoon, but it occurred to her that he and the dog were probably long gone and a swanky businessman with a pretty family was no doubt living in his huge house.

The door of her mother's study creaked as she opened it and Assia found herself cringing as she tried to dampen the noise. She decided not to switch on the light, as though it were in some way too irreverent a thing to do in this chamber of memories. The smell of old books and journals was so evocative of her childhood that Assia felt quite winded. She had stepped into one of those Einsteinian wormholes which took her back to her eighteen-year-old self, that girl with a gilded future who had just won a place at Oxford. She and her twin sister were objects of envy – they were beautiful, clever and being half-Russian made them seem exotic. The world was going to fall at their feet. Here and now, Assia felt envious of that younger version of herself, as though she was someone else entirely, someone she once knew and longed to be.

She picked up a copy of *Zhar Ptitsa*, the Russian literary and artistic journal published in the 1920s, from a large pile on the floor. The cover of the journal was a vibrant design by Natalia Goncharova with fiery reds and yellows arranged in a pattern depicting petals, stems and leaves. The shapes of the leaves were splayed so that they resembled the tail of the mythical firebird, whose feathers could light rooms, even when plucked from the creature. Goncharova's irresistibly vibrant pattern was reminiscent of the shaded cloisonné enamels found on Ovchinnikov and Kurliukov silverware of the late 19th and early 20th century, the *kovshi*, *bratini* and punch sets which would have decorated the sideboards and tables of rich Muscovites. Olga had loved Russian Revival pieces, the polychromatic celebration of this Byzantine form of decoration, even though it was directly at odds with the courtly classicisation of St Petersburg which Fabergé indulged in. Olga had always told Assia that Russians were inconsistent and contrary and that it was no coincidence that the Russian Imperial Eagle had two heads.

'Russia is always split, always mercurial. It's the Russian schizophrenia which gets people. Foreigners just can't pin our wings back in a display cabinet – we defy classification.' Olga had said this to the twins one chilly morning as they walked to St Alexis's for a service. 'Think of it – I am a Russian immigrant: I have left my country and despise many aspects of it but here I am, taking you to a service at a Russian church. I only have to hear the chanting and look at an icon and something happens to me – something atavistic over which I have no control. I long for my *rodina*, the motherland, with a yearning so strong it hurts, even though I couldn't wait to escape it. I don't want to live there, but I do want to be there. I am like the mutant eagle with two heads.'

Tanya laughed at the idea of a mutant eagle and put her mother's hand in hers, swinging it as they walked along. Assia frowned and looked up at Olga.

'Mama, would you say we are Russian, Tanya and I?'

'Of course you are, darling. Your father may be English, but he speaks Russian beautifully and knows the country well.

You're so young now, but when you're older, you'll understand the concept of *rodina*. It's a special Russian thing.'

'But we've only been to Russia twice.'

'Yes, but you're my daughters and I am bringing you up as Russians. You speak the language, you go to Russian church, you eat Russian food and you know all the Russian fairy-tales. As I said, when you're older it will all fall into place. When you go to Russia one day in the future, you'll have that feeling and I'll be so happy. My job as your mother will be complete.'

Assia opened and closed the drawers in her mother's Davenport desk. Some of them were quite stiff and she had to pull handfuls of crumpled manuscript printed on an Amstrad out of one of the drawers to be able to close it again. She didn't know exactly what she was looking for but she couldn't shake off the suspicion that Kostya would have given her mother something – some Fabergé presents – and she wanted to find them. She pulled up a beautiful chair painted in Georgian green with a crescent back and lattice seat and stood on it to open the cupboards above the bookshelves. She wondered if her father had looked through everything in the study or whether he had just closed the door on Olga's world and left it unmined and unexplored. She suspected the latter and she felt rather angry on her mother's behalf that all those balls she had been juggling before she died had just been left to settle and gather dust.

In the second cupboard she opened she saw a sizeable pale pink box lodged behind a ring binder which was so crammed with papers that the metal rings had split. She pulled the box out quickly and placed it on the floor. There was nothing to suggest what was in it, but Assia had a feeling that this was what she was looking for; the box was too pretty a colour not to have something precious inside and when she heard the rustle of tissue paper as she lifted the lid, she knew she had found something. Pressing down on the layers of crisp paper, Assia could see something colourful emerging and she lifted a magnificent enamelled silver-gilt casket out of the box.

She imagined that she was a young *boyarina* in a painting by Konstantin Makovsky lifting up a present from a boyar suitor and admiring it with a joyful expression. Her breath slowed and thinned as she held the *larets* in her hands and explored its every angle. The size of a large jewellery box, the casket was encased in a carpet of colourful enamel set in between tiny silver coils which formed shapes. These little coils, known as *cloisons*, when filled with enamel formed little pools of colour which were further enriched by painted details on the surface of these tiny lacquer lakes. As well as the swirls, there were little geometric details such as triangles and rhomboids in dark reds and greens set on a pale blue background. The decoration paid homage to the ornamental wood-carving from the Talashkino and Abramtsevo workshops as well as the bold simplicity of Ivan Bilibin's drawings. Kandinsky must have been inspired by this decoration, thought Assia – all these shapes are re-worked in his monumental abstracts and speak of Old Russia in a newly forged way.

Inside, the casket was gilded and shone with a muted glow when Assia held it up to the window. Immediately, she looked for an inscription just under the hinges, in the same place that Kostya had inscribed a dedication in the cigarette case to Yelena, but there was nothing on the casket. The marks on the underside of the box, where the Fabergé mark overstruck Rückert's initials, were perfectly authentic and signified that the casket had been made by Fedor Rückert, the enameller of great renown, for Fabergé in the years between 1908–1917. It must be worth at least £200,000 on today's market. She examined the inside of the casket with her loupe and then, as it caught the light, she came upon the inscription under the rim of the lid:

A dream of Old Russia for my darling Olyushka, with love from Kostya, Easter, 1987

Pins and needles prickled her feet which were folded underneath her but Assia found she couldn't move. If she moved, then the *larets* might disappear in a puff of smoke and leave her, hopeless and alone, in her father's house. She lifted the pale pink box out of the way so that she could photograph the casket and make notes and as she did, noticed that it was a little heavier on one side. She plunged her hand into the tissue paper and groped around until she felt something cold with her fingers. Her hand closed around a smaller box and she pulled it out, closing her eyes as she did so. When she opened them, the feeling of déjà vu which overcame her was so discombobulating that she had to look around her to remind herself where she was at present. The enamel on the surface of the fan-shaped box was exactly like the enamelling on the Livadia Egg – that beautiful chequerboard of painted enamel of the most exquisite quality inspired by the pattern on the top of the casket of the Trinket Seller.

She knew then, and laughed out loud. *Mama had always loved the Trinket Seller. You were leaving me a clue, Kostya, weren't you?* She was excited now and her heart raced in her throat as she turned the box over to look for the maker's marks. Smiling, she saw a small stamp with the Cyrillic initials 'K.S.' *And there you are.* He hadn't used Fabergé marks on this piece. This was K.S. for the maker Konstantin Stepanyan.

She opened the box to look for an inscription from Kostya but again, at first, saw nothing until she turned the box upside down and examined the inner rim of the lid.

An homage to our favourite Dresden masterpiece, with love, Kostya, Easter, 1992

The sky outside had a half-hearted opaqueness which was entirely dread and suffocating; the colour of chloroformed nothingness. Raindrops began to tap against the windowpane, intermittently at first and then more and more insistently. Assia was holding her loupe up to Yelena's cigarette case, which she had extracted from her bag, and was comparing the Fabergé marks with those on the *larets*. She observed that the marks were the same, the trough of the square was deeper on the right in both pieces. Acid spurts of adrenalin were pumping through her system and after a few moments she found that she couldn't hold the loupe without shaking: realisation had dawned.

She was aware that she had always known in the bottom of her heart but had not been able to acknowledge it. She had heard distant alarms from her subconscious but had found reasons to ignore them. Now, the truth itself was as unpleasant and menacing as the sound of the guillotine blade being hoisted up.

'Kostya made this, this, this and this.' While talking to herself, she touched the pieces which she had laid out in front of her as evidence. She had even taken off her pendant egg necklace and put it in the line-up. 'K.S. Konstantin Stepanyan. *And* he made the Livadia Egg – I know it. He made it all.' Assia shook her head, more in disbelief than in remonstration with Kostya. Had her mother known about his forgeries or had she believed that they were genuine Fabergé pieces? She must have known that 'K.S.' were his initials and that he had made the fan-shaped box, surely?

'What are you doing in here?'

He sounded forlorn, almost – as though she had left him out of something. She hadn't heard him over the sound of the rain and the swell of her heartbeat in her ears.

'Oh, Papa.' She spun around and got to her feet clumsily. 'I was just looking through some of Mama's books – perhaps Tanya told you that I'm editing her *Encyclopaedia of Fabergé Eggs* and adding new material. There's a lot of research involved.' Assia smoothed down her skirt and placed her hands over it neatly.

'Ah, I see.' Richard had a hand on the doorframe and looked down as he spoke, studying his Lobbs. He had developed a bit of a paunch over the years but it hadn't travelled to his face and he still looked handsome. 'I didn't know about that but – yes, it's a good thing that you're updating her book.' He looked directly at Assia and nodded sincerely. 'She would want it to be current. She couldn't stand not to be at the forefront of things, could she?' He offered the last two words tentatively, as a peace offering.

'Absolutely not, couldn't stand it!' Assia's cheeks were flushed and she could feel the warmth spread down her neck as she laughed. It was good to laugh here, in her parents' house, and her smile broadened when she saw her father laughing too.

She wanted to go over and hug him but she thought that might be too much for now.

'What are those things on the floor?' He frowned with curiosity, a look Assia had never seen before. It was the kind of look she supposed he reserved for particularly tricky aspects of deep, dark maths.

'Oh, yes, these.' She felt suddenly protective of them, like a lioness wanting to ward a predator off her babes. 'These are a couple of pieces I found in Mama's cupboards. I don't think they're anything, but I was just checking.'

Thankfully, the predator backed off. 'Ah, I see. You and Tanya ought to go through everything anyway and decide what you want to keep. I've been thinking I need to downsize and the house is worth quite a bit now. No point my sitting on a goldmine. Are you coming down for coffee? I can't be too long, there's a Senior Common Room meeting at four.'

She wrapped the *larets* and the fan-shaped box carefully in the pale tissue paper and placed them securely at the bottom of her large leather tote. She took one last look at the room before closing the door.

XXVII

'Oh, dear Lord! I'm so sorry, love, I didn't see you in here!'

Assia sat up in bed as the top light was turned on. She saw a skinny woman with dark cropped hair back out of the room dragging a hoover by its suction tube.

'It's not Tanya, is it? You're Anastasia. I'm sorry, love, your Dad didn't tell me you were in the house. I'll come back when I've finished the other rooms.'

'Thank you so much, I'm so sorry. I'll be out in a second.'

Gathering the clothing on the floor, Assia dressed hurriedly. She was running out of clean clothes and the bedroom was a tip. The contents of the bag she had brought from London were strewn over the floor and there was an empty wine glass on the bedside table. She had hidden the empty bottle from last night in the little cupboard on the other side of the bed and had planned to throw it away along with the others she had hidden. She had better do that before the cleaner finds them, she thought.

Apart from a trip to buy wine from the shop on the corner of Observatory Street, Assia hadn't left the spare room for the past three days. She had started to write an article about Kostya being the maker of the Livadia Egg and had even covered the wall of her old bedroom with photos of the Livadia Egg so that she could know its every detail. Her father had said she could stay in the house for a while but he hadn't really understood why she didn't want to go back to her flat in Pimlico. Or perhaps he hadn't wanted to understand.

'What's all this?' he had said, frowning and nodding at the photos on the wall when he walked past the bedroom one evening.

'It's just research, Papa,' Assia had said quickly, jumping off the bed when she saw him. 'I can't do it in my flat in London. You know I mentioned that I had had a break-in? It wasn't a burglary – nothing was taken. They were trying to stop me researching this new egg because they don't want me to prove it's a fake. That's why they left a copy of Mama's obituary on the table with the message "Cease and desist".'

'That sounds very odd.' He hovered in the doorway, his hands behind his back. Assia couldn't determine if he was lingering because he was concerned or because he was intrigued by the mysterious 'they'. He continued 'Who would do such a strange thing? And your Mama's obituary – are you sure it isn't an old copy that you just had lying around?'

'I'm quite sure. It's the people behind this new egg – the Russians. They left it for me in my flat so that I would find it. They don't want me poking around and revealing that it's an out-and-out fake. Look, Papa, this is key.' She pulled off a blurry sepia photograph of Fabergé eggs which had been plastered onto the centre of the wall with a drawing pin. 'This is a blow-up of a photograph of one of the vitrines from the Fabergé exhibition of 1915, organised in part by the Grand Duchess Olga as part of her role in the All Russia Red Cross Ladies Committee. Come up close – can you see this reflection here? You can just make out some tiny white shapes on the vitrine, can't you? This is a reflection of the real Olga egg, the one made by Alma Pihl in the design that Mama predicted. It's covered in white daisies – it's in the vitrine, but it's hidden here behind the Flower Basket Egg so that you can't see it directly.' She held the photo up to her father's face and shook it. 'Papa, this is huge: not only does it prove that Mama was right, but it proves that the Livadia Egg is not authentic.'

Richard took a step back into the hallway and looked over his shoulder warily. His mouth had hardened into a line and

Assia might have thought that he was angry if it weren't for the heaviness in his eyelids, weighted by sadness.

'Assia? We've been here before. Don't you remember? '

She might have felt more reassured if he had looked exasperated. But he hadn't. He looked at her with pity. She could see that he was peering at her computer screen, trying to decipher the eerie movements of the digital universe as it carried on multiplying and dividing under the thin glass of her iMac. His chin wrinkled a little with doubt, as though he were deliberating whether or not to fetch help,

'Papa, I know how this looks. I do. I know you must think that I'm relapsing to the state I was in when Mama died, but I promise I'm not. You remember Kostya - Konstantin, Mama's friend from Piter - don't you? Of course you do. Well, he made this egg, the one that the Russians are hailing as a new discovery. And he used a special motif on the egg, some chequered enamel, so that I would recognise it and know that the egg was a fake.' She took a deep breath and carried on, excitedly. 'This is all really positive stuff because I'm gathering evidence to prove that the Livadia Egg is a fake. I'm doing it for Mama – I owe it to her: to her memory and fine scholarship. If she had been alive today, she would have pronounced the Livadia Egg a fake – and people would have listened to her. That reflection in the photograph is too important to ignore.' She waved a hand at the wall of pictures. 'And I can't exactly include a fake egg in the *Encylopaedia*, can I?'

Richard nodded gently and pulled the door to Assia's bedroom so that it closed noiselessly.

XXVIII

The Moscow skyline was winning him over tonight. He had always been a Piter man, preferring the Rostral Columns and dome of St Isaac's to Tsereteli's absurd bronze of Peter the Great and the Soviet grandeur of Stalin's 'Seven Sisters,' the Gothic sykscrapers which surrounded the city like the wall of a fortress. And yet, this evening, as his car swept round Borovitskaya Ploshchad, Ivan felt quite moved by the vast new addition to the Kremlin precinct: the statue of St Vladimir.

The President and Ivan had originally signed off on a plan to erect the bronze of the prince, who had introduced Christianity to ancient Russia, on Sparrow Hills so that it would dominate the Moscow skyline, but a few overly vocal liberals had managed to muster public dissent and it was subsequently agreed that the statue would be placed just outside the Kremlin gates. Location aside, the most gratifying thing was that the Ukrainians were furious that Russia was paying homage to Prince Vladimir. They were whining that Volodymyr – as they called him – was their founding father because he had been based in Kievan Rus, but what they refused to understand was that Kiev had been flattened by the Mongols in 1240 and that Moscow was the natural successor to the realm and spiritual legacy of Vladimir the Great.

Ivan leant closer to the car window, lamenting the black-out windows which cast everything into a darker shade. The colossal Prince had been lit so that he shone a sort of gunmetal grey: upright, irresolute and determined. It rose above a series of graduated steps in the earth which were designed to represent the ripples of water which emanated from a baptism. Ivan liked to think of the Prince as the man who had cleansed Russia, plunging her into the waters of a new life, a birth into Christ. Tonight, against the night sky, the giant Saint was looking down on him, crucifix in hand and blessing his mission.

The General had readied his people. He himself, Ivan Borisovich Denisov, was ready. Soon Russia would be cleansed again.

XXIX

Edward looked at his watch in irritation. He was standing on the low stone steps outside, watching the spray of one of the dome-shaped fountains on the pavilion which spread before the neoclassical temple of the Moscow Manege. The area outside the exhibition hall had been roped off and a steady stream of guests emerged from the long queue of cars which moved smoothly alongside the building.

He had promised to wait for Madeleine and her daughter so that he could escort them into the exhibition, and here he was doing just that – waiting. People with money were good at making other people wait: eating up someone else's time was a form of conspicuous consumption. The English rarely did it; even the bride who keeps her groom and guests waiting too long is considered to be dancing on the margins of proper behaviour, but the Russians excelled at it. Since he had lived in Russia, Edward could barely recall a time when a meeting hadn't been interrupted by someone taking a phone call. He had become a connoisseur of the levels of fabulous rudeness displayed by rich Russians and he could even judge how keen someone was to cut a deal by their lack of manners. Edward knew that the oligarch who answered his phone without excusing himself was going to be harder work than the one who held up a finger to indicate that he needed a moment. And he had perfected the ultimate mask of nonchalance, his 'I'm not listening to the incredibly interesting conversation you're conducting in front of me' face, effected mostly by looking out of the window, fiddling with his own phone or looking at his knees. He had become used to being treated like a servant by rich Russians and it had made him more aware than ever of the importance of manners, not because the Russians so rarely had any, but because the delicate dance of politeness which he insisted on following acted as his refuge. Manners were a means of preserving *his* dignity so that the next time an oligarch neglected to apologise for being two hours late, Edward would be more polite than ever, knowing that he was laying a weightless veil of irony upon the head of the unsuspecting brute.

Madeleine Roseman, though, was a whole other matter. Edward imagined that the pair of them were probably in her car, and Madeleine was instructing the driver to do another lap of the square, taking just long enough to make him sweat. She was not being uncouth in her tardiness, rather she was deploying 'feminine wiles'. Edward laughed to himself at the thought of Madeleine toying with him with the girlish manipulation more suited to her daughter; he knew that she wanted him but he had hoped that he wouldn't have to play too many grotesque games. Although Madeleine could be described as handsome, Edward wasn't turned on by desperate women and he could smell her disturbing neediness underneath all that hairspray.

He looked at his watch again and sighed. Fiddling with his cuffs, he was uncomfortably aware of his agitation. The organisation of this evening's exhibition had been a challenge up until the last moment. Madeleine's Fabergé egg had been held up at Russian customs, its progress into Moscow halted by the need for various pieces of apparently unnecessary paperwork. Reluctantly, Edward had had to involve Ivan who had made a few angry phone calls and blasted the ears off the various petty officials who had spectacularly misjudged who they were playing with.

Edward wondered where Assia was right now and what she was doing. He cursed his heart for its foolish hopefulness and gritted his teeth every time it missed a beat on seeing a beautiful brunette process into the Manege. Madeleine had confirmed that Assia was not going to show up and he felt the echo of a deep sadness that they were no longer in each other's orbits. At the beginning, the Livadia Egg had pulled her closer to him, like a lodestar, but without warning, she had fled, shrouded in a sourness and hurt that he couldn't quite comprehend.

Assia had been one of the very few girls unavailable to him. He had courted her half-heartedly at Oxford but then circumstances had conspired to snatch her. At the time, Edward had been quite winded by the sorry saga of her mother's death; he felt cheated, as though he had been limbering up for a race which no one told him had been cancelled. A few times he had tried to visit Assia at home but Richard, her father, on the occasions when he chose to answer the door, had said that it wasn't a good time and that perhaps he should try again in a few weeks. From looking at Richard's unkempt state, Edward imagined that Assia probably wasn't faring much better and he even found himself examining the façade of the house to see if he could ascertain which was her window. He pictured himself throwing stones at her bedroom window, little pricks to bring her back to the light from the bottom of her pit of darkness. She didn't reply to his letters and eventually – even though he hadn't meant to – he forgot about her. Terms came and went and he spent eight months in Moscow for his year out. He met other beautiful girls – many of them Russian – and his life continued on its successful trajectory. A double First in Russian and Latin from Oxford led to a coveted placement in the Foreign Office, then a position in the office of the British Ambassador to Moscow. His grievous disappointment over Assia had just been a minor hitch.

The buzz and crackle of security radios multiplied as the guards standing by the large doors of the Manege appeared to be receiving a flurry of information. With fourteen Imperial Fabergé eggs inside the building, they had their work cut out, thought Edward. He spotted Madeleine and Athena getting out of their car and made as if to walk towards them without moving very far. In her stilettos, Athena lifted her feet slowly as though she was stuck in mud, clearly unused to wearing sky-high heels. Edward felt rather sorry for the large girl with overstyled hair as she was overtaken by sleek Russian women who no doubt went to the gym in their heels.

'Welcome to Moscow!' grinned Edward, holding his arms out wide.

Madeleine was thrilled to see Edward. She had spoken about him at length to Athena, hoping that it would encourage her daughter to muster some enthusiasm about a trip to Moscow. And although Athena had told her to 'shut up already about the English dude,' Madeleine was relieved to see her daughter perk up as they walked towards Edward in his tuxedo.

Just before they had got out of the car, much to Athena's amusement, Madeleine had pinched the apples of her cheeks to give them colour – something her darling mother used to do just before she gave the order for guests to be shown in. She felt so excited about tonight's exhibition: it was the first time the John D. O'Connor Fabergé egg had been to Russia and she hoped her Pee Paw would be proud of her and Athena. To be a guest of honour at this magnificent event in Moscow – just outside the Kremlin walls – was something she could never have dreamt of and she felt wonderfully, blessedly happy.

'My egg had better be in there!' she said as she embraced Edward, giggling. 'And this...' she placed her arm around Athena 'is my daughter, Athena.'

'How do you do?' said Edward, kissing a stiff-shouldered Athena on both cheeks. 'So, let's not miss a moment of this spectacular occasion. Why don't we go in?' He smiled kindly at Athena and ushered the two women inside.

The vast hall of the Manege was dimly lit within. On entering, guests were handed a map of the exhibition, a guide to the fourteen eggs on display. The installation company which had designed the interior space of the hall had come up with a theme, 'Tomb of the Pharaohs', which it was felt would excite guests and make them feel like explorers lighting upon treasure. In the centre was a vast square bar with an aqua blue neon top on which guests could lean and order drinks, while the waiters and waitresses with trays of champagne coupes and canapés wore black, their necks and arms bedecked with multicoloured neon light tubes.

Edward wanted to laugh at the spectacle, but he had to admit it worked. It was breath-taking and dramatic and he liked the fact that he could barely see the other guests. With the cabinets of the eggs illuminated in cones of golden light throughout the hall, it felt as though everyone assembled had wandered onto to the deck of an alien landing, its other-worldly eggs being sown in the earth: the beginnings of an occupation.

He swilled a mouthful of dry, creamy champagne over his tongue and imagined his taste buds sending frenzied signals to his brain as the expensive drink washed over them. He had come to need this boost on social occasions; that special fizzing power-pack in a glass. It made him a much nicer person: far more tolerant of the dull to-and-fro of conversation with people he didn't know and it excited him, helped him to fall in love with a gathering, with the moment. He liked listening to speeches with a full glass in his hand, raising it to a toast: congratulating a bride and groom, applauding the opening of an exhibition, the launching of a book, anything, cheering those instances when the world comes together. Glancing to his left he saw that Madeleine had already hurried over to her egg and he found himself smiling as he spotted her gazing into the cabinet and pointing out features to guests who had gathered next to her, like a proud mother allowing people to admire the baby in the pram. She seemed to radiate happiness as she bathed in people's wonder and fascination and there was something truly joyful about witnessing the moment.

'I got this from the bar. What is the drinking age here?' Athena appeared next to him holding a glass of something clear with a salted rim.

Edward raised his eyebrows. 'There are no formal laws on when you can drink it as such, but you can't buy alcohol unless you're eighteen. What is that? Vodka?'

'Yeah. The barman said it was just above freezing point. It feels really strange going down my throat.'

'Take it easy on the vodka front, young lady. It creeps up on you: you won't think you're drunk but suddenly dancing on tables will seem like a good idea.'

Athena giggled. 'Is that what you do when you get drunk?' She rolled the glass on her lips and looked up at Edward suggestively.

'Certainly not.' said Edward pretending to frown indignantly. 'Now, you won't have seen the Livadia Egg yet, will you? It's the new kid on the block. Let's have a look before all the long and boring speeches start.'

Five glasses of champagne and three speeches later, Edward was flying. He felt heady with the success of the evening: many of the Russian Forbes's – the super-rich of the country – had turned up tonight as well as the majority of the political elite. The President was out of the country but the Prime Minister had made a speech on his behalf and thanked everyone for gathering to celebrate the genius of Carl Fabergé and Russian artistry. He had remarked on the exceptional nature of the evening, how there had never been so many Imperial Fabergé eggs gathered together since Malcolm Forbes had lent his collection of eggs to the Kremlin Armoury in 1990 and how grateful they were to have the loan of the eggs of Madeleine Roseman and the Ferber Foundation. Edward had been standing next to Madeleine when she was thanked by the Prime Minister and she had held her drinks glass against her breast and bowed ever so slightly like an honoured knight. Edward had known that Ivan was about four people to his right, standing in a group with Arkady Kolesnikov, the Director of the FSB, known as 'the General' and he had glanced in his direction, pretending to scan the crowd but in actuality wanting to see Ivan's reaction to the Prime Minister's speech. Ivan had caught his eye and, looking straight at him had raised his glass in a congratulatory gesture with a wry smile.

Tapping his fingers on the neon blue bar in the centre of the hall, Edward felt a mixture of light-headed and elated. He was enjoying the exclusivity of the evening, its refinement. Here he was, part of this elite crowd of movers-and-shakers in Russia, surrounded by the rarest pieces of decorative art in the world. He had helped to make this exhibition happen and he had made Madeleine happy in the process. He was doing good things – important things – and enjoying himself in the process. *Only in Russia.* Only in Russia can you achieve everything, he thought. The barman handed him the whisky he had ordered and as he drank it, he noticed a beautiful blonde leaning on the bar across from him. She glanced at him coyly and he smiled back.

'Hey, here you are.' Athena sidled up to Edward. 'Mom told me to come and find you. She's busy showing people our egg. She was so *psyched* to be mentioned in that speech! Did you see her bowing? She is never going to stop talking about it!' Athena leant an elbow on the bar and clicked her fingers at one of the barmen. 'Yeah, a chilled vodka, thanks.'

Edward exhaled heavily through his nose and hoped that if he didn't say anything to her then she might go away.

'So, I think Russia's really cool. All my friends, when I told them I was coming out here, were like "I bet the food's disgusting" but the dumplings have been nice and you don't *have* to eat fish. And Mom's been ordering steak for every meal anyway for her diet. And you can order fries with everything if you want also.' She took a large gulp of her vodka and scratched an itch on her shoulder. 'So, did you study Russian at school, or something?'

Some shouts – men shouting – could be heard at one end of the hall. Frowning exaggeratedly, Athena put her drink on the bar and turned to see what the noise was about.

'Hey, what was… oh, my God! Oh!'

She ducked down underneath the lip of the blue neon bar and pressed her back up against it. Edward did the same and put his arm in front of her as they heard a loud burst of machine-gun fire. People screamed and fell to the floor immediately as the rounds of gunfire continued and the noise of shots being fired appeared to spread intermittently across the hall. Shrill female screams from a particular part of the room could be heard while some women covered their faces with their hands and the male guests looked around frantically from their prone position, unable to see much in the dimly lit hall.

From where he was crouching by the bar, Edward could make out that the men carrying guns were wearing balaclavas and spreading throughout the vast room from the back of the hall, returning fire at what were presumably shots from the security guards surrounding the eggs. He saw two gunmen shoot down a guard, spraying him with bullets so that he crumpled to the floor. His mind was treacle-like, struggling to make sense of what was happening in front of him. The gunmen had on the neon arm rings of the waiters and it was only later he would realise that they had been the waiters passing round foie gras before they went on their shooting spree. His breathing had shallowed and he was pressing his arm into Athena with such pressure that she pushed back slightly.

'It's OK,' he whispered when he saw that she was sobbing. 'They've moved behind us, I think.' He peered around anxiously, trying to ascertain where the gunmen had got to.

'That's Mom,' she whimpered through her tears.

'What?' he said hoarsely.

'That screaming from over there. That's Mom. I know it's her. I think she's been hurt.'

Holding his breath, Edward could feel his heart beating so hard that he thought it might pummel through the muscle and tissues of his chest. He strained to hear the screams – there were lots of them now, moans and screams, coming from all over the hall. He wasn't sure if one of the voices he could hear was Madeleine's – he didn't know what her voice would sound like when it was distorted by fear and pain. Did anyone know what another human would sound like screaming?

Another burst of machine gunfire sounded – higher up now, as though they had fired into the ceiling – over some triumphant yells from the gunmen. Edward couldn't make out what they were saying, but they weren't speaking in Russian. Their words had the breathy, guttural sound of Arabic.

Silence and screams. Not silence – the sound of no gunfire.

'They've gone!' someone yelled. Everyone stayed where they were, holding their breath. Athena pushed Edward's arm away and stood up, still trembling.

'Athena! Sit down! They might come back!' Edward tried to reach out to her and grabbed the hem of her pink dress. She pulled against him.

'The egg's gone!' Someone yelled from the middle of the room. 'They've taken the Livadia Egg!'

Edward's hand turned to lead and he dropped the hem of Athena's dress. She stumbled for a second before casting around for her mother, teetering pathetically in her heels.

'Mom! Mom!' she screamed. 'I can't see you! Mom, are you hurt?'

XXX

'Get out of the bloody way!'

Assia jumped to the right and onto the grey pavement stone. The cyclist whizzed past, standing on his pedals so that when he turned the corner he seemed to do so more sharply. She turned to watch him – his crop of blond hair and checked shirt disappearing along the lane. The way he had shouted at her hurt: his patrician vowels and the fact that he had sounded so angry stung her. She shouldn't be in his way, she wasn't worth stopping for, stupid cow. He was youthful and had a bright future ahead of him: he wasn't going to slow down for the likes of her. She wanted to run after him and explain that she was terribly sorry but it was so long since she had walked along Queen's Lane and she had forgotten about that particular corner and how bikes could take you by surprise. And did you know that I was a student here too and once upon a time I was worth knowing?

We've been here before.

Her father's words had scared her that night. She had thought she was doing the right thing: refusing to be cowed by the Russian intimidation, their order to 'cease and desist'. No! She was making a case – she had gathered good evidence. She was going to strip back their lies and prove the Livadia Egg was a fake!

But she had seen the alarm in her father's eyes. He had looked at her with that same mixture of fear and pity all those years ago after the accident when she had told him that she was not going back to her degree course.

And she had known then what she needed to do.

It was such a long time since she had walked around Oxford properly and she felt buoyed by the silent industry she knew was taking place behind the walls of the quads. Oxford had purpose, she thought. Bent over their books, the scholars were thinking and writing and churning out ideas: Oxford was the Coketown of the mind. Assia wondered if perhaps she should return to her College to finish her degree – maybe it was the thing she needed to do to feel complete again.

Walking along Queen's Lane, weaving her way behind the walls of the colleges, she had felt something close to happy. The thought of finishing her degree was like a peg on which to hang the heaviness she had been feeling – it didn't go away, of course, but she thought she had found something to motivate her to get up in the morning. She could push Fabergé to one side – leave all that anxiety about what is real and what isn't, all that decorative trickery and the need to prove it – all that could go. She'd tell her agent to find someone else to revise the *Encyclopaedia of Fabergé Eggs*– she was too close to it all to be able to do it. It was such a relief to be able to push it all off her table and she exhaled with a long, yogic breath. In the sun, glitter on the pavements shone and little bits of coloured paper bore testament to the triumphs that had processed up this lane. Happy undergraduates who had finished exams and stumbled exultantly, covered in glitter and flour, to The Turf to drink champagne and revel in the newfound freedom of having nothing to do for a summer. Assia had been imagining herself finishing her Finals when that Apollo on a bike had yelled at her. As she had watched him whizz off, she realised that the glitter was for him and his sort – the young ones.

You're avoiding it, Assia, aren't you? You just don't want to go there. Stop trying to find a reason to turn back.

XXXI

'A glass of champagne for you, Sir?'

The stewardess with heavily rouged lips leaned over Ivan to pass Edward a cold glass of champagne. Edward had been dying for a drink; if he could have smoked on the plane he would have lit up as well. He thanked his luck that Ivan was asleep in the seat next to him. He probably didn't approve of champagne, being a Western import, although Edward would have placed a lot of money on the fact that what Ivan did at home was probably very different to what he spouted in public. No doubt he had a large amount of the finest French wine in bond in Switzerland.

He took a sip of his drink and looked out of the small aeroplane window. They were gliding above an undulating carpet of cloud which obscured all view of the world below. He put his hand on the cold window and flexed it, stretching his fingers out into a star shape. He was willing his thoughts to take shape, to put the pieces together, but it was impossible. This had happened to him before, when Malaysia Airlines Flight 17 was shot down over Eastern Ukraine. He hadn't been able to understand how a plane full of innocent tourists, most of them Dutch and Malaysian, could have been blown out of the sky as a hecatomb for an Eastern European conflict – something which many people thought was just angry little men having a tussle over a remote corner on a map. His brain had spat the events out – refused to load the disc.

Yes, there they all were in their finery at the Manege – like passengers on the *Titanic*, tipped out of a grand occasion straight into disaster. The gunmen had stolen the Livadia Egg and shot eight people in the process, six of them dead.

She had looked dead when he had seen her lying there on the floor of the Manege. Her black satin dress was wet and sticky around her middle and Edward had felt sick as he realised that it was wet with the blood which was pooling at her back. She was no longer screaming and a Russian woman in pale blue chiffon was kneeling by her head saying prayers.

'Oh, my God. Mom!' Athena fell to her knees and cradled her mother's face with her hands.

Edward had tried to feel for a pulse, fumbling with Madeleine's wrist, but had stopped when he couldn't tell if there was one or not. He had felt so helpless and moved out of the way when the paramedics arrived.

And then, with a headache and sore eyes, he had come to in a chair in Madeleine's hospital room at the American Medical Centre and it had taken him a while to realise that the man standing by Madeleine's bed tapping out an email on his phone was the American Ambassador.

'Ambassador Steel,' he sprang out of his chair. 'You may remember me – Edward Baillie Aston. I worked for Sir Jeremy when he was here.'

'Edward, yes, of course.' The tall grey-haired man with teeth which protruded slightly beneath his finely trimmed moustache shook Edward's hand warmly. 'Thank you for looking after her,' frowning with concern he glanced at Athena who was curled up asleep in the other armchair next to Madeleine's bed. 'The consultant told me that they're concerned about associated abdominal wounds but that the operation to repair damage to the liver was successful. What have they told Athena?'

'The same. She doesn't know whether she should be relieved or worried. But I've heard they're good here, aren't they?'

'The very best. She's in good hands.' The Ambassador nodded reassuringly. 'The CIA will be wanting to speak to her later. We're taking this incident very seriously: an American citizen shot by Chechens in Russia. The White House wants a briefing. We're pleased that the Russians have already responded with force but the alarming fact is that this is leading back to Dudayev.'

'Aslan Dudayev?' Edward blinked.

'Yes. One of the gunmen was captured and he has admitted the involvement of Dudayev's right hand man, Murad Varayev, in the plot to steal the Fabergé egg. Russian Bumerang tanks are moving into Chechnya as we speak and the FSB have managed to identify a Chechen safe house near Tambov where they believe the egg is being hidden. This is going to get nasty, I can tell you. The Kremlin is not going to hang about on this one – the Chechens have humiliated Russia right on its doorstep, just a stone's throw away from its seat of power.'

Without warning, Edward's stomach had heaved. He had excused himself quickly and run to the room's small bathroom where he had coughed up spitfuls of bile.

Ivan's eyes were moving rapidly from side-to-side under the skin of his eyelids. Edward had been watching his face while he slept but this suggestion of mania was so sinister to behold that he looked away. He retreated in his tiny seat, pressing himself closer to the window in case Ivan should wake up and find his head grazing his colleague's shoulder – a familiarity which would embarrass them both. The strange physicality of a stuporous sleep was intriguing and revolting at the same time and Edward found himself studying Ivan's skin; the pores, the fine hairs and the shadow of stubble.

Ivan's eyes opened suddenly. He glanced at Edward: an expressionless look – a sort of matt white which gave away nothing. Edward nodded a hello and sunk back into his seat, his heart beating a little faster. He slipped his empty champagne glass into the pocket on the back of the chair in front of him and wiped his sticky fingers on a small square napkin.

'Good champagne? What exactly are you celebrating? You English upper classes can switch off so easily, can't you? Suppress a rioting mob and then return to your club for gin and tonic.'

Edward wasn't sure to which cliché of British Empire life Ivan was referring, but he thought it wise to let it go. He couldn't fathom whether the Russian was angry about the theft of the egg or just enjoying the opportunity to have a poke at the English. There was something about Ivan which chilled him to the core. He was an ancient god who needed the appeasement of smoke and prayers– a blue flame licking in a distant temple rather than a mortal red-hot bonfire. Edward didn't know how to deal with that sort.

'So does Madeleine Roseman like being on her back indefinitely? She looks like the masochistic sort, a real...' He leant closer to Edward and whispered a Russian term for Madeleine which was so disgusting and so far beyond the descriptive powers of English swear words that Edward was genuinely shocked.

The sound of rain lashing the side of the aeroplane woke Edward. He had turned his head to avoid Ivan and on closing his eyes had fallen into an unrewarding sleep of nothingness. The little crystals of ice which had flowered around the lower corner of the tiny window had – at first – looked like cracks in the thick pane and Edward peered at them closely to reassure himself that the plane was not falling apart. He let his head lean on the window and thought of how it was his fault that Madeleine was lying in a hospital bed. Assia would undoubtedly blame him for encouraging her to send her egg to Moscow, for leading her on, for letting her be in the path of a Chechen bullet.

Last night, after the Ambassador had left the hospital room, Edward had looked blankly at the screen of the monitor next to Madeleine's bed, the oscillating numbers and peaks and troughs of the digital charts which meant nothing to him. The back of her hand had an alarming-looking tube in it and so he touched the tip of one of her fingers, the little one on her left hand.

'I'm sorry, Madeleine, I'm so so sorry.'

XXXII

North Oxford is, essentially, Victorian Oxford. Assia loved the broad leafy streets and large Gothic Revival houses. Running off the Woodstock and Banbury Roads, these streets were hymns to ordered living and high thinking. More than just an estate agent's dream, there was a sense of purpose behind this Victorian suburb – the architects had built houses which would foster the thoughts of University dons. The gables and turrets on the houses echoed details of college quads, while the large gardens provided space enough for useful contemplation.

From St Giles, Assia had walked on the shady side of the Banbury Road, hugging the wall of St Anne's for the small amount of shade it cast. The heat of the sun was unforgiving and her skin prickled. In her sandals, her toes felt red and swollen and she considered resting on a wall on the corner of Bevington Road, but decided she would carry on as she was only a few streets away now. A white car with its windows down and drum and bass pumped up stopped at the lights and the pavement shook with the beat of the music. The bass was so loud that the car speakers sounded muffled and when the car drew off at the green light its many exhaust pipes spewed fumes, emitting a loud pop and then a deafening acceleration noise like a rocket launching. Assia's heart stopped momentarily at the popping sound and she put her hand on her chest with the shock. As she waved the fumes away she felt so angry at the fright the morons in the car had given her that tears pricked her eyes and she glared at the car in the distance, hoping the driver would register her indignation.

Glancing down North Parade as she walked past, Assia could see her mother, Tanya and herself walking along the narrow street. Her mother strode ahead, eager to get to the service on time, elegant in a black cashmere coat with a tie belt and the girls followed in their navy blue wool pea coats with velvet collars and velvet pocket flaps. Olga's blonde hair swung in a high ponytail and her side-sweep fringe gave her a fashionable edge. The twins, as nine year olds, had their long, wavy, dark hair flowing down their backs – Olga had told them that the Grand Duchesses wore their hair down until they came of age and then it was pinned up to show off their long necks and fine bone structure. Olga turned around to tell the girls who were walking along with one foot on the pavement and the other on the road to hurry up and stop being childish. The girls stepped back onto the pavement and trotted to their mother's heel, knowing that she would lose her temper if she had to ask them twice.

It was a potent memory. She hadn't invented the scene because it had been their ritual on a Sunday ever since she could remember, but the glorious technicolour of the vision made it feel like a mirage, a grandiose indulgence of the senses. Wasn't there a physicist who said that every moment of our lives was happening now, simultaneously? Here she was, the Assia further down the line from that hurried but happy twin, watching her young self from a hot day in the future.

That periscopic clip from her past was at the forefront of her mind as she shuffled along the hot pavement to Bardwell Road. Olga had started taking the girls to the Chapel of St Alexis the Wonderworker when they were too small to remember and there had barely been a Sunday when they hadn't attended – even when Olga was away travelling she would get Richard to take them. The Chapel was the foundation stone of Russian Orthodox life in Oxford and had been established by the strangest exile from the motherland of all: John Ernest Fairfax. Fairfax had taught English to the children of Tsar Nicholas II and had decided to go with the Imperial Family to Tobolsk when they were exiled to Siberia by the Bolsheviks in 1917. His devotion had not ended there: when the family were sent on to Ekaterinburg to the Ipatiev House, Fairfax had followed them and found lodgings in the city even though he was forbidden from seeing the family. After that fateful night in 1918 when Nicholas, Alexandra, the Grand Duchesses, the Tsarevich and a few of their retainers were executed in the cellar of the house by their captors, Fairfax had lingered in Ekaterinburg, trying to find out as much as he could about the shooting and how and where the bodies of the family had been disposed of. He gathered as many items from the Ipatiev House as he could, including a few items of the Tsar's uniform and some small icons belonging to the Grand Duchesses. Aware that his life was in danger when the White Army lost Ekaterinburg to the Bolsheviks, he travelled across the South-East border of Russia into China and settled for ten years in Harbin where many other White Russians fleeing the Revolution had arrived seeking refuge. In Harbin, Fairfax joined the Russian Orthodox Church, taking the baptismal name of Alexei in honour of the Tsarevich and stating that he wanted to bear witness to spread the word of the holy martyrdom of the Imperial Family. Within a couple of years he had been ordained and was made a priest and after some years an Archimandrite. Eventually, poor health and family concerns prompted a return to his native England in 1929 and Fairfax decided to make Oxford his home and set about creating an Orthodox congregation in his house on Bardwell Road in North Oxford. The chapel he made was founded upon both his deep Orthodox faith and the cult of the Imperial martyrs whose relics he had preserved and displayed there.

Father Alexei became a familiar figure in Oxford and was regularly sighted walking the streets in his black robes, brown beard flowing down over the chain of his gold pectoral cross, staff in hand. Although he could not be drawn on the subject of the Imperial Family, he did go to Paris to speak with a woman who claimed to be the Grand Duchess Anastasia. The interview upset him greatly and he had confessed to his adopted son

Sergei, that the woman was a 'faux Anastasia' and that he had stated as much in his affidavit. The woman, who spoke no Russian or English, had not recognised him and had not been able answer his questions relating to particular events which he believed the true Anastasia could not have forgotten during their precious time together at the Alexander Palace.

Father Alexei, the first English Orthodox Archimandrite in over a thousand years, died in 1966, one month before his ninetieth birthday. His devotion to the preservation of the memory of the Imperial Family had been tireless and his adopted son, Sergei Fairfax – also a priest, continued to run the Chapel and to serve the Orthodox community of Oxford. Like many Russians before her, attending a service at the Chapel of St Alexis was one of the first things Olga did when she arrived in Oxford and she became very close to Father Sergei before he died. She was adamant that her girls would be brought up as Orthodox Christians and not Anglicans like their father – Richard had not bothered to put up a fight, saying that if he'd had a son, he might have insisted on his being an Anglican but Olga could do what she liked with the girls' faith, as long as they were Christians. And so the Chapel of St Alexis the Wonderworker had become as familiar to Assia and Tanya as their own house.

The curtains of the large bay window at the front of No. 5 Bardwell Road were closed. The sun streamed through the chintz so that Assia could make out the pattern of fuchsias climbing a trellis. Glancing up at the first floor she saw the warm glow of gold paint on an icon in the upper corner of the room, an icon which she knew was the winged Archangel Michael holding a book of Gospels astride a winged red horse. As a young girl, she had once asked Father Arseniy why an Archangel with wings would need to ride a winged horse and he had taken her hand in his large, fleshy palm and brought her over to stand beneath the icon.

'My child,' he had said, kneeling so that his face was level with hers, 'look at the Archangel's face. What colour is it?'

'Um, red.' Assia's cheeks burned and she looked at the floor. She wished she hadn't asked the question.

'Yes, that's right. It is as red as his cape and his horse. The Church Slavonic at the top of the icon calls him "Chief-Commander Michael, the Terrible, Dreadful, Powerful Warlord of the Heavenly King". In the last book of the Bible, the Apocalypse, Arkhistratig Mikhail and his army of angels were tasked with fighting the dragon and casting him out of heaven. In essence, Michael has to defeat Satan and his minions and banish them from God's Kingdom for ever. A divine flame burns within him as a Servant of God, which is why his face is red. I also happen to think it is rather like divine war paint. If you had to fight the Devil you would want all the wings you could get, wouldn't you?'

The brass doorbell for the chapel was stiff and resisted any attempt to press it. Assia knocked on the door using the large brass ring and as she did so, lifted the letter box to try and peer into the hall. In the days when Olga and the twins attended weekly services, an old woman called Serafima always sat on a mahogany chair at the foot of the staircase and her job was to open and close the door and scare off the uninitiated with her throaty Russian and inability to speak English. She had adored the twins and Assia recalled sobbing fiercely aged twelve when told that Serafima had died in the John Radcliffe following a bad bout of pneumonia.

After a few minutes of waiting, Assia turned around and walked back out in front of the house, looking up at the chapel to see if she could spy anyone inside. It was four-thirty in the afternoon and she would have expected the priest to be getting ready for the five-thirty Saturday vigil but there was no sign of any preparation in order. Unnerved by the quiet in the house, Assia went back to the door and knocked firmly once more. She couldn't bear the idea of not being able to see the chapel now; she felt an overwhelming need to be in it and to surround herself with the icons she had grown up with. This was why she had come to the chapel: for the first time since the accident, she wanted to pray.

She was sitting on the wall outside the house, trying to Google a phone number for the chapel when she heard a voice.

'Can I help you?'

A middle-aged woman with a brown bob stood on the steps of the porch. She had a proprietorial hand on her hip and was frowning slightly.

'Oh, yes, hello.' Assia jumped off the wall and walked up to the porch. 'I used to worship here at St Alexis's and I was hoping to be able to go in.'

'It's closed, I'm afraid.' The woman gave what presumably she considered to be an apologetic smile but which instead looked more like a grimace. She turned to go back inside and Assia ran up the steps before she disappeared inside.

'Closed? For renovations?'

'No. Closed for good. My father is in a nursing home and the house needs to be sold to pay the extortionate fees. Alright?' The grimace again.

'Sergei Fairfax is your father?'

'Yes. I must be getting on, I'm afraid.' The door began to close.

'We have met before but I would have been rather small and you probably don't remember me. My mother's funeral was held here and I used to come here with her every Sunday. She was very close to your father, Father Sergei.'

'You're Olga's daughter?' The woman held onto the front door but did not shut it. 'Anastasia or Tatiana?'

'Anastasia.'

'I see.' She played with the long necklace of blue beads which she wore over a white linen dress. The skin on her arms had the deep brown tint of an Oxo cube while her bosom was crepey and speckled with brown spots. 'You'd better come in then.'

'Father Arseniy – do you remember him? He took over from my father – anyway, he died eight years ago. I was sad about that, I have to say.' Evgenia unlocked the wooden door of the chapel. 'Goodness, it's stuffy in here. I must open a window.'

Assia crossed herself and bowed before the altar while Evgenia wrestled with a window. She hadn't set foot in the place for sixteen years and although nothing had changed, she thought it all looked rather shabby and makeshift. Evgenia had said that there hadn't been a service there for four years – after Father Arseniy's death, they had found a priest but eventually he had fallen out with the Russian Orthodox Church in Exile and left in high dudgeon. After that, most of the parishioners had transferred their allegiance to a new Orthodox Church in Headington and Evgenia had felt unable to cope with the responsibility of the Chapel without her father's support. In particular, she was very worried about what to do with the icons and pieces which the Tsar and his family had given to her grandfather in exile in Tobolsk. Value aside (and really the items were only small bits and bobs), she felt the collection should be transferred to a museum or curatorial body which could preserve it and someone from an oligarch's foundation was coming to do an inventory next week.

'This is the piece which really troubles me' said Evgenia, touching the stand which held an icon with an image of the Empress Alexandra in it. 'It's rather important because my grandfather had it made and he was among the first to venerate the last Imperial Family as New Martyrs and Saints. He told my father that the painting of the Empress within the icon was given to him by the Grand Duchess Olga when the family was in exile. And apparently, just before he died, he kept telling my father that the icon was shining, emanating divine rays, and that he must guard it carefully.'

'I prayed before that icon for the first nineteen years of my life.' Assia stood before the smooth lacquered wooden *kiot* and crossed herself again. 'Icons leave their images branded on your heart. When you have been looking at the Mother of God of Vladimir or the Winged Archangel Michael ever since you were a child, you come to see their outlines in everything: the silhouette of hills in a landscape, the way a shadow falls, chestnut branches against the sky. You can be apart from these things in the physical world but they travel with you – whether you like it or not.' She caught Evgenia's eye and smiled ruefully.

'You stopped coming here after the funeral, am I right?' Evgenia paused next to a small table covered with a white lace cloth and small icons. Her fingers traced the smooth *repoussé* detail of the cloak on a small silver icon of the Mother of God of Iveria; over the years many fingers had touched this part of the *oklad* and the small engraved stars had almost softened to invisibility. She had asked the question tentatively, as though chary of the answer.

'It didn't feel right. Not for me – I mean, I felt it was wrong of me to come. The Chapel didn't deserve to have its precious sanctity despoiled by me. I felt as though I had killed *her*.' She pointed to the portrait of the Empress set into the icon. Her gaze lingered on the image of Alexandra, her fine aquiline nose and her imperious eyes.

'You poor girl' said Evgenia. Her head was cocked to one side sympathetically. 'I had moved to Australia by that point but Papa told me about the funeral and said it was the saddest service he had ever had to lead. He told me that you seemed to be in a trance that day.'

'I was numb; wrapped in some kind of protective shroud woven by my brain. It was trying to prevent me from self-destructing. It could have tried harder, frankly.' She walked up to the icon of the Empress Alexandra and touched the glass with the tips of her fingers.

'And you lost your faith.' Evgenia said this as a statement, nodding to indicate that she agreed with the conclusion she had drawn.

'Yes and no.' Assia brushed a strand of hair out of her eyes and turned to face Evgenia. 'It wasn't a clear-cut thing. I didn't rail against God, really – it seemed perfectly logical to me that he would abandon me. I mean, I was defective – no one else causes their mother's death because they're an awful driver, do they?'

'You're not the first it happened to, Anastasia, and you won't be the last either. Accidents happen.'

'I know.' She squeezed a clump of her hair in her hand – something she did when she was anxious. 'A while after it happened I felt that in some way it was pre-ordained. We both had it coming – we were being felled in some way: my mother for wanting too much from life, and me for being so unworthy, so incapable.' Assia looked around the chapel and waved her arm before her. 'My God is the cruel, Old Testament God. I thought I wanted nothing to do with him, but here I am – bowing to the icons and kissing them.'

'You're very hard on yourself.' Evgenia wore a pained expression. 'You know, God didn't want the accident to happen, he didn't want to punish you. He couldn't prevent what happened, but he understands your pain.'

Assia snorted lightly, channelling the breath out of her nose. She looked down at her feet, trying to blink the tears away.

'Oh, my darling. Don't cry!' Evgenia rushed over and wrapped her arms around her. 'My sweetheart! You remind me of my son – so full of anger and pain. He's only nineteen, but he's going through a hard time at the moment and he needs lots of love and someone to listen to him.' Evgenia pulled back so that she could see Assia's face. 'You, my sweetheart, need to be told that everything is OK. You're not defective and you're not a murderer. You need to forgive yourself and realise that no one else blames you.'

Evgenia smelt of something peppery, some kind of expensive cologne. Assia allowed herself to be suspended in the scent and the strength of Evgenia's embrace. Resting her head on the older woman's shelf-like bosom, she felt soothed and let her tears wet Evgenia's leathery neck. Olga and Richard had never been the cosy, hugging types and Assia had scorned those women who couldn't let their children do anything without cuddling them, but just now it felt immensely comforting to be held firmly by a maternal figure.

'This place is your home, sweetheart. God is welcoming you back to the fold.'

Assia closed her eyes. Her shuddering sobs began to still; her cheek rested in the groove of Evgenia's neck. In her mind's eye, the silhouette of the icon of the Mother of God of Vladimir hovered over them both as they stood there, embracing. The tilt of Evgenia's head towards Assia's echoed the tenderness of the Virgin whose cheek touches that of the boy Christ, and Assia, like the small Jesus, folded into Evgenia's all-encompassing maternity.

'Let me give you some time here alone, my sweet,' said Evgenia, stroking Assia's hair. 'I think you need to talk some things over with the Almighty.' She pointed heavenwards. 'When you've sorted things out, come downstairs and have a cup of tea, all right?'

'Thank you, Evgenia. You've been so kind. I'm sorry for…'

'I don't want to hear that word from you, young lady.' Evgenia shook her finger at Assia sternly. 'You don't need to apologise for existing, as far as I am concerned. I'll see you in a little bit.'

The door closed and the white net curtains billowed in response. Assia breathed deeply and took in her surroundings. It was a small chapel – just a large room with a high ceiling and some pillars which marked out the narthex, nave and sanctuary – but Assia thought it had always felt as charged with sanctity as any of the larger Orthodox churches she had been to. As a young girl, during services she would look at the icon of the Royal Martyr Alexandra and she would imagine Olga entrusting it to Fairfax. To think that the Grand Duchess Olga had actually touched the miniature in the icon! The thought electrified her young mind – she felt as though touching and kissing the icon was a way of reaching the spirit of the Grand Duchess and she dreamed for hours on end of what they would talk about if they met. She would have asked Olga what it was like being the daughter of the most powerful man on earth only to be arrested and bundled off into exile. How did they manage to exist in the Ipatiev House – how did she cope with having the windows whited and not being able to see outside? She, herself, would have found that very hard to bear – she loved her view of the houses and gardens of North Oxford. She liked to imagine that one of the gardens she could see was a secret garden which no one else knew about – not even Tanya – and there she would meet the Grand Duchesses and the Tsarevich Alexei and they would play all day and take photos of each other with a Box Brownie.

This place is your home.

Evgenia was right, thought Assia. This place – this chapel – *is* my home; far more my home than the house I grew up in. There I am reminded of all the pain I caused Papa and Tanya, but this place, this small and holy room, is where Mama communed with her *rodina*. She was herself here more than anywhere. The chanting, the icons, the prayers, the people – all of it reminded her of the beloved and accursed homeland which she had left behind. She felt safe here. She was able to soothe the wound that leaving her *rodina* had opened.

I am an exile too, she thought. The day that Mama died was the day I became an exile from my former life. And here I am now, useless and without hope.

Beloved Royal Martyr Alexandra, you were exiled from your former life as Empress of All the Russias but you bore the suffering with magnanimity and fortitude. The health of your poor son was a source of constant worry and anxiety – how much harder must that have been to endure when you were prisoners, away from all the medicines and doctors he needed! Look kindly upon me and grant me the strength and resolution to find purpose in my life. Help me to heal and to lead a life worthy of the one my mother lost.

She crossed herself and looked deeply into the sad, hooded eyes of the Martyr Empress. Alexandra looked back at her with steel, resolved to be Tsarina and wife of Nicholas II, whatever history may throw at her and her family. The peoples of Russia needed them, after all.

It began as a glimpse, something spied from a certain angle as a shaft of sunlight settled in a particular way and lit up the painting under the glass. Assia paused her veneration, distracted suddenly by what she just saw. *Surely not?* She went up to the iconostasis and picked up the icon of the Martyr Empress, holding it up to her nose so that she could scan it forensically. *Just here, I'm sure I saw a flash of pink. Just in the lower right corner as the sun glanced off the icon.* She held the *kiot* at an angle so that she could see it in a raking light. *Was it a trick of the light or a trick of the mind? Plenty would say I am prone to the latter…*

She turned around to check the door was still shut. She shouldn't do it, but the compulsion she felt was beyond her control – like a mole who has begun burrowing, she couldn't stop now until she hit stone. The *kiot* was locked. *Damn it.* Scrabbling in her handbag, she pulled out a small pair of nail scissors and used one of the blades to probe the locking mechanism. After a few moments of dextrous coercion, she smiled when she felt the pleasing motion of the lock turning and the lid of the *kiot* suddenly lifting away. She sat on the floor, legs straight out in front of her like a toddler, and prised the icon out of its velvet-backed nest.

The icon looked small out of its elaborate wooden casing. The border of the *oklad* was gilded, something which was not so discernible when it was in the *kiot*. Assia admired the engraved figures and painted faces of the Tsar and his children which surrounded the portrait of the Tsarina. Fairfax had commissioned the icon from a Russian silversmith when he was living in Harbin and, not having much money, the silver used was quite thin and unmarked but the overall effect was arresting. The Tsar and Tsarevich were pictured on either side of the Tsarina, while the Grand Duchesses were beneath her, two in each corner. Eastern Orthodox icon makers very often didn't render faces in the metal of the *oklad* but left oval holes in the silver or gold which would fit over a painted icon. This allowed an icon to display riches in the form of its precious metal *oklad*, sometimes with jewels or seed-pearls applied, as well as extraordinary immediacy in the painted face of a Saint or Biblical character. Although this icon had been painted in the early 20th century, the style of the painted faces was traditional, showing the Tsar and his children with oval faces, attenuated noses, small, plump lips and almond-shaped eyes which fixed you with their stare.

The miniature of the Empress was beautifully painted with delicate little brushstrokes which only emerged on closer examination. Gazing out at the viewer, she was shown from above the waist, wearing a square-necked dress with lengths of white embroidered chiffon gathered at the shoulders. She wore several strings of pearls, one further up her neck from which hung a large diamond which matched the large pendant diamond earrings she also wore. Her brown hair was pinned up with only the slightest suggestion of wispy curls around her forehead and a small gold coronet mounted with pearls sat atop her head. Her skin was a rich ivory with a slight apricot flush over the cheeks and the shading around her jawline and small, pointed chin emphasised the elegance of her bone structure. She appeared to be looking around and beyond Assia with a stare which seemed to dismiss and beseech at once.

It was the tiny little grey Cyrillic signature 'V. Zuiev' nestled in the white chiffon at the lower left of the Empress's dress which almost made Assia jump.

'Ah ha! Zuiev! Of course you are. This makes more and more sense.'

Trying not to warp the *oklad*, she pulled it gently around the sides to see if she could lift out the small silver nails which held it in place. She managed to coax two nails out this way and began to lift the rest with her nail scissors, all the while watching the door of the chapel anxiously. As the last nail fell onto the lacquered floorboards, Assia held her breath in a bid to quell the pulse beat which was racing at her temples. As slowly as she could, she lifted the *oklad* off the panel of wood.

The flood of warmth which rushed over her when she saw what was behind the icon cover both soothed and charged her at the same time. She couldn't believe what she was seeing and she glanced again at the door, worried that Evgenia would apprehend her. Resting in a velvet-covered niche was an oval-shaped frame of pink guilloché enamel which held the miniature of the Empress.

'My God,' said Assia, sliding her fingers under the silk and lifting the frame up. It was light and she held it up to her eyes easily, feeling the chill of the metal on her fingertips. Surrounding the small painting of the Empress was a slim border of pink enamel which was further surrounded by an intricate gold lattice inset with tiny pearls in a random pattern. The lattice was then encircled by another border of pink enamel on a wavy guilloché ground. It was so beautiful to behold that Assia scrunched up her eyes and opened them again to be sure that she wasn't in some prayer-induced reverie. Looking for the strut to the frame, she turned it around in her hand, expecting to find the standard ivory backing, tiny gold screws and a scrolled gold strut, but instead she gasped. At the verso of the miniature of Alexandra was a miniature of the Tsar in the uniform of the Preobrazhenskii Regiment with the duck-egg blue sash of the Order of St Andrew. His eyes were animated and Assia wondered if his expression harboured a hint of amusement. She looked at him again: 'So you found me!' answered his ice blue eyes, sparkling.

Ten minutes passed. Assia hadn't moved from her position on the floor, the *oklad* and small silver nails scattered to the left of her. She was mesmerised by the pink frame with pearls and couldn't pull her eyes from it, afraid that it might atomise if she looked away. She began cataloguing it with her eyes, taking notes in her mind: *Maker's mark for Albert Holmström, two rings of pink enamel intersected by a ring of lattice work set with half-pearls.* She stopped when she saw the small holes at the top and bottom of the frame. She rubbed her finger over them and without taking another breath, reached into the back part of the icon and lifted up the red velvet-covered backing board. An object spun around as the board was pulled off and Assia nearly choked when she saw something gold and white lying on the dark wood. Still holding her breath, she grabbed the object, a gold and white enamel cockle shell, opened its two beautiful halves and depressing a small, articulated spike in the outer rim of the shell's mouth, she inserted the frame so that it was suspended within the shells and could spin around.

She breathed out and marvelled. Cradled in her hand was an ingenious creation by Fabergé which had not been seen since John Fairfax hid it in an icon at least eighty years ago. The shell was truly exquisite: the ribs, which ran vertically along its body had been rendered in gold, while the troughs were filled with translucent, pearly white enamel. It was everything Fabergé was famous for – taking inspiration from nature and enhancing it so that the piece was both familiar and other-worldly at the same time. Girls love shells and little boxes and things they can keep secrets in – this was such a clever design for a present for a young woman. It just cried out to be clutched and hidden and then its secrets revealed in an intimate moment. She spun the miniatures and watched as the images of Nicholas and Alexandra whirled around, moving so quickly that his eyes became hers and her mouth his. She wondered if the Grand Duchess had done the same thing, sitting in a window seat in the Alexander Palace, looking out at the endless lawns and trees and thinking of the young man she loved. Maybe she planned to commission a miniature of him for the shell?

Questions swam in Assia's mind like a shoal of fish heading upstream, suggesting themselves and then darting away again. *Is this piece recorded? Which of Fabergé's designers created it? Why did Father Alexei hide it away?* But her mind kept rounding in on a concept which both alarmed and intrigued her: *the cockle shell and miniatures are the surprise for an egg.*

A parade of surprises from other Fabergé eggs assembled in her head: the ten-panel screen in the Danish Palaces Egg which unfurls to show perfect miniature paintings of the Empress Maria Feodorovna's favourite palaces and residences in Russia and Denmark; the (still-missing) folding red gold and sapphire miniature frame with six leaves from the 1896 Twelve Monogram Egg; the miniature articulated swan from the 1906 Swan Egg and the darling little elephant automaton from the Royal Collection which had only recently been identified as the surprise for the 1892 Diamond Trellis Egg. Holding the delicate shell in the palm of her hand, Assia dared to believe that it was the surprise to an egg. *Could it even be the surprise to Olga's egg? The real Olga's egg?* She felt as though she were bearing the key to another world, a world in which she and her mother were right and stood proudly like statues of Justitia and Prudentia shaming the St Petersburg Museum and their faux egg with their presence.

The shoal of fish leapt out the water to negotiate a waterfall and re-entered it, a volley of little silver bodies: *Where on earth could the egg be? Did it still exist? Did Father Alexei have it and if so, had he hidden it somewhere even more ingeniously than he had hidden the surprise?*

The floorboards creaked on the stairs outside the chapel door. Panicking, Assia began to gather everything up, slotting the miniatures into their niche in the velvet backing and lowering the *oklad* back on top. She was on her knees now, pressing the silver nails back into the icon cover when the door opened.

'Are you all right, sweetheart?' Evgenia hovered in the arched doorway, not wanting to intrude. Assia's position on the floor must have alarmed her because she rushed up to where she was sitting and knelt next to her.

'Dear God, what happened to the icon?'

'You need to see something, Evgenia.' Assia shuddered and tried to overcome her reticence. In that moment she didn't know if she was confessing something punishable or bringing Evgenia the best news she had ever heard. Evgenia's forehead wrinkled as she steeled herself for what the solemn-faced Assia was about to say.

Like a naughty child awaiting a smacked hand, Assia extended her arm slowly. Her fist was balled and she twisted it so her fingers faced the ceiling. Gradually, she peeled her fingers away to reveal the pearly white shell in her palm.

'What's that?' said Evgenia with the whip of anger in her voice. One side of her upper lip curled with confusion.

'It was hidden in the icon.' Assia touched the *oklad* approvingly. 'It's a gold and enamel cockle shell by Fabergé and it holds this miniature of the Tsarina in the icon. There is a miniature of Tsar Nicholas on the back, as well. My gut feeling is that it's a surprise for an egg.'

'Surprise? I don't know what you're talking about, Assia. Evgenia stood up and brushed the back of her dress. 'Can I hold it?'

'Of course.'

Assia handed the shell to Evgenia and opened the icon again to retrieve the miniature. She picked up the *kiot* to move it so that she could sit next to Evgenia and show her how the miniature fitted into the shell. Lifting the wooden case briskly, she sensed something; it was as light and imperceptible as a fingertip smoothing down silk.

She froze.

XXXIII

Ivan Borisovich Denisov stood next to one of the large lights with a white screen behind it which was pointing at the President. He watched a makeup artist fuss over the President and smiled to himself, knowing how much it would annoy his friend. The Russian flag was hanging from a small pole which had been positioned behind the President. He batted the makeup woman away and leant on the right arm of the gilded chair in a way which was more stiff and business-like than casual. His close-set eyes shrank into his face behind high, waxy cheekbones.

As the camera men set up, Ivan crossed his arms in a relaxed attitude and sensed the thread of a thought which had preoccupied him just before he fell asleep last night. He had read Aristotle's *Poetics* as a young man and it had occurred to him that Aslan Dudayev's life had been an ancient tragedy according to Aristotelian precepts. The Chechen leader had risen to fame and power in the beginning, but his fatal flaw had been to abuse this power and he had neglected to rule his kingdom properly. Then there had been the *peripeteia*, the grand reversal of fortune, when it appeared that Dudayev had been behind the theft of the Livadia Egg. Finally, all the loose ends had been tied up and Dudayev's tragedy was about to come to an end. Yes, he thought, this is good. I must share this with the President, it will amuse him no end.

Ivan congratulated himself as he watched the final act.

CAMERAS ROLL. THE PRESIDENT SPEAKS.

'Just a few months ago, I unveiled the first monument to Prince Vladimir the Great outside the Kremlin.

PAUSE. INEXPRESSIVE GAZE. LOOKS DOWN AT HAND.

'In doing so, I was honouring the founder of our nation state and recognising the sacrifices he made for the glory of our great nation. Few Russians can deny that we stand on the shoulders of history.

PAUSE. TRADEMARK DRY COUGH. MOUTH BRIEFLY COVERED WITH FIST.

'Five days ago Chechen terrorist-traitors stole the Livadia Fabergé Egg from an exhibition at the Moscow Manege. Their deadly attack on guards and guests at the exhibition was an abominable crime, a strike against the heart of Russia and it will stay with us for ever.

LONGER PAUSE. STROKES LARGE & HEAVY WATCH.

'What they do not realise is that history cannot be denied. Russia has always dominated the Caucasus and where necessary, stepped in to stop the people there destroying themselves. But these filthy Chechen terrorist-traitors have learned nothing from history. Historically, Russia has always sought retribution. It has always been inevitable. But Aslan Dudayev bit the hand that fed him. He knew about the plan to attack Russian people and heritage and he sanctioned it.

'Since this evil attack, Russian forces have not ceased in their mission to punish the perpetrators and recover the Livadia Egg for the Russian people. Aslan Dudayev has been eliminated and the Livadia Egg has been recovered in a Chechen safe house near Tambov.

'Russia has always fought terrorism in all its forms consistently. As part of this show of strength, when the damage caused by the philistine terrorists has been repaired, the Livadia Egg will continue its tour of Russia, a symbol of our dominance and invulnerability.'

ANOTHER EXPRESSIONLESS STARE. END OF SPEECH.

XXXIV

Mongolia, September 1918

The train drew to a halt again. Not that it took much to halt; it had barely picked up any speed to speak of since they had left Hailar. His eyes had become used to the soft grasslands of Mongolia; at first the vivid, lush green of the landscape looked so lurid it had made him rather queasy, but now he found that he felt a little peculiar if he couldn't see it on the horizon. He had come to need its piquancy in the same way that one comes to need a spice in cuisine.

He leant his head to the left, stretching out the muscle which ran along the right side of his neck to the shoulder, along the collarbone. Looking out of the window for long periods of time was beginning to take its toll on his lower back. He had tried sitting on the opposite side in the booth, but he couldn't stand to sit against the direction of travel – it disturbed his digestion. Occasionally, he liked to walk along the corridor and stand by one of the open windows, letting the cloud-steeped air smooth over his eyes and face, blowing away the visions of death which had woven cobwebs on his brow.

The sight of three women hanging from a tree by the tracks had upset him in particular. They had only just left Ekaterinburg and with the train moving at the usual snail's pace he hadn't had time to blink and miss the scene. One of them had a board dangling from her neck which declared in spindly letters 'We are counter-revolutionaries'. They were young women, late teens he surmised, and they wore their hair in short bobs, just like the Grand Duchesses when they were growing their hair back after it had been shaved during a life-threatening bout of the measles. He couldn't see the face of one of the girls because her thick hair hung over it like one of Anastasia's rag dolls, while the other two faced the railway tracks, their heads cast to one side in a gruesome pastiche of girlish coquettishness. He thought of the poor Grand Duchesses and the sobs burst out of his mouth in a coughing fit. He hadn't seen their bodies and he was torn between not wanting to believe they were gone and knowing it to be an absolute truth; he had seen the pit at Ganina Yama and the jewels, buckles and pieces of bone, but the bodies had gone.

Now, dangling before him were sweet young girls, strung up by filthy, Godless, Red Army soldiers. The Grand Duchesses were every young woman murdered by revolutionaries; the Empress, every mother weeping over a slaughtered son; and the Emperor, every man crucified, flayed and burned in this Apocalypse. Fairfax didn't want to leave Russia, but he had no choice now; he had to get out while the Whites still controlled the Trans-Manchurian line.

He took it out at least once a day and read it. Now they had left Russia and were deep into Central Asia, he read it more often so that their memory was stronger. He unfolded it carefully, aware that too much handling would wear it out of existence; the paper was jagged on its left side – torn from a diary, no doubt.

Ipatiev House,
Ekaterinburg,

Saturday, 13th July 1918

Dearest Fairfax,
    I hope Father Storozhev can get this to you safely.
    The house is much cooler this morning after last night's rain. Mama is feeling much better now that the heat has lifted a little. It had been so hot that we had barely been able to sleep a wink.

Do you ever catch sight of us out there? They raised the height of the fences around our small garden but naughty Anastasia still likes to jump and stick her hands up in the air when we take our walk. She likes to think that someone will see her hands and wave back, even though she wouldn't be able to see them waving.

I think of you when I read to our Alexei. He misses you too – he says being ill is no fun when you only have your family to torment. Dr Derevenko is our only visitor now – soon we shall forget that there is a whole world out there.

I should be so grateful if you could do something for me. Could you give the enclosed to Dmitri Shakh-Bagov? He is an officer of the 13th Life Yerivan Grenadier Regiment and I would like him to have it. They are stealing things from us here, from our trunks in the shed, and I don't want one of the guards to take it. It should go to Mitya.

Don't stay in Ekaterinburg, Fairfax dear. Go back to St Petersburg, find Mitya and then go home to England. We are not living in Russia anymore. Russia has gone.

With my love and thanks,
Olga

He pulled the linen bundle out of his leather case and cradled it gently. He didn't want to unwrap it again – it was too risky on a train full of strangers, especially a stopped train, but he drew comfort from holding it. Outside, a mother carrying a little child with dark plaits and nut-brown cheeks flushed with red stopped on the path which ran alongside the railway tracks to observe the train. Fairfax saw the little girl gazing at him curiously and he waved.

XXXV

Just the thought of what had happened leaked a euphoric shot into her bloodstream. It was impossible to sleep, especially as she could hear Evgenia snoring in the neighbouring bedroom. She sat up and the bed creaked loudly. She was staying in one of the spare rooms at the Chapel House: heavily patterned floral wallpaper and a tiny bedside lamp with a paper-thin shade. She got up to open the flimsy curtains and gazed at the night sky. The leaves on a tall chestnut in the garden twisted in the breeze, shining in the moonlight like silverfish. Was there someone outside watching her? Perhaps, but they had no idea what had gone on in the house – they could never have guessed at this.

You won't believe what happened today, Mama. Well, in fact, you will, because you were there with me, weren't you? You guided me – you must have done! How else would I have known what to do? Evgenia simply couldn't understand what I was doing when I held up the kiot *and ran my fingers along the cool grain of its wood. It is so beautifully made and my fingers were only just able to detect the opening, but that was enough. With a little pressure I managed to prise open this 'back door' and there, nestling innocently in a velvet lining was our lode star.*

Everyone dreams of making a great discovery – that Howard Carter moment when a hot and dusty dig becomes the gold-coated tomb of an ancient pharaoh, but until it happens, you cannot know how you will feel. I felt calm, so calm. No gasping – Evgenia was the one doing the oohing and aahing – and no sweating palms. Fate moved my hands and so it all happened without thought, without

239

prior knowledge – I was just acting instinctively and lit upon this small package. It was wrapped in calico, I think – something soft and pliant which had yellowed with age. The material unfurled easily – this was no brittle and dusty embalmment – and it rolled out, pure and brilliant, as fresh and exquisite as frost on a leaf. Your egg, her egg: Olga's egg.

Daisies, Mama! Clusters of fat milky white daisies cover the egg at random, just as they flower in crops in a meadow. And it's her – it's Pihl all over, as you knew. The egg is covered in a gorgeous pale green matt enamel which has been stippled to look like grass and is inset throughout with rough-cut emeralds and microscopic diamonds for dew drops. Olga's Cyrillic cypher of 'ON' is on the top and then there's the surprise of the cockle shell and the miniature portraits of Nicholas and Alexandra. The whole piece is an inspired mixture of classicism and the avant-garde – it's the most amazing work of art I have ever seen.

There was a letter folded up in the egg and I cried when I read it. It was written by Olga to her love Dmitri Shakh-Bagov and she says how she has entrusted the egg and its surprise to Fairfax – our Father Alexei – as a present to give to him. She writes movingly of hope and the belief that things will get better – 'from winter comes spring' – although to read it, you feel that in all actuality she has lost hope and is handing its torch to someone else. She knew that she was going to die and I think she was saying farewell to the world.

Father Alexei must have asked for the secret compartment to be made when he commissioned the icon and its kiot in Harbin. Of course it made sense to hide such an outrageously beautiful remnant of Imperial luxury while he was on the same continent as the Reds but Evgenia couldn't understand why her great-grandfather didn't display the egg in the chapel. I don't think she can grasp the idea that the Egg was like a splinter of the True Cross for Father Alexei. Olga entrusted it to him and it was a relic of the family he loyally served and loved. It was his mission to give the egg to Dmitri and perhaps he hoped that he would be able to find him one day – I am certain that he never stopped looking. Now that I have held the egg, I think I can understand some of what he must have felt – it was her *egg! It was made for her and she would have spent many hours looking at it and picking it up; the egg is so redolent of her that Father Alexei must have been transported back to the Alexander Palace and his time with the family when he held it. He was a devout man and he would never have sold the egg but perhaps he thought that his descendants would and hiding it so ingeniously was the only way to prevent it.*

To think, Mama, you were right about Olga's egg! Can you believe that it was here all along? All those Sundays we came here, bobbing before it and kissing it – we had no idea that the egg was right at the back of the icon. I like knowing that it has been in the same place for so long; the chain of its provenance has been unbroken and our link to Olga is the stronger for it.

We now have proof that the Livadia Egg is an out-and-out fake: we have the genuine article here in the Chapel. Evgenia has hidden the egg now – just for tonight – I suspect a part of her thinks I'll run off with it. I told her that we need to be very careful about the moves we make from now on and that I was followed and intimidated in London. I didn't know I would be leading them to the real egg when I came here. I am worried: not only is the egg enormously valuable, but the Russians will want to get it off us. They won't want their fake egg being upstaged and invalidated.

I'm not sure I trust Evgenia to handle it all correctly. Once we had digested the enormity of what we had found and took it downstairs to the kitchen, she cracked open a bottle of champagne and behaved as deliriously as a lottery winner. I suppose, in some ways, this egg is a winning lottery ticket for her – she is the sole heir to Father Alexei's property and therefore the egg is hers. She kept asking me what it was worth and I tried to deflect the question by saying that nothing like this has ever been on the market. I'm worried that she's already told people about it; she was fiddling on her phone after her fourth glass of champagne. She's probably announced it on Facebook. She doesn't realise what will happen if the Russians get wind of this. I don't even want to think about it.

I don't want her to sell it. I don't want her to be involved. This isn't about money – it's about you and me – and Olga Nikolaevna.

XXXVI

The hostess showed a party of Russian businessmen to their table. A herd of Cerruti suits, they followed her to a booth and filed along the seats of drum-tight leather.

Why do they always have to look so miserable? From a smaller booth, Edward watched the businessmen progress through the restaurant. *They're in one of the best restaurants in town, their wallets are fit-to-burst with cash and they probably have model wives at home. Surely they can't have expected such luxury when they were growing up in tiny little apartments in Kupchino?*

A bored waitress with a leather-apron stuffed with various shellfish-gouging tools appeared at his table and in a monotone asked if he was ready to order. Edward thought about smiling at her at her but decided against it – it would only alarm her and why break a habit he had spent years perfecting while living in Russia? He ordered twelve garlic snails, a plate of foie gras sushi and a bottle of French chardonnay which was wildly overpriced.

When she had gone, he pulled the pages with torn edges and placed them on the table in front of him. The booth was lit with a series of Danish low-hanging lamps and the drawings lay half in darkness and half in a pool of warm yellow light. The lamps swang softly in the wake of bustling waitresses and their light coursed over the designs like a searchlight.

The waitress returned to the table with a brushed silver wine cooler and the Chardonnay. He said he didn't need to try the wine but she hovered at the table as he took his first sip so that he had to dismiss her. He picked up the designs again and wondered how he had got here, to this point – sitting in a jazzed-up seafood restaurant near the Mariinsky Theatre, looking at some torn pages and thinking that he needed to leave Russia.

Had it begun on the plane, on that flight back from Moscow? Ivan had been repellent in his attitude towards Madeleine and it had upset Edward more than he himself had realised.

No, it wasn't just that, he thought. Ivan had proved himself to be some kind of vile misogynist, but that revelation hadn't really surprised him. Russia was full of racists, xenophobes, women-haters and gay-bashers; there were plenty of people who could intellectualise the supremacy of Russian Christians and under the current president, they were having a heyday.

No, it wasn't just that: it was the particular alchemy of circumstance, knowledge and suspicion which had put his hackles up. Assia's stubborn doubt, the promise of her love and then its absence, the harsh and sudden recognition of Ivan's power and threat. The payment: yes, the payment.

Ever since he had seen that payment listed, it had all begun to fall into place. He had tried to find ways to smudge the pattern into random happenings, incidents and coincidences, but his brain kept spying the ice-cold logic behind everything.

This was how it had all happened: at the start of the week, he had called in on Ivan's office. Marina had looked up from tapping away on her phone and smiled immediately when she saw him.

'You must be rushed off your feet. Would you like some chocolate-coated coffee beans this time?

'Thank you, I'd love one. It's been non-stop since the theft, of course. As you know, we're stalling the tour and it's caused a vast amount of upset and painful administration. Our insurers are not happy either. Actually, I wonder if you could help me – Galina's not here, is she? I need to double-check something on the donors' report against the amount sent to us. I'm caught between the insurers and the donors and it's not pretty.'

'No, she's not here. Sick again, apparently.' Marina rolled her eyes. 'Try me, though. My talents are infinite.' She held her hands over the keyboard and flexed her long and elegant fingers, poised to help.

'It would be amazing if you could. I need to check payments into Pegasus Holdings – the Panama account. You have access, don't you?'

'Of course I do. As much security clearance as Galina – probably more. As Ivan Borisovich's assistant, I have to be able to access these things.' She lowered her chin defiantly.

'Could we just pull up transactions from January of this year? The Mamontov Foundation for the Arts say they sent £800,000 from their UK account for the Nizhny Novgorod leg of the egg exhibition but I only have £745,000 recorded here. I just need to check what arrived in the account – it should have been in January.' Edward leaned over Marina's left shoulder and watched as she tapped away on the keyboard. She wore one of those sweet scents pushed at young women by the big brands – Dior or Armani, or somesuch – and the smell reminded him of airport duty-free shops and sex. She opened various windows on her computer screen and Edward found himself mesmerised by the deft movement of her hands and her upright posture – the way her back curved in slightly above her derrière. He wondered what kind of company she'd be over dinner and considered asking her out.

'So, I'm in the account now,' she said, glancing back at Edward. Her eyes were lined with kohl which made the whites of her eyes shine Disney white. 'I just need to scroll through… hmm. Not that.' She stroked the small red wheel on her mouse and scrolled through page after page of transactions for the account. Edward watched and read the data as it sped up the page: at first his brain refused the feed of information but then it began to flick through it as quickly as one might pick through paper files in a drawer. Marina was scrolling through the year from the bottom up, trying to get to January – he saw multiple payments in from Rorke LLC and out to Vesta Cape, along with many other company names which were as anonymous and neutral sounding as their owners hoped they would be.

Suddenly Marina stopped scrolling. 'Hang on, I think I've been in last year's book. Is that right? I'm not sure.'

The screen was static and Edward's eyes continued to scan it. And then he read it:

02SEP   KONSTANTIN A. STEPANYAN   600,000 USD

The page disappeared as Marina clicked into other windows.

'I'm sorry, I was in the transactions for last year, not this year. They make it rather easy to do, which is so silly. You would have thought a bank which handles such major transactions would have a better online platform.' More clicking. 'Right. Here we are. I'm scrolling up again to January.'

'Wait, could we go back again to the previous page?' Edward pointed at the screen.

'Why?'

'I just thought I saw a donor name I recognised.'

'But I'm in this year's book now – I thought that's what you wanted?' She sounded wounded and turned to look at him, frowning.

'Don't worry, it's fine. It doesn't matter. Carry on.'

'No, no, no. Let's go back.'

A few more clicks. There it was: he hadn't imagined it. The Museum's offshore holdings account had paid Konstantin Stepanyan $600,000. Why on earth would it have paid him such a vast amount? Had he bought something for the Museum's collection and they were reimbursing him? There could surely be no other reason why it would pay him over half a million dollars.

'OK, thanks, Marina. Let's go back to this year.'

After that, it was all he could think about. He tried to dismiss this newly acquired knowledge, to pretend that it was inconsequential, but it was impossible. At night, after a long day, his mind crawled over it; clattering across the plane of the subject, touching every aspect with an arachnid leg. It plagued him in the same way that a phone number scrawled on a book of matches in her husband's trouser pocket troubles a wife. He started to question what he knew: Konstantin had been a Fabergé specialist and restorer, hadn't he? That was what Assia had told him and from what he knew, he hadn't led the bountiful life of someone who had just been in receipt of a rather large sum of money by most people's standards. The only explanation he could land on which sounded vaguely plausible was that Konstantin must have made a discovery of an important piece of Fabergé and sold it to the Museum. But Ekaterina Arkadievna Vavilina, the longest-serving curator in the decorative arts at the Museum, when asked, said Konstantin was just a restorer for the Museum and had never sold them anything to the best of his knowledge.

'Kostya? Oh, no – he wasn't a dealer. He loved Fabergé too much to trade with it. He might have made the odd good find privately, but he would most likely keep those pieces and live with them before selling them on, reluctantly, and only to the right kind of connoisseur. None of those buffoons with more money than sense.' She sniffed and looked out of the window, trying to blink the tears out of her eyes and regain her composure.

'He was such a darling, that boy. He used to come here all the time when he was younger – you couldn't keep him away from the collection.' She sighed with a sad smile. 'I always used to laugh when I saw him at our door, waiting to get his hands on our Fabergé. Some days I would arrive home late because he had insisted on looking at all the Imperial Presentation boxes in the collection, or wanted to open our archives. But you know, he was never a nuisance. We all loved him and he taught me more about Fabergé than anyone else. We'll never find a better restorer than him – there were times when I did actually ask myself if he was the reincarnation of one of Fabergé's workmasters.'

Before he had left Ekaterina Arkadievna looking out of the window wistfully, Edward had told her that had bought his mother a miniature Fabergé pendant egg which needed restoring and asked if she had known of anyone who could do the job – perhaps someone who had worked with Konstantin Alexandrovich? Without blinking, she had waddled over to her desk and, flicking through her address book which was full of crossings-out and bits of paper, had copied something onto a Museum-headed compliments slip. She explained that Pyotr Shemetilo was the man to do it. He had trained under Konstantin and had a studio in the same block.

Driving away from Tsentralny Rayon and along the pylon-lined Vitebsky Prospekt to Pyotr's studio in Frunzenskiy, Edward wondered what the hell he was doing. This was the kind of crazy behaviour of which he had accused Assia – following a trail and refusing to turn back, like a sniffer dog whining by an empty car. He had thought she was utterly deluded and unhinged for questioning the authenticity of the Livadia Egg, but here he was now, speeding under a broad, blue Russian sky, desperate to find something – anything – that might support his hunch.

In his stuffy studio, Pyotr had offered him tea and a chocolate-covered plum to dip in it, presented on a small tray. Lanky with sloping shoulders and a sullen, down-turned mouth, he smiled broadly when Edward mentioned Kostya.

'Genius. Complete bloody genius.' He took a long draw on his cigarette. 'I was very lucky to learn from him. He was an alchemist, really – the first person to be able to enamel like the workmasters. He understood the science of metalwork but he had aesthetic vision as well. You need that to work with Fabergé.'

Sitting on a wooden stool in Pyotr's small workshop, Edward marvelled at all the tools and instruments stored neatly above his workbench. There were hundreds of little wooden drawers in a large dresser which ran up the wall, each of them labelled with their contents, 'Sheaths,' 'Files,' 'Lock-rings' and so on, and then hanging in order of size on racks of hooks were wrenches, spanners, pliers and other things which were used to manipulate metal and make it bend to the will of art. To the right of the large window which captured light from the east was a small icon of the Kazanskaya Mother of God.

Edward took a deep breath. 'Do you mind if I ask you something? Kostya was very close to a friend of mine and, well, I want to know: do you think he could have committed suicide?'

For a moment, Edward wondered if Pyotr had heard him. He was looking out of the window, his eyes fixed on a point beyond.

'It's a lonely life,' he said finally, without looking at Edward. 'You're committed to your art in a way which is very anti-social.' He crossed one long leg over the other. 'Even the way we have to work is not conducive to socialising: you have to bend over your bench for hours on end, looking at items in high magnification. You forget about the outside world.' He dipped his plum in the tea and nibbled at it. 'What I'm trying to say is that we are isolated out here. And Kostya was the brooding sort. He felt things very strongly but couldn't always express that strength of feeling in the right way. All geniuses are flawed, right?'

'OK, this is going to sound strange,' said Edward, moving onto his next difficult question. 'Do you think Kostya could have made the Livadia Egg?' He curled his fingers around the thumb on his left hand and squeezed it tightly.

'What?' Pyotr put down his teacup and frowned. 'The Livadia Egg? The one that has just been stolen? What are you talking about?'

Edward unfurled his fingers and placed his hands squarely on his knees. 'Apologies, Pyotr, I'm being clumsy here. It's easier if I explain it like this: my friend, Anastasia Wynfield, was very fond of Kostya and that is how I came to know about the sad news of his death. For a while now, Assia – you must know her? – has been convinced that the Livadia Egg is not authentic and recently I came across something which made me think that perhaps Kostya himself made the egg.'

Edward held his breath, waiting for Pyotr's reaction.

'Of course I know Assia,' muttered Pyotr, waving his long fingers. 'The mournful beauty of the Fabergé world.' He sighed. 'Well. Where do I begin? The Livadia Egg – it's not my favourite, granted, but that doesn't mean it's fake. It would be impossible for one person to fake a Fabergé egg anyhow. They were great collaborative masterpieces – no single person made them because so many different elements were involved. The best engraver, the best carver, the best artist, the best enameller; all of them were needed to make the greatest works of decorative art ever made.' He used his unusually curved thumb to push the rest of the chocolate plum into his mouth and he carried on speaking while sucking on the plum. 'But here's what I'll say on the matter – if anyone could make one, if anyone *had* to do it, it would have been Kostya. You know what they say about restoration being the midwife to forgery. And now I've said that, you'll have to tell me why you think he made it.' He raised his eyebrows.

'Well, I just found out that the St Petersburg Museum paid a sum of $600,000 to Kostya and I believe they paid him to make the Livadia Egg. I have looked into every other explanation, and that is what I came up with. Am I insane?' He threw his hands into the air in frustration. 'Listen, if Kostya had *found* the Livadia Egg and sold it to the Museum, he would have sold it for a lot more than half a million dollars, wouldn't he? And he didn't sell them anything else because I checked with the Fabergé team there.'

'Perhaps the $600,000 was a part payment and you don't know about the other twenty million dollars they sent him for it. On the open market, that egg would worth at least thirty mil.'

'Maybe. But when you have that kind of money, it's hard to hide it from everyone around you. It would have been news pretty quickly. And don't you think he would have told the world that he'd made the most exciting discovery in the history of art? I'd be screaming it from the rooftops and cashing in on the publicity.'

'He wasn't like that.' Pyotr shook his head and wrinkled his nose as though disgusted by the concept.

Edward persisted. 'Did you ever see what he was working on in his studio?'

'Occasionally. But he would mostly pop in here for a cup of tea and a chat and to take a look at what I was working on. His studio was broken into after he died and they took the safe where he kept his materials and things he was working on. That kind of thing happens quite regularly round here. The management are pretty hit and miss on security.'

'Who's in the studio now?'

'No one, as far as I know. But I have quite a few boxes of Kostya's books and paperwork.' He waved at a pile of boxes which were stacked precariously next to a small table groaning with towers of books. 'Kostya's sister cleared it and she asked me if I wanted his library and workbooks because she didn't know what to do with them. I've been meaning to go through them but I haven't had time.'

'May I?' Edward was already unstacking the boxes and pulling out books.

'Well, yes, er... please can you keep some semblance of order? Yelena Alexandrovna was careful to replicate Kostya's shelf system when she packed the boxes.'

Edward grabbed a book from the box and began flicking through it quickly. A cloud of dust rose in the sunlight as the pages snapped past like a pack of cards.

Pyotr put his teacup down on the work table so that the spoon jangled exaggeratedly. He swivelled his stool around to face Edward who was crouching over the second box he had opened.

'You know, up until he died, I didn't see Kostya much. But there was something which stuck in my mind. People other than us jewellers don't come here much, so you always notice a new face.' He began to fiddle with his chin as he spoke, as though debating whether or not to speak.

Edward put down the books he was holding. 'Yes,' he said this gently with only a hint of a question, not wanting to distract Pyotr's train of thought.

Pyotr decided to continue, frowning slightly with the effort of recollection. 'I remember thinking that he dressed very smartly. He would have been handsome in jeans, but he cut quite a figure in his Brioni suit with brogues and his black saffiano leather case. I'd only seen him in the papers but I got quite used to seeing him here – he came at least once a month over the past year. Kostya said he was an old childhood friend. They knew each other from school – they ran some art history club, or something. In fact, you'll know him from the Museum, he's a Trustee.'

'Who was it?' Edward sounded impatient. He wanted Pyotr to say the name.

'Ivan Borisovich Denisov.'

XXXVII

Konstantin Stepanyan's Studio, St Petersburg, Eighteen Months Earlier

Kostya unwrapped his fifth Kis Kis toffee and smoothed the wrapper with his large thumb before placing it on the pile he had built next to his teacup. He pushed the bowl of sweets towards his visitor.

'I've given up the sweet tooth of my childhood.' Ivan pushed the bowl back towards Kostya.

'I don't seem to be able to. It's a congenital defect in my family. You should see how many Alenka bars Yelena can eat in one sitting.'

'How is Lena these days?' Ivan pulled at the knot of his tie and took a sip of his boiling hot tea.

'Oh, you know. Widowed. Bored. In need of grandchildren. She bothers me instead.'

'Ha.' Ivan laughed half-heartedly and shifted on the stool he was perched on. 'How can you sit on these things all day?' he asked reproachfully.

'Better for the back. And I need something which swivels so that I can grab various tools and the like. A normal chair with arms would get in the way.'

'It's quite a set of tools you have here.' Ivan nodded admiringly at the banks of tools. 'The studio of a true master of his art.' He tipped his head back slightly and looked at Kostya down his nose.

'I don't know about that.' Kostya fumbled with another sweet.

'It's what I've heard on the grapevine. And it makes perfect sense; you were always deft with your hands, even way back when. Do you remember that beautiful birch wood box you carved in the shape of a heart? The one you gave to me so that I could win over that sexy girl Katya? It was quite a piece – even the President still remembers that box.' He laughed loudly as he reminisced. 'And it worked! I bedded her on our first date.' He shook his head with amusement. 'Girls are just magpies really. They'll do anything for a trinket.'

'Hmm.' Kostya looked down at his hands awkwardly.

'Now.' Ivan drummed his fingers on the work surface. 'The reason I'm here. Didn't you once tell me that Fabergé made an egg for the Grand Duchess Olga Nikolaevna and that it's missing? No one has ever seen it?'

'Yes, that's right.' Kostya straightened his back. 'Olga Morozova's research led her to believe it was made.'

Ivan slammed his hand down on the table excitedly. 'Olga Morozova! That's right! The love of your life! How could I forget? Is she still with that English chap, the one who was so obviously a spy?' He leant forward animatedly, eager to consume any emotion Kostya might register.

'He wasn't a spy.' Kostya pursed his lips and held Ivan's greedy gaze. 'Olga's dead. She was killed in a car crash thirteen years ago.'

'Ah, oh dear.' Ivan grimaced exaggeratedly. 'The heart is a cruel organ. It takes a long time for the hurt to fade, doesn't it? I hope the bastard responsible was punished.' He was serious now, angry.

'Her daughter, Anastasia, was at the wheel.' An intense plush spread up Kostya's throat. 'She's been punished enough.' He picked up another sweet and held the twists between his thumb and index finger before putting it down again. 'She's a well-respected Fabergé expert now, like her mother. She managed to put her life back together, which is more than I can say for myself.'

'Listen.' Ivan put the sweet Kostya had rejected back into the bowl. 'The egg – the Grand Duchess Olga's egg …'

Kostya narrowed his eyes expectantly when Ivan let his words trail off unfinished. 'Yes?'

'That egg. Make it for me.'

XXXVIII

Edward took a large swig of whisky and gazed at the charming little Dobuzhinsky watercolour which hung next to his bookshelf. It was a beautiful stage design for Tatiana's drawing room in Petersburg for a 1935 production of Tchaikovsky's *Eugene Onegin*. The spire of the Admiralty rose on the horizon, seen through a window draped with heavy tasselled curtains. The room had all the attributes of a salon where a society woman would receive her esteemed guests. Here, Tatiana would receive Onegin and observe him coolly as he declared his love for her, as she herself had done to him all those years ago as a young girl preoccupied with romance. Dobuzhinsky's style was light and deft – the architectural detail of the ornate mouldings in the room rendered expertly with quick lines and flourishes. Edward liked to stare at the watercolour and play out the scene in his head – if you owned a stage design you were obliged to populate the stage every night in your head; it positively demanded it of you, he thought. In some of his stagings Tatiana would laugh at the supplicant Onegin, ridiculing him for being too late to win her; in others, she wept with him kneeling at her feet – fat tears rolling down her pale cheeks as they both lamented the fickle and empty life of a gentleman who had missed his one chance to be happy without realising it.

'You were right all along. I believe you now. I'm sorry.'

He read it again. He could see that she had received and read the text two days ago but she still hadn't responded to him. He couldn't blame her really, it was a pathetic message. He had hoped that she might be intrigued by his change of heart and moved by his apology, but he should have remembered that Assia was stubborn and she was almost certainly still furious with him, no doubt blaming him for putting Madeleine in harm's way.

'I have proof that Kostya made the egg.'

He had another swig of whisky and pressed 'send.' His little dart flew through the night skies, dodging the million other darts fired every second; with hunter's precision, it landed right in her phone.

His phone rang immediately. He looked at it and smiled happily, acknowledging at the same time that he had had far too much to drink.

'Hello!' he cheered, his voice thick with booze.

'You're a moron. And a drunk one. Don't send things like that on your Russian phone. Get your English phone and Skype me. And if you're in your flat, go outside to do it otherwise they'll hear you.'

The line went dead. Sprawled on his sofa, Edward looked sheepish. He hauled himself up with an old man's groan and staggered to the bedroom where he riffled in his bedside table for his English phone.

Outside in the pale blue Petersburg night, he looked around half-heartedly and leant against the wall of his apartment block while he fiddled on his phone.

'Hello? Assia? Can you hear me? I can't see you.'

'I know you can't. I've switched the picture off. I can see you though. Can anyone hear you?'

'No, I don't think so.' He looked around again. He was shivering slightly.

'So. Tell me. The proof?' She sounded impatient.

'Drawings. Kostya's drawings. I found his designs for the Livadia Egg. They were stuffed into one of the books from his studio and Petya Shemetilo and I found them. They're incredibly detailed. He made the Livadia Egg, Assia! And…

um… and I saw a transaction in the Museum's accounts. They sent him $600,000 from an offshore account. I don't know what for, but it has to be for the egg.' He was speaking quickly, nervously, as though he were reporting to an angry superior.

'My God. OK.' A pause. 'You need to send me pictures of the drawings right away, and can you get proof of that payment to Kostya?'

'I can try, but it's going to be difficult.' He looked around anxiously and cupped his hand over his mouth. 'Petya said that Ivan Denisov had been to Kostya's studio many times. He saw him there.' He said these last words slowly, emphasising the significance of what he was relating to Assia. The devil had been sighted.

'And where is the Livadia Egg now? Is it back on display?'

'No. They're sending it to Petya for restoration. The terrorists did not treat it gently, apparently.' He took a deep breath. 'I want to quit, Assia. I want to come back to England. Back to you.'

'You can't, Edward. You need to stay there, please.' Her tone softened marginally. 'Please. And listen, I need you to ask a favour of Petya – a big one.'

Edward pulled his phone headphones out forlornly. It was 11pm and the sky was milky with a stain of blue, as though a paintbrush had been dipped into a jar of cloudy water. He felt as though he was just sloping out of an all-night party with a bad hangover and a black eye. *Damn this wretched city.* As he turned to go back into his apartment block his heart stopped as it registered someone melting away from the corner of the yard.

XXXIX

Three Weeks Later

For the first time in as long as she could remember, Assia realised that she missed her mother. She ran her breath through her nose and listened to the slow exhalation and the animal noise of her breathing. For years she had fought this feeling, squeezing it in her fist and moulding it into something sharp and ugly to hurt herself with. Her father and sister were allowed to grieve – grief was the indulgence of the victims of her crime – but she was only allowed to repent of her actions and lead a small life in apology. Dr Morton, her psychologist, had, at some point during their many sessions, suggested that she was a fervent adherent of Jung's concept of psychic synchronicity because she believed that her role in her mother's death was a punishment sent by the universe for being defective. According to him, she spent too much time wrestling with the great Hydra of coincidence and occurrence, all the while refusing to accept that she was just a tiny little ball bearing in the random explosions of life.

'A colleague of mine reminded me of a scene in *American Beauty*, that film with Kevin Spacey. Have you seen it? Do you recall the scene where one of the characters films a plastic bag being blown about in the wind because he sees beauty in it? It is rather wonderful, isn't it? Imagine, Assia, that you are that white bag. Let yourself be blown about and buffeted by life's extraordinary randomness. Don't fight it. You are using all your energy fighting something you cannot control and it is making you ill.'

The rhythm of her breathing calmed her and loosened the knot in her stomach. *Riddle me this, Dr Morton. How many floating bags does it take to magic a Fabergé egg into a wooden box which you have been staring at your whole life?*

She tried not to think about tomorrow's event because every time she pictured it, the cold hand of adrenalin grabbed her insides and she felt as though she might faint. Tomorrow was the day she took on Goliath and she needed to be in the best possible frame of mind. Her father had asked if she wanted to join him this evening at high-table at St John's to take her mind off things and she had been truly touched by the gesture. Without really meaning to she had told him some of what she was planning to do tomorrow and he had put his hand on her shoulder and pressed it warmly, saying 'Courage, ma chérie!' Assia had surprised herself by hugging him back and he responded by putting his long arm around her and stroking her head. It was such a modest show of affection but it had been enough to make her weep hot snotty tears. Her father held her back to look at her blotchy face.

'You need no instruction in how to take on the Russians, but I think you'll find that a cup of my Turkish coffee in the morning will help. Cardamom is very soothing. Your mother always found it set her up well for the day.'

In her father's hallway, she straightened the picture in front of her, one of the prints from *A Rake's Progress* which hung in walnut frames with ivory mounts on the chalky Georgian green walls. She knew the engravings well from sight but she had never really engaged with Thomas Rakewell's rackety progress. In the print before her, Tom was kneeling on the floor of a gambling den, shaking his fist at the Almighty. His wig lay on the floor, pulled off in frustration, and a little dog barked excitedly, its front paws quivering on the chair Tom had knocked over. Behind the luckless Tom and the eager card players, smoke was billowing into the panelled room unnoticed.

XL

The dome of the Radcliffe Camera rounding on the horizon brought a sting of tears to Edward's eyes as the taxi drove up the High. He turned to look out of the car window so that Ivan, who was sitting next to him, couldn't see his face.

'It's a long way to come for a bloody book launch,' muttered Ivan tapping on his phone disdainfully.

Edward chose not to comment and smiled to himself. Thankfully he hadn't been next to Ivan on the flight from Petersburg but he had barely been able to stand being on the same plane as the man. After a few moments he leaned forward to direct the driver. 'Can we pull up here, please? Ivan Borisovich, that's your hotel just there. The Old Bank.'

'Where are you staying?' frowned Ivan as he climbed out of the car.

'I've made other arrangement with friends. I'll see you at the Ashmolean.'

Edward gave the taxi driver his friend's address and they sped off up the High and down along St Aldate's on the circuitous route to West Oxford. He was longing to get away from anything to do with Russia. Everything so far had been a poker game, but he couldn't reveal his hand quite yet. Even when Kostya's drawings had been stolen from his apartment a couple of weeks ago, he had known to bite his tongue. The way they had turned everything over, ripped pages from books, pulled his Dobuzhinsky off the wall and stamped on the glass: all of it felt like a slap. There was nothing he could do while he was in Russia. Everything was acknowledged but nothing was spoken. Turn the other cheek.

Yes, it was good to be in Oxford. This was his turf, a city he knew like the back of his hand. The Russians would have to think harder about how to provoke him in his own land – it would have to be something elaborate, something more fantastic than a cup of irradiated tea or a padlocked bag. He had escaped Piter and he wasn't going back now, back to where the skin between his shoulder blades prickled every second for fear of a gun being pressed into it. Kostya had preoccupied his thoughts ever since he had worked out what had happened to him – this man, whom he had never met, suddenly loomed large in his St Petersburg life. He found himself wondering if Kostya had seen the view from this angle of the Anichkov Bridge or whether he had eaten at the small café on Favorsky. Kostya became his friend in fear – when he had a sense of foreboding that today might be the day, he thought of Kostya and derived a certain comfort from knowing that someone else had known what it felt like. It did occur to him that perhaps Kostya hadn't been scared – surely he must have known that his days were numbered when he made the egg? But he had made it anyway. Maybe he didn't want to be around anymore, mused Edward. After all, Olga, his great love, was dead and someone at the heart of the Kremlin was commissioning fake Fabergé eggs.

It was on a particularly beautiful July evening in St Petersburg, walking in the Summer Gardens and pausing to look at the river through the delicate grille of cast-iron railings suspended between elegant granite columns, that he had become aware of an affinity with Kostya that went beyond that of shared fear. *Did you stand here and think of her, as I am thinking of Assia now? What actually happened between you and Olga? Was she like her daughter, blowing hot and cold all the time? Was it easier to love her from afar?* He leant his cheek on the cool iron and pressed it gradually harder so that he could feel the perpendicular ridge of the railing grind against his cheekbone. He wondered why he was still here in Russia and why he hadn't just upped and left and gone back to a safer, softer life in Britain. He rolled his cheek, allowing the cool iron to knead the strings of muscle on the right side of his face. *I'm waiting for something*, he thought. *I'm waiting for life to happen to me.* There and then, gazing through the railings, he saw Kostya. Yes, there he is, pushing open the door of his daughter's apartment block, pausing as he inhales the cold outside. I can see him. He's following the path which has been cut through the snow, head down, gloved hands in pockets. You can't see his eyes beneath his hat and his mouth is just a grey-blue line above black stubble. Now a skinny young man is coming out of the apartment block behind him, huge shiny black headphones bulging beneath his hood. His large red hands are shoved deep into the pockets of his navy blue puffa jacket and he's nodding his head slightly as though keeping time with a beat. He seems to be walking in the same direction as Kostya, striding along the tarmac which is lined with muddy slush on either side. Kostya crosses a patch of virgin snow to meet another path and the youth crosses too, stamping in Kostya's footprints on the snow. He takes his phone out to look at it, puts it in his pocket again, glances around and speeds up so that he is just a couple of yards behind Kostya. *Kostya, turn around! I think you need to look behind you. Kostya! Kostya?* The young man takes something out of his pocket – a gun – and presses it into the small of Kostya's back. At first Kostya doesn't notice and the skinny youth continues keeping pace behind him, stretching his hand forward so the gun is still in place. Then Kostya stops suddenly – perhaps the youth said something to him – but he doesn't turn around, instead he looks up at the sky through the bare and gnarled branches of the tree above him and smiles.

The taxi pulled up outside the small Victorian terrace and Edward used the brass knocker to bang on the glossy green door. He could hear a child crying and a woman's voice reasoning gently. The crying came closer to the door as it was opened and a blonde woman appeared.

'Ed, hello! This is Mummy's friend, Edward,' she said to the red-faced toddler in her arms who immediately buried his head in her shoulder. 'Come on in. Let me take your bag.'

'Goodness no, Toni, don't be silly. It's light as anything, anyway. It's great to see you.' They embraced and kissed each other on the cheek. 'I hope I'm not disturbing nap time or anything?'

'Not at all! Grown-up company is always in demand here. Have a sit-down and let me put the kettle on. Could you watch Ivo just for a second? Thanks.'

Edward sat on the deep sofa in the sitting room which was connected to the kitchen by an archway and looked around at the beautiful high-ceilinged room. Piers and Antonia had some wonderful pictures – a few enchanting small watercolours by John Varley along with a handful of old master landscapes which they had hung against an earthy Etruscan red – and sitting in the strong summer light streaming through the large bay windows, Edward imagined the sun infusing him with its strength. He started at the clink of mugs and opened his eyes to see Ivo grinding some PlayDoh into the carpet. Periodically the little boy stared at him, mouth slightly open, watching unashamedly in the way that only children can. Edward put his thumb on his nose, wiggled his fingers and blew a raspberry, feeling a surge of unexpected pleasure when Ivo giggled infectiously.

'So how is Russia, land of the Tsars?' Antonia came into the sitting room with a tray of mugs, biscuits and a large cafetiere. 'Is it as romantic and exciting as it sounds to a stuck-at-home mother of a two year-old?' She leant on the pommel of the cafetiere so that the filter sank down slowly.

'You're living the dream, believe me. Beautiful house, beautiful child, safety and security. Russia is the opposite. It's still the land of the Tsars, the only difference is that the current Tsar is known as the President.' He took the mug of coffee Antonia handed to him. 'Thank you, just what I need.' He stuffed a cushion behind his back on the sofa. 'It's Manichean,

Toni: dark and light. What you see happening there is onstage – it's what they want you to see – and what they don't want you to see happens backstage, in the dark.'

'So not particularly romantic then. And there was I thinking it would be all fur hats and *Doctor Zhivago*.' Antonia sat on the floor with her coffee and picked at the PlayDoh on the carpet.

'It's funny you should mention *Zhivago*. I was thinking about it the other day when I saw the spine of the book in someone's library.' Edward leant forward and stroked Ivo's head as the little boy ambled over. 'Toni,' he addressed her urgently. 'Did you know that the CIA submitted the manuscript of *Zhivago* to the Nobel Committee and they bought thousands of copies of the book to turn it into an acclaimed bestseller? Their plan was to get it to win the Nobel and hence enrage the Communists and compromise the reputation of the Soviet Union. They used the novel as a weapon, a Trojan Horse of sorts. This is what the Russians have been up to with the Livadia Egg – the one that was stolen. They've been using it to manipulate events. It's the ultimate post-truth tool.'

'Hell, Ed, I live such a bloody sheltered life. Oh, crap, I keep forgetting not to swear in front of Ivo.' She laughed and covered his ears with her hands. 'I use motherhood as a means of putting distance between myself and geopolitics. It's quite a good tactic – you should try it.' She laughed. 'Distance, I mean, not motherhood. You should try that though – fatherhood, of course. Talking of which, are you and Assia still dancing around each other? And what's her book about? Are you sure she wants me to come to the launch? I haven't seen her since the accident.'

'In answer to your first question, I have no idea. I adore her, but you know what she's like: *splénétique*, stubborn, totally unpredictable. Everything you want in a woman!' He paused to smile as he thought about Assia, before blinking and returning to the moment. 'And yes, she really wants you to come. The book is very important to her, it's her mother's *Encyclopaedia of Fabergé Eggs*.' His phone rang and he took it out to check the screen. 'I'm so sorry, Toni, I've got to get this. One second.'

Chewing on a Sticklebrick, Ivo studied the man with the phone solemnly. When the man raised his voice and stood up quickly, Ivo hurried to his mother.

'Is everything OK, Ed?' Antonia said, concerned.

'No, not really. Sorry, Toni, I've got to go. Classic Assia. Classic self-destructive behaviour.' He shook his head and narrowed his mouth angrily before lightening as he waved at his hostess and her child. 'Sorry, I'm so sorry. I'll be back later.'

'... and hot beverages and biscuits will be brought out and put on this table at the end of your talk by the staff from the coffee shop downstairs. The biscuits are gluten free and the milk is organic and there is soy milk available too.' She kneeled and pointed to a wire taped to the floor. 'There's a power point here for your publisher's card machine and please let people know that your book will soon be stocked in the Gift Shop downstairs, all right? Oh, and just in case anyone wants to know, these are known as the Arundel Marbles and the Randolph Sculpture Gallery is available for hire to anyone like yourself, all right?' Polly Marshall waved her clipboard at the colonnade of sculptures which lined the gallery and pushed her designer glasses back on her nose. 'I'm in my office if you need me, all right?'

Assia watched as the Operations Manager for the Ashmolean strutted back along the gallery to her office, clicking her heels along the way. She thought how absurd she looked passing the white marble sculptures of gods and goddesses in her tight high-street trouser suit, believing that all the world needed was a Microsoft Outlook Calendar and soy milk. Assia approached the sculpture of an Amazon on a plinth and ran her finger along the folds of cloth which clung to the torso. The Amazon was headless, armless and her legs stopped at the knee but she was perfection in her deathlessness, her shoulders arranged so that you could imagine her reaching back to pluck an arrow from her quiver. Assia thought that this gallery of ancient marble was the right place in which to make her offering to the world of objects which survived men.

Glancing at her watch, she sat down and flicked through her notes again. She had checked and double-checked that the computer was hooked up to the projector and she'd been through her slides so many times that to do so again would be ragingly neurotic. She sprang up, smoothing her Diane von Furstenberg wrap dress and walking over to the table which was stacked with heavy books with glossy dust-jackets. She picked one up and smelled the pages – that gorgeous scent of thick, processed paper which was an opiate for bibliophiles. The title page read '*The Encyclopaedia of Fabergé Eggs/ by Olga Morozova Wynfield/ revised and updated by Anastasia Wynfield/ with an appendix on the Imperial Egg of Olga Nikolaevna/ In Memoriam Olga Morozova Wynfield, 1952–2002*'.

'My God, Assia, this is amazing!' Tanya suddenly appeared by her side and stroked the cover of one of the books. 'Mama would be absolutely thrilled. It looks really beautiful. Are you nervous? I'm nervous for you.'

Assia jumped when she heard Tanya's voice and then laughed at her exaggerated reaction. 'Thank you, Tanyusha! I'm glad you think it works. I hope Mama would have liked it. It's been a labour of love really, and of repentance.'

Tanya frowned, her pretty little mouth puckered into an angry 'O'. She took Assia's hand and stroked it. 'You have nothing to repent for. Understood? The only thing you need to apologise for is for not having allowed yourself to be happy a long time ago.'

Assia squeezed her sister's delicate hand and decided to believe her. 'I'm still not convinced that Papa will ever feel so kindly towards me though.'

'You're probably right' said Tanya, adjusting her belt buckle, 'but that's nothing to do with you and everything to do with him. I know you think that while you've been out in the cold as the pariah, he and I were comforting each other every evening and hating you, but that just wasn't the case. I think she realised that he couldn't love us in the right way without Mama there – she was some kind of conduit to his emotional pool and when she died, he raised the drawbridge. Anyway, damn him. I'm going to fetch the old bugger. Save us some seats. *Bonne chance, ma chérie.*'

'I'll keep some at the front for you!' said Assia as Tanya wound her way back through the rows of silver chairs. A few people drifted into the gallery through the large rotating glass door of the Museum and sat down at the back, fiddling with their phones and getting pens and pads out of their bags. Seeing unfamiliar people there didn't cow her, in fact she preferred addressing strangers – it was the familiar faces which floored her, the people who knew her and would quite reasonably surmise that she couldn't pull off what she planned to do right now. The tide of anxiety which she had been keeping at bay began to creep higher, eroding her nerves and wearing away the bulwark of confidence she had carefully erected. A flush spread up her neck and red strips flared under her cheekbones. She could feel her face reddening and began to panic that no one would take a girl in a fancy wrap dress with Dutch doll cheeks seriously.

The crowd that had gathered was standing and sitting in clumps throughout the gallery. People leaned over chairs to talk to each other and Assia could see their lips moving but couldn't hear what they were saying. She was as remote and separate from her audience as an animal in an enclosure. She felt annoyed with them, angry even. Yes, she had summoned them here, but there was something about their expectations which made her want to scream.

The sound of hurried footsteps drew her eye to the back of the gallery and she saw Edward coming towards her, waving and nodding at people in the platitudinous and dismissive way that only an Englishman could. Her stomach folded in on itself at the sight of him: the profile he cast when he glanced to one side, the slope of his shoulders, the little V where his crisp shirt collar met above his tie – all of the code that the wretched mind learns involuntarily as part of some Darwinian script.

'Hi! You made it!' She stepped back as she smiled at him, perturbed by the way he made for her, as direct and sure as an arrow. He glowered at her, his hands shaking slightly as he grabbed her shoulders. She could feel his fingers pressing through the thin cotton of her dress, rigid with tension.

'What the hell are you doing?' He moved her roughly to the side. 'Are you insane? Do you have a death wish?'

'What do you mean?' Her eyes widened. She had never seen him so angry.

'Ivan Denisov knows about the *Encyclopaedia*. He knows you're not putting the Livadia Egg in it. He just rang me and I had to tell him that it was news to me too. He has ordered me in no uncertain terms to stop you. I thought we agreed that you would keep the Livadia Egg in the book and that the police would deal with the evidence we gave them?'

'I couldn't, Edward. I'm sorry. I just couldn't bring myself to include it. It felt like a betrayal of Mama. I can't include something fake in the book just to keep the Russians happy.'

She looked at her feet like a chastened school girl.

'You can't launch the book,' he said. 'You'll have to back-pedal and then get it re-published with the egg in it. And have you even been to the police?'

'Yes and no.' She bit her lip in an attempt to indicate guilt and appear endearing at the same time. 'Mark Smith from the Art and Antiques Squad at New Scotland Yard is coming to the talk. I've told him I'm revealing something important.'

'Oh, for goodness' sake, Assia! This isn't an art crime – it's a crime against humans. A murder! So, the police know nothing about what they did to Kostya? Don't you think they'd want to know? The CIA are interested – a few agents are accompanying Madeleine here today.' He breathed out heavily and looked up at the heights of the gallery as though entreating the gods. 'And you're planning to provoke the Russians now by declaring to the world that you're not putting the Livadia Egg in the *Encyclopaedia*? Nice work. Really well planned.'

'Do you think you could just wait and listen to my talk? I've…'

'You know they'll take you down because of it,' he continued hurriedly. 'They'll go for you in every way that they can. These are not people you mess with. You're behaving as though you don't know about all the journalists and opposition voices they've had killed.' He longed to shake her and bring her to her senses. 'Denisov is already apoplectic. If you doubt the authenticity of the egg then you're blowing the Russians' pretext for killing Dudayev and subjugating Chechnya.' He looked around them anxiously.

'I don't live in Russia, Edward. I can say what I like here. And I have to present this in public. It's the only way to hit them where it hurts. Appearances are everything to the Russians and if I can pull back the mask, that's the war won. Listen, I haven't told you everything that's happened recently – I couldn't because they're following you and it would have got out. *Please* just wait and see and all will become clear.'

'You're mad. You know I can't protect you if you do this, Assia.' He released his grip and looked away sadly.

'You have to believe me, Edward. I can do this. I have an ace up my sleeve and I know what I'm doing. It's not over yet and I need to finish it.' She stepped into his line of vision and looked up at him earnestly. 'I owe it to Mama.'

'*That's* what worries me, Assia. You feel you owe her everything and you don't. You can't keep destroying yourself in apology for what happened.' His voice was flat and thinned with disappointment. He waited for her to say something and when she didn't he turned and walked to the back of the gallery and out of the revolving door of the museum.

XLI

There was only a small amount of standing space at the back. An excited charge cracked in the air as people chatted and waited for the presentation to start, occasionally glancing back to see how full the gallery was. The Director of the V&A, the Senior Curator from the Royal Collection, Heinrich, the Hermitage: they were all there except the contingent from the St Petersburg Museum. Assia hadn't expected so many people to attend and she began to wonder if Edward had been right. This was bigger than her. Attempting to control it was like trying to steer a vast articulated lorry on winding icy road. Her stomach began to tighten and she could feel the familiar brick of nausea travel up her throat.

Tanya and her father were sitting on the right-hand side, a few rows back from the front. Richard looked solemn. He was staring straight ahead at the projector screen and Assia thought how old he looked as she studied his face. His hair was still thick but had more grey than colour in it now and broken capillaries gave him an unnatural flush over the bridge of his nose and at the top of his cheeks. His eyes had grown a more brilliant sapphire blue with age, a burst in intensity like the bloom of a firework in the sky. That kind of azure couldn't last – it was too beautiful. Eventually it would glass over into a crystal translucency before milkiness and cataracts would dim it forever.

She must have caught her father's attention because he looked at her suddenly and smiled eagerly. Perhaps he's as anxious as I am, thought Assia. At that moment Madeleine appeared, propelled past the rows of chairs in a wheelchair pushed by Athena. Assia was taken aback by how thin Madeleine looked but at the same time by her air of imperiousness. She was holding her head high and dressed in a red Hillary-style trouser suit, she looked ready for business. Two men in dark suits followed her – presumably the CIA men Edward had spoken of. Athena parked her mother a few rows back from the front and handed her a black quilted Chanel handbag over which Madeleine folded her hands as though it were a lap cushion. Assia thought Madeleine looked more empowered than ever.

I can't hold this off any longer. Breathe. Time to begin.

'Good afternoon. Thank you for coming.' Her voice sounded muffled and she twisted the tiny microphone on her dress out slightly, the tapping of her fingers resounding like a sonic drum.

'Today marks the launch of the newly revised *Encyclopaedia of Fabergé Eggs* which was first published by my mother, Olga Morozova Wynfield, in 1991. Now, in 2017, I have updated this book and made a significant new addition. As with all great discoveries, there is a story which needs to be told, and it begins in 1918 in Ekaterinburg, at the Ipatiev House where the Imperial Family, the Tsar, Tsarina, the Grand Duchesses and the Tsesarevich are being held prisoner by the Bolsheviks.

'You know how this tale ends, I am sure, but there is another story which needs to be told in tandem and this one begins in 1960s St Petersburg.' Assia paces to the side and back. She looks at her audience and continues. 'The story starts with Konstantin Stepanyan and Olga Morozova: two children who grow up in the same apartment block. Konstantin's father is an Armenian dissident writer who was taken away by the secret police one night, while Olga's parents are toe-the-line intellectuals. Konstantin and Olga live in each other's pockets, even though her parents frown on her friendship with the child of a pariah. They love art and history. They haunt the great museums of the city. As time goes on, Olga excels at school and is tipped for the top. She reads History and History of Art at St Petersburg University – she is glamorous and beautiful and wants to see the world beyond Soviet Russia. Konstantin's calling is more vocational. He is a craftsman, an artist, and he wants to work with his hands. He could never leave Russia. They are the closest of friends, but Olga knows that Konstantin would like more than friendship.

'At University, Olga meets Richard Wynfield, an English graduate lecturing in maths abroad. She is the most beautiful girl on campus and he is exciting, foreign and the object of every girl's affection. Olga wins his heart and they leave Russia to get married. They settle in Oxford and have twin girls. Olga publishes books on Russian Decorative Arts and Fabergé and becomes famous in her field. Back in Russia, Konstantin works at the Hermitage and practises restoring Fabergé. He marries and has a daughter, Viktoria, but continues to love Olga. He can't forget her. He goes to see her in England, occasionally, and they meet when Olga travels to Russia. They begin an affair. His wife tires of the second woman in their marriage. They divorce.

'Just before she is killed tragically in a car accident, Olga announces to the world that she believes that Alma Pihl, who worked for Carl Fabergé, designed an egg for The Grand Duchess Olga Nikolaevna. An elderly art student of Pihl's in Finland contacted Olga and when they met, revealed that Alma Pihl confided in her that she had designed a Fabergé egg which the world didn't know of. Olga begins researching in the hope that she will uncover the egg and she believes that she has discovered the preliminary designs for "Olga's Egg".

'Sadly Olga died before she could continue research into the existence of Olga's egg. Her family and Konstantin are devastated by her death. Konstantin throws himself into his work and becomes more and more depressed and isolated. When his grandson is born with cerebral palsy, he decides to do something that he would never have dreamed of doing: he takes a commission to make a Fabergé egg. An egg for Olga.'

Muttering can be heard in a few places among the audience. Assia doesn't see Ivan Denisov entering the hall and standing to the side.

'Ladies and gentleman, here you will see the "Livadia Egg" as it is known. The St Petersburg Museum announced that this egg was discovered recently in the apartment of a woman whose father had rescued it from the Baryatinsky Mansion after the Revolution and kept it out of the hands of the Communists. They say that the egg was offered for sale and bought by the Treasury and donated to the Museum for the nation. The egg features miniatures of the Crimean palace of the Tsar as well as Crimean flowers. But the egg is a fake.'

Gasps. Some members of the audience look around anxiously to gauge reactions.

'It is no coincidence that the design has a Crimean flavour – the mandate Konstantin was given was to create an egg which celebrated the Crimea and its place in Russian history so that the egg could be used to drive home the fact that the Crimea had belonged to the Russians before it was handed over to the Ukraine in 1945. It is also no coincidence that the egg was stolen by Chechens when it was exhibited in Moscow. All of it was pure theatre for your benefit. The conception, theft and recovery of the Livadia Egg was orchestrated entirely for political purposes; as a justification for renewed suppression of Chechnya and the elimination of her wayward leader, Aslan Dudayev.

'Theatre is one thing, murder is another. After Konstantin had been paid for his exquisite craftsmanship, he was silenced and shot outside his daughter's apartment and the death was absurdly passed off by the police as suicide.' Assia clicks a small monitor in her hand and a recent photograph of Konstantin appears on the screen.

'But Konstantin was an honest faker. He loved Fabergé too much to let his own works be passed off as the work of the great man himself. He left tiny little clues throughout the egg which are his language, his message that the egg is a fake. Here on the egg,' she clicks to a photograph of the Livadia Egg, 'you can see that this cloison curls in on itself like a snake, something which a Fabergé workmaster would not have done – and Konstantin knew this better than anyone. And here, you can just make out – with a loupe – that one of the diamonds has a little 'S' for 'Stepanyan' scratched into its verso.' She clicked again and a close-up of the miniature of the chapel of the Livadia Palace appeared. 'Here, you'll see that the roof tiles of the Livadia Palace chapel are black but that in this photograph from 1915' –another click – 'they're white.

'All of these small elements are not just flaws, the tiny mistakes of an inexperienced workmaster – they are flaws by design. Konstantin purposefully included these miniature flaws as a way of subtly declaring his authorship of the egg. Here is a copy of one of his many pages of detailed designs for the egg which were found hidden in a book in his library. You can see, here' – she moves a small red dot over the screen – 'that he was writing these flaws in – this note here says "curl tail of this cloison", while this note on the next slide says "miss one diamond out here". It may not surprise you to know that these pages of Konstantin's designs were stolen from the apartment in which they were being kept, but I also have further evidence of his authorship which I find irrefutable.

'While examining some of the other pieces in the Fabergé style which Konstantin had made and given to his family and my mother, I noticed that he always inscribed them with a date and some form of dedication; he wanted the recipient to think of him.

'Following the retrieval of the Livadia Egg from its so-called captors, it was sent to a restorer who could tend to some of the damage to the enamel and hardstones – they are, after all, Philistines, those Chechens, absolutely no idea of how to treat a work of art. The restorer needed to examine the egg very closely and to access the enamelled areas, he had to lift off the slim gold band which covers the lower hinged lip where the egg opens. Just by the hinge, on the silver rim, was an inscription so light and delicate as to be dismissed as a play of the light.

'And here it is…' Assia pressed her monitor, this time without a click, and an image filled the screen. The brightness of the translucent pink enamel and the silver made most people blink as their eyes adjusted to the enlargement of a detail of the egg. There, inscribed in Cyrillic were the words

To Olga Mikhailovna (1952–2002), my love and my life, from Konstantin Alexandrovich (1952–2016)

The gallery fell silent. After a few seconds, those who couldn't read Russian began to whisper and ask what the inscription said. Assia's eye was caught by motion at the back of the gallery and she saw Edward walking in. Trying to compose herself, she looked down for a second and blinked quickly to push back the tears which she knew were coming.

'Konstantin had made an egg for Olga, but not for Olga Nikolaevna, the Grand Duchess of Russia. Instead, he had made an egg for Olga Mikhailovna Morozova, my mother, the woman he had always loved. He knew that he would be killed for making this egg – to have the maker of such an important piece wandering around St Petersburg would have been untenable for the people who wanted to present the egg to the world – and that is why he added his date of death to the inscription. Pure Russian fatalism.'

Pausing, Assia chose not to look at her father. A voice in her head willed him to understand why she had to talk about Konstantin loving her mother. *You always knew, Papa, didn't you? Please forgive me. You'll see why I'm doing this.*

'With Konstantin out of the way, the individual who commissioned the egg from him thought that he had the floor: through the egg, the world would see and understand that the Crimea had always been Russian and they would marvel at Carl Fabergé's Russian genius. They would orchestrate the theft of the egg by the Chechens and then the Russians would punish them for it. So many political birds were killed with one stone.'

A new slide appeared on the screen showing John Fairfax in his Archimandrite's robes.

'But the people behind the Livadia Egg have a problem. They hadn't reckoned upon the unswerving faith and devotion of an Englishman named John Fairfax. Fairfax had been taken into the employment of the Imperial Family as an English tutor when it emerged that the Grand Duchesses were speaking English with a broad Scots accent, passed onto them by their previous tutor. The Grand Duchesses and the Tsarevich grew to love their solemn teacher who hid a wicked sense of humour behind a formal exterior. After years teaching the girls and entertaining the Tsarevich on his sickbed, Fairfax decided to follow the Imperial family faithfully in their exile to Tobolsk and then to Ekaterinburg.

'Fairfax spent many days watching the Ipatiev House where the family were imprisoned. He was horrified when the windows were boarded up and his beloved pupils were denied fresh air, light and glimpses of the world outside. He had not been allowed to stay in the house with the family but he had been able to smuggle letters in via the nuns at the local convent who brought eggs, milk and bread for them. A few days before she and her family were slaughtered in the basement of the house, Olga sent Fairfax a letter and a small package. In the letter, the young Grand Duchess, who was beginning to despair of her fate, asked Fairfax to do something for her, a task which he would spend the rest of his life trying to complete.

'After years spent in Harbin where he converted to Orthodoxy, Fairfax returned to England and settled here in Oxford. Now known as Father Alexei, he set up the Chapel of St Alexis the Wonderworker in North Oxford and built up a small congregation. In pride of place in the Chapel was an icon with the Vladimir Mother of God framing a miniature of the Tsarina. For Fairfax, this icon was an object of worship – a reminder of the beloved family he had lost in Russia – but also a reminder of the task the Grand Duchess had given him, for inside the icon he had hidden the object she had entrusted to him' –

Click.

– 'her egg.'

Collective intakes of breath are rarely heard outside of cinemas or theatres. In this instance, the gasps came intermittently, almost one-by-one as people deciphered what they were looking at. Projected on to the screen was a video of a beautiful egg covered in white daisies which was turning on a socle. Next to the egg was a small cockle shell, opened to hold a miniature portrait of the Tsar Nicholas on one side and the Tsarina Alexandra on the other.

'Oh, my God!' someone cried out. 'This is incredible!'

The hubbub grew louder as people exclaimed and remarked upon what they were seeing. Some even held their phones up to record the video on the screen. Assia scanned the audience, desperately looking for Edward who was no longer standing where she had last seen him.

'Ladies and gentleman, this is Olga's Egg, the *real* Olga's Egg. The one commissioned by the last Tsar of Russia for his daughter, the Grand Duchess Olga.' Assia pointed with an outstretched arm towards the screen. '*This* is the egg designed by Alma Pihl for Fabergé's workmaster, Albert Holmström, to bring to life. *This* is the egg she never spoke about after the Revolution until she told a favoured student that she had designed it.' She paused. She spotted Edward who was standing next to Madeleine in her wheelchair. He had his hand over his mouth and at first she felt alarmed before realising that he was covering the broadest of beaming smiles. His eyes glistened and he nodded at her encouragingly.

'Ladies and gentleman, *this* is the egg that my mother fervently believed existed having seen some designs of Pihl's and *this* is the egg that I found in a photograph of one of the vitrines from the Fabergé exhibition of 1915.' The photograph appeared on the screen and with a red laser pointer pen, Assia outlined the white dots reflected on the glass of the vitrine.

'Just at the back here, you can see the small white daisies in the reflection of the glass. Although you can't see the egg itself because it is behind the Flower Basket Egg, you can see that the reflection corresponds with the height and shape of Olga's Egg.'

A woman approached Assia on her right-hand side. She was wearing a long black dress and flat tan leather sandals and carried a small box in both hands. Assia took the box from Evgenia and, opening it, brought out the Egg covered in daisies and held it in her left hand like an orb.

'As you can see, the flowers which carpet this miniature masterpiece are daisies. Alma Pihl was inspired by "White Flower Day", a charitable event for the Anti-Tuberculosis League which the Tsarina began in Yalta. In this photograph of Alexandra and her daughters, the staffs they are carrying are covered in *belyie svetki*, white daisies, just like the egg here. Pihl's design has emulated the abundance of flowers with its carpet of daisies and Olga would have been reminded of this happy occasion when she and her siblings would sell flowers to the crowds from baskets full to the brim with bouquets. The egg is marked for Albert Holmström, the workmaster, and his execution is flawless. Everything from the plique-à-jour enamel of the yellow centres of the daisies, to the way the egg opens like a flower, splitting into segments just as petals unfurl to be warmed by the sun – all of it is infused with the genius we have come to expect of the House of Fabergé.

'The design of the egg's surprise is also wondrous. This beautiful cockle shell, which nestles inside the egg, opens to reveal a double-sided miniature of the Tsar and Tsarina which slots into the mouth of the shell just so.' Evgenia appeared again and took the egg from Assia so that she could demonstrate how the surprise worked.

'With the cockle shell, Pihl was alluding to hidden things, secrets that are kept deep within the heart until prised out. This exquisite cockle shell even has a secret compartment, a false bottom of thin gilded silver which opens when you press the floor of the shell gently. Sadly there is nothing in it to hint at the secrets which occupied Grand Duchess Olga, but what I discovered when I found the egg in Father Alexei's chapel illustrates Olga's state of mind just before she died.

'When I pulled the egg out of Father Alexei's icon where it had been hidden for over ninety years, I found two letters rolled up next to it. One letter was to Father Alexei – "dearest Fairfax", as Olga referred to him – and the other was to Dmitri Shakh-Bagov, an Officer and Olga's last love. Olga had entrusted her Fabergé egg to Fairfax. She wanted him to give the egg to Dmitri along with this letter:

Ipatiev House,
Ekaterinburg

Saturday 13th July, 1918

My dearest Mitya,

Much has happened since we last saw each other. My nursing days at the infirmary seem like a lifetime ago – all our friends there, where are they now? Where are you now?

I hope you are in good spirits and bringing laughter to those around you. We try to think of ways to occupy ourselves here but they make it harder and harder. I have been suffering ever since they painted out our windows. Life without a view is much poorer than I could have ever have imagined. Seeing people gave us hope. I wonder what you are looking at now?

Alexei is much improved but Mama's heart still ails her. Papa laments the reduced time for walking and exercise in the yard outside. We all take comfort from the small services that Father Storozhev comes to conduct.

I have sent instructions for dear old Fairfax to give the egg which accompanies this letter to you, if he can. You'll remember it from when I brought it to the infirmary once to show everyone, to cheer them up. Do you recall how we all marvelled at the shell and how you said it should have your portrait in it instead of Papa's and Mama's? I want Monsieur Fabergé's egg to give you hope in these times of darkness – think of me when you see daisies and know that from winter comes spring.

Khristos Boskrese!

With all my love
Olga

When Assia had finished reading the letter out, she fell silent and bowed her head. A few in the audience did the same and Evgenia tried to wipe her tears away with the inside of her wrist.

'Every day that passed in the Ipatiev House ate away at Olga's reserves of hope and happiness. The longer they were held there, the plainer it was to the family that they were not going to be rescued. When Olga wrote this letter, she was passing the baton of hope to Shakh-Bagov and laying herself on the altar of her fate. And yet through the egg, through her love for Mitya, she was hoping to be remembered. The letter is testament to a spirit that has not quite broken – Olga was reaching out to the person she loved and hoping that he could bear the flame of her spirit.

'As you can imagine, Fairfax bore the egg and letters on his protracted journey back to England from Russia like splinters of the True Cross. During his time in Harbin, he sent enquiries as to the whereabouts of Shakh-Bagov but was not able to locate him in the chaos of the Civil War and Revolution. After settling in Oxford and establishing the Chapel of St Alexis, Fairfax's correspondence reveals that he continued to search for the young officer, repeatedly asking for news from Russian emigrés in Britain, France and Germany. He had heard that a Shakhbagov had commanded a military detachment resisting the Red Army in Echmiadzin, Armenia, in 1920, but then the trail had gone completely cold. And ever since, the icon with the egg and letters hidden in it took pride of place in the Chapel, waiting to be handed over to Dmitri.

'This beautiful egg has a number of untimely deaths associated with it: the murder of the Grand Duchess Olga, the unrecorded death of Dmitri Shakh-Bagov and the death of my mother, who had come to know of its creation but never knew that it was hiding in the icon she had knelt before and kissed for decades in the Chapel of St Alexis. This is why I want the story of this egg to come to fruition here and now.'

A small ring of applause came from the second row. Tanya was clapping excitedly until her father put his hand on her shoulder to quieten her. Assia caught Tanya's eye and breathed in slowly, drawing strength from her sister's excitement.

'This egg will finish my mother's story. I have included it in my revised and updated edition of her *Encyclopaedia of Fabergé Eggs*. As soon as I discovered the egg I rushed to halt publication of the book with the St Petersburg Museum's fake Livadia Egg in it and instead replaced it with the real egg belonging to Olga Nikolaevna, the "White Daisies Egg".

A shoulder and the back of a head threading though the crowd from the right side of the gallery caught her eye. She hadn't realised he was there.

'Ivan Borisovich! Stop! Don't go!'

Heads turned back in a kind of beautiful synchronicity, like sunflowers in a field, so that everyone faced the back of the hall in a matter of seconds. The man in the navy blue suit stopped, took another step away and then stopped again before turning round.

'Ivan Borisovich, you knew Kostya well – you were old school friends. Were you honest with him from the beginning? Did you tell him that he would have to die when he had finished the egg you commissioned from him? Did you really not trust an old friend to blab? Does the President know about the killing?'

The man's left hand contracted into a fist. Assia wasn't sure if he had heard what she said because he didn't say anything and looked as though he could hear a sound from far away.

She spoke more loudly this time.

'Kostya inscribed his death date into the egg. I think he knew he was going to die, don't you? Don't go, please. You'll find there are some gentleman from the CIA in the audience who would like to speak to you. *Kostya made a deal with the Devil, didn't he? But he had the last laugh.*'

She said this last bit in Russian and he turned to look at her reproachfully, his eyebrows inverted, as though she had wounded him. He clenched his jaw and opened his mouth to say something but thought better of it, shaking his head and muttering 'half-breed' under his breath. Someone in the audience began a chant of 'Out! Out!' insistently, clapping as he did so. Ivan looked at the source of the commotion and saw Edward glaring at him as he moved his hands together like cymbals, his chant increasing in speed and volume. Person after person followed suit until the entire hall had taken to its feet and the exhortation to leave was resounding.

Ivan Borisovich Denisov took a step back and regarded the rows and rows of chanting Western liberals with disgust. He saw two men in dark suits approaching him with intent. Americans – they thought everything was their business. They had no idea how far behind the tide they were. He wasn't going to waste his time making them feel as though they were in control. Forget diplomacy – the time for that was long gone. If they really wanted to see where they stood in this game of chess then they would be shown. All in good time.

He spun on his heel and walked out of the Ashmolean.

Assia watched, dumbfounded, as the chanting turned into applause when Ivan Denisov left. People cheered and whooped and turned back to look at her at the front of the gallery. Although she had rehearsed today's event over and over again, she couldn't think what she had planned to say next and she smiled wanly as face after jubilant face stared at her expectantly. Ivan's departure had thrown her and she felt light-headed with what she supposed was excitement.

She sensed someone looming over her, fumbling with her collar. Looking up she saw Edward. He squeezed her arm reassuringly and unpinned her microphone while she tried to work out what was going on. He pinned the device to his jacket, swept his hand over his hair and addressed the audience.

'Ladies and gentlemen, you have witnessed something extraordinary today because of Assia Wynfield. You have clapped eyes on a newly-discovered Fabergé egg which has not been seen in public since it was first exhibited in 1915. It is a piece of exquisite craftsmanship, redolent of all the privilege, power and tragedy of the last Tsars of Russia.'

Edward glanced quickly at Assia who was standing to the side with her arms crossed. He could see the dimple in her left cheek and took this to be a good sign.

'But, there is more to this egg than beauty and history – its very existence invalidates the Livadia Egg which claims to be the egg made for the Grand Duchess Olga Nikolaevna.' He held his hands out and shook them, remonstrating with the room, urging them to outrage.

'This is a patent lie propagated by a few ideologues in the court of the President who want to make the world choke on Russia's supremacy. And yet the truth is out now and truth – as we know – is no friend to regimes which peddle myths.

'But rather than view the Livadia Egg as a flagrant fake, I want us to think about the other story it tells, the story Russia doesn't want you to know. Think of it: a young Konstantin Stepanyan stays in his hometown of St Petersburg while the woman he had always loved, Olga Morozova, left Russia to follow her English fiancé to England. Many years later, she is married with twin daughters and a world expert on Fabergé, while his life has fallen apart. He is divorced, depressed, and then he learns that Olga has been killed in a car crash. He knows that just before she died she spoke in public about her theory that Fabergé had made an egg for Olga Nikolaevna. When he is commissioned by Ivan Denisov to make the Grand Duchess Olga's missing egg, he purposefully does not make it in the design which Olga Wynfield thought the egg would have been made in. He didn't want to sully her theory with his false egg. Instead, he followed the brief to make an egg which celebrated the Crimea and he did a marvellous job – the egg fooled almost everybody. Only Assia Wynfield, here, thought that the egg might not be right. From the very first time she saw it, she doubted its authenticity and she persisted in her belief where others might have given up. It is entirely due to Assia that we are witnessing Fabergé history today and that we now know that Konstantin Stepanyan made the Livadia Egg not for the Grand Duchess Olga Nikolavena, but for *his* Olga, Olga Mikhailovna.'

Richard Wynfield stood up and clapped. His clap was strong and resonant, the kind that comes from palms and not finger tips. Tanya joined him, catcalling Assia and gesturing for her to come back out from the side lines. Soon, the whole gallery was on its feet again, clapping in earnest.

Assia walked over to Edward and took his outstretched hand.

Epilogue

No. 5, Bardwell Road, Museum of the Chapel of St Alexis the Wonderworker, Oxford

They had reached the front of the queue. A museum guard unhooked the red plaid rope which hung across the entrance to the room. As they walked in, the long queue behind them which snaked back down the stairs of the Chapel House and out of the front door shuffled forwards slightly.

Raised up in her father's arms, a little girl with long brown hair wearing a navy-blue woollen coat with a velvet collar peered into the tall glass cabinet before her. She craned her neck and her father took a step forwards so that she could get as close to the glass as possible. Her mother watched her, enchanted by the expression of wide-eyed wonder on her daughter's face.

'What's that?' The girl pointed to a beautiful silver-gilt icon displayed on a stand towards the back of the cabinet. The quizzical look on her pale face, the slight knitting together of her delicate eyebrows made her mother smile.

'That's the icon in which Father Alexei, the founder of this chapel, hid the White Daisies Egg, this egg here. Isn't it spectacular?' The little girl's mother pressed her head next to her daughter's so that they gazed through the glass together. In the cabinet's artificial light, their faces looked luminous.

'They look like daisies, but they also look like bright stars. I love them, Mama.' The little girl beamed and her mother felt her smooth cheek swell slightly next to hers. She turned to catch her daughter's look of wonderment.

'Carl Fabergé made it in 1914 as an Easter present for the Grand Duchess Olga and then the egg disappeared. No one even knew it existed, apart from your grandmother, Olga Morozova Wynfield. She always believed in the egg, even though there was very little evidence to suggest that it existed. It is just as much her egg in a way.'

'But Mummy found it' said Edward, leaning in so that his head was above those of his wife and daughter. 'It's Mummy's egg, really.'

'Mummy's egg!' laughed the little girl.

Assia kissed her daughter's cheek and looked at the egg again. 'Yes, I suppose it is.'

Glossary

Alexandrite – A rare variety of the mineral chrysoberyl, named after Tsar Alexander II; notable for shifting from a green to red colour in different types of light.

assay master – The officer overseeing the identification and calculation of the precious metal content of an object prior to hallmarking it.

boyarina – A noblewoman of Muscovy, late medieval Rus'.

bratina – A Russian loving-cup.

cabochon – A precious stone which has been rounded off on one or more sides but not faceted.

chased – Used to describe metal which has been engraved or embossed by use of a hammer and punch.

cloisonné enamel – Enamel melted into compartments *(cloisons)* formed by thin plates or silver or gold wires applied on a flat surface; these remain visible in the finished piece.

cypher – A monogram-like device typically consisting of the initials of a royal or imperial personage.

en grisaille – Monochrome painting in grey.

enamel – A hard decorative surface created by fusing powdered glass onto metal using heat.

Galanteriewarenhändler – 'The Trinket Seller,' an early 18th century Baroque pearl figure group of a trinket seller and his Dalmatian by an unknown goldsmith in the collection of the **Grünes Gewölbe**, Dresden.

GARF – The State Archive of the Russian Federation.

Grünes Gewölbe – The Green Vaults Collection in Dresden, founded by Augustus the Strong in 1723 and one of the oldest museums in the world with the largest collection of treasures in Europe.

guilloché enamel – A repetitive pattern etched into a metal surface, usually with machine tools (a rose engine or geometric lathes), which is visible through translucent enamel; with sunburst guilloché, the pattern recalls the rays of the sun radiating from a central point.

hardstone – A general term used to describe any opaque stone capable of being carved for use in jewellery-making.

Holmström, Albert – a Fabergé **workmaster**. His workshop produced the 1913 Winter Egg and the 1914 Mosaic Egg, both of which were designed by Alma Pihl.

Kazanskaya Mother of God – In Russian iconography, an icon of the Mother of God is a type, named after the place or church where its 'master copy' was located; 'Our Lady of Kazan' was venerated in Kazan where it was said to have been discovered in the 16th century and was subsequently revered as a palladium of all Russia; notably it shows the Child standing and the Virgin chest-length.

kiot – A case for an icon, typically a wooden box with a hinged, framed glass door in the front in which the icon is placed; some are highly ornamental with carved, gilded inserts.

kovsh – A traditional Russian drinking vessel, shaped as a bird.

kokoshnik – A traditional Russian head-dress worn by women; the image of a woman in profile wearing a *kokoshnik* was used for the hallmarking of precious metals between 1899 and 1917.

Kurliukov – Orest Fedorovich Kurliukov, a **workmaster** and owner of a gold and silver factory active in Moscow between 1884 and 1918; known for his cloisonné work in pastel shades.

larets – An ornamental chest.

moss agate – A variety of chalcedony, the term 'moss' agate arose because deposits of ferrous and manganese oxides infiltrated the stone, so forming dendritic and moss-like patterns.

nephrite – A soft form of jade, green and often slightly veined; sometimes referred to as 'Russian jade'.

oklad – A pierced metal cover for an icon which exposes various elements of the painted imagery such as the face and hands, often applied with enamel decoration and precious gems.

Ovchinnikov – A firm trading in fine silver and enamelling, founded by Pavel Ovchinnikov in Moscow in 1853.

Piter – A colloquial term for St Petersburg.

plique-à-jour enamel – Transparent enamel that is melted into compartments that are not backed, achieving a stained-glass effect when light filters through.

pominki – Funeral repast; wake.

repoussé – A term used to describe metalwork which has been hammered from the reverse side to create a design in low relief; also known as embossing.

rodina – Homeland.

Shtandart – The Imperial Russian yacht, launched in 1895.

surprise – Of only three rules established by Alexander III for Fabergé relating to the Imperial Easter egg commissions, one was that each egg should contain a surprise for the Empress; a well-known example is the miniature train wound up with a golden key inside the 1900 Trans-Siberian Railway egg, although the surprise was not always an object separate and distinct from the egg, for example, the 1898 Pelican egg itself unfolds into a screen of eight ivory miniatures.

Vladimir Mother of God – In Russian iconography, an icon of the Mother of God is a type, named after the place or church where its 'master copy' was located; the Vladimir Mother of God is a Byzantine icon depicting the cheek of the Virgin tenderly touching the cheek of the Christ Child and it is presently displayed in the Tretyakov Gallery, Moscow.

workmaster – A master goldsmith who oversaw his own workshop (staffed with highly-skilled craftsmen) which produced jewellery, silver and *objets d'art* for the House of Fabergé.

Author's Note

Olga's Egg weaves fact with fiction. Fabergé never made an egg for the Grand Duchess Olga that we know of, but he did make Easter eggs for recipients other than the Dowager Empress Maria Feodorovna and the Empress Alexandra.

In their excellent book *Fabergé Eggs; A Retrospective Encyclopaedia* (Scarecrow Press, 2001), William Lowes and Christel McCanless divide the known Fabergé eggs into four categories: 'Tsar Imperial' (any egg given by Tsars Alexander III or Nicholas II to either Maria or Alexandra Feodorovna), 'Imperial' (a small group of eggs known to have been in the possession of Maria Feodorovna, most probably gifted to her by family or friends at Easter but not by her husband or son), 'Kelch' (a series of seven eggs commissioned by the Russian magnate and industrialist Alexander Kelch for his wife Barbara) and 'Other Eggs' (particular eggs made for high-ranking Russians and foreigners, such as the Duchess of Marlborough).

The eggs with the most value are the Tsar Imperial eggs and it is no understatement to consider such a Fabergé egg the equivalent of a winning lottery ticket worth tens of millions of pounds. At present there are seven missing Tsar Imperial eggs, three of which have no visual record (we now have a very real sense of the design of the missing 1888 egg courtesy of astonishing detective work by Anna and Vincent Palmade who – from a photograph – discerned its outline in the reflection on the glass of one of the vitrines of the von Dervis exhibition of eggs in St Petersburg in 1902), and up until 2014, when the 1887 Third Imperial Egg was discovered by a scrap-metal merchant in Mid-West America, the tally was eight.

The egg belonging to Madeleine Roseman in the novel, the Alexander III Medallion Egg, is, in fact, one of the seven missing eggs, as are the two belonging to the fictional Ferber Foundation, the Mauve Egg and the Royal Danish Egg.

The whereabouts of the missing eggs is an endlessly fascinating topic, ever expanded by specialist research. In tandem with the opening up of Russian State archives in the 1990s, Kieran McCarthy of Wartski, the famous West End jewellers specialising in Fabergé, was able to trace the provenance of the missing 1889 Nécessaire Egg and subsequently identify it in the background of a photograph taken at a Fabergé loan exhibition held at Wartski in November 1949. Until 2008 when McCarthy spotted the egg in a photograph where it was nestling in the bottom of a cabinet next to the Countess of Suffolk and Sacheverell Sitwell, no picture of the egg was known to exist. Going through Wartski's ledgers, Mr McCarthy discovered that the firm sold the egg in 1952 to an anonymous English buyer and since then it has never been seen again.

With only grainy, indistinct images and spare written descriptions of some of the missing eggs, recent discoveries have been received with a healthy dose of scepticism. In 2001, a conglomerate named the 'Russian National Museum' declared that it had purchased the 'Karelian Birch Egg,' one of the two eggs designed for presentation to the Empresses in 1917 but which were never delivered because of the Revolution. It was only in 1999 after Fabergé's great-granddaughter, Tatiana Fabergé, published drawings of the designs that scholars learned that eggs for 1917 had been designed but it was presumed that they had not been completed. According to the RNM, the egg had been purchased from the descendants of a Russian émigré who had kept it in a vault in London along with accompanying documents of provenance.

For some experts, the appearance of the Birch Egg so soon after its existence was discovered is too much of a happy coincidence and plenty consider the egg to be a clever modern creation. Interestingly, the Russian millionaire who fronted the RNM, Alexander Ivanov, also announced his acquisition of the other 1917 egg, the 'Blue Tsarevich Constellation Egg,' while the large majority of Fabergé scholars consider the original to be in the Fersman Mineralogical Museum in Moscow (where it was discovered by staff in the museum's storerooms in 2001). Ivanov's egg is presently on display at his Fabergé Museum in Baden-Baden.

'The young genius' Alma Pihl – as Olga Wynfield describes her in the book – deserves some further mention. Born in Moscow in 1888 to a family of jewellers who on both the maternal and paternal sides worked for Fabergé, at the age of twenty Alma began work with her uncle, Albert Holmström, Fabergé's head jeweller. She quickly gained a reputation for herself as a talented jewellery designer with an eye for discerning beauty in the everyday, and famously drew inspiration from sunlight shining through a frosted window of the workshop for a series of 'ice' brooches commissioned by Dr Emmanuel Nobel. She was the designer for two Tsar Imperial Easter eggs – the 1913 Winter Egg and the 1914 Mosaic Egg – for some, the most exquisite of Fabergé's eggs. To be given the task of designing these Imperial commissions was both a challenge and an honour for the young designer and again, it was the discovery of beauty in a moment of quotidian domesticity which moved Alma to conceive the design for the Mosaic Egg. On a winter's night in 1913, Alma had watched her mother-in-law working on her cross-stitch embroidery and when held up to the light, the inspiration had come to her: she would design an egg patterned with petit-point embroidery, a design which would appeal to the Empress Alexandra who so enjoyed her needlework.

Following the Revolution and the closure of the Fabergé firm, Alma and her husband left for Finland in 1921. There Alma found work as a drawing and calligraphy teacher at a school in Kuusankoski where she taught for twenty-four years, never speaking of her former life as a designer at the House of Fabergé.

The letters from the Grand Duchess Olga Nikolaevna to John Fairfax and Dmitri Shakh-Bagov are entirely invented by me, the former recipient being fictional and the latter a historical personage for whom Olga Nikolaevna did have true affection.

A Georgian adjutant in the Life Grenadiers of the Erevan Regiment, Dmitri Shakh-Bagov arrived as a patient in May 1915 at Their Imperial Highnesses' No. 3 Hospital at Tsarskoe Selo where the Tsarina and the Grand Duchesses Olga and Tatiana were Red Cross nurses. Olga was immediately taken with the new arrival and on Shakh-Bagov's readmittance shortly after his initial discharge, it became clear to all those working at the hospital annexe that the couple were in love. Olga spent many hours at Mitya's bedside keeping vigil or chatting, playing draughts and reading each other's palms and the handsome and good-natured young officer stole her heart. His departure from the No. 3 Hospital in January 1916 left Olga melancholic and despondent until he visited Tsarskoe Selo in May of that year. When he left again in June, Olga gave him an icon and for her own part, clung on to everything and anything that he had touched. Apart from a brief encounter in October and then in December 1916, she was never to see him again and with Rasputin's murder and the not-so-distant rumble of revolution on the horizon, events served to scatter the pair across Russia. In June 1917, Shakh-Bagov left his regiment and nothing of his fate is recorded after 1918 aside from a possible sighting in 1920 of a commander named 'Shakhbagov' leading a detachment fighting the Red Army in Echmiadzin.

The character of John Fairfax, Father Alexei, is in no small way inspired by Charles Sydney Gibbes, 1876–1963. A Yorkshireman, Gibbes went to Russia after leaving Cambridge and deciding against entering the Church. He was tutor to the Romanov children from 1908 until 1917 and devoted himself to the Imperial family. When they were sent into exile in 1917, Gibbes followed them to Tobolsk and then onto Ekaterinburg, although he was not given access to the Ipatiev House where they were held and executed. After their murder on 17th July 1918, Gibbes stayed on in Ekaterinburg and made many visits to the House of Special Purpose, as the Ipatiev House was known. There he took part in the investigation into the death of the family undertaken while the city was under White Army control and collected mementoes of the family from the house, including some of the Tsarevich's bloody bandages, one of his pencil cases and a bell, a pair of the Tsar's felt boots, exercise books belonging to Maria and Anastasia, and a chandelier which hung in the bedroom of the four Grand Duchesses.

When it became too dangerous to stay in Ekaterinburg, Gibbes went to Harbin, China, where he stayed for almost twenty years and joined the Orthodox Church in 1934. He was ordained a priest and took the name Father Nicholas in honour of the Tsar. He returned to England in 1937 and in 1941 moved to Oxford where he set up the Chapel of St Nicholas the Wonderworker at 4, Marston Street. There he hung the chandelier rescued from the House of Special Purpose, placed the Tsar's boots by the altar and adorned the walls with icons which had been given to him by the Imperial family and which he had salvaged from Ekaterinburg. The chapel acted as both a place of worship and a shrine to the Imperial Martyrs. Father Nicholas died in 1963 and is buried at Headington cemetery, Oxford.

In August 2000, the Moscow Patriarchate proclaimed the last Imperial Family of Russia Passion-Bearers and elevated them to Sainthood.

Further reading on the last Romanovs:

Helen Azar, *The Diary of Olga Romanov; Royal Witness to the Russian Revolution,* Westholme, Yardley, 2015, and her website: theromanovfamily.com

Paul Gilbert, his websites (royalrussia.news and angelfire.com/pa/imperialrussian/) and the journals *Royal Russia Annual* and *Sovereign*

Helen Rappoport, *Four Sisters: The Lost Lives of the Romanov Grand Duchesses,* Macmillan, 2014, and *Ekaterinburg: The Last*

Days of the Romanovs, Hutchinson, 2008

Simon Sebag Montefiore, *The Romanovs*, Weidenfeld & Nicolson, 2016

Frances Welch, *The Romanovs & Mr Gibbes*, Short Books, 2002

Further reading on Fabergé:

Cynthia Coleman Sparke, *Russian Decorative Arts,* Antique Collectors' Club, 2014

Toby Faber, *Fabergé's Eggs; One Man's Masterpieces and the End of an Empire,* Macmillan, 2008

Tatiana Fabergé, Lynette G. Proler, Valentin Skurlov, *Fabergé Imperial Easter Eggs*, Christie's, 1997

Tatiana Fabergé, Eric-Alain Kohler, Valentin Skurlov, *Fabergé: A Comprehensive Reference Book,* Slatkine, 2012

Caroline de Guitaut, *Fabergé in the Royal Collection*, Royal Collection Publications, 2003

Géza von Habsburg, Alexander von Solodkoff, *Fabergé: Court Jeweller to the Tsars*, Studio Vista/Christie's, 1979

William Lowes and Christel Ludewig McCanless, *Fabergé Eggs; A Retrospective Encyclopaedia*, Scarecrow Press, 2001

Christel McCanless, her website: fabergeresearch.com and its quarterly *Fabergé Research Newsletter*

Kieran McCarthy, *Fabergé in London,* Antique Collectors' Club, 2016

Geoffrey Munn, *Wartski: The First One Hundred and Fifty Years*, Antique Collectors' Club, 2015

A. Kenneth Snowman, *Fabergé: Lost and Found; The Recently Discovered Jewelry Designs from the St Petersburg Archives*, Harry N. Abrams, Inc., 1993

Ulla Tillander-Godenhielm, *Fabergé: His Masters and Artisans*, Unicorn, June, 2018

Annemiek Wintraecken, her website *Fabergé's Imperial Easter Eggs:* wintraecken.nl

About the Author

SOPHIE LAW was born in London in 1981 and studied at Oxford University and the UCL School of Slavonic and East European Studies. She began her career as a Russian art expert at Bonhams Auctioneers in 2006. After a number of years as head of the Russian Department at Bonhams and as a UK Board Director, she now acts as a Russian art consultant. She lives with her husband and daughter in Oxford.

© *Laura Gaze*

Acknowledgements

I would like to thank Sean Gilbertson, CEO of Fabergé and Gemfields Ltd, and John Andrew of the Fabergé Heritage Council, whose artistic vision and support have granted *Olga's Egg* a part in the never-ending story of Fabergé.

CPSIA information can be obtained
at www.ICGtesting.com
Printed in the USA
BVHW030227130323
660312BV00004B/126